LAIR OF THE DARK ELVES

As the door fell inward, Kilgore felt hands grasp him and yank him inside before he could shout a warning. The door slammed shut with a crash. Kilgore leaped to his feet, drawing the humming sword. In the semi-darkness, he saw a rude little room of beaten earth, not quite as nice as a troll hole. He also saw five crouching figures lined up against the door, their eyes flinty with hatred.

Then all five attacked with a clashing of swords. With one stroke, the magic blade of Kildurin shattered two swords. The figures backed away for a whispered consultation. Then a distant clamor came from the back of the room, and Kilgore realized there was a tunnel behind him.

Whirling around, he saw a glow bobbing toward him and heard the racket of many feet approaching. Dark Alfar! Now he was truly captured. Holding the sword, he waited.

Also by Elizabeth Boyer
Published by Ballantine Books:

THE ELVES AND THE OTTERSKIN

THE THRALL AND THE DRAGON'S HEART

THE WIZARD AND THE WARLORD

The Sword
AND
The Satchel

Elizabeth Boyer

A Del Rey Book

BALLANTINE BOOKS • NEW YORK

A Del Rey Book
Published by Ballantine Books

Copyright © 1980 by Elizabeth Boyer

All rights reserved under International and Pan-American
Copyright Conventions. Published in the United States by
Ballantine Books, a division of Random House, Inc., New
York, and simultaneously in Canada by Random House of
Canada Limited, Toronto.

Library of Congress Catalog Card Number: 79-91716

ISBN 0-345-30986-3

Manufactured in the United States of America

First Edition: May 1980
Second Printing: August 1983

Map by Chris Barbieri

Cover art by Robert Florczak

For Kimo and Loke

CHAPTER 1

The Ramskell troll was generally blamed for the Year of the Blight, although Sciplings hadn't bothered to believe in trolls for nearly a hundred years. Valsidur of Shieldbroad, chieftain of the rich Western Quarter, secretly sent a delegation to bargain with the troll, certain that gold would soothe any grievance. There was indeed a huge cave at Ramskell and a local legend about the troll that was seven hundred years old, but there was no troll to be found. After a quick peek inside, Valsidur's retainers rode home again as fast as their fat, sturdy ponies could carry them. It was unfortunate, but after all, it was none of their business that all the fjords and creeks and lakes in the Northern Quarter had stayed frozen all summer and the sun never warmed enough to bring the green to the land. In Shieldbroad the placid Codfirth had broken up on schedule and the fields and flocks were more prosperous than ever, from the least peasant farm to the numerous upland shielings of Valsidur.

In the midst of this plenty and contentment, the Midsummer Thing was held as usual at Valsidsness, where the participants had tented their booths for seven centuries, dating from the landing of Valsid the Kling-Bearer at Valsidsness. The doorposts that he had cast overboard to guide him to a homesite now formed the doorposts of the Brandstok hall. The great tree that grew in the center of the hall, spreading its limbs over the black thatch, was the same one that had sheltered Valsid seven centuries ago on his first night on the shores of Skarpsey—or so it was said.

The Thing was the traditional meeting of the Sciplings to settle lawsuits and feuds and to arrange weddings and divorces. Valsidur opened up the great hall and its cellars, and the kitchens were as hot as forges with continuous roastings and stewings and seethings. When all the legal affairs were settled, the feasting and contests began. The most popular contest was held in Brandstok hall. The entire hall was jammed elbow to elbow with the combatants whose object was to destroy as much fish, mutton, and fowl as possible. Up in the barrow hills a few rough fellows supervised the horsefights, frowned upon by the gentlefolk, but one of Skarpsey's most dearly-held traditions.

The year of the Blight promised the usual festivities. Valsidur and his nine retainers awaited the arrival of the northern chieftains, and along with them waited the son of Valsidur, called Kilgore. He was at the age Sciplings call standing tide—neither boy nor yet man.

Kilgore was in a surly mood. Lately his father and the fat old retainers had taken to pouncing on him and drilling some valuable bits of advice into his head about governing Valsidur's quarter. Unfortunately, Kilgore did not care two sticks about the mighty position he was supposed to inherit. He was more interested in old legends than in ledgers, and would have traded all the honored traditions of the Brandstok for a good sword any day. With no serious adult supervision for most of his life, Kilgore grew up on a diet of peasants' stories about elves and magic. He drank in the stories of trolls and barrow ghosts and treasure mounds and wizards until he imagined a troll under every cow byre and fancied he heard elven pipes moaning of a windy night.

But lately, to augment this obnoxious belief in magic, he had taken to carrying around a rusty old sword and asking questions about the Great Wars in Gardar. Right gladly Valsidur told him everything he knew. Valsidur took it as the bitterest of personal affronts that his father and five older brothers had ridden to Gardar and died as heroes without him. It made no difference that the bones of his famous sire and brothers had been picked by wolves and birds instead of being decently burned. Fate had dealt Valsidur an unkind blow and he was determined to wage his own wars, so he became a general in the war of prosperity.

But all Kilgore heard was the glory. He would gaze at the old relics, battered helmets, rusty swords and shields, gently hefting the fearsome weapons which had cloven skulls and lopped off limbs. Valsidur and the retainers were relieved, believing that he had given up magic for a more acceptable form of entertainment. For a week Kilgore never entered the hall without giving a petrifying bellow, which he said was his grandsire Wulther's battle cry. Even more annoying, he persistently pestered the old retainers to consider contriving a glorious end, such as a sea voyage or an impossible quest, rather than retiring peacefully in Shieldbroad.

Kilgore hated state occasions. As his father's heir he was forced to sit through all of them. He had already wasted the better part of the week at the Thing watching lawsuits, when he would rather watch the horsefighting, and now he had to be on hand to greet the northern officials. It was insufferable. Covertly he gouged his knife into the bench and sighed. The smells from the kitchen were absolutely marvelous. Sighing again, he caught a glare from Valsidur and scowled back.

At last the northern chieftains arrived outside. Their ponies were thin and few, with that anxious look that bespoke a fear of the stewpot. Kilgore looked at the ponies and their riders narrowly, wondering. Eating horseflesh was a horror to Sciplings. The mere accusation of it was grounds for a feud.

Valsidur greeted his old friends with a pleased roar and sat them down in the best seats, pretending not to notice their poor clothing and lean looks.

"My dear friends and neighbors!" he thundered. "It's been too long since we last met. How—er, how are your crops and flocks and fisheries?" He smiled un-

3

easily, knowing he was among unfortunate and desperate men.

Thlasi of Whaleness shook his head silently. Erin of Neck refused to even answer, and Therin of Heroness spoke with false, heavy cheeriness: "Well, this will be the last Midsummer Thing we'll celebrate together, Valsidur. All of us are leaving the north and going to the Southern Quarter."

All the retainers gasped and began exclaiming, "You won't like it. Nobody knows if there's habitable land there, even. Too many strange beasts, and what about the weather? No one has ever gone to settle beyond Willowdale."

Valsidur rapped for silence with his fishing spear. "This is a drastic decision, neighbors. Are you sure you want to give up your comfortable homes and all that is familiar?"

Thlasi of Whaleness answered flatly, "Of course not. But what else can we do besides starve to death? Last fall an early storm ruined our crops and killed at least half our sheep in the fells. We barely survived the winter by eating all our cattle. And this year the winter never left. The boat stands are frozen fast, the few lambs that were born were deformed or frozen, half the ewes died, and the other half was starving without grass. Now we have started to eat our horses. Nothing is left in the Northern Quarter. We'll take what little we have and our few ponies and go south."

Valsidur rubbed his chin. "Then it will be a bad year for trade," he murmured almost to himself. "But friends, I have enough gold, wheat, firewood, livestock, and ponies to lend you. You don't need to leave. What are neighbors for?"

"There are limits to hospitality," Erin of Neck said. "We might be a burden on you that would ruin you too. And we have our pride. We would rather start over in the south. Perhaps when the Blight passes some of us will return."

"You ought to come too," said Vigfus of Goatnef gloomily. "You'll get the Blight too, perhaps this fall. It's creeping further south each year."

4

"It's just a freak of the weather," Valsidur said. "Surely you won't pull out just because of one year's crop failure. Why, the crops failed every year for five years not long ago and no one packed up and moved. Stay just one more year."

The men of the north looked at one another a moment. With reluctance Therin said, "Well, this may sound strange, but we believe it's something to do with magic. You know something peculiar happened in Gardar after we lost the Wars. No one could get in, no one got out. I've heard the place is under a blighting cloud the same as we are and the trolls and wizards run about in broad daylight. It isn't a natural cloud, you know, that deforms animals and kills all green things it touches. I'm afraid to go out at night because I'm sure there are trolls or sendings under my barn. We've all had enough; we're leaving."

Kilgore was acutely interested. "I've always wanted to see some trolls and sendings. It's about time Skarpsey saw a little excitement, since the Wars are over."

"Tush! We don't believe in magic here in Shieldbroad," Valsidur snapped with a withering scowl at his son.

"No?" inquired Erin of Neck. "Then we must've heard a lie when we heard you sent someone to find the Ramskell troll."

Valsidur looked ruffled, like a disturbed barn owl. "Well, it did no harm, since we found no troll."

"But one always wonders about the old legends, if there's not a grain of truth somewhere," said the old retainer Onnund, glancing uneasily at some old amulets hanging on the wall.

"If there are wizards in the Northern Quarter," Kilgore declared, slapping his old sword, "I say let's raise an army and drive them out instead of running away. We're not cowards. Our noble ancestors—"

But nobody listened, and nobody listened in the days to come when the migration started. Trains of ponies and carts and a few sad-looking sheep and cows passed Valsidursknoll, making a dusty new road southward. It was an exciting but saddening time. Kilgore watched the travelers with envy and irritation. He tried to corner a few of them and demand information about the Blight, but all were unwilling to talk. They only said, "You wouldn't believe it if we tried to tell you."

Kilgore lost patience and began demanding, "Why don't you stay and fight for the land you love?"

"You can't fight wizardry," was the answer, and on they went.

Privately Kilgore believed the so-called Blight was indeed the magic of wizards from Gardar to frighten the people away. They had already won the entire north of Skarpsey and now they were working their way southward, driving the sciplings before them. He was haunted by the thoughts of what would happen when all the refugees were crammed into the Southern Quarter with no place left to flee except maybe into the ships that had carried the sea traders' merchandise —leaving Skarpsey to the powers that had possessed it centuries before the first Sciplings landed on its shores. Try as he might, Kilgore could not arouse even the faintest interest in raising an army. The comfortable Shieldbroadsmen propounded that the cold weather and clouds could be nothing but a mere fluke of nature's unkind side, and the fleeing northerners were too frightened to think of anything but escape.

Finally one evening in the Brandstok hall, Bork the Fat and Onnund of Wolfskill managed to loosen the tongue of one of the travelers.

"I'll tell you, then, and swear that it's true upon the barrows of my forefathers," declared the traveler, looking around the crowded hall. "As my name is Grimulf of Grimsness, son of Grafar, I have encountered wizards in the Northern Quarter. I used to raise horses there, but the grass and the horses are gone. I was caught in a blizzard this spring, searching for three mares, and I came upon a house on the fell that I know never existed before. I was freezing so I stopped there. Three bearded men in fine cloaks made me welcome and gave me a bed for the night. My dogs wouldn't come near the place, which should have

6

been warning enough for me. I became suspicious when the food and drink I had began making me sleepy, so I refused to eat it. And when I lay down in the bed, I saw a sending sitting in the rafters grinning at me. It looked like an old corpse in rags and it vanished when I held up Thor's lucky amulet. I made my escape and never saw that house again, even though I spent days searching for it."

An uncomfortable silence filled the hall. Against the walls the old banners and shields stirred and rang softly in a stray breath of wind.

"Stuff!" Onnund of Wolfskill squeaked, sputtering on the dregs in his cup.

Valsidur pulled his beard and grunted. "Fellows like this ought to be fined for spreading rumors. That would solve the problem in a week. I can't believe rational and civilized people would stir themselves into such a frenzy over a pile of myth and superstition."

"Magic is not myth or superstition," Kilgore said, eager to show off his knowledge. "It's a force as real as the fire and ice of Skarpsey, and people used to practice it as a fine and ancient art to—"

Valsidur clutched the arms of his chair and bellowed, "Let the trolls take all the fine and ancient arts! What I want to see is a reasonable explanation for this miserable cloud of cold weather creeping down on us fjord by fjord, and magic is not a reasonable explanation."

"It's as reasonable as anything else you might think of," said Kilgore. "Some things don't have to be reasonable. We know there are volcanoes and geysers inland, but does anybody have a reasonable explanation for the way they work? What we ought to do is raise an army and get ready to fight for Skarpsey."

"No armies," Valsidur declared. "If something is causing this trouble it must be men, and we know that gold is a better way of dealing with men than swords." With that, he rose and stumped away to bed.

Since all the wine had been consumed, the neighbors all left, leaving the hall to Kilgore and a score of travelers. The fire died down to coals and most of the homeless ones were preparing for sleep on the tables, benches, and floor. Kilgore discovered a toothless old scop who mumbled himself to sleep right in the middle of the story and no amount of shaking and punching would rouse him. The hall became silent. In the amber light, the old weapons and banners did not look so faded and eaten by time and decay. Kilgore sat looking at them for a long time, wishing those warriors from better times were still around to defend Skarpsey from this mysterious attack.

Finally he yawned noisily, stretched, and curled up in someone else's cloak to sleep. He was almost asleep when the great front door which sported the beak of Valsid's ship ponderously creaked open with a gust of wind. He thought about rising to shut it, but that would entail threading his way among bodies, benches, dogs, tables, and scattered cups and plates. Besides, it was a warm night. Let the ones closest to the door shut it if they got cold.

Suddenly the coals on the hearth leaped into crackling flame, casting a bright glow in the mahogany darkness. He heard light footsteps and he felt the hem of a long cloak brush past him. He fell asleep before he could investigate.

In what seemed like only half an hour or so, someone woke him by unrolling him from his borrowed cloak, and sunshine streamed in on him brightly. Feet were trampling the boards in great activity for such an early hour. All the retainers were there and more local people and travelers. Kilgore groped around for his old sword, grumbling, "What's all the excitement Leave off stepping on me or—"

"Get out of the way, Kilgore," puffed old Snorri. "Must you always be underfoot?"

Kilgore rubbed his wooly head, relinquished his borrowed cloak to its indignant owner, and plowed his way through the crowd around the Brandstok oak with the intention of getting outside as soon as possible. Everyone was wide awake and cackling all at once like a bunch of chickens. His father was in the midst of them, trying to make himself heard and almost smothered by wagging beards and hands plucking at his cloak.

"What's all the uproar about?" Kilgore demanded. "Did we have thieves in the night?"

"Worse than that!" said Bork the Fat. "We've had some sort of wizardry right here in the Brandstok hall."

With a quivering hand he pointed to the Brandstok oak. When the crowd cleared for a moment Kilgore shoved closer. There was the hilt of an old-style sword stuck into the tree with not even an inch of blade showing. It was made of gleaming gold, curiously wrought with all manner of runes and designs. The guard was shaped like an eagle's talons curving over the wielder's hand. Impaled to the tree under the sword's hilt was a scrap of parchment. Kilgore snatched the paper and read the faint spiky writing: "Whoso pulls Kildurin from the tree shall rule over all the minions of Surt, to the confusion of the wicked and the confounding of their Power."

CHAPTER 2

In the days that followed, hopefuls from all the Quarters came to try their luck at the sword. Valsidur issued an official proclamation that everyone must try it, however humble or obscure, lest the sword king spend the rest of his life cleaning fish or herding sheep. A fishing boat, a new house at Willowdale, and a hundredweight of salt cod annually were promised to the man who brought the sword king to the hall. Everyone from the wealthy to the vagabond wanderers was instructed to try the sword, and almost every night a revelrous gathering tested another batch of prospective kings, always ending in a consolation feast.

To Kilgore the whole enterprise was painfully embarrassing. He felt torn two ways. In spite of his belief in magic, it was still disquieting to witness a genuine magical manifestation in such a staid and stodgy spot as the Brandstok hall. Or worse, the sword was a farce to make Shieldbroad look ridiculous—a dangerous hoax, perhaps, that would oust the family of Valsid from the chieftaincy of Shieldbroad. As the self-appointed guardian of the sword in the Brandstok, he sat glowering worriedly with his old sword across his knees during the foolish attempts to withdraw the weapon from the tree. He disdained the idea of making himself look ridiculous by sweating and straining at the sword with that greedy glint in his eye that all the candidates wore. He was certain that an object so holy and mysterious would never be withdrawn in such a carnival atmosphere.

Almost overnight authorities on elven magic sprang

up and hastened to the Brandstok hall to advise everyone else. A galloping trade in amulets, lucky tokens, and petty spells flourished among the people of Shieldbroad and the southbound travelers. It seemed that everyone had always believed in wizardry and elves and had just been waiting to expound his knowledge of the topic. They alternated between fearless bragging and terror lest wizards carry them off, which was relieved only by a new amulet or dead lizard, or when a new hero came swaggering up to try the sword. Their spirits then rose to a feverish pitch as they swept inside the hall like the sea. Their disappointment afterward never failed to delight Kilgore.

Disappointment hit old Valsidur the hardest of all. He would glare at the innocent sword, muttering, "Now why shouldn't it be me? The Valsids have always been kings and warriors. If anybody in Skarpsey deserves it, it is I!" Then he would pounce from his chair and try to wrest the sword from the tree by main force. It never budged in the least. Yearningly, gloating, the retainers all tried it several times, pulling till their eyes popped, to no avail.

"What are we to do with this troublesome king when he does appear?" Valsidur grumbled. "He's worse than the Blight. He'll take the best of everything for himself, unless we enlist him somehow."

"Or buy the sword from him," old Snorri suggested slyly. "A stranger with no friends about him, perhaps a poor man, he would have his price. Every man has a price, even if it is his life."

"Oho," chuckled Valsidur. "I see your meaning. It's worth a try, to preserve such an honorable institution as the Brandstok."

All the old men grinned and winked. But a week passed and still the sword stubbornly refused to be withdrawn.

Another week passed and the novelty seemed to be wearing thin. No new heroes had come to try the sword for several days. The old retainers came to the hall to drink wine and tell lies. People began remembering the Blight to the north and the old unease about wizards returned. Kilgore hoped the sword craze was over and people were returning to their senses. Any day now they would see the wisdom of raising an army and marching north. His father was certainly gloomier and grouchier, a sure sign that everything was returning to normal. Valsidur sat morosely where he couldn't see the sword and refused to be amused.

The loud knock at the door one evening was sudden and welcome. The guests and travelers brightened hopefully. A servant opened the door with a flourish and escorted in the traveler. Pompously the servant announced, "Helgi Thinbeard of Bank. Desires a word, sir."

"Well, come in, come in," commanded Valsidur. "Who sent you and what is your business?"

Kilgore observed with a grimace that the fellow smelled of fish and smoke and was not well clad, though he seemed properly respectful. He was dressed in rough-woven russet, coarse sailcloth breeches, a hairy leather hauberk, and a barbarously ornate belt. On his feet he wore thick rough boots that a Shield-broader would have worn to work in the fields. He looked fairly youthful of countenance, sun-browned and keen-eyed, but his beard was silver-streaked and he had a knowledgeable look about him. Leaning on a tall black staff, he looked around at the occupants of the hall.

In a placating tone he began, "I bear you greetings from Bank, and a peculiar message."

"Well, go on with it," Valsidur said impatiently. "Who's it from?"

Helgi Thinbeard bowed slightly and looked around the attentive hall with a faint smile. "I myself bring my own message to you. In regard to this—" He waved his hand toward the sword.

"And who are you to bring your own advice to us?" grunted Onnund of Wolfskill critically.

Helgi smiled and combed his sparse beard with his fingers. "If it pleases you, I and all my fathers before me were called soothsayers."

12

"A soothsayer!" everyone in the hall cried, echoing and re-echoing.

Valsidur sat up and clutched the arms of his chair. Kilgore braced himself for the explosion that was sure to follow.

"Soothsayer, eh?" Valsidur studied the fellow with narrowed eyes. "Well, make yourself comfortable, soothsayer," he continued gruffly, and imperiously invited Helgi Thinbeard to dine and refresh himself. After ordering that fat and livers and curds be brought, he commanded the harpist to begin a song. "You must try our famous Brandstok ale," he said. "The best in all Skarpsey. Your health, soothsayer."

Kilgore observed his father's altered mood and crowded closer to the soothsayer. The fellow still looked and smelled like a mere chapman off the boats. Helgi Thinbeard stared back at him, as if he had read Kilgore's thoughts. Then Kilgore noticed a knife with a well-polished horn handle thrust into the soothsayer's belt. Surprised, he felt inclined to be more respectful after that.

The soothsayer at last finished his meal and leaned back and began stuffing a black pipe with a strange fragrant herb. Then he ignited it with a coal and began puffing clouds of greenish smoke. Politely he asked how the summer was advancing in Shieldbroad. Valsidur returned the proper answer and inquired after the state of affairs in Bank, a settlement in the Southern Quarter. They bantered the usual questions back and forth until Kilgore was fuming with curiosity.

At last all the preliminary requirements were satisfied. Valsidur offered a deep "Hem!" and looked serious.

Taking the hint, Helgi Thinbeard began, "You remember that I said I had a message for you?"

Valsidur grunted and tried not to look too eager, having never spoken with a soothsayer. "Yes, I recall something of the sort. My sire and his sire back to Valsid always listened to soothsayers."

"And died by violent means," Snorri couldn't help

13

murmuring in the safety of the darkness, since the fire was dying.

"Let the soothsayer speak," Valsidur ordered. "I'm sure he speaks for the benefit of Shieldbroad." He meant profit. Kilgore could see his crafty old face in the red fireglow.

The listeners drew closer and the soothsayer puffed solemnly on his pipe before speaking. "You shall gain, and you shall lose. Something more dear to your heart than your gold and this hall." Kilgore wondered what on earth that could be. The soothsayer continued. "See these moths?" He pointed to the little flitting shadows flashing around the burning whale oil lamp. "Before these die, you shall see the sword drawn out of the tree by the only hand that has not tried. Before the dark of the moon, wizards will come into this hall as in the old days, and one will do you good and the other ill. There are many things in and under Skarpsey which you do not know and which you blind yourselves to. Remember that you are in a very ancient land, newcomers to an old order. Eventually mankind will rule all of Skarpsey and the old order shall cease." He reached for his staff and fastened his cloak and hood.

"Wait!" a dozen voices cried.

"An army! I told you so!" Kilgore shouted.

"Silence!" bawled Valsidur. "Now explain all that nonsense. What have moths to do with the sword king? And what about these wizards? And you know as well as I that men have ruled Skarpsey for seven centuries. As if anyone else could rule! I think you know more than you are telling us. Who is the sword king? Is he in this hall? Come, I'll make you rich for the rest of your life if you tell me his name so I can help him rise to power. A very great deal depends upon it, I assure you. Now tell us, Helgi Thinbeard of Bank, what is the name of our hero?"

Helgi shook his head and smiled a thin smile. "The power you speak of and the power the sword king shall assume are worlds apart. I am not permitted to tell you more. But this I will add, Valsidur of Valsidsness and the Brandstok, it is not men who rule this land."

"Oh, it is not?" Valsidur's tone caused the hall to become still and brittle. "I suppose you are speaking about elves and wizards, then. Perhaps you yourself are one of these—wizards."

Helgi said calmly, "I came only to warn you to be on your guard. Do not attempt to meddle with that sword, or the world will be everlastingly sorry. Now farewell."

"I can make you rich," Valsidur said. "Allow me to give you this." He offered Helgi a small black pouch from his own pocket which contained many marks of gold and silver.

"No, thank you," Helgi said. "Remember that I warned you." He bowed low and turned toward the door.

"Seize him!" commanded Valsidur, rising from his chair.

The mob crushed forward. Kilgore jumped on a table to avoid being trampled, yelling, "He's the one! He put the sword there! Offer him more gold and you'll see! He'll be back!"

But the noise drowned out his words as they eagerly sought to lay hands upon Helgi Thinbeard. Suddenly the fireplace, thought to be the best in Shieldbroad, gave a great belch of soot and choking smoke and sparks and the fire vanished. The hall was in total darkness. Instead of stopping calmly until the light was found again, everyone blundered around knocking over benches and tables. Kilgore felt around on his table and discovered a lamp that hadn't been spilled. He managed to light it and stood holding it until order was restored. By this time, of course, Helgi had escaped. Everyone sat down sheepishly.

In high excitement, Valsidur announced, "The sword king is one of us in this hall tonight. One of you has not tried, or is waiting for me to make an offer. For the last time I shall speak. If one of you pulls this sword out tonight I shall give you twenty marks in

15

gold, twenty bolts of cloth, twenty cows, twenty horses and I shall adopt that man as my second heir."

The hall exploded with the news and several fellows lunged for the door to tell the rest of the settlement. But Valsidur roared, "No one is to leave the hall until he has tried the sword! If the soothsayer is right, tonight is the chosen night for the king to make himself known. Tonight and no other night. We'll find him if we have to haul everyone from his bed. Prepare yourselves to welcome the king of Skarpsey." So saying, he crossed the hall hastily to the sword so he could try it first, in case it would now come out for anyone. Modestly he tugged at it. Kilgore grinned in the sudden hush. Everyone fully expected it to come out. But no amount of yanking and muttering would encourage it. The sword remained as obstinate as ever.

"It could be a hoax," said Snorri soothingly as Valsidur stalked away to his chair and began swatting moths with vengeful glee. "Whoever does get it won't be near as deserving as you."

"It's a wizardish humbug," muttered the audience as the last of the hopefuls tried the sword. An ugly rumble went around the hall. "We'll find that traitor Helgi and then we'll see."

"Cut down the tree," someone suggested and pandemonium broke loose. Half the crowd thought it an excellent idea, and the other half thought that the very mainstays of Shieldbroad were being attacked. It was the tree of Valsid the Kling-bearer, the First Father, and as long as it stood, Shieldbroad would prosper. The others pshawed their sentimentality until everyone's ire was aroused.

"Silence before I clear out the lot of you!" Valsidur roared, but no one was listening to him except Kilgore and sly old Snorri.

"That's what you get for impoverishing the Brandstok and elevating some churl as another heir," Snorri said sternly. "For centuries Shieldbroad has been the land of the Valsids and now you propose to divide it. You'll only cause wars and disagreements in the future and Shieldbroad will become a battlefield.

And all because of that sword hoax. There's a man waiting somewhere for you to draw yourself in over your head in promises of wealth and power and then he will come and pull out his cursed sword and turn us out of the Brandstok hall to starve. What then? I suggest you hush this up and deal privately with the hoaxer when he shows up." He glared at the sword furiously as if he might pull it out by sheer wrath alone.

"He has a point," ventured Bork the Fat timidly.

Valsidur closed his eyes tiredly. "Leave me alone to think." The old roarer sat with his head bent down in thought as the hall cleared. The nine retainers waited quietly, as much a part of the Brandstok hall as the knots in the floor boards or the soot on the beams. One by one they nodded off to sleep as the bright fire died down. Kilgore yawned and looked impatiently at Valsidur, who seemed to be carved of stone. But something caught his eye in the amber shadows and the door squeaked as if it were opening very softly.

"Who's there?" Kilgore rang out sharply, reaching for his old sword.

"Just me, sir," a hoarse, anxious voice answered, and a ragged bit of shadow detached itself to hover on the edges of its native element, visible only in snatches as it sidled along the rim of the lamp light.

"Come forward and explain yourself," Kilgore commanded with an officious brandish of his old sword. "There are stern penalties for spying on secret Brandstok councils. What are you doing here and how long have you been listening?"

"Eh?" said Bork in the middle of a snore, hastily brushing away the ash on his sleeve that had fallen out of Thredell's drooping pipe.

The small creature shuffled backward and forward. "I meant no harm. Everyone on the road said I could find lodging here for the night. All the southbound travelers, you know. If I'm not in the way, I'll just curl up here on the doormat and do no harm at all and I'll be gone in the morning."

"See that you cause no trouble then." Kilgore put up his sword.

"Who is this?" bellowed Valsidur suddenly, enraged. "I said I wanted everybody out. I want it quiet so I can think!"

"He was spying on us," Kilgore said. "Came slipping in as quiet as a ghost."

"Stranger, come forward," Valsidur ordered. "I fear a greater fate brings you to this hall tonight. State your business."

The intruder shuffled into the light. His eyes were wild and bright like a hare's. Black brows met in a scowl over a beak of a nose, which sported one of several black-haired moles. A mingled, yellowish beard bristled all around his narrow face and hung nearly to his waist. The color of his cloak was a greasy maroon and it hung in tattered festoons around his ankles, which were shod in ponderous reindeer boots, crudely sewn and hairy, with long, curling, clumsy toes. He seemed to have a habit of shuffling, even when standing still, which a gimpy leg rendered even more peculiar. The rest of his outfit consisted of a gnarled walking staff and a dirty black satchel stuffed under one wizened arm.

The apparition made a stiff, quick bow, darting glances on all sides, "I wasn't spying, kind hosts. At least not on purpose. That is to say, I heard what you said, but it was against my will, although I came for the same purpose. That is to say—"

"You'd better explain yourself better than that," Valsidur rumbled.

"Certainly, certainly. First let me introduce myself. I am called Warth of—er, no particular place, since I have no lord or allegiance. In this part of Skarpsey, at least. You see, I have heard of your difficulties with a certain sword, I believe, and that you have made certain offers, shall we say. I believe that I can be of service to you, in a small way, perhaps."

"You?" snorted Valsidur. "What can you do, wanderer?"

"I can remove the sword."

Valsidur sat forward on his chair with a gleam of triumph in his eye. "I don't believe it."

"But I can," Warth insisted.

"You, a king over the minions of Whats-his-name? Over all the island of Skarpsey?" Valsidur's expression was an inscrutable knot of disbelief.

"Unless the sword is a hoax," said Kilgore, "and this is the joker who put it there. I don't like his looks. What sort of a king would this fellow make? He looks more like a beggar, or a—"

"Wizard" was on the tip of his tongue, but something in Warth's bright, vindictive eye silenced him. He felt exactly like a dog with its hackles up.

"If it is a hoax and you're responsible—" Valsidur clutched his spear, his shrewd old eyes hidden in scowls.

"Oh, no, not me," Warth protested with a squeak. "You see—" He shuffled closer, glancing around, and his voice fell to a croaking whisper. "I have in my possession certain—ah, spells and charms. Minor magic and sorcery have been a harmless little pastime of mine—"

"A wizard!" shrieked Torfi of Swansknoll. "That dreadful boy was right about all this magic stuff! Whatever shall we do?"

Kilgore felt no elation. He kept his hand on his sword and felt a peculiar chill tingle his spine whenever he happened to catch Warth's wildly roving eye.

"Lock the doors, Kilgore," Valsidur ordered. "Make sure no one else is hiding in the shadows. Step forward, wizard. I believe I offered ten marks in gold and a holding in Willowdale and a fishing boat to the one who could remove this sword."

Warth grinned and scratched his ear, pulling it quite out of shape. "But it seems to me you promised something else. Adopting an heir, wasn't it? And wasn't it twenty marks in gold?"

"Twenty marks in gold it was," agreed one of the retainers sagely.

"Then twenty marks it is," Valsidur growled. "But you have to ensure that the sword is mine, if you actually do possess the magic to pull out that sword

19

yourself. I'd gladly give twenty marks in silver if I were the one to pull it out."

"But I'm sure it was gold," hinted Warth.

"Let's get the sword out and then decide on terms," Onnund advised officiously, as steward of the treasury.

"Good idea!" Valsidur said at once. "Proceed, wizard. But wait. Are you sure the magic will work for me? I was not able to pull it out myself."

"I am positive it shall," Warth declared, hobbling briskly to the tree to take a look at the sword. "Or else I would not have come so far in the beastly summer heat. But the situation in Gardar is so grave that I had to resort to extreme measures." He leered and grimaced, rubbing his yellow, knotty old hands together. "When I heard of the sword I came as fast as I could travel, you can be sure, my dears, just to get it out for you so we will all be saved. Not for the world would I see the race of mankind frozen and driven out of Skarpsey by nasty wizards and trolls and frost giants and dark elves." He listed them with eager relish.

"And that's what the sword king has to fight?" Valsidur asked.

"Aye," Warth replied. "Thousands of 'em. But if you've changed your mind, I'll find another mortal who will be sword king. I understand how you'd rather not attempt such heroics. At my age I wouldn't dream of possessing such a dreadful sword as that."

"Bah!" Valsidur said, rising up majestically. "At the age of one hundred my great-great-grandsire Thorold the Squinter still went to war. The descendants of Valsid are never taken by age, but only by acts of peril and bravery. Use your spells and charms, wizard, and I shall do the rest to save Skarpsey."

"Those are the words I wanted to hear," Warth said with a caper of glee, showing his teeth like a fox. Then he began looking through his black bag, shaking and punching it to rearrange the contents.

The retainers all winked and grinned at one another. Valsidur sat with his eyes fixed upon the wizard.

20

"Tell me, wizard," he asked, "is the sword very magical?"

"Very!" replied Warth. "It can cut anything. Ice, stone, wood, or metal. And it makes the wielder of it perfectly invincible in battle. There is nothing its owner couldn't do. Nothing!" His voice rose to a squeak, and his glittering eyes reminded Kilgore of a rat's eyes.

"And wouldn't you like to have it yourself," Kilgore said.

The shriveled wizard favored him with a disdainful leer. "Not I. I much prefer the twenty marks. Besides, it has a curse on it, so I wouldn't touch it for the world."

"The minions of Surt?" murmured Kilgore.

Warth darted him a chilling look, but his tone was fawning. "Of course I understand that the brave descendants of Valsid would not be at all frightened by a mere curse. Very brave, you Sciplings."

"Naturally!" Valsidur snapped. "Frightened of a curse, indeed. What kind of a curse is it?"

"Oh, I'm sure it's nothing," Warth hastened to explain. "The fairest of prizes always have a purse attached to make them more attractive. I mean curse, not purse. Speaking of purses, did we finally agree upon thirty marks in gold?"

"Something like that," Valsidur said. "How long does this curse take to work? Is it an immediate affair, or will it wait and show up three generations from now?"

"I could look it up in my book," Warth said, hauling out a volume as thick as two Brandstok ledgers. "It may take awhile—"

"Oh, never mind," said Valsidur. "Just get your spells working and remove that sword. I'll wear an amulet or something when I use the sword."

"If he can draw it out for you, that is," Kilgore said. "I think we were all safer when you disclaimed all magic and wizardry."

"Quiet, Kilgore," Valsidur commanded.

Warth leafed through the ponderous book, mum-

21

bling and puzzling and arranging small devices of bone, horn, stone, feathers, and fur. At last he drew some curious marks and circles on the floor and said pompously to the hovering retainers, "Now I have it. Stand back, there, or you're liable to find yourselves mixed up in my spell. Now, my lord Valsidur, stand ready and you shall draw the sword from the tree."

So saying, he raised his arms, screwed shut his eyes, and began slowly enunciating a long spell in some strange language, accompanied by cryptic gestures and movements. Kilgore shuddered, feeling an inexplicable uneasiness. Warth's magic certainly was not one of the fine and ancient arts the peasant folk had talked about. It was sinister and cold.

"Now pull it out!" Warth ordered in a taut tone.

Everyone trembled as Valsidur laid his hand on the sword and pulled. Nothing happened.

"Hmm," mused Warth disappointedly. "I'll try another. This elven magic is hard to unravel." This time he carefully drew runes with chalk around the sword on the rough bark of the tree.

"This is pure deception," Kilgore said. "And robbery."

"Silence is absolutely essential for the workage of magic," Warth warned, raising his skinny arms again.

"Silence, Kilgore, or leave." Valsidur did not take his eyes off the wizard's antics.

Kilgore didn't leave. He folded his arms and sat down between Warth and the nearest door. Warth was not going to escape with his father's gold or the sword if he could help it. As long as Warth was anywhere near either, Kilgore did not intend to remove his eyes from him.

The spell failed, and Kilgore muttered, "He's not a real wizard, if he's really any sort of wizard at all."

Snorri and Onnund gouged their elbows into his ribs from both sides simultaneously, hissing at him angrily.

Another spell failed, and another after that. Valsidur was beginning to look fierce and snappish. All the retainers glared like gray old roosters. The wizard smiled fawningly and consulted his books.

"Have no fear, I have spells by the barrow load," he said. "Here's a beauty that's bound to work." In utmost concentration, he shut his eyes and said the words and Valsidur pulled and nothing happened.

Kilgore snorted. "It's a shame we have to stay awake all night because of this trickster. I doubt if he could make cream rise on milk."

Warth glared as if longing to exchange insults.

"We shall keep trying tomorrow," Valsidur said. "Perhaps a night's rest and food and drink will refresh your magic."

"Thank you, kind sir." Warth sighed. "You're right. I'm a very old and tired wizard, and soon I'll retire to some pleasant cave—er, hut to live out the remaining days of my wretched life, and all I desire is a few pieces of gold to comfort my old age. I shall always remember your kindness." The covert leer he darted Kilgore belied his mincing tones.

After they were gone, Kilgore exclaimed in a rage, "Why, it's plain to me that we'll all be murdered and robbed by that sly hoaxer! He'll probably burn the hall over us tonight. Don't trust that weasely character, even if he's not a wizard. You've all lost your senses. You'll see. You'll be sorry you swallowed all his lies. Just like a lot of codfish, all of you."

He mumbled the last epithet, knowing that the retainers thought he was too impudent for his age.

"Bah!" old Thredell growled, blinking his red eyes like a bear. "It's you who will be surprised when that sword comes out. I warrant you'll believe in magic then." He drained a couple of half-empty cups of ale and stamped out of the hall, soon followed by the other thanes, grumbling and holding onto one anothers' arms.

Kilgore poked at the dying coals with his old sword. The blade was wavery and discolored, chipped and pitted with rust. He sighed and hung it on the wall with the rest of the old relics and threw the stiff old sheath into the fire. His eye fell on the soft plain sheath of the mysterious sword, hanging on the back of Valsidur's high carven chair. Furtively he walked to the tree where the gold hilt gleamed softly in the red light of the dying coals. He studied it closely. The workmanship was finer than anything he had seen in Shieldbroad. Designs in the gold depicted battles and monsters and ships. It was a weapon worthy of a great warrior—surely not a calculated hoax engineered by a creature like Warth. Kilgore felt an ache in his throat as he gazed at it, as often he had felt when he listened to Valsidur telling of the old glories now gone. Well, they were gone forever now. No one in Shieldbroad wanted or needed such a weapon now. A good hay fork would be more highly prized.

Kilgore started to raise his hand, hesitating to make sure everyone had gone. Touching the gold hilt curiously, he jerked his hand away in haste. Some sort of thrill had tingled his fingertips, but that seemed impossible. His imagination was tricking him. For a moment he stared at the sword, then grabbed it with both hands for a good firm yank. Instantly he let go and leaped back. No mistaking it this time; it had quivered like a live thing. Perspiring, he stared at it a second time, working up his courage to touch it again. Ignoring the tingle, he slowly took a double-handed grip on the great sword and pulled strongly. It slipped from the tree with a soft ringing sound. A white light glimmered from the long fine blade. Tangled runes ran together like molten silver; as he gazed, the spiky figures suddenly made sense.

"No night shall overtake the sons of Ask and Embla."

He marveled that some unseen and ancient power should extend this token for the protection of mortal men. He turned the sword over to admire every detail. It felt light and efficient in his hand, as if it had been weighted and balanced just for him.

"Kildurin," he murmured, and the sword hummed in response.

He was startled from his enchantment suddenly by the soft quick padding of footsteps in the passage.

Quickly he thrust the sword back into the tree, amazed at how easily it sank into the thick trunk. Then he dived into the shadow under a table and hugged his knees to his chest. He didn't want to break the spell of what had just happened, not by talking and explaining what he was doing in the dark hall.

The intruder glided up to the tree and stopped. With a chill, Kilgore recognized the ragged cloak of the wizard Warth. His heart thudded, and he reached for the old sword but it was gone. Warth stood still in the moonlight that flowed through the open door, staring at the sword and the tree. Then with choking sounds of rage the wizard threw his satchel on the floor and stamped on it five or six times. Snatching it up, he glided away, still snarling and muttering.

Kilgore crept out of the shadow when he was certain Warth was gone. Looking at the sword again, he felt his protective temper rise when he thought of Warth trying to get it for some unscrupulous purpose of his own. Then he noticed that the sword was a good two hands above the gash where it had been. He grinned to himself, understanding the wizard's outrage at realizing the sword king had beaten him to the sword.

He spent the night curled up at the foot of the tree, so it was the first thing he saw when he awoke early the next morning. No one else was about yet, so he touched his sword lovingly, wondering how on earth he was going to announce to all of Shieldbroad that he was the sword king. Their disappointment would be intense, after hoping for a hero and having to settle for Kilgore. He frowned, and decided to spend the day hunting badgers in the barrow hills by himself.

CHAPTER 3

Even Kilgore was not prepared for the furor in the Brandstok hall. He had planned to return and issue a modest statement before the assembled populace of Shieldbroad and perhaps demonstrate how he withdrew the sword. But the confusion overwhelmed him utterly. Everyone had come to inspect the new position of the sword personally. He was stepped on and shoved about until he bumped up against his father.

"Kilgore!" the old man roared in a fury. "Someone has moved that hoax of a sword in the night! You were the last one in the hall. Did you see who did it?"

"Yes, I did it myself," Kilgore said.

"Bah! Take yourself out of here and don't let me see you until you can keep a civil tongue in your head." Valsidur hadn't been so furious since a storm sank all his fishing boats. "Did it yourself! Bah!"

Kilgore let himself be jostled into one of the darkest corners where he sat quietly beside old Snorri who had drunk too much. He said to Snorri, "If I told you I could pull out that sword, would you believe me, Snorri?"

"Why, certainly I would," said Snorri, rather mushily. "But you didn't, did you? You're a bright young fellow, but you're just not ambitious. Now when I was your age——"

"Help! Help ho!" came a shout from the door. "It's another one of those dratted troublemakers. We don't need any more wizards, thank you!" Half a dozen of the retainers sprang to his aid.

"One side, you bloated winesack!" came the strident

26

shout. "I hear the sword king has appeared at last and I've come a thousand miles to see him. Now get out of may way or all your grandsons will be toads and lizards."

"He looks like another wizard!" babbled old Balthar as the retainers tried to hold the door shut. But they were all so fat that only one could get close enough to it to push. "Careful! Ouch! Oh, posh, he's getting in!"

"If a traveler wants our shelter, let him in," Valsidur said.

"But he's a wizard," puffed Bork the Fat, "or you can pluck out my beard, every strand!"

"Then I shall, unless you let him in!" Valsidur replied.

Reluctantly, the retainers opened the door and the traveler shoved his way through them with the irascible shout, "Make way! I came to see the king. Now where are you hiding him?"

A saffron cloak and hood surged in his wake and men and dogs hastened to get out of the way of his large, stamping, black boots. A dusty white beard flowed in a tangle down to his waist, where it was cinched under a wide leather belt. He carried a dragon-headed staff decorated with runes and a small black satchel was tucked under one arm.

"Well, what's your name and your business?" Valsidur demanded.

"Skanderbeg is the name and my business is none of your business. I came to speak with the owner of that sword." He nodded toward the tree. "But I wouldn't refuse the comfort of a warm fire and a cup of wine."

"I'm the ruler here," Valsidur said. "See here, you haughty old vagabond, in this hall you must be on your best behavior or you will spend the night on the road with the wizards and thieves."

"Hum! So!" mused the traveler to himself. "Well, then you may consider me on my best behavior. Now do tell me where I can find the man who pulled out that sword."

27

"Your guess," Valsidur said, "is as good as ours. He came here last night and moved the sword about two hand spans and hasn't made himself known yet."

"Oh, a modest one." Skanderbeg sighed, appropriating a cup of wine from one of the retainers. "Thank you most graciously, sir. Then I shall have the dickens of a time finding him. I certainly hope he presents himself soon, after waiting nearly two weeks to get the sword out. Time's a-burning." Busily he removed his gloves, unwound a long silk scarf, and took off his boots as he talked. "I say, would someone mind bringing a chap a bit of dinner? I've had a frightful journey and I fear there's a worse one before me. Do be a friend and kick that log onto the fire, won't you? These old halls are wonderful for tradition, but rather drafty, don't you think?"

Kilgore pushed forward. "You say you're here to talk to the owner of that sword in the tree?"

"Certainly. For such a large sprat you don't pay much attention," Skanderbeg retorted, looking him up and down. "But the whole lot of you can count your lucky stars that you weren't changed to icicles, with that ice wizard you let in. Excellently dull, really."

"Ice wizard?" murmured Kilgore. "Warth?"

"One of the worst I know. Invited him right in, you did, and you're lucky he didn't hoodwink you out of the sword for himself—but that's neither here nor there." The old fellow sat back comfortably in his chair with a long traveler's sigh. "Fetch me another pot of this lovely wine, will someone?"

"What are these things you speak of?" demanded Valsidur. "I think you are a wizard, old man."

"Yes! echoed Onnund boldly. "Who and what are you?"

The traveler had shut his eyes. Now he opened them to regard the scowling ring about him. "Aye, who and what. As to the who, I am who I said. As to the what—" He produced a pipe and began stuffing it with brown leaves. "Let's say I'm merely an itinerant handy-man. Wherever there's work that needs doing, I have a way of being there. Whether it be

28

treasure seeker, giant or dragon slayer, exterminator of other pesky brutes such as wizards, trolls, ogres, spirits, and whatnot; unicorn catcher, sleuth, or just a plain, ordinary general genius, I'm the man for the job." Pressing a finger in the pipe's bowl, he drew on the stem until the pipe began puffing clouds of fragrant blue smoke. "Now if anyone cares to discuss any matters of importance, he may meet with me in my chamber. Is my dinner ready? I think I prefer the privacy of my rooms. Just trot the trays to my door."

"One moment there," said a voice from the back of the hall. A figure materialized in the gloom and came forward, hooded, and holding a tall staff. "So! Skanderbeg, you troublesome old dragon!" Warth tossed back his hood and planted his feet firmly. "How dare you menace these innocent people with your lies and frightening tales? They should rightly fear you, with such talk. I came here to help these kindly folk. You came only to threaten!"

"Hence, varlet!" Skanderbeg roared, rising to his full height. "And just empty your satchel of Valsidur's gold and provisions before you leave. Thought you'd line your pockets anyway, since you couldn't steal the sword, didn't you?"

Warth showed his teeth and simpered. "No one believes you. I can and shall remove that sword."

"Bah!" Skanderbeg said. "You can't."

"Liar!"

"Thief!"

"Prove it!"

For a moment the two wizards glared at each other. The men of Shieldbroad cowered back. Then Skanderbeg rubbed his ear and Warth's black satchel burst open. A ham and other provisions tumbled out, plus a good many other things.

"Why, there's the family sword!" Valsidur exclaimed. "I never gave him that, you can be sure!"

"And my good cloth and silver!" the kitchen steward added.

"Thief! Robber!" With an angry grumble the crowd

shifted forward. Warth stood his ground for an instant, then scuttled toward his fat volume of magic spells.

"Stop that creature!" roared Kilgore.

Warth turned, bristling like a rat. "And I have a word for you, spying and creeping under tables. Just remember that Kildurin has a curse upon it. Whosoever wields that sword shall also die by it. The sword king will die, or by my bones, I'm not Warth the wizard!" Sucking in his cheeks, he began to blow. An icy wind blasted the relics off the walls, overturned tables, and sent everyone tumbling. With a wild screech, Warth blew himself up the chimney, sucking the fire after him.

With a thunderous rush, the hall was cleared of everyone but Skanderbeg, still smoking his pipe by the fire, which he restored with a nod. Kilgore crept from the shelter of an overturned table and blinked in the brightness of the fire. The wizard piled on about a month's firewood and the greedy blaze set all the shadows dancing. The wizard then sat down and lifted his voice in mad song. The words were in a strange dialect Kilgore had never heard before. When the wizard stopped for breath, Kilgore presented himself.

"Here I am, sir," he said.

"Well! So you are. What do you want?" The wizard was sitting so close to the fire it was a wonder his beard wasn't singed. "I suppose there won't be anything to eat tonight?"

"I'll find you something," Kilgore offered.

"No, I'll manage with my own provisions. Do sit down and join me. Do you like strawberry jam?" From his satchel he laid two covers and produced a small black teapot.

"I'm sure to," Kilgore said. "What is it?"

"Fruit grown in a more hospitable land than this. Help yourself, lad, and have a piece of toast."

"Delicious," Kilgore said. "What is the land called where this strawberry grows?" He was always fascinated by far lands.

"Nothing. It hasn't a name yet, but it's a lovely

place for a castle. Right in the mountain pass to guard
the plain below, just like a cork in a bottle. But another fortress is needed to the south where the river
bends around in a big loop. You see, it's situated like
this—" He whipped a rolled-up leather map out of
his satchel and marked castles and fortresses and enemies with knives, a bowl, a jug, and the black teapot.
"In days to come this will be the most valuable holding in Skarpsey," he said. "But there's another loca-
tion you might like better further inland—"

"Sir," said Kilgore.

"Skanderbeg, if you please. I'm not a sir. I'm a
jack-of-all-trades. Master of all."

"I'd like to get down to business, if you don't mind."

"Business? Business? I thought eating was your
business, by your style in dispatching toast and jam.
What business have we to discuss?"

Kilgore rose and walked into the amber shadows
around the tree. When he returned, he laid the gleaming sword across the table. "I wish to discuss this," he
said.

Skanderbeg's eyes flew open. "Great Hod," he murmured. "So it's you. By the wizard's gizzards, and
you're little more than a boy. I suppose Elbegast knew
what he was doing—" He shook his head.

"Now I want to know the truth," Kilgore said. "Is it
really elven? Do elves still exist, if they ever did? And
if you are a real wizard, just what are you? Also—"

"Stop! I shall tell you everything, and then we'll see
if you have any questions," Skanderbeg said. "To
begin with, where the land is now was once nothing
but a vast nothingness, except for a lot of ice and the
great cauldron of Muspell boiling away. One day it
ran over and to make a long story short without going
into the giants and dwarves and elves, the land was
created, complete with Skinfaxi and Hrimfaxi—"

"Do they really exist? Bright-mane and Frost-mane
were a story my grandmother told me, and how the
sun and moon are chased by wolves. Are they real
horses and chariots?"

"I won't go into that. You seem to be slightly edu-

31

cated, which is a marvel in this place. Then you know that mankind are the sons of Ask and Embla, the two ash trees. Good. Don't interrupt. So now I shall tell you about Surt. He is the great ice wizard who rose from the first awful darkness and who is constantly striving to return the earth to the Fimbul Winter so the evil creatures of the dark can thrive."

"Trolls? Giants?" Kilgore asked. This fellow was an admirable storyteller.

"Aye, and a good many others you mortals have never seen on these pleasant coasts. They were here from the ancientest of times even when you newcomers first arrived."

"Seven centuries is nothing to scoff at," Kilgore said.

The wizard sighed and looked at Kilgore. "Time is more accurately measured in centuries to give the proper perspective. Where you men have claimed Skarpsey seven, there are those who claim it for a couple of hundred centuries. You frail creatures are but an insignificant blink in time, yet it is true you shall someday possess Skarpsey for your own and we of the ancient orders will be gone."

"How ancient are you, Skanderbeg?" Kilgore asked.

"Nearly eighty."

"Centuries?"

"There are others far older than I," the wizard said testily. "Allow me to continue. One of these ancient orders is the Alfar, or elves as you mortals persist in calling them in your fairy stories. The Alfar order is split into Light Alfar and Dark Alfar, referring to their respective tastes in climate. The king of the Light Alfar is Elbegast and it was he who placed the sword in the tree. You were the one he chose of all the mortals to perform this little chore for him, which I shall tell you about in a moment."

"Well!" Kilgore said, admiring the sword. "I've always wanted a sword like this. How did he get it to stick in the tree when anyone else tried it?"

Skanderbeg took a large swallow of tea. "I can't imagine, unless it was magic."

"I suppose. It's a good thing I've always believed in magic."

"I rather imagine you'll believe a lot more fervently when you get back from Gardar," Skanderbeg said.

"Gardar! Nobody who goes there can expect to come back," Kilgore said with a worried smile, wishing someone else were around to help deal with this wizard if he got too extreme. "Am I to take this sword and go to Gardar with it?"

Skanderbeg pressed his temples. "Yes. And with it you shall locate and slay the wizard Surt. The last war in your grandfathers' time was the tail end of the Sixteen Centuries' War, in which Surt was captured and thrust into dwarf prison, twenty leagues underground in a stone cell without a door; but we have recently discovered that he's been in Gardar these past sixty-five years, causing all manner of grief. This was his last chance. We've given him opportunities to redeem himself, but he'll never change, so Elbegast has taken the sword out of hiding. If it hadn't been for Surt, there would be no Dark Alfar and no ice wizards and no threat of the Fimbul Winter that has ruined your Northern Quarter."

Kilgore pondered the wizard's words. "Then Surt is causing this coldness that is descending on us?" The wizard nodded. "Then I say let's raise an army and march on his southern borders, burn his cities, attack his garrisons—"

"Wouldn't work. He doesn't operate that way. March an army into Gardar and you'll march out a bunch of icebergs. He's got eyes everywhere, even here in the Brandstok. And do you really suppose a wizard such as he would fight by mortal rules and means?" A stern eye held Kilgore in thrall and the wizard whispered: "And now I shall tell you the greatest secret of all. Nothing can destroy Surt. He has suffered death by every weapon we can think of, and he returns stronger than ever each time. This sword is the last attempt, and it will be the bane of Surt. Now, any questions?"

"The only question a sane and sensible person

33

could ask is do you expect me to buy such nonsense, but—"

"Well, blow me to Padbury!" exclaimed the wizard, flinging up his hands. Instantly the room was full of wind. Papers and books flew everywhere, relics fell down from the wall, and the old banners shook themselves to shreds. "No, no, no!" shouted Skanderbeg. "Stop!"

The wind ceased as if someone had put a cork in. Skanderbeg recaptured his papers and rearranged his rumpled clothing, beard, and hair, muttering in a wrathy fashion. He began putting on his boots and packing up his things in a most peculiar fashion. When he stabbed his finger at a spoon or map, it immediately hopped into the satchel. Kilgore stared in fascination, unable to speak for amazement.

"I shall tell Elbegast he made a dreadful mistake," said the wizard. "Put the sword back in the tree and he will come for it, but probably not before that cloud gets to Shieldbroad. Farewell."

"What? Wait!" Kilgore grabbed Skanderbeg's cloak. "I'm sorry, but you misunderstood. I never said I was a sane and sensible person, Skanderbeg. Nobody has believed in these things in Shieldbroad for years, except the poor people who live close to the fells and firths. And me, of course, much against the will of my father. Tell me more about magic. How do you make things jump around like that?"

"Sane and sensible!" growled Skanderbeg, sitting down again. "And listen, you've got to realize there are simply things you don't need to know about, being a mortal. I didn't learn what I know and earn these silver locks sitting in a chimney corner hobnailing with witches' sprites. I suppose you want proof that magic is a real force, even in Shieldbroad. Well, can you read the runes on the sword blade?"

"Certainly. They say—"

"Hush!" The wizard clapped his hand over Kilgore's mouth. "No one can read those runes but you, and the only others who know that key are in their tombs. I can't read it, in spite of my skill. And look

34

here at this." He removed a smooth green sphere from his pocket. It was about the size of an egg. Kilgore looked into it curiously and saw Shieldbroad in miniature, a green jewel between two black arms that welcomed the peaceful Codfirth almost to the doorsteps of the settlers. Beyond he could see more fjords and nesses and a vast dark cloud that poured slowly and heavily like ink into a green fjord as he watched.

"What is this? I can see all over." Kilgore wanted to look longer but Skanderbeg took it away.

"It's a tool. It's not good for mortals to get too close to it. Now is that proof enough that Surt exists?" Kilgore nodded. "Good! That's progress. Now a word about this sword. Keep it close to you every moment so it won't get stolen. It will protect and warn you about danger with a humming sound which other ears will not hear. It will cut wood, stone, metal, and you are the only one who can wield it. Kildurin has a spirit of its own and fights of its own will. But no more for now. It is time to retire. I must wish you a good night. Be ready for an early start at the darkest hour before dawn."

"But wait—wait! You haven't explained a thousand things!" Kilgore protested. "What armies do we have? Where exactly are we going? I want to see this Elbegast, if there is such a person, or elf. How did you know about this sword? And speaking of the sword—"

"Just follow my advice and you won't go too far wrong," the wizard said sleepily, rising to usher Kilgor to the door.

"What did you say about an early start?" demanded Kilgore. "Do you mean just the two of us? Shouldn't we tell Valsidur? Shouldn't we—"

"I said we must retire early if we are to make one. And the answer is no, and probably no again. Goodnight. Mind the darkness. Don't fall over anything, and watch out for enemies."

"Enemies—" Kilgore muttered in a daze. The door was open and it would have been rude to insist on staying. He mumbled, "Goodnight," and stepped into the dark corridor. In a positive muddle, he shuffled toward his quarters. A cold breath made him look up, just in time to see a flitting movement in the gloom. Suspiciously he hurried after it, through the silent Brandstok hall where a few last embers glowed on the hearth. The front door creaked, and he caught a glimpse of a dusky red cloak slipping out. Warth the wizard, he marked to himself grimly. But the thought was crowded out of his head with speculations about the morrow.

CHAPTER 4

At the darkest, most desolate hour of the morning Kilgore was awakened by a smart rapping at his door. "Be silent as you can. We must be off with as much secrecy as possible."

With a strong thrill of excitement, he dressed hurriedly in his most rugged clothing. The wizard adventure was not only a dream, he told himself with wonder as he made his way to the main hall. There he stopped short, seeing the worst tangle of barrels, boxes, ropes, kegs, and all manner of strangely shaped objects he had ever witnessed. In the midst of it all, the wizard was flinging boxes and sacks and all manner of things from his black satchel. Obviously more magic at work. Kilgore shuddered and stared in fascination.

"Good day," Skanderbeg said after a moment. "Just the person I was looking for."

"May I help?" Kilgore asked dutifully, without enthusiasm.

"You haven't any choice, since this is mostly your business. What you may do is divide everything in half, equally."

"What! All this is going with us?" Kilgore exclaimed, looking about him.

Silently the wizard stuffed a wine barrel into his limp little satchel; miraculously, it disappeared into the black folds as if such feats were everyday occurrences.

Kilgore shook his head slightly and fell to work dividing the mountain of provisions. There was enough to supply ten men food for half a year, and equipment for a regiment. One heap alone looked like an entire larder.

"Now then," Skanderbeg said at last, handing him a pack, "put your half in here. My share I shall put into my satchel, although there's little enough space already, with my books and bottles and things. You must hurry faster than that, you know. We can't dilly-dally around until the household awakes. I've a feeling already that our purpose is known to the wrong people. Hasten, hasten! Don't worry about getting everything in; the pack will hold anything you put into it."

"Whatever you say!" Kilgore said and discovered, to his surprise, that there was ample space for everything, no matter how large or bulky.

"Now for breakfast," Kilgore suggested when it was done.

"Of course. You're quite right," Skanderbeg agreed and filled Kilgore's pockets with dried fruit and nuts and hung a little flask around his neck. Then on went the pack, and they were on their way.

"Eating is such a bother when something important is afoot," Skanderbeg said as they crossed the door-yard, striding along so fast that Kilgore abandoned his doubts about the old wizard's strength. He would be fortunate indeed merely to keep from slowing Skanderbeg's pace, let alone outdistance him.

The pack was astonishingly light, and the pre-dawn dimness was delightful and still. Overhead, the stars still shone as if it were midnight, and the air was fragrant with ripening grain and mown hay. A few larks and throstles chirruped hopefully from the brakes and marshes.

"What a pleasant time for beginning," Kilgore said, his boots making long strides across the lush pasturage. The firth smelled cool and fishy.

"Aye, and high time for our undertaking," Skanderbeg agreed in a preoccupied manner, his eyes fixed upon the misty north where lurked the Skull Mountains in shrouds of blue mist.

"Why must we be so secret about our journey?"

Kilgore asked when they had passed the last homestead of his father's thanes.

"The more it is kept a secret," Skanderbeg replied, "the fewer people will know we're gone." And he strode on.

"But wait—" Kilgore caught up with him and demanded, "I think you ought to tell me your plans. After all, I have a right to know, since I'm carrying this sword." He touched it in its leather sheath where it hung at his waist, weighty and unaccustomed.

"Just a minute. I shall explain." Grumbling, Skanderbeg paused and hurriedly scratched on the earth with his staff. "Here is Shieldbroad. Neck is to the north, Heroness further north against the foot of the Skull Mountains. On either side of Heroness, Coldbeck easterly and Goatnef westerly. Now the Skull Mountains are actually two great ranges, the Briarthorne and the Burnt, and behind them lie the Trident Mountains, barred from the Briarthornes and Burnts by a great chasm that once led a mighty river to the sea. The river is gone, but the Gardar Road lies there now, leading to a pass into Gardar just east of the triple peaks called the Trident. I plan to take us up the Skull Mountains, over the tops, and down into the chasm. And then we shall rush through the Gardar Pass, if we arrive there alive. Needless to say, Surt's minions are guarding the pass very closely, since by now word has leaked out that you are coming. Barring any worse calamities than I've planned for, we should be returning to Shieldbroad next spring. If all goes well, that is. At least, as well as it can. Any more questions? Good." He scratched out the map, and left Kilgore musing at the scratch marks.

"What shall we do in Gardar? How do we go about finding—you know who?" Kilgore asked, hurrying after Skanderbeg.

"Finding Surt will be no problem whatsoever. In fact, we shall be lucky to remain undetected long enough to be effective."

"Oh, I see." Kilgore walked in silence, thinking of the scratched map and Skanderbeg's words about the

39

expedition lasting until spring. And to think—no one at Valsidursknoll knew where he had gone, except that he'd disappeared the same day as the wizard. Kilgore himself was little more enlightened, and here he was rushing off with a strange magical personage into dangerous territory that no mortal had seen since the deaths of Wulther and Valsidda, almost sixty-five years ago. That was the sobering part. He had no idea of the dangers that waited ahead.

But as he strode blithely across the rocky pastures and windy beaches of Shieldbroad, the horrid perils seemed far away. Kilgore felt quite competent to deal with any of them, and he touched the cool golden hilt again. He squinted into the velvety gloom of oak woods, half hoping to see a troll or dragon or a child-snatching monster lurking about. Not that he knew what to look for, but he'd heard plenty of old tales from his grandmother, made more fascinating by the disapproval of his elders. He was on the point of asking Skanderbeg if he supposed they would encounter any of these beasts when he noticed the wizard frowning often over his shoulder behind them.

"Are you practicing being cautious?" Kilgore demanded as they puffingly scrambled up a hillside. "And why are we punishing ourselves by climbing this hill? As you can see, it just goes right down the other side again."

"So it does. All to our purpose when we descend. I like to rest on a hilltop, particularly when it has such large lovely boulders on top. Very like a fortress, don't you think?" He sat down gratefully in the shade of one of the rocks, since it was hot.

"How peculiar to make such an ordeal of resting," Kilgore said, and sat down also. "I would rather find a pleasant grassy level and lie down for a nap in the sun. Rocks and brambles can't compare to green, beautiful—"

Skanderbeg was not paying the slightest attention. He hauled the various parts of a large telescope out of his satchel and gleefully assembled them like a boy with a new toy. It was brassy and new and had silver

40

engravings in runic all over it. Kilgore was impressed and curious in spite of himself.

"Never used it before," the wizard said proudly. "But I always knew it would prove useful someday."

"Hum! You'll have to wait a while for the moon to come up," Kilgore suggested.

"There are other natural phenomena to observe besides the moon, and these strange bodies don't mind the time or season," Skanderbeg replied as he aimed the instrument southward and squinted into it with one eye. "Ha! and there is is. I knew it would be shortly following the dawn. Have a peek."

"If you insist," Kilgore said with an indulgent sigh. Nevertheless, he stooped eagerly to look into the telescope. The distant landscape leaped at him, startlingly clear and close. It was the wood that bordered the last thane's homestead, which they had crossed earlier. There was an odd sound in his ears, like trees rushing in the breeze. The trees in the telescope were moving, but there were no trees on their hilltop. A bird twittered—a brown throstle in the bush he was looking at with the telescope. Hastily he shook his head and backed away from the device.

"Very pretty," he said, trying not to sound impressed. "But I saw nothing more dreadful than old Bork's wood—nothing I didn't see hiking through it."

"You don't say. Perhaps you're looking at the wrong things," Skanderbeg said, taking a quick glance. Then he demolished the telescope with one word. The heap of legs and segments was stuffed into the satchel. "Let us be off. I have decided we've got to be at Haelfsknoll by the end of next week." Motioning to his satchel, he made it snap itself firmly shut, very businesslike.

"Why, that's only thirteen days. A man on a strong horse might do it, but not we two on foot. We must cross all of Neck yet, and then into Coldbeck or Goatnef to get around the Sloughs of Heroness. You can see very plainly on your map—"

41

"Not on my map, I couldn't," the wizard answered shortly.

"We are not going through the Sloughs," Kilgore said flatly. "That vile place has swallowed good men for centuries."

"They must have been rather foolish to attempt it, knowing how dangerous it was, eh?" Skanderbeg said. "I suspect it swallows fools and sages alike. But you, sirrah, have other concerns than bogs and the beasties in them. I shall get you safely to Gardar; you shall worry about conquering Surt, and other incidental giants, ogres, and so forth. Contrary to what you mortals think, the Sloughs are perfectly navigable, although not without certain dangers, I will admit. Trust this old head for once. I didn't get this old by staying stupid, and you shan't get much older if you remain so dense either. Now let me worry about the important things. You worry about sorcerers and giants."

Before Kilgore could ask what things were more important than giants and sorcerers, Skanderbeg had collected his satchel and bounded to the bottom of the hill. Kilgore hurried after him. He was scarely rested, but Skanderbeg seemed as lively as he had been that morning. Noonday, he hoped, would provide a long rest, a decent meal and a nap in a grassy hollow out of the wind.

When the sun was straight overhead, Kilgore called a halt. Skanderbeg grumbled and made much noise about getting to Haelfsknoll. He pointed out the dangers of traveling at night: trolls, dark-elves, wolves, or falling accidentally into a greedy bog.

"I refuse to move until we have eaten," Kilgore declared, unpacking. "We shall hurry twice as fast afterward."

"You mortals think the sun being straight up is a signal for you to be hungry. I would have stopped soon enough," the wizard growled, nevertheless eyeing the dainties fondly.

They dined hastily, and Kilgore felt strangely uneasy. They had stopped in a rather unpleasant grove of knotty old trees with lumps and boles that looked like twisted faces with eyes. He observed the wizard looking about with a suspicious air and frowning. In a very short time the provisions were repacked, and Kilgore was glad to be on the way again.

At the end of the first day of the adventure, they camped on a hilltop overlooking the tower that marked the boundary of Shieldbroad. Here the road forked. To the east, the Coldbeck road; to the west, Goatnef, and the middle fork led to Neck. All night long the travelers heard horses and oxen and all manner of traffic on the roads below, creaking or plodding steadily southward through Shieldbroad. Kilgore thought of the green fields and forests of Shieldbroad, and how lucky were those wanderers traveling that way.

The following morning he looked his last on Shieldbroad—for a while, anyway, he told himself sternly. But words of Skanderbeg lingered in his mind. Perhaps he wouldn't get back for a long time, or not at all. He shook his head to clear it of these dreadful thoughts, not liking to think about the possible consequences of this adventure.

Neck was not a pleasant land. There were few homesteads and villages, and the countryside was rocky barrow mounds of forgotten wars and grassy swales where the chill wind raced. Bands of gray and black mottled sheep grazed to the hollow tune of a single bell clonking, while the fleece-clad shepherd stood outlined with his staff against the cloudy sky. In silence sheep and man watched the travelers pick their way across the windy barrow mounds. Kilgore plodded at Skanderbeg's heels, desolately thinking it was a shame that Neck had not progressed from the wild, dark past as Shieldbroad had. He had an uneasy feeling the country was barely civilized. A gang of wandering warriors on their shaggy horses might come sweeping down upon them, waving their crude weapons, and in this barren place there was no place to hide. Shuddering, he looked around at the old barrows, hoping he wouldn't see anything to frighten him. All he saw that was alive was a shepherd with a twisted staff and whipping cloak, black against the bleak sky.

For seven days the curious maps of Skanderbeg led them over hills, through cold valleys, until Neck was behind them. They met no one, as was Skanderbeg's plan. Kilgore constantly complained about the trackless going, declaring that there were few enough people in Heroness and even fewer now, so what would it hurt to travel on the road and thereby avoid the Sloughs? Skanderbeg turned a deaf ear, when he was in one of his patient moods; usually he snapped, "By the great wizard's gizzards, this isn't a pleasure trip! It's dangerous enough already in these lands. All you do is complain. And what a prodigious appetite! You'll have us eaten out of everything by the time we get to the Gardar Road!" And more. Kilgore had done more enjoyable things than travel with a wizard.

Heroness, if anything, was more disappointing than Neck. It was flat, and the once-famous smooth pastures for swift horses were now rank and gummy. Dead grass covered the earth in a mat. Only the most noxious of plants survived, liked nettles and thorns and tiny burrs that snarled the hems of their cloaks. There had once been stands of poplars and sycamore, but now the great trees lifted bare white branches to the sky. The pretty lakes were now seas of cracked mud. Reeds rattled like bones in the nipping wind. The land had a smell of early winter about it, of frostbite and frozen mud. Only a plentiful supply of ravens and kites remained to crouch in the bare treetops and flap squawking at the approach of the travelers.

In the six days spent in Heroness, they saw not a living soul. Most of the granges and villages, Kilgore knew, were on the eastern and western borders where traffic from other lands was heaviest. The interior of Heroness was traversed only by far-roaming flocks of sheep and goats and a few solitary hermits. Here the climate was still and hot and smelled of the Sloughs to the north.

44

Kilgore inhaled the smell of things rotting. The Sloughs were ahead—a black line across their path, shrouded in mist. He felt a crawling sensation just thinking about entering that sorrowful place. At the very least it was haunted by spirits, and he felt like reminding Skanderbeg of this fact, but was embarrassed to admit that he feared such things.

It was late afternoon when they reached the green perimeters of the Sloughs. Skanderbeg paused and leaned on his staff. "Well, we have made it this far. If you come through the Sloughs well, I'll have few fears about taking you on the rest of the journey."

"Thank you," Kilgore said when the wizard paused significantly. It wasn't much of a complaint.

"Now I shall warn you. Stay very close to me. Don't break or tear any of the trees or plants you see. Watch out for snakes and don't eat anything. We shall be safely on the other side by nightfall. Even I would hate to get stuck here after dark. Oh, yes, and if you hear any singing, stop up your ears, for more than likely it will be a gaggle of undines—nasty slimy creatures. They'll charm away your senses and drown you in a bottomless pool if you let them. Now, any questions? Good; we must hurry. This would be an awful place to encounter slipping, spying creatures."

"Of what sort?" asked Kilgore, ready to turn back. He was chilled with dread already.

"Any sort. Just be on your guard, always." With resolute strides he hurried away, and Kilgore was quick to follow.

The turf became grassy underfoot, then sedgy. Green reeds scratched at their legs, waving black-tipped heads with the wind. A multitude of frogs kept up a lugubrious croaking and creaking. Giant sycamores stood in the middle of a sea of green water, with trailing veils of moss drooping into the murk. Reeds and grass grew out of sluggish pools, where a few flowers of some sickly, poisonous sort bloomed on the surfaces. As far as Kilgore could see, the place was nothing but willows, brakes, and motionless

45

water. The only things he could see or hear were the frogs and a pair of cackling ravens.

"Skanderbeg, there's no way we can get across that," he exclaimed, and sat down on a green hummock. "I refuse to go any further, unless it is east or west around this horrid swamp. We wouldn't get more than ten paces before we found ourselves in to our necks. Not to mention the spirits, bats, spiders, brutes—"

"I am aware of all that! Do you think I'm new at this business? Certainly not! I've crossed far worse bogs than this one."

"But have you crossed this one before?"

"Well—one bog is very like another."

"What does that mean?"

"Oh, it means whatever I said it means!" Skanderbeg exclaimed, glaring at him. "I have a map of this hideous place, if you really must know!" He flung down his satchel and looked inside, grumbling. "I don't see my map case. Did you put it in your pack?"

"I don't remember. I quit noticing. There was so much stuff—"

"Well, we must unpack then. Dradgast it! Look at the sun. Not four hours of traveling light left. Quick, quick, let's hurry." He began hauling things out of his satchel with both hands, and Kilgore followed suit. In a few moments, there was a terrific heap of loot.

"Foul fish livers," Skanderbeg muttered. "I still don't see it. I suppose we have left it somewhere. I don't know what we shall do without it, and it's the only one of its kind. I got it from a quaint old necromancer who runs a shop in Oldstead, and he got it from an old trunk he'd bought from a sea wanderer —but that's of no importance. I know I brought it. Do you remember a long tube, painted blue and silver and red? That was its case."

"Why, yes I do. It was in my pack. But its not here now, and I haven't seen it since—I don't remember. But the first time I saw it was on the first day, in that little wood in Shieldbroad, where we stopped for lunch. I remember—yes! But I'm certain I packed it again. At least I thought I did. We were in such

46

a hurry though—" He looked around, feeling that same uneasy feeling he'd experienced that day in the wood. To reassure himself, he touched the sword, and was startled to find that it quivered finely.

"Skanderbeg!" he called in alarm. The wizard didn't respond; he was searching through the mountain of boxes, boots, staffs, and one huge red and blue silk tent.

"Ha!" cried Skanderbeg in delight. "Here it is! Sitting right on this tuffet. It's a wonder we didn't see it."

"Yes, it is. Skanderbeg, I think something awfully strange is going on, and I don't like it. Listen to the sword. It's ringing, ever so softly, and it trembles. It gives me the most peculiar feeling, and I have felt it before. That very day I mentioned, when the map case disappeared." He put his hand on the sword. "It acts as if it wants to be drawn."

Skanderbeg was shuffling through the maps in the case. "So it was made, lad. It's nothing to worry over."

"But what causes it to do that?"

"Something malicious is near. An ice wizard or something. We must be off; the time is very short. You repack and I shall examine the map." He shuffled through the maps, frowning over the yellowed, frayed material.

Kilgore touched the sword again, and the mysterious thrumming had stopped. The presence that caused the warning was now gone. More reassuring yet, the map was found again.

Kilgore finished repacking, and Skanderbeg tucked the map case into his satchel. Boldly he struck off into the gloom and mist of the Slough. Kilgore clung to his heels, stepping in the same tracks and treading often on the hem of Skanderbeg's cloak. There seemed to be no path. Very quickly Kilgore forgot which direction was back to dry earth. Underfoot the going got mushier, until they were hopping from hummock to hummock, and the hummocks were getting fewer and farther.

"Skanderbeg," he called at last. "Do you think the map is wrong?"

"No, there's nothing wrong with the map, I see the way perfectly clear. Follow me."

They found themselves on an island with a dead tree. The wind hissed in its naked branches. All around them was black, still water.

"What unusual directions," Kilgore commented, disheartened.

"Not at all. You must remember this is a wizardous map." The wizard cast about the island. "Look here. I've found the way."

Kilgore stared into the water. "All I see is an old rotten tree which is probably slippery and the hiding place of countless snakes. Besides, where would it take us? Surely the map is wrong."

"We shall get to those hummocks yonder. I think I see dry land ahead." Skanderbeg stepped onto the mossy log, tapping the way with his staff.

"I'm no wizard," Kilgore protested. "I can't live a dozen lives."

"You only use one at a time anyway. Come along; it's quite safe."

Kilgore inched his way along the log. It was indeed slick. "Is this on the map?" he asked.

"It is, although by the trail one wouldn't know it was a dead tree. Ha, just as I suspected. These willows are growing on dry earth. Perhaps it will show us a decent road."

Kilgore thankfully pushed through the willow screen. To his relief, the earth was grassy and only a little soggy and dank. There were hedges of thorns and ancient willow trees with their gray trailing leaves hanging almost to the ground. It smelled of decay. Kilgor thought it must be an excellent place to grow mushrooms, the black and deadly kind. He shuddered, and hurried after Skanderbeg.

"Ugh, those tree roots look exactly like a pile of snakes," he said.

"Don't say such things. It gives 'em ideas. Or your eyes may start deceiving you. In places like this it is

48

easy to make things into what they aren't." He surveyed the area, fist on hip, and consulted a small shining device in his hand—an oracle, he called it.

After they had been walking some time, Kilgore called a halt to tighten the laces of his boot. "Look!" he cried. "There's someone else crossing the swamp. Footprints."

Skanderbeg took one look and sat down on a mouldering stump. "It wasn't what I feared, but something just as bad," he said. "That proves that expecting something to be bad will make it worse or at least as bad as what you'd hoped."

"What is it? Something dreadfully evil, like— Warth?"

"Not so evil. These are our own tracks."

"What a relief!" exclaimed Kilgore. "I'd thought Warth was following—"

"No, nothing worse has happened than getting ourselves lost in the Sloughs of Heroness, and it is almost sundown. We shall head straight north, bearing west to avoid going in a circle."

Accordingly, they walked briskly, bearing to the west. At last they paused to survey their progress. Kilgore pointed ahead. "There's a clearing. We can look at the map there."

"It seems to me—" Skanderbeg began, slowing his pace and eying the clearing, "—we've been here before. Yes, remember that tree? I'd never forget that. It has a broken branch like a skeleton's hand—" He stopped and stared at the tree. The broken limb pointed across the surface of a scummy green pool. "I wonder what it is pointing to?" he speculated. "Let's follow it."

"What about the map? How can we get across that?" Kilgore regarded the muck in horror. "It must be terribly deep. And who made this tree marker? How do we know it's not some unpleasant joke?"

Ignoring him, Skanderbeg prodded ot it with his staff. "Just as I thought. It's not water at all, but turf growing on the pool. See, this is grass. It will easily hold our weight."

49

So saying, he stepped onto the curdled surface. It undulated with each step like a greenish-brown carpet.

Kilgore followed, testing each step gingerly. When he reached the far side, Skanderbeg was waiting.

"Hurry, hurry! There's another tree pointing the way." He began jumping hummocks again. Yet another pointing tree waited, and they cautiously crossed a bed of soft black mud that oozed and bubbled. A grim old pine pointed steadily across a sea of waving tules. A straight young cedar sent them plunging into a forest of moss-draped dead trees. The ghostly peeling trunks became denser, and the fern more plentiful. It was gloomier too, with the sinking of the sun.

"I see a clearing," Kilgore said. "Why, it looks as if there's some kind of—" He stopped himself before he said something foolish. He thought he had seen a house lurking among the trees.

"A house!" Skanderbeg exclaimed. "Upon my body and soul! I've never heard of it before. No, it can't be." He stole stealthily to the edge of the clearing and Kilgore followed.

The stead rose right up from the swamp. Frogs creaked around its mossy gray walls and ravens roosted in its shaggy black thatch. At the east and west doors rotted the old beaks of long-forgotten dragon ships. The black portals gaped lonesomely as they sagged in ruin.

"This must be more ice-wizardry," Skanderbeg muttered.

"It looks like any old deserted place to me," Kilgore said. "Why don't we spend the night there?"

"You may if you want to get whisked away with it at some wizard's capricious whim," Skanderbeg said. "I'm certain that it is an unhealthy holding. Perhaps it was even placed here specifically to trick us. That sword is a valuable token. But I never suspected that Warth could conjure something so imposing. If it is Warth's, of course."

"And whose else could it be?" Kilgore inquired.

But Skanderbeg refused to answer, which seemed to be a wizard's prerogative. He only began to withdraw from the house, muttering, "Blasts upon those trees. I'd like to make matchwood out of the treacherous brutes." He looked at them darkly.

"But we can't go back. Let's go around the stead then, if it distresses you so. The map has taken us thus far—"

"I should have told you. There is no map. Oh, there is, but we don't have it. Remember that strange occurrence with the map case? And the sword singing? I have a feeling our map's thief was right under our very noses. Several times. Once to steal the Slough map and once to—I don't know what. But it is the only map missing from the collection. He's up to something. Probably altered every one of my Skull and Trident maps to lead us into every troll and ogre's den between here and Hel's kettle. Drat that nosey, sneaking—"

"Warth?" asked Kilgore. "Why, if only I'd taken the chance I had to end his miserable life. The night before we left Valsidursknoll I was sure I saw him in the corridor outside your chamber, no doubt listening. I could have tried the sword on him."

"And accomplished nothing. He's far too cunning and cowardly to let you kill him. But that's all past now."

"Why would he steal our map, when it's the sword he wants? And just what could he do with the sword if he stole it?"

"He stole the map so we wouldn't know where we're going. And he wants the sword so we won't have it," Skanderbeg replied shortly as he consulted a fat yellow-leaved book.

Kilgore touched the golden hilt of the sword and frowned. "But it's useless in his hands. What can he do with it?"

"If he should manage to decipher the Alfar runes he could become more powerful than Surt. If he is in league with the rebellious ice wizards' clan, who are most certainly in league with Surt, they could unitedly bring down the Fimbul Winter. Or perhaps he'd take his knowledge to Surt and sell it for a staggering price. I really don't know what the little savage would do, since he's half troll and therefore more than half insane. Now do quit bothering me for just one instant while I try to use my oracle!"

Kilgore went and sat on a stump. His spirits sank with the sun. With growing discomfort he watched the shadows getting longer and blacker while the hoots and howls and other doleful noises grew more frequent. He began wondering why he had ever impetuously consented to accompany this unreliable magical personage on such a fool's voyage as crossing the Sloughs with no map with night approaching.

Kilgore kept up with Skanderbeg as best he could, but the wizard hurried along at such an incautious rate while Kilgore looked suspiciously at every step and was forever glancing around behind him. Lagging as usual, Kilgore stopped to catch his breath. He caught a glimpse of something running through the brush, hunched over and dragging some flapping bird after it. Kilgore was about to dash away after Skanderbeg when he noticed the path the strange creature had taken. It was perfectly dry and well-trodden and terribly inviting after all their slogging through ankle-deep mud.

"Skanderbeg!" he called. "I found the trail!" With a bound, he gained the trodden place and set off whistling.

At a small distance, Skanderbeg stopped, hearing his shout. "What did you say? Come along, you troublesome boy. This is not the place to be a laggard."

Receiving no answer and hearing no sound of sturdy boots squashing along in the muck, he turned around and saw no sign of Kilgore. He muttered, "Blasts and boils. Kilgore! Come back here! Halloo! Kilgore!"

There was no answer. The slough seemed to soak up the sound of his voice. The only reply he received was the hoarse croaking of a drove of frogs.

CHAPTER 5

Blithely Kilgore strode along the spongy path. It was Skanderbeg's turn to catch up with him for a change. The thought was so cheering that he quickly covered quite a distance before he realized that Skanderbeg ought to have caught up by now. He halted in his tracks and called, "Hallo, Skanderbeg!" Turning around, he was dumbfounded by what he saw. Or rather, what he didn't see. The wide easy path he had so cheerfully followed was not there behind him where it belonged. Instead, he saw black pools, toadstools, and clumps of wiry grass and fern. He looked ahead and there it was, innocently leading him on. Behind, it was gone.

Woefully he sat down on a log as the dusk purpled around him. Hungry insects hovered in humming clouds. Bats began their nimble flights and the mists were gathering. Croaks and grunts and rustlings were all around. Something came splashing heavily toward him and he decided it would be better to keep walking in the hope the path would eventually lead him out of the Sloughs, and he would wait for Skanderbeg on its edge.

He hurried onward through the curtains of mist, thankful that the trail was broad and easy to follow. One moment he was in the clear and the next he was groping and choking in the fog. It had a hideous odor of rotting vegetation. Drawing his cloak tighter around him, he gripped the sword and listened with dread for its warning note.

Listening, he stopped suddenly. Ever so faint, the sound of voices came to his ears. Somebody was singing. Undines, he thought with a chill. But no, as he stood straining to hear, he realized these were the voices of men, upraised in joyous song. Kilgore started toward them eagerly, picturing a pleasant fire and a safe place to spend the night. It would be wise, he decided, to have a staff in case he had to defend himself. They might be robbers. He reached for a stout young sapling and bent it to him to cut it. With a hiss and a snap it sprang from his hands and stood trembling. The other trees nearby began to rustle and thrash their lower limbs. Hastily Kilgore abandoned the idea.

The mysterious singing started again, nearer now. He stopped to listen. It was uproariously gleeful, as if a large group of friends had come together. "Now, if the singers were monsters or something wicked," Kilgore reasoned to himself, "how could they sing so jovially? Wicked hearts harbor no mirth, my father used to say. These fellows sound like the thanes of the Brandstok—lusty, cheerful souls. Why, I must be almost out of this gloomy place, if there are people living near. Ha, won't Skanderbeg be in a state when he finds me waiting for him. I shall look positively bored, as if I'd been waiting forever."

He hastened now, ignoring the shadows and sounds around him. His head was full of puddings and fires and roast fowl and sweet wine. He bid the swamp a disdainful farewell, glad that nothing worse had happened to him than being lost from Skanderbeg for a few hours.

A square black outline appeared among the trees. He could see doors and windows glowing with cheerful light. The inviting uproar was drifting out to him, along with the delicious aroma of something cooking. Almost by themselves, his feet found the path. He scarcely noticed the rotting ship's beak beside the door, nor did he recognize the house where the crows were nesting in the broken roofs. He had eyes only for the yellow lights ahead.

Reaching the door, he did remember to knock politely. At once the singing stopped, and there was some hurried whispering. Then the door opened wide and a voice exclaimed, "Well, come in, come in! I declare, a traveler. Are you lost in the Sloughs, my friend?"

The speaker was a tall, wrinkled old fellow whose hood kept flopping over one eye or the other. Kilgore could scarcely see his face and the dimness of the room didn't help. The inviting yellow light was made by a small fire in the kitchen hearth. Around the fire sat four more hooded men. They looked like travelers; each was dusty and ragged, and all carried bulging dirty satchels. They stared at him silently—hardly the type to sing so merrily.

Uncomfortably he answered, "Not really lost. I'm traveling with a friend who's lost, though. I stumbled upon the path quite by accident."

"Surely you have a map!" said the first man in horror.

"We did have, but through some devious means our map was pinched by a rat of a wizard."

"Eh! Really!" Everyone marveled, exchanging glances.

"Are you certain it was a wizard, my boy?" the first asked, ushering Kilgore to a stool beside the fire. "I've never heard of such a thing in these enlightened times."

"Ah yes, it's unfortunately true," Kilgore said sagely. "You may not know it, but it's rumored that the greatest ice wizard of all has escaped from prison in the dwarf kingdom. His evil henchmen have held the land of Gardar captive these three score and five years. And now that he is free, things here in Heroness are getting pretty cold and barren. I have inside information that he is plotting a take-over." He nodded mysteriously, pleased at the open-mouthed wonder of his five hosts.

They all gasped and shook their heads in dismay. The one closest to the fire, an unhealthy, poxy sort, spoke up and said, "I don't believe it. Tell us how you happened to find out. Was it elves that told you?"

"Now, you needn't make fun, it's perfectly true," Kilgore said, nettled by their indulgent attentiveness. "I can't tell you who told me, since it involves a great many important details too vital to discuss."

"Well!" remarked the fellows. The poxy one said slyly, "It sounds to me as if Surt has escaped."

"Oh, then you know about Surt?" Kilgore asked in surprise.

"It's no secret," the first one said. "Few people don't know. The fact that Surt has conquered Gardar at the expense of many human lives is well known. We have been aware for years that he planned to enter the lands south of the Trident and Skull Mountains. And we also know that the elves and fire wizards are doing everything they can to stop him and the mighty body of ice wizards he is calling from all the darkest points of the earth."

"Oh, indeed?" Kilgore murmured, eying the roasting ducks hungrily.

"Where are you from, lad?" another traveler asked. "And what are you called? The lot of us come from Whaleness."

"Kilgore of Shieldbroad." He bowed solemnly. "Retainer to Valsidur."

"Really," the first said. "I am Mord, and my companions are Nord, Gullni, Gerpir, and Trollni." They nodded and mumbled in turn. Kilgore had seen uglier men, but not as a group, although misshapen noses, warts, and hairy moles were common enough afflictions. Mord continued, "We are traveling to Oxbarrow and decided to spend the night in this abandoned house. You are more than welcome to share it. Ah, did you say your companion expects to find you here?"

"Certainly, if this is Haelfsknoll." Kilgore looked longingly at the ducks. They glistened golden with dripping grease and the smell—

"But we're still in the very heart of the Slough," Nord said. "The place you spoke of is a day's journey from here."

Kilgore looked around, disconcerted. "Then we passed this house earlier. It is only an ice wizard's conjuration, I'm afraid."

"It looks substantial enough to me," Gullni said in alarm. "You don't suppose we'll all be whisked away to some realm of the black arts, do you?"

"I think you're just trying to frighten us," Trollni said with a hoarse chuckle.

"You must be famished," Mord said kindly. "Would you like to help us put away this brace of ducks? They are easily caught and killed."

"I didn't intend to trouble you." Kilgore sat down at once and took out his knife. "But the hospitality of Sciplings cannot be refused."

"Our pleasure," Mord said. "It's not often we encounter someone so knowledgeable in the affairs of wizards."

"I'm dreadfully afraid to sleep in this house," Gerpir said anxiously. "Do you suppose we'll be all right?"

"I hope so," said Nord, a squinty fellow who was always winking.

Kilgore observed the winking all through the meal with mounting irritation, but he was too polite to mention it. Finishing the last of one entire bird, he said. "I thank you for such hospitality. Do go on with another song. I heard your voices when I was far into the swamp, and I said to myself 'What fine singers!' Won't you sing another?"

They looked at each other as if suddenly shy. Then Gerpir choked and turned quite green with coughing. Mord thumped his back for him and said, "Gerpir's the best. Now that he's out, we couldn't bring ourselves to sing another note. Besides, it's terribly late. I'm almost asleep." The others yawned enormously and blinked their eyes. "We must hie ourselves away to bed. Travelers have to get early starts."

"Yes, that's true," Kilgore agreed. "But tell me first where the lot of you are away to? Not much this way, except Gardar and Surt."

"We're going south," Gerpir said quickly. "To— to Oxbarrow."

"We've relatives there," Trollni added.

57

"But isn't Heroness dreadfully out of the way for you?" inquired Kilgore. "You ought to have gone straight east from Neck to the Wildefeld, then—"

"He means Coldbeck," said Gullni, of the pox.

"Yes, of course. What was I thinking of?" Gerpir murmured.

"Still," Kilgore said, "you never should have come into the Sloughs. The road branches at the southern edge, east to Coldbeck—"

"Ah, true, but we never pass up a chance to admire the countryside of Heroness," Mord explained. "Now tell us—will you stay the night? We have a whole house, but this is the only room in decent repair. It's far too dangerous for a lone traveler in the Sloughs at night."

"In fact," Gullni said, "we insist. I can't remember when we've had a more welcome guest."

"Say," spoke up Trollni, "what have you heard about that peculiar sword they found in the lord Valsidur's hall? Wasn't it one of his sons that pulled it out of the tree?"

"Yes, it was," Kilgore said, smiling. "Which one I don't know—"

"There's only one," Nord interrupted.

"But it is a marvelous weapon," Kilgore continued. "It is said that Surt would do just about anything to steal it."

"What does it do, exactly?" Mord asked. The others paid strict attention to Kilgore's reply.

"Well, being only a retainer, I don't know all of course," he said, enjoying himself. "It's elvish, they say. The owner of it can slay anything at one stroke. It fights of its own accord, and will not be sheathed until it has tasted evil blood. And that's about all I've heard of it," he finished, realizing he was getting a little too eloquent.

"My, my, a prize indeed," Nord said loudly, and winked rapidly. "I suspect this fellow who has it is just as powerful as Surt."

"Every bit, if not more," Kilgore said offhand. "Now I'm quite ready for a night's rest. Show me, if you will, where I may place my things, and I won't trouble you further."

At once a space was cleared beside the fire, and he lay down. The other five arranged themselves closer to the door. Soon the fire died low, and the place fairly quivered with hearty snores. But more than one pair of eyes were wide open all the while.

Kilgore absolutely could not sleep. The sword under his head kept up a disapproving hum, and he kept hearing rustlings and thumps. Rats, he thought. Or hoped, rather. Skanderbeg had seemed very certain this house was charmed. But rats did not whisper and mumble. He caught words like "Spell" and "Stiff as ice" and "Sword." Fully alert, he looked around the huge old kitchen chamber cautiously. His five hosts were still huddled under their blankets in five large mounds, all still sleeping soundly. Now he must protect them from the evil, ice-loving brutes that infested the place. That would be the heroic thing to do, but he wished that Skanderbeg were on hand. He wasn't experienced in this sort of thing.

While he debated, a movement so near him it was frightening caught his eye. A rat or a spirit! But no. It came creeping toward him from the direction of the lump that was Nord next him, and it was nothing more than the fellow's hand. He was probably cold, thought Kilgore, and groping for his cloak in his sleep. So he arose and carefully spread his own blanket over Nord and wrapped his cloak about himself.

Then he must have dozed, in spite of the strange noises and whisperings, for suddenly he realized a glow was filling the room. Dawn, he thought, and shook the sleep from him. But something was amiss. The glow was inside the room instead of outside where it belonged. In fright, he seized the sword and sprang to his feet. The sword sang and blazed with a brilliant white light, impelling him forward by a will greater than his own.

"Flee!" shrieked a voice, and the light was snatched away. Feet clattered on the stone floor. By the time Kilgore's dazzled eyesight recovered, he

59

found himself standing in the center of the room, holding the sword like a torch. Its light was slowly dimming and its song diminishing. Feeling foolish, Kilgore tiptoed back to his place. The five mounds of blankets did not even stir. They must be weary indeed, he thought with a smile, and yawned. He was asleep almost as soon as he lay down again.

It seemed like only moments later that he was jarred from his sleep. With a clashing of swords and shields, the door was flung off its hinges and a band of warriors burst inside with hideous cries. Kilgore was on his feet with Kildurin in his hand before he was quite aware of it. By the sword's outraged gleaming he could see strange devices and foreign arms and armor. With a shout—more of alarm than challenge —he raised the sword. All stopped at once and whirled in their tracks. Encouraged, Kilgore dashed after them, just close enough to be menacing. There was a crush at the door he hadn't anticipated, and he almost fell in his hurry to stop. The last warrior turned with a guttural roar, raising a long black spear. Kilgore ducked its thrust, then boldly clove the fellow's shield in half with the sword. The enemy fell back to draw his sword, but the next blow of Kildurin took off his head, helmet and all. Then the doorway cleared and the others departed in a clatter of armor. Kilgore started after them, still dazed. But the ancient courtyard was silent and empty of any figure except a statue of an immense warrior on a horse, now mossy and weathered.

He returned to examine his first slain foe, wondering if he should have to pay a blood-price to his relatives. At any rate, he could keep the armor and weapons. He stooped to see the face in the helmet. To his everlasting surprise, helmet and armor both clattered emptily on the flags. He felt an uneasy chill as he looked around for the others. The courtyard was empty. He shivered, feeling as if he had broken into a barrow mound. Next he observed that his five hosts were gone without taking their belongings. Probably startled out of their wits by the enemy attack, he decided. They had seemed like mild, timid fellows and he hoped they were hiding safely somewhere. If they blundered into those fierce warriors they would certainly fare the worst. When daylight returned he would search for them, or their corpses.

Sleep was out of the question, so he sat down to wait for morning. He kept an uneasy eye on the armor in the doorway until he fell asleep after a short while, wondering uneasily what his father would say.

The early watery sunlight awakened him. He unwillingly went to have a look at his battle loot and stood marveling at the curious armor. It was nothing like any he had ever seen, strangely shaped and made of some black material that looked almost like ice. It was also cold in spite of the warming sunlight. When he looked at it more closely, he saw that it was dissolving like mist. In a few moments there was nothing left but the sun-warmed flagstones.

With the sun, his curiosity and enthusiasm returned, although he found no traces of his five hosts. He searched the old house from top to bottom and discovered nothing more dramatic than rotting furniture, a few bird nests, and some old clothes. No dungeons full of rotting bones, secret corridors, or mystic trappings to remind him of the glorious past. His imagination, however, told him that the place must be of some peculiar significance or it would never be in a wizard's incantation. Thus satisfied, he went outside to investigate. The warrior's statue stood as if guarding the entrance. It was an uncommonly ugly wood carving, with Thor's staring eyes and a berserk grin. In one crude fist, a hammer was raised aloft.

"What tales you could tell," murmured Kilgore. His voice sounded peculiar in the empty courtyard. Then he added merrily, "By the sword of Elbegast, I command you to speak, statue! Who are you and where do you come from?"

He laughed and turned to go through the gate to find Skanderbeg in the Sloughs. With a crash the statue fell over, raising a cloud of dust. Kilgore leaped to the corner of a wall and peered around it warily, his heart in his mouth.

"Help! Help!" came a muffled shout and a thumping noise from the fallen carving.

Kilgore advanced, dumbfounded. The statue had split when it fell and there was something inside it. With a branch he pried the two halves apart and jumped back. A small figure crawled out of the cavity, covered with dust and wood chips. It was a boy about the age of Kilgore, carrying a large battle hammer meant to be thrown.

"Where am I? What happened?" the stranger demanded. "Did you have something to do with this? If you're a wizard, I'm sworn to kill you. But tell me quick, has Valsidda taken Gunnarsmound?"

"No," said Kilgore. "He was overtaken and slain and all his men before they got there and that was three score and five years ago, besides. Now who are you? Wraith, wizard, or man?"

"None of those. I'm a girl. Asny of Gardar, princess to the Wolfganger throne, and I don't believe your story." She shook her fair hair out of her eyes and raised the hammer as if it were the weight of a feather. "I'd be about eighty years old and you can see I'm not. You don't look much like a wizard to me either. Who are you and how did you get here? What is this place?"

"It's part of an ice-wizardly conjuration and I wandered into it crossing the Sloughs of Heronness. I come from Shieldbroad to the south, where my father Valsidur rules in the Brandstok hall." Kilgore looked curiously at her great rough boots, coarse breeches, and long embroidered shirt, belted with a wide leather girdle decorated with gold nails and peculiar symbols. "You don't dress like the girls I've seen. And you can't really throw that hammer can you?"

She eyed him contemptuously. "In Gardar the girls are as good as the male warriors. Being a princess I was encouraged to go to war so the people will have faith in me when I am queen. But what of my country? Tell me quick. Is my mother the queen dead?"

"It is all gone," said Kilgore. "Surt has taken everything. A cloud covers the land and trolls and wizards prowl by day and night. No one goes in, few have ever come out. We lost the Wars utterly. A great many good warriors went into the mound—the ones who weren't picked by birds and wolves."

"Ah! Well." Asny sighed, lowering her hammer and fastening it at her belt. She regarded her toes in silence. "Then I am the queen of Gardar. For seven hundred years, the line of queens has not been broken. Fate has preserved me by means of this wizard spell so I can return and save my country." She examined Kilgore with large dark eyes that had a queenly look to them. "I believe that sword is of Alfar manufacturing. Where did you get it? Weapons like your sword and this hammer are given to specific persons by the Alfar themselves."

"Elbegast gave it to me," Kilgore said pompously. "And that is all I will tell you until I can trust you. Now that you are freed from your imprisonment, what do you intend to do?"

"Free Gardar and kill Surt," she said immediately. "I don't suppose you could point the way out of this swamp, could you?"

"I could, if my friend Skanderbeg were here," Kilgore said. "As if happens, we are bound for Gardar ourselves on a secret mission which I dare not even mention in this place. Five men were mysteriously kidnapped last night—"

Her eyes were as round as the moon. She clapped her hands over her mouth. "Wait, stay a moment!" she whispered. "You must be the bearer of the sword! Elbegast promised that he would come forth to save Gardar from the final destruction. We all waited and hoped, but then I was snatched right in the battle and put into this hideous enchantment. Tell me, are you the one? You don't know how many scalds and songs were made about you. You certainly took your time to appear. I hope you're not too late."

"Everybody but me knows everything about this business!" Kilgore exclaimed indignantly. "We had no scalds in Shieldbroad. We didn't even believe elves and wizards really existed. Why wasn't I told that I was the only one in the dark?"

"As long as there are trolls," Asny said, "no one is ever really alone in the dark. Well, I am truly pleased to run into you, Sword-bearer. What is your name?"

"Kilgore of Shieldbroad, son of Valsidur, son of Valsidda. Our ancestor was the first Valsid," Kilgore replied with a touch of pride. "Valsid made the first holding on Skarpsey, you know."

"An outlaw from the eastern islands, I believe?" she asked. "Now tell me about this Skanderbeg you're traveling with. The name has a wizardish ring I don't much like. Can he be trusted?"

"Certainly! And what do you mean by calling Valsid an outlaw?"

"Good. Then we shall get along together, if you are positive he's a safe wizard. I suggest we find him and begin the journey immediately. If the defeat of Gardar wasn't its final crisis, then the real one must not be far off, whatever it is." Asny tightened the laces on her boots and straightened.

"Why, who asked you to join us?" Kilgore demanded in outrage. "You can't come along even if you are the queen of Gardar. Your hammer may be elven, but if we have to carry you besides it all the way, we'll never get there!"

"You're likely to need all the help you can get," Asny said scornfully. She pointed behind him. "I suppose those are the five men you thought were kidnapped last night?"

Kilgore turned and saw Mord, Gullni, Trollni, Gerpir, and Nord scratching runes on the ground, consulting books of spells. Mord raised his staff and a cold blast whitened the toes of Kilgore's boots.

"Wizards!' yelled Asny. The hammer made a singing noise as she whirled it and let it fly. It glanced off Mord's helmet with a solid clang and came spinning back to her hand. Mord threw himself flat and the other four dived behind heaps of fallen stone.

"Wait!" Kilgore exclaimed in horror. "Friend Mord,

are you all right? Last night it was wraiths and now this wild girl—"

"Attack! Rush them!" Asny charged the mound where Trolli was hiding. In midair the hammer shattered a peculiar black lance that looked and sounded like ice. Gerpir popped up and hewed at Asny with a sword, but one smash of the hammer sent him scuttling. Kilgore could only stare in shock until an axe almost looked him in the eye. As he drew the sword, it leaped in his hand and the axe vanished in a puff of cold air.

"So that's how it works," Mord declared, weaving a mighty spell. A swirling white cloud gathered and took the shape of a huge frost giant. It gave a bellow, filling the courtyard with icy wind and driving snow pellets. From its eyes, hidden far above in a cloudy beard, bolts of ice darted wherever the creature glanced. It swung a black sword viciously, fanning Kilgore with a breath more icy than the winds from the lands of ice in the north. In the screaming windstorm, Asny appeared by his side and yelled, "You take the frost giant. I'll manage these wizards!"

Protesting, Kilgore again felt the sword drawing him. It parried several of the great ice bolts, reducing them instantly to water particles, and dissolved the giant's sword. With no effort it pierced the giant's body, which thinned away to nothing and disappeared, like a cloud of mist.

"Truce!" declared Mord from the corner where he and the others were trapped by Asny. "We wish to negotiate with the sword king for our lives!"

"You'll do your negotiating with me, wizards," Asny said, holding her hammer aloft very sturdily. The wizards cowered and looked longingly at their staffs which Asny had taken from them. "Well, Kilgore, your first captives. What do you wish to do with them? I never favored taking prisoners. Too much bother."

Kilgore looked at the five prisoners in bewilderment. The sword was howling in his hand. "I thought—" he began.

"It's all a misunderstanding," Mord said smilingly.

"Do forgive us and let's sit down to talk about this. Obviously there's been a case of mistaken identity here. We are your old friends from last night, if you will remember, and not wizards as your friend here seems to think. No harm has been done, after all. Let us sit down over there with our possessions—"

"And wizard staffs!" Asny said. "Never! You tried to steal the sword by conjuring that frost giant, but the sword is too strong for that poor sort of magic. You're pretty cheap wizards, aren't you? Back up there against the wall, or this hammer will smash you into a thousand pieces. I've seen ice wizards melt, believe me, and Kilgore would not hesitate to finish all of you off."

"Bah. We know what a dolt Kilgore is," Nord said. "The five of us unarmed are more than a match for the two of you, so why don't you do the sensible thing and put down those weapons and flee? We are merciful souls; all we want is that sword and you may return peaceably to Shieldbroad where such troublesome things as magic do not exist. Remember, Kilgore of Shieldbroad, that we had mercy on you and spared your life when you wandered right into our kitchen. Had it been any other ice wizards, you would certainly be cold and stiff by now under a dozen ice spells."

"Yes, you tried only twice to murder me," said Kilgore, his cold pallor dispersing as he thought about being awakened twice from sound slumber. He waved the sword cautiously. "I venture to boast that none of your spells could have touched me anyhow, with Kildurin to protect me. I wasn't fooled last night by you, not for an instant. Knowing full well you were ice wizards, I sat down to join you with no fear."

The wizards scowled at the sword and the other four shoved Mord out in front to use him for a bulwark. "Cowards!" Mord sputtered. "Come, let's rush them. A stupid mortal and a small female with a hammer are no obstacle!"

"But Kildurin and the hammer of Kari Wolfganger are," Asny said without yielding an inch of ground. "This hammer has been in the hand of a Wolfganger queen for five centuries, and it still is now. As the

66

queen of Gardar, fallen or not, I have sworn an oath to rid Skarpsey of such vermin as you."

"A Wolfganger!" Gerpir said gloomily. "At least this is the last one we shall have to deal with. Surt took your seven brothers, as I doubt you know, and changed them to vargulfs. Half man and half beast and forever in the thrall of Surt. But as we are traveling to join Surt, we could beg pardon for them, if you would let us go now."

Asny laughed and tossed her head. "I will free them myself when I get to Gardar and you I shall throw into the deepest pits under Grimshalg when I take my throne there. Kilgore, what is your wish for your captives? We could use them as hostages, if Surt cares anything about them, which I doubt."

Kilgore kept the sword at ready. It refused to be sheathed, humming angrily. "We shall wait for Skanderbeg," he said. "I have the feeling he will find us here very soon."

"Skanderbeg?" Mord said. "That's the last wizard I want to see. I once succeeded in a plot to lock him in a tower for several thousand years. It was only a joke, but he never forgave me, although we were the closest of friends."

"I hope he roasts you alive," Nord remarked.

While the wizards fretfully exchanged a few threats, a rusty and unkempt crow sat on a wall chuckling hoarsely. Kilgore had seen him first just before the frost giant appeared. He seemed uncommonly brave for a raven and was certainly given to fits of wheezing and cackling. Spreading shabby wings, the raven sailed to the ground with a thump and began picking among the wizards' belongings with his huge black beak.

Mord stared at the raven. Snatching up a stone he hurled it with all his might at the bird and gave a screech of triumph at the explosion of black feathers that abruptly swirled into something quite different—and Skanderbeg himself stood there holding a peculiar dead lizard distastefully by the tail. Tossing it away, he gathered up a feather-covered cloak on the ground and stuffed it into his satchel.

"Skanderbeg, you old fire dragon!' Mord exclaimed, hurrying forward. Asny closed behind him. "I haven't seen you since we went to the Guild school. What a privilege to see you again!"

"Bah!" Skanderbeg said just as Mord's outstretched hand made a plunge toward his staff on the ground. Skanderbeg didn't appear to notice, rubbing his nose casually. Mord's staff, once it was clutched by its owner, suddenly transformed into a loathsome snake. Mord dropped it and leaped back with a shriek.

"Heroics never pay off," Skanderbeg said. With a nod to Kilgore and a nervous glance at Asny he commenced setting fire to the wizards' staffs and belongings. With a greedy hissing sound, the purple wizard flame ate up the staffs and baggage and melted a hole in the stony ground. Underneath was marshy grass and a rotting log.

"And now, Mord and dear friends," Skanderbeg said, as the walls began fading around them, "Your magic is destroyed and you are as helpless as mortals. If you wish ever to be wizards again, you will march yourself south to the Wizards' Guildhall and ask the Chief Fire Wizard for pardon. If you ever set so much as one toenail on Skarpsey again, I shall be after you with the hounds of Hel. Tell the Chief you are the first of many I shall send. Now scat."

The wizards moaned. "It's thousands of miles to the Guildhall. Two oceans to cross and seven mountains. You can't expect us to make it without any magic."

"Oh but I do," Skanderbeg said. "Believe me, I shall be watching you too. If you so much as hesitate too long tying your boots, I can send a bolt of fire a thousand miles to roast you in your tracks. If you should even think about—"

"We're on our way," Mord said with a sigh, looking around at the willows and bog pools of the Slough. He started slogging in a southerly direction, not looking back or caring whether the others followed or not. Grumbling, they followed in his tracks.

When they were out of sight, Skanderbeg said, "Well, if they get out of the quicksand they're heading for, there's always the undines. Who's this elfin creature you've adopted, Kilgore? You can't expect to take it along, you know." He looked at Asny in surprise as she drew herself up for an answer.

"Allow me to speak for myself," she said haughtily. "I am Asny Wolfganger. Doubtless you know who I am if you were around during the end of the Wars. I desire that you grant me a boon."

"It shall be granted," Kilgore spoke up. "That hammer is Alfar, Skanderbeg. We could use her help. She's worth an army, in spite of her misfortune in being a girl."

"As far as brains go," she said, planting her feet, "I think I've got you beat, Kilgore. Muscles aren't everything." She was slightly built, and the glint in her eye was pure stubbornness.

"Well, I suppose I know what the boon is." Skanderbeg sighed. "I don't see how we can refuse, since you have defended Kilgore in a situation that could have been awfully sticky. Join us and welcome, Asny Wolfganger, and be warned that you will be expected to do a man's share on this journey. I am acquainted with the fame of the queens of Gardar. The Fighting Queens are a noble tradition."

"Were, you mean," Asny said. "You won't regret my company in troll country. We hunted them for sport, when there was no serious fighting to be done."

Kilgore found he could sheath the sword after the humming stopped, quite a while after the wizards had disappeared. He looked darkly at the position of the sun in the sky and announced, "I think we should be finding our way out of this wretched place. Perhaps if we hurry we can reach Haelfsknoll by dinner time."

"Dinner time," muttered Skanderbeg. He was examining a map. "I think if we bear a little to the east we'll find the traces of an old road. It was the Thorsknip Road at one time."

"Then I know that road," said Asny. "I rode through here several times with my mother and her troops. I think I see one of the landmarks, a great tree, but it is dead now. Nothing changes like the passage of sixty-five years."

Calling out the landmarks, Asny led the way with caution and Skanderbeg brought up the rear. Gradually the land became drier and the road more pronounced. When the Slough gave way to Haelf the farmer's hay meadows, they stopped on a low knoll to look back at the Slough. Mile upon mile it lay steaming and black, filling the air with its reek. Then they crossed the hay meadows, waded a shallow icy creek, and arrived on the green home tun of Haelf. Amid the cackle of geese and blattering of lambs, Haelf welcomed them, and his household at once began preparing a royal feast. He gave them fleece slippers and the best seats, saying, "In Skarpsey no guest goes unhonored. Skanderbeg, it's good to see you again in this country. It's been a good many years, hasn't it? But things have changed now, I fear."

He looked sad but refused to cast a cloud upon the festivities. A host of shaggy children from neighboring farms pestered Skanderbeg for magic tricks until he conjured a full size dragon-ship right in the courtyard of Haelfsknoll.

When the sun began to set, Haelfsknoll became noticeably less merry. The neighbors who had come to visit with the guests slipped away quietly. Haelf looked gloomy and his sons were grim as they finished their evening chores.

"We are glad to have you with us tonight, Skanderbeg," he said in a low voice. "In a little while you are bound to see why."

CHAPTER 6

As guests, Skanderbeg and Kilgore and Asny were expected to take the best beds in the house, which were the sleeping lofts above the hall and ground-floor rooms. Asny declared that she would sleep on the porch outside, not being accustomed to the easy life of roofs and bed and board.

"Besides," she added, "I have seen the preparations you and your sons have been making. It's obvious that you expect trouble. Are you feuding with someone, Haelf?"

Haelf uttered a great sigh or moan and sat down in his chair. "Someone or something is certainly feuding with me. Since last fall we've been plagued by a sending. Sometimes it is the ghost of a small child and sometimes it is a flayed cat which tries to sit on a sleeper's chest and suffocate him under an unnatural weight. No one will stay here after the sun is down because of him. At the very least, he upsets all the milk pans in the dairy. Several times we've heard a terrible moaning and bellowing up on the fell which drives the cows insane and sends them rushing over cliffs or into the river. But the very worst happens when someone is left alone in this house. They are never seen again and I suppose the sending has killed them. He always appears when there are guests and looks them over very carefully before scaring them out of their wits. We haven't lost a guest yet, but no one will ever see one shepherd and three servant girls we've had."

Asny weighed her hammer in her hand, scowling professionally. "I've never dealt with a sending before, but I've slain my share of trolls," she said. "Let your sending come in here tonight, Haelf, and there are Alfar weapons that will be waiting for him."

"Alfar weapons!" Haelf shook his head. "What are these times coming to? Some of my guests have been Alfar folk, I'm certain. The sending went absolutely wild with fury, but he couldn't come in. Perhaps I'll have to find an Alfar weapon of some sort to get rid of him. This certainly doesn't work." He held up a sheep's rib which he carried in his shirt for protection.

Skanderbeg stood thoughtfully beside the dying fire. "Any idea who it might have been? An enemy you had that has died? Has anyone been murdered by any of your family on this property?"

"No. I've never had an enemy that I know of," Haelf said with a ghost of his old smile. "I am not extremely bright, Skanderbeg, but I have my theories about this sending, and I believe the same thing has brought him here that has brought you here to the foot of the Skull Mountains. In my father's time the Wars were lost and the Gardar Gap road was closed, separating Gardar from the rest of the Northern Quarter forever. Since then we have seen a good many strange things. Trolls prowling our upper pastures in broad daylight, companies of horsemen racing northward in the night toward the Gap, and peculiar travelers have become commonplace." Haelf chuckled and lit his pipe with shaking hands. "Haelfsknoll has become a port of call for the wizards as they travel between Gardar and the south. I've been summoned out of bed at midnight to host a dozen or more ice wizards when they meet. Of course, I'm watched carefully so I won't overhear anything; but even so, I've gathered a bit here and a bit there until I think I know something dreadful is going to happen."

"It already has happened," Kilgore said. "A cloud of cold weather is creeping down the Quarter from Gardar and everyone is moving out. In a matter of months, it may reach Shieldbroad. I suppose you've noticed the shorter growing season."

72

Haelf shook his head. "Haelfsknoll hasn't been touched, although the neighbors are suffering from the Blight. I can't explain it in rational terms, but there was an old story my grandfather used to tell me. At one time a man lived here who was highly favored by the gods of Valhalla. When he died he was put into a mound—one of these mounds nearby—and the gods refused to let the snow whiten his barrow as a sign of their favor. I don't know if it is a true story or not, but the hills of Haelfsknoll seem to be holy hills, in spite of all the wizards do to drive me out."

"Then you'll stay here?" Skanderbeg asked.

"Until I die," Haelf affirmed. "I'm not afraid of wizards." He rose slowly from his chair and began fumbling with a lamp to light his guests upstairs.

Outside the door of the hall, a deep rumbling moan came from something on the porch. Boards creaked under a great weight. Asny pointed to the unshuttered window with a gasp. The huge head of a vicious-looking bull was framed by the timbers. It looked inside for a long moment, rumbling low in its throat, then turned away with a toss of its black horns, rolling tiny, red-rimmed eyes. It gave forth a shrieking bellow that echoed on the fell and set the farm to pandemonium. The cattle bawled and bellowed in their stable and the ponies raced past the hall in terror.

"Is that your beast?" Skanderbeg asked, cautiously peering out the window. Then he leaped back with an exclamation. "By the beard of Hod," he muttered, grabbing his staff. "It's the flayed bull. Kilgore, the sword!"

Kilgore had it in his hand before he was aware of it. An angry buzzing filled the hall. It impelled him out the door onto the porch with Skanderbeg holding his staff like a torch behind him. Asny crowded after Skanderbeg.

"Where is it?" she whispered.

"There," said Kilgore, swallowing drily and trying to steady his shaking knees. "On the roof of the cow stable."

The creature gave another shrieking roar of challenge. Kilgore reluctantly let himself be drawn toward the cow stable. The beast snorted wildly, its eyes glowing like coals. Kilgore advanced with care toward the huge shadowy shape that was only a blackness on another blackness. Timbers creaked and pieces of turf fell softly to the ground. He could feel the bull studying him, and his skin prickled with a barrow mound feeling. For a long moment they looked at each other appraisingly. Then the bull silently vanished. Kilgore could not see well enough to watch it go, but he knew by the difference in the atmosphere. He breathed easier as he circled the cow stable, listening to the din inside. By the time he returned to the porch of the hall, the sword was quietly sheathed.

"The sending," Haelf said. "This was a different form. It doesn't bode anything but ill, I fear."

"Did you get a good look at him?" Skanderbeg asked and Kilgore nodded, feeling strangely tired. "Well, what do you think of him? How did the sword behave? Did he run away from you?"

Kilgore only nodded again. "Listen!" he said suddenly and they heard a faint bellow up in the fell.

"That's on the Gardar Road," Haelf said grimly. "The beast is heading for Gardar. I hope it doesn't ever come back."

Skanderbeg drew his knife and began carving runes into the house timbers. "This will hinder him some if he ever does come back. The other wizards will read it and stay away too."

"Wizards," Asny said. "Was this sending a wizard, Skanderbeg? How do you know he won't come back?"

"Because he is intent on getting to Gardar and waiting for us there," Skanderbeg said, finishing up his carving and sheathing his knife. "Kilgore, you're rather quiet. Are you having second thoughts about making this journey?"

Kilgore shook his head. "First thoughts are bad enough. I never really suspected or believed the safe pleasant world I lived in was so insignificant. Wizard spells, sendings, and that terrible bull. I feel like I'm a hundred years old. What was it, Skanderbeg? Was it you-know-who?"

"Surt? It may have been," Skanderbeg said, ushering them back inside and bolting the door firmly against the night. "Haelf, I suddenly feel starved again. I hate to trouble you but—"

"No sooner sought than done," Haelf said, disappearing in the direction of the scullery.

"Was it really Surt?" Asny demanded. "Why didn't you kill him, Kilgore? It would have saved you a journey to Gardar."

"If it was him, the time wasn't right," Kilgore said. "But the challenge has been issued. Now he knows where we are and what we are going to do. I wish Elbegast would help us. How does he expect us to do this thing by ourselves? Surt has all sorts of tricks and disguises and all we have is Skanderbeg. Is there any hope, really?"

Skanderbeg snorted wrathfully. "There are worse liabilities. But I'm glad you've had a couple of scares now. Perhaps we can make some progress on this little field day of ours, now that you have realized what we're up against."

Kilgore sighed and said nothing, thinking fondly of Shieldbroad. Already it seemed he'd been gone a lifetime.

Haelf returned with a fat loaf and a round of cheese and a crock of berries and sour cream. Kilgore mechanically ate half of it all before climbing up the ladder to the sleeping loft. There was a small window to let in fresh air, a clean straw mattress, and quantities of soft fleeces. In the adjoining room he heard Skanderbeg's sawing snores begin, which would not leave off until it was time to wake up.

In the morning Haelf made a great fuss about their departure, aghast that they had no intentions of staying another day or two to rest and visit. But since they insisted, he had no choice but to invite them cheerfully to return another day. "I may not be bright," he said with a broad wink to Kilgore, "but it's an honor to have such folks in this old hall. As I said, I know nothing about Surt and Gardar and the sword stuck in that tree in Shieldbroad for the one who is to kill Surt, and should I ever be asked if I knew the sword king I'd have to say no; but regardless, I send my blessings with you, young lad. And with you too, young fellow," he said shaking Asny's hand seriously.

Asny opened her mouth to protest heartily that she was the uncrowned queen of Gardar, not a young fellow, but she saw him wink again and he made a low and respectful bow. Seizing his hand warmly she said, "Thank you, Haelf. The day will come when I can repay you for sheltering us here at so much risk to yourself."

Skanderbeg tucked his satchel under his arm. "There's one fellow I should like you to beware of," he said in a low tone as they stood upon the porch to go. "He's a small trollish thrall with a wild eye and a great wart on his nose. Delay him as long as you dare. Watch for the Alfar."

Haelf nodded and walked with them as far as his boundary. The old farmer wiped a tear from each eye and shook hands all around once more.

"Dear Haelf!" Skanderbeg said. "We shall see you on the way back. Watch for us on the Old Road."

"I shall, but I fear all I'll see is the monsters who have slain you," Haelf replied stubbornly.

"Tush," Kilgore said gently. "Don't look so mournful."

"Ah, we shall see," Haelf replied glumly, adding, "by the gods!"

"Farewell! Goodbye!" they called and started up the rocky trail.

Haelf stood and waved until his shape disappeared from the traveler's view. The trail inclined upward, steadily winding its way into the mountains. By noonday the cloud had lifted and they could see the Skull Mountains in all their awesome ferocity. Dingy clouds still hovered around the highest ice-clad peaks. On the Trident side the three sharp spires rose from a sea of blue mist, still very far away but grim and imposing nonetheless.

"See those three sharpest peaks?" Asny asked, pointing with her walking staff. "That is the Trident of the Skull Mountain giant, who is said to be merely sleeping until the end of the world when he will awaken to fight for the evil forces in the last battle. You can see he has been asleep a long time indeed, because there are trees growing on his slopes."

"A giant?" Kilgore looked closely at the great blue expanse that was the Skull Mountains. "If that's true, I sincerely hope I'm not here on the day he awakens. Why, a giant that size could step across all four Quarters in a dozen strides, or from the Southlands to the Northlands. And nobody can hurt a mountain giant, since he is all stone."

"Well, it shan't happen today or tomorrow," Skanderbeg said briskly as he scanned the mountain slopes at hand.

"Is it possible, Skanderbeg?" Kilgore asked after a space of vigorous walking.

"What? The giant? Oh, it's only an old myth. Times may never get that extreme. If we are successful in routing Surt this time, that is. Now put it out of your mind and think about what Haelf said about trolls and giants and stop bothering me about it. I've got important things to think about." He produced a hard-boiled egg from his pocket and began peeling it with grave concentration.

The Briarthorns steepened around them. They had passed the easy foothills and now walked among gray shoulders of mountain and ventured across slithering slopes. In places the trail was almost obliterated by sheets of loose scree and here the going was perilous. One slip and a person would go sliding clear back to Haelfsknoll. To make things even more unpleasant, a chilly wind blew from the east, rattling the dead briar thickets like old bones and spinning away the dry leaves. It moaned and muttered among the wind-carven peaks like witch voices.

Kilgore was the first to notice the rock bouncing

down from above. They were crossing a slide of scree which was carrying them downward faster than they could cross it. Looking up, he saw only the stony face of the mountain side. As he watched, a sizeable boulder detached itself and came bounding toward them, gaining speed.

"Look out!" Kilgore shouted, sliding out of its path.

Asny saw the boulder and wound her hammer over her head and let it fly. It struck the rushing rock with an explosion of dust and chips. The boulder was smashed to pebbles. The hammer returned in time to be hurled at another crashing stone. As quick as Asny could throw, the hammer shattered the rocks, which were coming huger and faster.

Skanderbeg was struggling with his satchel and staff and trying to keep his balance long enough to cast a spell. "Get to solid ground!" he cried. "Run! Asny, leave off that except when absolutely necessary. Hasten!"

The three scrambled to the edge of the avalanching stone and found themselves in a rocky, narrow little valley between two gloomy humps of mountain. A few rocks still bounced after them from time to time, but all fell short.

"Well!" Kilgore puffed, looking back uneasily. "I've never seen a rock-fall quite like that one. I'd swear somebody was doing it on purpose."

"Ha! One would suspect that," Skanderbeg grunted, "if one didn't already know it was trolls."

"Trolls!" Kilgore exclaimed with a delighted shiver. "I wondered if we would get to see any. Do you suppose they'll bother us again?"

Skanderbeg only grunted; he had assembled his telescope and was examining the landscape behind them. Asny answered Kilgore's question. "Almost certainly," she said cheerfully. "They're almost impossible to get rid of when you're in their territory. Especially when they're hungry, and these fellows probably don't see many travelers."

"Hungry!" Kilgore said. "You mean they eat people?"

78

"Only when they're hungry and if sheep and cattle are scarce."

"I thought trolls turned to stone in daylight," Kilgore said, and hastened to add, "at least that's what my old grandmother said."

"It is the cloudy weather that makes them so bold," Asny answered. "And this cloud is very different from ordinary clouds."

"Hullo! I saw something in that clump of trees," Skanderbeg said. "We'd best be on our way. My map shows a trail through this gorge and something else that may save us from the cooking pot. Follow me!"

They hurried, then hastened, and finally began to run. All about them stones clattered or bushes rustled with trolls. Kilgore could see them occasionally, flitting from rock to rock, bold as brass. They were dark and squatty, with over-large, lumpish heads and hairy, pointed ears standing up over small, close-set features. Kilgore had the feeling they had tails but he didn't pause to look long enough to make certain. Each troll carried a clumsy bow or club over one stooping shoulder.

"I'd work a little magic on them if they'd get close enough," growled Skanderbeg. "But they know it too, drat their hides."

As they fled, they began noticing how their gloomy little valley was narrowing. Beginning imperceptibly, a low steady roar was growing in volume, first as a deep vibration in their ears, then a throaty rumble. It was the sound of water crashing far below in a deep chasm.

"Running water!" Skanderbeg panted. "We're saved! They can't chase us across running water. Next best thing to a stubble field. Once on the other side, I'll send a fireball and really roast those little blighters!"

"That sounds like a terrible lot of water," Kilgore gasped, holding the sword's hilt with one hand as he ran.

"Perhaps there's no bridge," Asny said.

"If there's not, I'll conjure one!"

"I see a bridge!" Kilgore exclaimed. "We're saved!"

"Not yet we're not," Skanderbeg corrected. "I see a tollkeeper and, in situations like this, the toll is likely to be quite extravagant. Let's walk so he won't think it's urgent."

"Is the tollkeeper a troll himself?" Kilgore asked, seeing the squat, scrawny figure of the fellow.

"We shall see."

The bridge keeper saw them and came out to stand on his bridge on the far side. "Hurry, hurry!" he shouted over the bellow of the water. "Look out for the trolls! Run!"

With an angry gibber, the trolls sprang from their hiding places and scuttled after their escaping prey at top speed. A few arrows were flown, but all went wide. The travelers dashed for the bridge. Their feet thudded on the stout wood planking.

"Safe!" declared Asny and turned back to the trolls clustering on the other side. She made a menacing gesture with the hammer. At once the trolls hailed her with a shower of rocks. Sulkily they lurked among the rocks on the other side of the chasm.

The tollkeeper hobbled out to meet them at the gate. "Hee, hee, hee, just in time," he cackled. "Not a moment to spare. Now then, what are you prepared to pay as toll?"

"Red gold, my good man, however much you want!" Skanderbeg declared.

"I would prefer a weapon," the old man whispered, throwing back his hood and revealing an awful enough sight. His old head was large and hairless, warty, and blotched with liver spots. One eye rolled around merrily of its own accord, and the old chap had only half a dozen yellow teeth.

"Weapons? Well, look at this." And Skanderbeg produced a large curving scimitar with a jeweled hilt; but the little fellow shook his head vigorously.

"Something longer. I have to fight trolls and wolves with it."

Skanderbeg pulled a long bronze sword from his

satchel, but the keeper shook his head. "Too big and heavy. I want something large and easily wielded, with tremendous power."

"Hum," said Skanderbeg. "Something—magical?"

"Why, yes. Yes, that's a lovely idea!"

"Then a staff like this is invaluable," the wizard said, handing him Kilgore's ordinary oaken staff. "Watch what mine does." He pointed across the gorge at a clot of brave trolls squatting at the end of the bridge. Without a sign, they turned suddenly into a crooked black tree.

"No. I want a sword. A magic one, which cuts metal and stone, invincible in battle, has magic runes to advise its master—"

"There is no such sword," said Skanderbeg firmly.

"But I have heard of one, to be sure. Last night in Haelf's hall."

"Indeed. Well, I can't help you. We have red gold, jewels, food, whatever. Take your pick. We have no magical sword to give away."

Suddenly the little man took hold of his chin and pulled away his face, which was only a mask. "Aha! I caught you in a lie, Skanderbeg!"

"Warth!" they exclaimed in disgust. "Might've known," Skanderbeg added.

"The sword, the sword!" He danced up and down gleefully.

"You'll never get it," Kilgore said fiercely. "Stand aside, or I shall let it slay you. Hear how it sings for your blood!"

"Give it over or I shall destroy the bridge!" he countered.

"Bah!" Skanderbeg grunted, eying the trolls who were eagerly crowding around the other end of the bridge.

"I can let the trolls have you, I suppose," Warth said, his eyes glittering. "But I'm sure, my dears, you'd rather just hand it over."

"And what would happen to us after we did?" Asny inquired, her hand closing over the half of her hammer. "You'd betray us anyway."

"Hah! You'd like to dash my brains out, wouldn't you?" Warth pointed a long yellow finger and Asny was frozen stiff as she stood. "You'd better learn proper manners, you young northern brute. Shall we continue our negotiations, my dear friends?"

"You have no friends on this side of the river," Kilgore said with a glance at the trolls.

Warth snorted. "Never judge a person by the company he is forced to keep. It is always worse or better than he deserves. A great genius is often forced to work with inferior substances. Now surrender that sword, or I shall demonstrate the ferocity and hunger of those same inferior substances!" He raised his reedy voice to a shriek and the trolls began dancing up and down in a frenzy of anticipation, hugging their lean hairy sides with long bony arms and grinning.

"All right," Skanderbeg said, taking a better grip on his staff. "Of course you are prepared to duel for it, I suppose?"

"To the finish!" Warth said with relish.

"You are not afraid of the consequences?"

"I'm sure there shall be none, as well known as Warth the Magnificent is throughout Skarpsey." He puffed out his thin chest and planted his feet in a war-like stance. "Why, I'm known from Ramfirth to Ness to—"

"Never mind!" Skanderbeg interrupted with annoyance. "State your challenge and be done with it. My patience is getting gaps in it." He began looking through his fat volumn of sorcery and scratching a few runes in the dirt.

"Very well," Warth said, drawing himself up with ridiculous stiffness until Kilgore had to smile. "I, Warth the Fierce, the Bloody, the Inconquerable, do take this staff and this occasion to engage in a duel to the death the usurperous, the cowardly, the lowly—"

"Oh, come on with it!" Skanderbeg exclaimed. "I'm ready, if you're not. Your weazand will get your head snatched off, if you keep it up."

"Don't interrupt," Warth said. "I'm not challenging

you. My quarrel is with this Kilgore of Shieldbroad creature."

"What? Me?" Kilgore had been watching with great pleasure and confidence, looking forward to Warth's next banishment by Skanderbeg. Now his joy faded considerably. "I have no personal grudge, Warth. At least none I can't forget. But actually, it would be an unfair match. I mean, a gust of wind could blow you away, and I'd feel reluctant to fight a weaker enemy. It would be a nithling's deed, I think—"

"Don't worry about him," Skanderbeg said in a pleased tone. "He is a wily old wizard, in some respects. You'll have a good, heroic fight, never fear."

"I wasn't thinking of that—" Kilgore began hastily.

"Are you ready, mortal?" Warth demanded, rapping his staff upon the ground.

"No. Yes!" Kilgore unsheathed Kildurin slowly. It hummed like an angry beehive in his hand.

"Hah! Cheat! You churl, I get to choose the weapons!" Warth declared.

"Well, then, choose," Kilgore said. "Axes, maces, choppers, spears—"

"Magic, I believe," Warth said with a grin only a troll would think pleasant.

"But first," Skanderbeg interrupted, "I insist we have lunch. And you must unfreeze Asny so she can enjoy the duel. Shall we sit on that pleasant patch of grass?" He pointed and it appeared like a square of green carpet, complete with wildflowers, bees, and butterflies.

"Ugh!" Warth shuddered. "I despise butterflies. They don't taste anything like real butter. Nasty things! Be off, you little harpies, or I'll eat you out of spite!" Grumblingly he lifted the spell on Asny and began stalking the blackbirds in the blooming wild rose bush.

Asny gasped and shivered, as if she'd just had a cold bath. "What happened? Where's Warth?"

"Still here, unfortunately," Skanderbeg said. "He's challenged Kilgore to a duel of power after lunch. We must be civilized about these things, you know."

"Duel of power?" Asny stared at Kilgore. "What power?"

During the meal Warth ate the daisies and bolted an entire loaf of bread and stuffed his satchel with other dainties when he thought no one was looking. He'd been living on roots and snails and fish and bats for years, growing meaner and more miserable by the meal. Fondly he drank vinegar with pepper in it and snatched a wineskin when he got the chance and stuffed it into his satchel

"Now are we ready?" he demanded when the cloth was shaken.

"If you still want to continue," Skanderbeg said.

"Yes indeed!" Warth hopped up at once.

"Wait," Kilgore said. "What are the rules?"

"There aren't any. That way, nothing is unfair." Warth said.

"Skanderbeg!" Kilgore whispered. "I don't know any magic! What'll I do?"

"Just act calm and pretend you know what you're doing. If you can't fool an incompetent ragbag like Warth, then I'm ashamed of you. Here, put on my cloak and hat. You'll come through this quite handily if you'll put a little effort into it."

"But Skanderbeg, I don't know how to defend myself against magic!"

"You're absolutely positive you don't have any power?"

"One hundred times over positive."

"What's that you've got in your pocket there?" asked Skanderbeg.

"A flint and steel, but what's that got to do with it?" Warth shook his satchel. "Are you ready, Scipling?"

"More than ready," Skanderbeg replied.

"But—" Kilgore began to protest, but Skanderbeg was walking away, leaving him facing Warth across a level little bare space.

"And you may strike the first blow, Warth," Skanderbeg said, "since you have the weakest power."

"Weakest? I, a centuries-old ice wizard of the first rank, and this half-grown Scipling mortal?" Warth almost choked. "For that piece of arrogance, wizard, you shall pay dearly. You shall lose both sword and a dummy to carry it." He raised his arms.

Kilgore flinched, and Skanderbeg's retort effectively silenced his protest. "Go right ahead," the wizard boomed. "We're waiting."

Warth uttered his spell in a loud voice and made the appropriate gestures. Closing his eyes tightly, he struck the earth with his staff.

Kilgore cautiously opened his eyes. "Are you finished?"

"No!" Warth looked up and down, as if he might have missed something important. His papery countenance began to glisten.

"I believe that caused a snowfall in Oxbarrow, south of Shieldbroad," Skanderbeg said thoughtfully.

Warth glared, then squeezed his yellowish face up in an awful expression of concentration and started the spell over. Kilgore closed his eyes and held his breath. Warth whacked the ground again with a triumphant screech, but nothing happened.

"This isn't half so bad," Kilgore said, with an uneasy grin.

"What's the problem?" Skanderbeg demanded. "Is there something wrong with you, Warth? I'll give you one more chance, and if you can do nothing this time, Kilgore shall take his turn. I wonder if he'll roast you slowly over coals, or do you prefer to be fried at once?"

Warth showed his teeth and clenched his fists. Beads of greenish moisture stood on his brow. After a moment of concentration, he suddenly dived into his satchel and pulled out his book of magic spells. After thumbing through dozens of spells and curses and plagues, he found the right page and read and reread it. Throwing the book down, he scratched in the dust with his staff. Confidently he lifted his arms and intoned a lengthy spell, eyes shut tight, and struck the ground with his staff with a grand flourish. Nothing happened, so he opened his eyes cautiously, staring at Kilgore—still intact—with disbelief.

85

Kilgore gave a wheezy laugh, greatly relieved.

Warth hurled his satchel to the earth and jumped on it. "Foul, base trickery!" He tried to break his staff over his knee. "The fire wizards always get the best of everything, and we ice wizards get the old worn-out leftovers! Now even these wretched, ignorant Sciplings are getting power. It's not fair! It's not—"

Warth had been punctuating each sentence with a hearty kick or stomp on his frayed little satchel, but suddenly it decided to retaliate. A muffled explosion went off with a bang and a fizz inside the satchel. Colored fog and staccato reports filled the air. Warth attempted to smother the disturbance under his cloak, but suddenly a louder explosion belched blue clouds of mist and swirling snowflakes into the air. Choking at the smell, Kilgore and Asny retreated while Skanderbeg whacked at several writhing snakes and strange winged creatures that flitted about, chittering like bats. When the smoke cleared, nothing of Warth was to be found.

"Escaped!" Asny exclaimed in disgust. "But say, Kilgore, how did you keep from being ice-magicked? You don't know any magic, do you?"

"Just because I come from Shieldbroad, do you think I'm totally ignorant?" he demanded with wounded pride.

"Yes," Asny said. "Tell us how you did it."

"You'll have to ask Skanderbeg," Kilgore grumbled.

Skanderbeg smiled. "In all modesty, I must admit it was an ingenious accident. Kilgore, show Asny what is in your pocket."

Obligingly, Kilgore pulled a salt shaker and a hard-boiled egg from the pocket of the cloak.

"No, no, your own pocket!"

"I see. I have it now. Flint and steel"

"Certainly. Now place them back in this box. Everyone knows that flint and steel inhibit the fine and unstable arts of magic, to a greater or lesser degree. The lesser the wizard, the greater the inhibition. Just to be safe, I keep them in a special box, except when Kilgore absent-mindedly pockets them as he did at our informal tea party this afternoon. I realized that probably nothing Warth could do would harm you, unless he took up mortal weapons, which he is far too cowardly to do."

"And why," Kilgore asked, "didn't anyone tell me all this before? I was petrified!"

Skanderbeg was gathering up his possessions. He wrapped his long scarf around his neck. "A little petrification teaches one a great deal. In other words, fear is the sauce that makes life exciting. As soon as one forgets to be afraid of fear, he can even cultivate a taste for it. You'll need a tremendous appetite when it comes to facing Surt." He unrolled a map and looked at it doubtfully.

"I think we're lost," Asny said cheerfully. "But we can't fail to reach Gardar if we follow this trail. Knowing the character of the brutes who made it, I'd say it can't lead anywhere else."

"Then we're likely to run into more trolls," Kilgore said.

"Exactly," Asny said, sounding pleased.

The trail led them into high and steep places. For several days they marched with their heads against the gray cloud ceiling, but ahead were ranks upon ranks of grim mountains reaching beyond the clouds. There was no break in the towering barrier of stone except the great cobalt crack that was the Gap. Skanderbeg charted a course parallel to the Gap, thus avoiding for a few days longer the trolls and beasts that waited there.

"Take a last look at the sea," Skanderbeg said. "We won't see it again until Surt is slain and Gardar freed."

CHAPTER 7

By the time they reached the summit of the Briarthorns the travelers were wearing fleece-lined cloaks from Skanderbeg's satchel.

"Knew we'd need them in the Tridents," Skanderbeg said, "but I didn't expect it would be so cold so soon. This is almost as bad as the Tridents will be."

Kilgore looked ahead at the awesome, ice-capped mountains ahead. Evening was growing blue-black and mysterious. No light, not a single homestead, not one friendly soul waited ahead.

"We'd better camp," Asny said. "I shudder to think what the night may bring out in this place. There's almost no limit to the trolls in these valleys and the wolves are legendary. In my time they said they were vargulfs."

"Let's make camp then," Kilgore said. "I thought I heard a howl. I don't care if there's no water, if there's a good defense."

There were plenty of niches and corners in the cliffs. The one finally chosen had a small trickle of water seeping from the stone. Skanderbeg put up the tent beside a deep little pool, carelessly waving a hand at it and uttering a few words; instantly the tent was up. Where the terrain permitted its use, the tent was their most valuable asset. Its silvery sides seemed to give off heat; and when something prowled too close at night, Skanderbeg never failed to know about it.

When the camp was set up, Kilgore still felt watched, although one side of the camp afforded a plentiful view of their backtrail, while the other sides were protected by the rugged cliff and two concealing shoulders of stone. There was even a rough little path over one side for an emergency route. It seemed safe and sheltered here as they gathered firewood, unpacked their provisions, and prepared for the night. Darkness soon hid the surrounding mountaintops from them, and the bed of coals cast a cozy red glow on the tent's sides. The teakettle babbled pleasantly to itself, as if it were on the grate at Valsidursknoll instead of far into the wild Briarthorns.

"Do you think our fire will attract trolls?" Kilgore asked as the bread toasted over the embers.

"No more than are probably already here," the wizard said cheerily. "Pass the cheese, if you please, and the wine."

After the little fire was no more than a few red, glittering points in the ash, Asny was already snoring, Skanderbeg had his head buried under a pillow, and Kilgore was wide awake. It wasn't because he was hungry, nor was he too tired to sleep. The day had been rather exciting, true enough, but that wasn't the problem. His bed was comfortable. His feet weren't cold. There were no gates he'd forgotten to shut, nor livestock to worry about. He still felt that ominous, waiting feeling, as if it were going to snow. He felt as if he really must go outside and reassure himself there wasn't a ring of gray trolls all around the tent waiting impatiently to pounce.

Stepping outside, he was able to see nothing in the moonless night. The clouds felt very close. He could discern the two shoulders of rock around their camp. That made him feel safe, and he turned to go back inside the tent. At that same instant he heard a wet snuffling noise and the splash of water by the pool. Skanderbeg's snores sputtered and went out. He put his head out and whispered, "Something is setting off an alarm. Kilgore, be on your guard."

Kilgore nodded and squinted away into the dark. The sword gave no indication of the presence of trolls or wizards, just a tiny thrill now and then. Wondering what it could mean, Kilgore stepped away from the tent a bit to see the water hole better. It was all lumps and blocks of shadow, but he could still hear a slight disturbance in the water. The creature gave another snort, which was a very familiar sound to Kilgore's ears, though he couldn't remember it. Then he heard slow, heavy steps coming around the water, grinding the stones together under considerable weight and crackling a few branches of thorn bushes. A large, black shape came out of the shadow into the paler darkness lit by the sky. Kilgore leaped back, his hand on the sword. "Skanderbeg!" he whispered.

"What is it?" the wizard asked. "It looks like a horse."

"In these mountains, with all these trolls?" Asny whispered behind him. She shoved past him to join Kilgore. "Why, it does look like a pony. He must be lost."

The pony walked up to Kilgore and shoved his big nose into the pocket where there happened to be a handful of dried fruit. In amazement, Kilgore felt the horse's ears and neck and mane. "It really is a horse," he said with a laugh. "I wonder if we ought to keep him. He could carry our packs, or we could take turns riding."

"But nothing eats like a horse," Skanderbeg said dubiously. "On the other hand, if he runs out of natural forage, we can always eat him."

"A Scipling would die before eating this horse," Asny said in an insulted tone. "Besides, he's been somebody's pet. Look how tame he is."

"Yes, indeed," Skanderbeg said as the pony took a mouthful of his beard. "He's very friendy, the little beast. If he's still here in the morning I guess we could put him to work."

The pony was still outside the tent in the morning and favored Kilgore with a friendly whicker. He was a handsome beast of a silvery color with a black mane and tail. After breakfast he allowed Skanderbeg to fit his head with an old halter, which the wizard had discovered in the bottom of one of the packs. They loaded all the packs and the tent and Skanderbeg's satchel onto the pony's wide back. He looked back at the load almost disdainfully, as if it were nothing at all. When they started off, the pony trotted ahead eagerly or pranced light-footedly behind, pausing to graze whenever he saw anything green, catching up with the travelers easily with a burst of amazing speed. At the end of an exhausting day's climbing, his hide was completely dry instead of sweaty, and he capered around the camp in an excess of energy and spirit.

"That pony is as strong as an ox," Kilgore grunted wearily. "I think tomorrow we ought to take turns riding him."

With a rider on his back and all the packs, the pony still pranced mincingly along the path and seemed to welcome the opportunity to gallop ahead with Kilgore to see which fork of the trail was the easiest to negotiate. Even with Skanderbeg's greater weight, the pony seemed to be stronger than ever. At the end of the day he had not turned a hair. The creature was evidently indestructible. Skanderbeg looked often at his maps and seemed pleased at the progress they had made. Kilgore was certainly pleased to be rid of the weight of his pack and it was glorious to ride along on a sure-footed horse part of the time so he could look around at the mountains and valleys and glaciers. Even when it was not his turn to ride, he sometimes held onto the horse's long tail for an extra pull up the steep places.

After a week of traveling with Sleipnir—which was also the name of Odin's marvelous eight-legged horse —they reached the summit of the Briarthorn Mountains and began descending into the misty foothills on the other side. Kilgore was entralled by the eerie beauty of the place. Stands of birch and pine were delicately etched against the mist, and rocky stream-lets of glacial water tumbled down ice cold and sparkling from the Burnt Mountains above. Most of the springs were hot, forming pools of various sizes and temperatures. Geysers erupted steam and spray into the air at irregular intervals, which explained the country's misty disposition. A lake of silver lay behind almost every hill and every cliff or crag was ornamented with a filmy veil plunging into a pool at the bottom.

"It's too beautiful not to have something wrong with it," said Asny in a practical manner.

"The only thing wrong with it is the fact that it won't last," Skanderbeg said. "I expect the Burnt Mountains to be positively dreadful this time of year—or any time, for that matter. Since it's too late in the afternoon to expect to get into the Burnts and camp, I suggest we camp at the next lake, if it has a hot pool. I feel like a long, luxurious hot bath."

While Skanderbeg was soaking, Kilgore and Asny unpacked Sleipnir and let him wander untethered about the camp like a large dog. He put his head into the tent and humorously sniffed the dinner pots as Kilgore attempted to cook. While the tea was brewing, the pony nibbled at Kilgore's back until he whirled around in irritation to chase him away. To his surprise, it wasn't Sleipnir. He was nose to nose with a dappled gray pony with a pink nose and white forelock. The pony wagged his head and flapped his ears affably, glancing over his shoulder at two more ponies as if to say, "We're just in time for tea!"

This piece of fortune was too good to ignore. Quietly Kilgore tethered all the ponies, who seemed to be the best of friends with Sleipnir, and dashed to tell Skanderbeg.

The wizard was almost boiled alive and showed no intention of getting out of his hot pool. But he sighed and said, "I suppose it is time I had a look at those horses. Kilgore, I have a suspicion about them all, even Sleipnir, which I had better tell you and Asny about before something happens."

"Suspicion? What about? Do you mean we'll have to leave them?" Kilgore demanded. "With horses we could get on the road and race all the way to Gardar without having to fight trolls quite so often. I often wondered why we didn't start out with horses."

"Because it's dangerous to get dependent on something that can stick its leg in a hole and break it, or get eaten by something, or get its silly self lost." Skanderbeg huffed his boots on, still red in the face from the boiling he'd had. "And now of course, it's too late to take the horses to Gardar because there's no way to get them down into the Gap from here. Tomorrow our path turns to climbing places where no pony can keep his legs under him."

Kilgore looked around at the tremendous variety of terrain. "Why can't we change our route? I think we ought to keep the horses for as long as possible. It's much nicer to ride."

Skanderbeg snorted and shook his head. "It's much nicer to fly too, but you don't have any wings." He was about to go on, but Kilgore wasn't listening. He was pointing to the far side of the lake, where the water was dancing in the last rays of the sun. Two silvery horses were playing in the shallows, dashing the water into the air as they raced along the shore, turned together, and reared up to playfully bite at each other; then they stood pawing the water with their hooves.

"When we get back from Gardar," Kilgore said excitedly, "I'm coming back here to capture some of these horses. Surely they've never seen men, which is the reason they are so trusting."

"A good enough reason," the wizard said. "But I suspect there are better horses elsewhere. Now where's Asny? Isn't anyone watching our camp? What if a bunch of trolls is waiting for their chance? Drat that girl, she's riding off on one of those infernal ponies! Asny!"

She was loping toward the lake on a white pony. Hearing Skanderbeg's shout, she turned easily and slid to a stop right at the toes of Skanderbeg's boots.

"Well!" she exclaimed. "We'll be in Gardar by this time next week. I have a theory that the owner of these ponies was killed somehow and they escaped to this place. Isn't that fate for you? Someone failed so that we might succeed."

Skanderbeg shook his head. "We'd all be troll food in two days. The ponies stay here. Tomorrow we begin climbing that." He pointed to the steepest, most jagged face of the mountain. "And that is no way a horse can go."

"Then let's go another way," Asny said with a rebellious tilt to her chin that indicated she was used to having her own way.

"No," Skanderbeg said, stomping toward camp. "No, no, no!"

"I think he's made up his mind." Kilgore sighed, patting the neck of the white pony. "And it's such a shame. I've never seen nicer ponies than these. If they're all as strong as Sleipnir, I know we could make it to Gardar if we had to ride day and night."

"Drat that old wizard. I don't see why you had to bring him along," Asny said. "There's plenty of ways to Gardar besides the Gap. They're long ways, but with ponies—"

"Listen, what's that?" Kilgore searched the trail. A reedy yelling seemed to be following them. In another moment a small, bent man appeared on the crest of the hill, put his hands to his mouth like a trumpet and bellowed, "Horse thieves!"

"Does he mean us?" Asny asked, horrified, as they hurried back to camp. Skanderbeg was also listening with one hand behind his ear.

"Horse thieves, eh?" the wizard said. "It appears we'll have a feud on our hands in another moment, thanks to these bothersome beasts. At least they'll be going back to their proper owner instead of being a millstone to us."

The owner of the horses came, bellowing at every other step, into their camp. "Horse thieves!" he roared one more time, glaring at the travelers. His face was large and red, and his nose was its largest and reddest feature. Mournful little eyes blinked at Skanderbeg from under a red cloth cap of the type usually worn by wagon drivers. Black boots came up past the stranger's knees to meet a dirty blue coat with gold braid unraveling off the cuffs and collar.

"Horse thieves?" Skanderbeg said. "See here, you vagabond, we haven't stolen anybody's horses. If these are your beasts we have a bill for you for their care and

94

feeding and I suggest you pay it at once, for I am not a patient person by nature. Now who are you and what are you doing in these mountains?"

"I'm a merchant," the fellow said, pulling on his red nose and screwing up one eye. "I load my wares upon my horses and go a-traveling until all is sold, but for the past week I've been trailing you to retrieve my beasts of burden. Then I shall resume my journey into Gardar to barter with the inhabitants there."

"You take horses to Gardar?" Asny asked. "How do you manage it?"

"Why, I point their heads north and ride along behind them and we don't stop until we get there," the merchant said in great irritation.

"And what is Gardar like?" Asny demanded. "Is there still a queen on the throne? How many people are there? Does Surt rule it?"

"What nonsense," the stranger said. "If you're so desperate to know, I suggest you go there. For a price, I would rent you one of my horses, but I have no desire to ride with horse thieves."

"And we have no desire to go anywhere with you," Skanderbeg said. "Now take your animals and begone from our camp."

"No, we want to join you," Asny said. "Name your price, sir, for we are determined to get to Gardar. You can name your price or we shall seize you and your horses and compel you to direct us, since this is a time of war and we are in grave need."

The little man snorted and pulled on both ears, a lifetime of which pulling had stretched them down to his collar. "Well, I'm not at all eager," he said haughtily, "but I suppose I consent."

"Keep your consent," Skanderbeg said with a furious glare. "We are not interested."

The stranger had started to sit down. Now he stood up. "Then I shan't stay another moment!"

"Oh yes, you shall!" Asny declared and he started to sit again.

"Not if you want to live!" Skanderbeg roared and he jumped up.

For a moment Skanderbeg and Asny glowered at each other. Then Kilgore intervened. "Well, the least we can do is offer the traveler our fire and food and a place to sleep for the night, while we decide whether to follow his route or not. Scipling hospitality calls for that much at least."

"Indeed it does," the man said indignantly, sitting himself down with a wary eye on Skanderbeg.

"Very well," Skanderbeg said, sitting in turn, with his staff across his knees. "But hospitality won't be all you get if you don't keep a civil tongue in your head. Hm! I don't recall ever hearing of a pony train to and from Gardar. What do you sell?"

"Various things, just various things," the trader answered. "I am called Ketil the Vendor by those who know me, and I believe I have the honor to be traveling with Skanderbeg the wizard, do I not?"

"I wish you did not," Skanderbeg said. "And I suppose you learned that precious bit of information at Haelfsknoll?"

"Aye, Haelfsknoll. I stop there on every trip. And what are the names of these two young people?" He looked keenly at Kilgore and Asny.

"Kilgore of Shieldbroad, Asny of Gardar," Asny said. "In the morning I shall ride with you, even if no one else does."

"You're a brave fellow," Ketil said.

"I'm not a brave fellow, I'm a—" Asny began indignantly but the wizard cleared his throat with a violent choking growl.

"I believe the dinner is ready," Skanderbeg said.

While they ate, Ketil sat himself down beside Kilgore, after a series of furtive sidling movements when Skanderbeg wasn't looking. In a leathery whisper he said, "I see you have a worthy-looking sword. Tell me, do you anticipate trouble if we travel together?"

"I certainly do," Kilgore whispered back. "You'd be much safer not to travel with me at all. There are individuals who would like to end my life tomorrow."

"Eh! Is that so!" Ketil said. "Dear me, this is getting complicated. We shall have to be very careful, although

96

I'm sure no one in the world knows about the road I take to Gardar. Perhaps we would do well to travel by night. As an experienced traveler of these mountains, I know there are strange beasts out at night, but from experience I've learned that night is better than day for secret travel. Believe me, I know these mountains inside and out. You couldn't do better for a guide to Gardar than Ketil the Vendor." He nodded fiercely and tapped himself on the chest.

Suddenly Skanderbeg swooped down upon Ketil the Vendor as if he were about to pluck him up by the hair of his head. "Nobody wants you for a guide to Gardar," he snapped. "And now as your kind host I will direct you to your sleeping arrangements. There is a blanket and you may put it anywhere you like." Skanderbeg stamped away and disappeared into the tent. The snoring commenced almost immediately.

"I think we ought to go with Ketil the Vendor," Asny whispered to Kilgore. "If we wander around in these mountains much longer we'll get winter-bound or frozen or at least eaten by trolls. We won't have this opportunity again to ride to Gardar in the space of a few days' time. If we let him leave us, we'll have to walk and maybe not get there."

"Skanderbeg doesn't trust him," Kilgore said.

"Pooh on that wizard. I haven't seen much evidence that he's a very good wizard at all. If he doesn't want to come, we'll leave him," she said decisively.

Kilgore frowned. It didn't seem quite right. "Elbegast sent Skanderbeg to travel with me to slay Surt and I don't think I shall undertake it without Skanderbeg. I'll try to change his mind. But if I can't, I think we should both stay with him even if we have to walk all the way to Gardar on our hands. He's an extraordinary wizard—I think."

"If he has any sense he'll come with us," Asny said. "Really, it makes little difference if we lose him or not. You have the sword. Why don't you tell him what to do?"

"Nobody tells wizards what to do," Kilgore said gloomily.

"If we start at all," Ketil the Vendor spoke up with a sly grin, "I suggest we go by dark. In half an hour we can be on our way."

Kilgore shook his head and stood up. "We'll decide in the morning." Unconsciously he rested his hand upon the sword. To his surprise, he found it vibrating and shrilling a warning in his ear. Curiously he looked at Ketil, who was also looking at him with a speculative eye.

"That looks like a marvelous sword," the Vendor said. "I don't suppose you'd show it to me?"

"I dare not." Kilgore said. "Once it is unsheathed it will not be sheathed again without the taste of blood. Particularly evil blood."

"Eh! You don't say!" Ketil said. "It must be magic."

"Somewhat," Kilgore said, striding toward the tent. "Now I must bid you a goodnight, since I'm sure you want to see to your ponies after such a long separation. Asny, Skanderbeg wished to instruct us about something, I remember. I wonder if he forgot too?"

He nudged the snoring lump in the tent but it never missed a snore, so he rolled himself up in his cloak and a blanket in one corner where he could occasionally lift the fabric and peer out. He could see the four ponies standing with their chins resting on each other companionably, and Ketil was still sitting beside the dying fire. The small fellow was rubbing his hands together and chuckling softly to himself. In the fire-glow, his nose looked redder than ever. He pulled it several times and tugged his ears as if he were very pleased.

The humming of the sword kept Kilgore awake most of the night. Twice it shrilled an intense warning that sent Kilgore bounding to the tent flap, but he saw nothing in the darkness. Skanderbeg never awakened from his contented snoring. Kilgore reached down and prodded the wizard. The lump didn't feel much like a wizard; more like a wadded blanket, which was exactly what it was. The snoring came from a small lizardlike creature which he discovered curled upon the pillow. When he grabbed it and hastily let go again, it silenced its bullfrog snoring except for a grunt or two, so he stuffed it into his pocket to return to Skanderbeg later. Quietly he slipped outside and hesitated uncertainly. An aged fire wizard certainly needed no help prowling around in the dark with all the unnatural beasts of the magical realm. Perhaps he was even invisible or in some other form. Kilgore scuttled back inside the tent and curled up at the entrance. He intended to watch; but the next thing he knew, Skanderbeg was doing some sort of dance on top of him, nearly killing him with his huge black boots.

"Kilgore, you're always in the way!" the wizard grumbled. "Whatever are you doing sleeping there?"

"I wanted to give you this." Kilgore put the lizard in Skanderbeg's hand. Immediately it began to snore, winking its beadlike eyes apprehensively.

Skanderbeg shoved it into his pocket almost without looking at it and said impatiently, "Would you mind hurrying yourself up so we can leave? Ketil is ready with the horses and I've been awake for hours. Don't dilly-dally, Kilgore, we must be off immediately."

"Then we're riding with Ketil?" he mumbled, but the wizard had gone to bellow something at Ketil.

"Well, I'm glad he came to his senses," Asny said, rolling up her blanket in a neat roll.

The ponies were equipped with bridles but no saddles. Skanderbeg officiated the distribution of the luggage, grumbling all the while at the delay. Then the procession started, led by Kilgore with Skanderbeg trailing in the rear as far as possible from Ketil the Vendor. The ponies were full of energy and mischief as they trotted along the trail, and the gray one carrying Ketil tried to dump him off over its head. If the sun had been shining, it would have been an ideal day, but even the misty sky seemed pleasant. It cast a silvery sheen over the lakes and rocky crags and birch stands until Kilgore thought he had never seen a more enchanting place, particularly when every lake seemed to be the gathering place for several of the pony bands that occupied the misty valleys. Watching five gray ones playing in the shallows he asked Ketil, "Are there always so many wild ponies here? Why hasn't anybody claimed them?"

Ketil smiled with his pointed teeth. "Why, somebody has. These ponies we're riding came from here. Anybody can tame them with almost no effort. They love people, but the only peculiarity they have is that you must never mention their names around them or they will go wild."

"Sleipnir didn't seem to mind," Kilgore said.

"Ah, but that's not his real name," Ketil answered. "And I can't say it out loud or all the ponies will bolt."

Kilgore rode in silence, fighting down his curiosity. "What if I called him by his real name by accident?"

"Then you would be without horses, and possibly in great peril."

"Well, I won't try to guess his name. But would you whisper his name so he can't hear it, so I would know, at least?" Kilgore asked.

"Certainly. When we get to the place where the path climbs the side of the mountain beside the lake I shall tell you the names of the horses." He winked slyly and pulled on his nose.

The path steepened and began winding among the crags of the mountainside. Below shimmered a dark lake that looked particularly deep. Kilgore slowed Sleipnir's eager pace to a cautious walk. Asny's pony behind him gave Sleipnir a nip to hurry him up, which caused the pony to lay back his ears and kick at the other horse. Then with no regard for the narrow trail or the perilous drop to the water below, he tried to turn around to nip at the horse behind him. Skanderbeg gave a warning shout as Sleipnir pivoted on his back legs and Asny's nippish pony backed up hastily.

"Sleipnir!" shouted Kilgore, hauling at the improvised bridle with all his might. "Sleipnir, you ninny!"

For an instant all four ponies snorted and rolled their eyes in alarm.

"Ninny! You dumb ninny!" Kilgore yelled, trying

to get the pony to turn the right way on the trail again. Instead, the horse reared and gave a loud squeal of rage, then dived over the edge toward the water below. Kilgore slipped off over his tail. By the time he sat up, the pony made a terrific splash, followed by a lesser splash which was Kilgore's share of the equipment and provisions. Then Skanderbeg's pony sailed gracefully into the air and dived into the water, closely followed by Asny's and Ketil's.

"Nykurs!" Skanderbeg exclaimed, with dust in his beard. "I thought so! Where's that double-dealing mercenary? I've a mind to roast him to cinder. Ha, you horse-dealing rat! Try to escape, will you?" With a roar Skanderbeg charged after Ketil, who was scrambling away, shedding his cumbersome coat and boots and hat and various other things as if he were molting. Glancing desperately over his shoulder, he saw Skanderbeg raising his staff for an incantation. With a last wild scramble, the little man leaped over the edge into midair. There was a puff of gray mist and a brief flash of greenish scales as a small slim shape plummeted into the water below.

"Drat!" Skanderbeg said, lowering his staff. "Kilgore, you were right in the way or I would have zapped him but good. And why didn't you warn me that you were about to holler 'ninny' at the nykurs?"

"I didn't know I was," Kilgore said, still dazed.

"They never came up," Asny said. "Did they drown?"

"Don't be silly. Those were water horses, or nykurs," the wizard told her. "They're the strongest beasts alive and very willing to carry you on their backs, until they have to cross a river. Then they're liable to lie down and drown their riders. Their blasted neighing can drive cows mad with fright and if you'll notice their tracks in the dirt, the prints lead in the opposite direction from the way they are going. From the way that Sleipnir beast appeared at the water hole I ought to have been warned and driven him away at once."

"Nykurs!" Kilgore said, watching the far side of the

101

lake where he could barely see the misty forms of horses playing in the shallows.

"Nykur, nennur, ninny, it's all the same," Skanderbeg said. "They flee like field mice to the nearest water when they hear their name. We might have been drowned, you know, thanks to that vicious Ketil creature."

"It's all my fault," Asny said. "I insisted instead of listening. And now we've lost everything."

"Not quite everything," Skanderbeg said, holding up one of the saddlebags in triumph and giving it a shake. "You can be sure I'd grab this. My satchel's in here, so all's not lost as long as I have that much. Don't be absurd, Asny, and stop blaming yourself. I wasn't sure either until it was too late." Shouldering the remaining pack he led the way up the path, tapping ahead with his staff.

By some great stroke of fortune, Kilgore's small backpack had fallen from the nykur's back and lodged partway down the cliff in a crevice. He climbed down to it and hauled it up. But all told, the incident had cost them about half their supplies and equipment.

"It could have been all of us at the bottom of that lake," Asny said with a shudder.

"And what about Ketil?" Kilgore asked. "I'd swear he turned into a fish at the last moment. You can call me crazy if you want to, but I know what I think I saw."

"Do you indeed?" Skanderbeg didn't slow his pace. "Then I won't argue with you. That harmless little man is now a fish."

Kilgore abandoned the subject, recognizing Skanderbeg's explosive predisposition. As he passed Ketil's red hat, he picked it up curiously to examine it. The sword at his side gave a shrill warning and continued to do so as long as he held it. Several times he nearly put it in his pocket, feeling strangely loth to part with it. As he hesitated, he had an alarming vision of the cap's owner, only the face he saw was not the red, too-large face of Ketil. What he saw was Warth the

102

wizard. With a quick movement he tried to toss the cap toward the water, but at the last moment he decided to stuff it into his pocket.

Skanderbeg saw him do it and snatched it out with a horrified exclamation, as if it were a poisonous snake. Hastily he flung it away and incinerated it with a wave of his staff. "Foolish boy! Do you want every ice wizard this side of the Trident to sniff us out? Never, never keep anything of an ice wizard's!"

"Particularly that one," added Kilgore with a shudder.

By midday the nykur valley was forgotten. A raw wind gusted from the high white peaks of the Trident. The trail was a tortured track among crags and wind-maimed trees, seeming to scrabble along the ground looking for hiding places. Tough bristly grass and thorns tore at the hems of their cloaks. Kilgore blew on numb fingers and grumbled, "My idea of saving Skarpsey isn't freezing to death in these hateful mountains. Trolls, vargulfs, or whatever sound better in a scop's song."

"Hum," Skanderbeg said. "You've never heard about Wulther and Valsidda starving during the winter in Gardar, or how miserable the glorious warriors were marching for days without water or supplies, or how dismal it must have been when—"

"Oh, never mind," Kilgore said. "A fellow needs to complain once in awhile, doesn't he?"

"You never stop," Asny said, wrapped up in her cloak. "Everybody can't be a hero, you know. Most people think it's too much work. But one thing you must remember, Kilgore. You and Kildurin must make it to Gardar, even if we have to tie you up and carry you. For me there is no alternative. I have no warm Brandstok hall to go back to hide in, as you keep moaning about doing. The trouble with you, Kilgore, is that you don't have anything you would die for. That's what puts grit in your gullet, not the memory of an easy life."

"And Shieldbroad won't be nearly so inviting with the fjord frozen and trolls galloping about everywhere," Skanderbeg said. "I predict that unless Surt is stopped now, within the year Shieldbroad will also fall to the Blight."

"Who said anything about turning around and going back?" Kilgore asked gloomily, huddling his cloak around his ears. "Going back is as insane as going forward, so let us go forward by all means. But I just hope the scops write a poem about these mountains and our misery. They always make it sound so delightful to be a hero, when it certainly isn't."

While they talked, Skanderbeg scanned their back-trail through a pocket spyglass. "Rats!" he suddenly exclaimed.

"Something's following us," Asny declared. "Get ready, Kilgore! What is it, Skanderbeg? We'll make him wish he hadn't."

"No, no! I mean, I have a peculiar feeling I'm missing something important. Something has been forgotten."

"Shall we go back?" Kilgore asked, liking and hating the idea at the same time. He thought of the pleasant fires at Haelfsknoll; but also the same cold trail would await them a second time.

Skanderbeg answered, "No, nothing is important enough to go back for, when time is as short as it is. If we delay much longer, winter will descend upon us, not to mention the evil slaves of Surt. But I wish I could remember—" He went on mumbling and scowling.

Kilgore thought nothing of his absent-mindedness. After a little hot tea to warm themselves, they were on their way. Kilgore trudged wearily in Skanderbeg's footsteps, groping for handholds in the steep places. Often the rocky trail disappeared under slopes of shale or ended abruptly at a vertical cliff's face, and they had to go back until they came to a fork in the path. All day long Kilgore told himself, "Just a little further, then I'll call a halt to rest."

But the sun was slipping westward by the time he at last called out to Skanderbeg, "Isn't it almost time to start thinking about a camp site now?"

Skanderbeg paused only for a moment. "Why, yes, we could stop now before we really have to. But if we slouch along and dawdle at the beginning of the race, how are we ever to win? We must keep going until the sun sets. The Plateau is scarcely half a day from us, and then the going will be easy. Until we assail the Burnt Mountains, that is."

"Plateau?" Kilgore echoed. "I thought we were nearly over the Burnt Mountains after all of this." He almost groaned, but concealed it at the last moment with a sigh.

"Certainly not," Skanderbeg said. "Didn't you look at the map? Here, I'll show it to you again."

"No, don't bother," Kilgore said. "I remember now. Besides, the satchel is packed away and we'd have to unload your pack to get it."

"We have barely arrived at the beginning place. The Plateau is a kind of breathing space before attempting the Burnt Mountains. The Briarthorns are only foothills compared to the Burnts."

"Oh yes," Kilgore murmured. "Foothills." Desolately he looked at the cliffs and rocky precipices and deep gorges around them. In some places a fly would have trouble navigating the steep walls, and these were mere foothills.

The wind sharpened as they climbed higher, shrieking and howling with a vengeance as if to defy them. Kilgore voiced no complaints; the numbing winds made speech slow and stiff, if not incoherent. Each step upward was a noteworthy accomplishment, and several times they had to make agonizing backtracks to find a place they could climb. Often the rocks underfoot were frost-rimed and slick, and those that weren't were usually loose and rolled as they were stepped upon, bouncing against the next person's shins almost by design. Kilgore tried to keep his eyes shut as Skanderbeg precariously skirted a vast chasm; he had the sinking feeling that the wizard was going to expect him to do likewise. His heart sank to his bootsoles when the sun dipped behind a cloud with no intentions of showing itself again that day.

The west began to glow softly red, then the clouds flamed. Looking behind and below, Kilgore could see only spires and peaks gouging through a blanket of red mist. The far southern horizon, where Shieldbroad lay, looked impossibly distant and was veiled in mist. The pleasant easy years spent there seemed like a fond remembrance or a dream of something that never existed.

The red sky had faded and still they climbed upward. The top—if there was one—seemed no nearer. Kilgore looked forward only as far as the next handhold. What a fine joke it would be if there really were no Plateau waiting above. He almost believed it and was almost ready to stop and say, "No farther!" But suddenly his cold, grasping hand felt grass and turf instead of stone. In amazement he looked up. Instead of more stern cliff, he saw the topmost peaks of the Skull Mountains, still bathed in the setting sunlight. He gasped. They were so close he could see more than a hazy blue form of a mountain. He could see the rugged detail of canyons, gorges, cliffs, and parapets. Icy crests were flung on high to impale the gray bosoms of clouds on their spires. Never had Kilgore realized the size and grandeur of the mountains from his safe distance at Shieldbroad. Even there, he had known they were fierce mountains, but now, right at their feet, he was awed. The wall of the Burnt Mountains still separated them from the Skull range, and even the Burnt Mountains were wilder and gloomier than anything in Shieldbroad. But his eyes were drawn almost irresistibly to the blue summits of the Skulls. Without realizing it he grasped the pommel of the great sword as he stared.

"Well, let's get camp set up!" Skanderbeg commanded briskly, startling him from his contemplation. "Astounding, aren't they, lad? They always cast a spell on a body the first time."

"We could never cross them," Kilgore said. "Not

if we had a million years. They're a fortress wall, almost."

"Aye, indeed. But we don't need to worry our heads about crossing them. Or so I hope. If it weren't for the Gardar Pass Gap we would never make it, and may not still, the way Surt's trolls are fortifying the Road." He pointed to the northeast. "And there it is—the black crack between the Skull and the Trident. That is the only way to get over these mountains. I would despair if I thought we didn't have at least a slim chance of getting through the Gap. But this map of mine shows the secret shortcut men have sought for years. Straight into the Burnts it goes, then westerly. I'll show everyone on the map."

After studying the Burnt Mountains a moment, Kilgore said, "Seems to me going over the Burnts is almost as bad as traveling all the way to Gardar on the Old Road. Certainly it will take longer."

"The longer it takes is just that many more days to stay alive," replied Skanderbeg grimly. "I couldn't guarantee absolute survival if we took the Road from Haelfsknoll."

"And who's to say," Asny added, already with an armload of dry wood, "that fighting every step of the way wouldn't take us longer?"

"That's right," the wizard agreed. "And time, you know, is our bane."

"But with the sword—" Kilgore began.

"Oh, yes, probably it could get us through it all," Skanderbeg replied. "But hacking our way through a forest of hungry trolls is nothing short of brash speculation."

"I still don't see the difference between those dreadful cliffs which we may fall over any moment and a few trolls," Kilgore said.

"I can see there's no convincing you," Skanderbeg said. "If it's fighting you want, then we'll go on the Road. If it's getting Surt you want, it's the mountains. But possibly there's another way out. Let me get my map case and we'll see." He got up stiffly and walked away to find his satchel.

Kilgore made himself comfortable on a flat stone. Suddenly Skanderbeg uttered a terrible screech. Whirling around and drawing the sword, all he saw was Skanderbeg with both hands pulling on his hair in a distracted manner. "It's gone!" he cried in a voice of despair.

CHAPTER 8

"What's gone?" Asny demanded, dropping a load of sticks to grab her hammer.

"The maps again? Oh, no!" Kilgore clutched the sword.

"No, not the maps, although they're gone too. Oh, this is the worst thing that could happen. How could I do it?" the wizard mourned, sitting down on a stone and holding his head.

"Well, what is it?" Kilgore demanded impatiently.

"Are we doomed?" Asny asked.

"Yes," Skanderbeg said with a sigh. "Someone or something has stolen my magic satchel with our maps, bedding, tent, telescope, and most of our food. The provisions and equipment I could live without, but not without my magical apparatus and supplies and my book of spells, without which I am totally helpless."

"Totally?" Asny gasped.

"Well, not really. I can still manage a few basic things. But if there were a crisis—" He sighed and wrung his hands.

Kilgore pondered the significance of the satchel's loss a moment, then said sternly, "What I'd like to know is how you got this far without having any idea you'd lost something that important."

Skanderbeg answered promptly, "With much practice one becomes accustomed to such things. We were following a plain trail and had no need of the maps, nor anything else in the bag, blasted creature. I know it was in this pack after the nykurs jumped—no, the last time I saw it was at night when I planted that snoring salamander. After that, anything could have happened to it." He pulled on his beard musingly, his brow gathering into a scowl.

"It was Ketil—or Warth," Kilgore said. "He must have pinched it last night or this morning while we were packing up. Blast him, next time I get the chance, Kildurin is going to sever that scrawny neck of his."

"I think we ought to go back to that lake and look for him," Asny said, shoving the hammer into her belt. "I'll go alone. I know I can catch you again."

"No, I'll go. I've got the sword, Kilgore said.

"No, we'll both go. Agreed?"

"Agreed." And they shook hands.

"Disagreed," Skanderbeg said. "Nobody is going back. I have a rather crude little compass and a few extra devices in my pockets, and there's enough food to last until Beortstad, the Alfar outpost. If we go back now, Surt will make sure we never get this close again. Does everyone agree?"

Asny and Kilgore nodded dubiously.

"Good. For dinner tonight we'll have tea and whatever else we can scratch together. We'll begin rationing our food at once."

He produced a travel-worn pouch which was filled with some sort of grain and began instructing Kilgore in its preparation. Although it tasted all right, the grain must have had magical properties. A very little seemed to make an awful lot of porridge, and it was certainly filling. It settled in his stomach like a bucket of plaster. That night he dreamed of the feasts in his father's hall—whole oxen, fowls, swine, all roasting in the huge pit that was the hearth in the hall of the Brandstok.

He awakened from his pleasant dreams to more tea and the grain made into a kind of cold thin pudding. There was scarcely even time to complain about it before Skanderbeg was packing things and rushing to get started. The night frost was still thick and crusty when they started on the trail along the Plateau. The turf was springy with the dead grass and walking was strangely effortless. A few thorn bushes clawed at the hems of their cloaks and the round, bald tops of rocks stood up to the weather like lichen-blotched sea monsters. In sheltered swales grew a hardy variety of evergreen that seemed closely related to the thorn bushes. On the Plateau there were a few birds to break the brooding silence, and once in a while some furtive rodent scurried across the path or piped a shrill chitter as they passed its den.

The sun stayed buried behind the huge bulk of the Skull and Burnt Mountains until almost midday. Far below, to the south, the rocky valleys and cliffs were lit with the usual gray light that sent the mist clouds huddling in the shadowy places, while the travelers marched along in predawn dimness. Kilgore felt cheated out of his daytime until sunset. Then the sunlight lingered on the stern Plateau long after all below was hidden in night. Like a red eye, the sun glared over the cloudy rim of the horizon; as long as it delayed the travelers hurried over the Plateau.

After two days of rapid traveling, the Plateau began to rise. Hills appeared, and rocky spines of mountains had to be scaled. Skanderbeg had his compass out and consulted it frequently with satisfied mutters and grunts. After one such consultation he announced, "We shall be at the Gap in exactly three days, or the following day at the latest. Losing our map hasn't thrown us off schedule much at all, considering we're already far behind where we should be. But if we weren't, we'd be going well indeed."

"Do you really hope to find the secret path down into the Gap without the map?" Asny asked doubtfully.

"Almost certainly I can," the wizard replied quickly. "It's all right in my mind. Yes, I can clearly see the way to go. You needn't worry yourselves about that." Confidently he struck off into the growing shadows, ignoring Kilgore's half-hearted suggestion that it was time to stop.

When he did stop, they made another hungry camp. Skanderbeg declared that a man didn't need a full stomach to sleep on, so supper consisted of tea and gruel again. Kilgore was beginning to feel rather surly about the situation, since for three days now the eating had been mighty spare. After the scanty meal, he strolled around the fire, looking into the surrounding darkness and hoping to see an edible beast drawn by the light. With a sigh he sat down by the fire again alternately to warm his back and then his face. While half a person was chilled, he discovered, it made no difference how hot the other half was; he was still cold. He wrapped his cloak around him and followed Asny's example of leaning against a fire-warmed rock and trying to go to sleep. But just as his head would begin to nod, Skanderbeg would clear his throat with a loud rasping noise or mutter something under his beard. Kilgore glared at the wizard where he sat hunched over the coals, his eyes two shadowy pits under the protruding beak of his hood.

"What are you brooding about, Skanderbeg?" Kilgore asked.

The wizard sighed and leaned on his elbow. "About the satchel. Its loss is not so bad; we could manage without magic. But what I worry about is who has it now. There are spells in that bag which would render even a sorry excuse of a magician into a first-rate sorcerer. I'm afraid that is exactly what has happened."

"So Warth has it now," Kilgore said. "How much of a threat is he really, Skanderbeg?"

"Enough to sink this whole venture, especially if he uses some of my own spells for his evil purposes. I made most of those spells myself in Cutshall Castle in my experimenting days. Why, there are spells in that bag that would give him enough power to—" He didn't finish the thought aloud, but Kilgore could read it in his face.

"He could steal the sword," Kilgore said. "Then he'd join forces with Surt. Or maybe he has his own wicked ideas. What could he possibly do with it? It's almost as long as he is and certainly too heavy for him to wield. Could he translate the runes, Skander-beg, with the magic in your satchel?"

Skanderbeg didn't answer. He only said, "It's time we got some sleep. You never lay aside the sword, do you? Good. Keep it close to you at every moment. I shall make a guardian ring around our camp tonight, since we're getting into country where one needs these things. Fortunately I don't need any props for this spell. My teacher made me learn it by heart and I've never forgotten it." He arose and dusted off his robes and gathered up his knotty old staff. He patted its dragon head affectionately before starting his incantation.

Asny, ever alert to danger, stirred suddenly and began listening. Her eyes slowly searched the wall of darkness beyond their little fire.

"What is it?" Kilgore whispered.

"Nothing, mostly," she answered. "Just a peculiar feeling. Someone or something out there in the dark, watching, waiting—"

"Save your monsters for the daytime," the wizard said. "We want to sleep tonight." However, long after Kilgore and Asny were asleep, he continued to brood beside the small fire. He clutched his staff in one hand, glancing now and then at its faintly glowing head. Suddenly he sat up, staring toward the edge of their camp. There, glowing softly, sat his own satchel.

"So you've come back," he said sternly. "I sent for you enough times. I hope you'll behave yourself this time and not get lost again."

He snatched it up, but something about it was different. It felt quite ordinary and lifeless, not at all magical. He looked inside and found nothing but feathers and sticks and a bird's nest. A cheap imitation of his own priceless satchel. With a sigh he threw it in the fire and sat down again, doubly vigilant. Warth must be in the area, he decided grimly. On tiptoe, he crossed the campsite to the sleeping lump that was Kilgore and stooped to see the sword in its sheath, right under his hand where it was safe. With a sigh he returned to his rock and sat down to watch.

Kilgore slept restlessly. Once he awakened, or thought he did, to see Skanderbeg burning his satchel in the fire. After that, he couldn't get warm. The ground beneath him was like ice. He dreamed he was lost in the Skull Mountains, wandering in a white wilderness of driving snow without any cloak or hood or sword. All around him were shadowy shapes like trolls and giants and wolves that followed him soundlessly. A desolate howling surrounded him in his dream, a sound full of almost human misery and despair. Instinctively he closed his hand on the sword, reassured by the feeling of the cool metal.

He slept dreamlessly, but the menacing howling of his former dream returned. It became louder and more insistent, almost to the point of awakening him. Suddenly he did awaken and sat bolt upright. The night was still black around him and Skanderbeg was sitting by the fire's ashes. He was only a blacker shadow in the gloom.

"Be quiet," he whispered. "It's vargulfs in the Gap. Wake Asny. I think we'll have a fight on our hands."

"I'm awake," Asny said. "Let's move to the top of that hill over there and we'll have the advantage. How much of the night is passed?"

"Dawn is only a few hours off," Skanderbeg said, "but that's still enough time for them to get us and run back through the Gap to Grimshalg before dawn."

"I wish the sun would catch them all," Asny said. "It would be better to be dead than held in Surt's thrall as the vargulfs are."

"You mean that's what he did to his prisoners?" asked Kilgore, who had shivered at vargulf stories all his life. Now he shivered in earnest.

"Many of Wulther and Valsidda's men, as well as the former inhabitants of Gardar, are now wolves by night and prisoners in Grimshalg by day," Asny said. "That was the fate of my seven older brothers."

The dismal wails echoed in the Gap and seemed to fade away. Then Kilgore realized he was hearing them on the Plateau, now on a ridgetop and now in a swale. "Don't they ever get tired and have to rest?" he asked.

"Not in a million years," Skanderbeg said. "Surt will hold them forever in thrall. If a vargulf is slain, it springs to life again with another body. All we have to hope for is a cloudless dawn."

In another moment they could hear the sound of feet pounding over the rocky hilltops, dislodging stones with a clatter. In the pale light from the coming dawn, Kilgore saw half a dozen black shapes pouring down into the place they had camped, circling and sniffing. Then the vargulfs came racing straight up the hill toward them.

"Ready!" Skanderbeg said tensely, holding his staff out with a fearful look of concentration on his face. A jet of orange flame shot out to meet the leader; by its light Kilgore had his first glimpse of a vargulf. The body was like a huge black wolf, with a brushy tail and sharp ears, but the face was flat instead of pointed like a wolf's. The facial features were mostly obscured by black fur, but they were more human than wolfish, with small eyes and white even teeth.

He drew the sword and waited for its response. It made no sound and felt heavy in his hand. Glancing at it, he was dumbfounded when he saw no shimmering light or golden runes. It was lifeless. Asny's shrill yell startled him just in time to thrust the sword into the neck of a vargulf as it leaped on him. Rolling over in a tangle of legs, he shoved the dead creature away as another attacked. By the time he had dispatched the second one, the first had leaped again to life with redoubled fury. He could hear Skanderbeg hewing away with his sword and trying to remember spells. Suddenly the wizard found one for green flame, which drove the vargulfs back a moment until they discovered it was without heat. Then they surged forward again.

"Oh, drat!" Skanderbeg exclaimed. "Yellow flame it must be then!"

Asny swung her hammer right and left, killing a vargulf with each blow. Kilgore was not having such

115

good luck. He disabled more than he slew and the wounded ones fought with greater savagery than the others. One ripped a huge rent in his cloak and another with a broken back got his foot and would have bitten through the leather if Asny had not struck it dead, temporarily.

"Eureka!" Skanderbeg shouted suddenly, brandishing his staff. "I have it this time!" Instantly the hilltop flamed with a lurid light and the vargulfs fled like shadows, streaking away toward the Gap without a backward glance.

"I did it," the wizard said proudly. "I remembered just in time. Knew I could do it, in a pinch. A true genius comes through when the pressure is on. Why, I—" He stopped, looking around suspiciously.

"It's sunlight," Asny said. "The sun is peeking through a tiny notch in the wall of the Trident. But at least we're saved. Kilgore, how many vargulfs did you kill? I counted thirty-six for myself."

Kilgore was staring at the sword and scarcely heard her. In a dreamlike voice he said, "Skanderbeg, this is not my sword."

"What? Of course it is. How do you think you killed those vargulfs then? Let me see it." The wizard took the sword gingerly, then handled it with more authority. "Well. You're quite right. No Alfar ever made such a sword. In fact, it's a very bad copy."

"Ridiculous!" Asny said. "You didn't take your eyes off the sword for a moment last night. How could it be a different one?"

"Very easily. I was fooled by another bad imitation," sighed Skanderbeg. "I thought my satchel had returned and for a moment my back was turned. Our thief slipped in and exchanged swords." For a moment he ground his teeth in silent rage. "When I get my hands on Warth again, he will wish all of the Skull Mountains were heaped upon him to hide him from my wrath. He will wish his troll ancestors had never descended from the Fimbul Winter. He will wish that such a thing as fiery torments had never been invented by the mind of Skanderbeg the fire

116

wizard!" He ended his speech in a roar of fury and struck the earth with his staff until sparks flew.

"What shall we do now?" Asny asked. "Are you sure it was Warth?"

"As sure as I am sure my name is Skanderbeg," he replied in a wrathful voice. "And what we are going to do is track that little rat of a beggar to his lair and burn it down around his ears, after we cut them off. Any objections?" His tone said there had better not be.

"Yes, I object," Kilgore said, sheathing the fake sword. "How do we track a wizard who can fly, or make himself perfectly invisible, or change into any form he wants? And look at what we have to track him in." Gloomily he stared at the labyrinth of peaks and gorges before them.

"I can track the west wind across the ocean," Skanderbeg said, striding around the campsite looking for clues. "Didn't you hear me say sleuthing was one of my better skills? Why, I can find the aeries of eagles, the lairs of sylphs, or the secret halls of Elbegast, if I so desired. This Warth creature shall give me no trouble—above what is to be naturally expected. A single thread, a frost-nipped bud, a peculiar smell are all ample evidence."

"Whatever you say," Kilgore murmured. He was so dejected he wasn't even hungry. The sword and the satchel were both stolen, and they were lost in the troll-infested and vargulf-haunted Skull Mountain.

Their plight seemed to lend Skanderbeg amazing energy. All day he strode along, full of confidence. Often he stopped abruptly to examine his pocket instruments; then he would dash away with renewed vigor. By nightfall they were at the feet of the Burnt Mountains. Their camp was in a desert of black basalt and spiney plants. Long ago one of Skarpsey's many volcanoes had spewed forth a mighty eruption of lava that hardened into the fantastic cliffs and crevices that were called the Burnt Mountains. The wind sang like a witches' chorus among the broken rock, and from an ice-bound glacier somewhere

117

above came booming moans and sharp cracks as the ice inched its way seaward. No camp in such surroundings could help being desolate, but the travelers were too tired to feel more than mildly gloomy.

At the earliest possible moment they were off again, skirting the tumbled flows of lava. By noon they knew exactly where they were being led. Skanderbeg called a halt and sat down to think. A nasty wind nipped at his nose and ears but he didn't seem to notice.

"Traveling the Gardar Road without the Alfar sword is the last thing I have in mind," he said. "Even with it, it's a fool's venture."

"But what if Warth takes the Gardar Road to get to Surt?" Kilgore asked. "We'll have to follow."

"Yes, and we'll get to Gardar all the quicker," answered Skanderbeg, "but it will no doubt be in a troll's stomach."

"Listen to me," Asny said. "Warth is too greedy to share his prize with anybody, especially Surt. I think he'll try to set up his own kingdom. Perhaps he'll cross the Gap to the old troll empire of Reekness."

"Reekness!" Skanderbeg muttered. "I wouldn't be surprised at all. Ha, what's this? Look here, anybody can see that someone carelessly hurried through here not long ago." He pointed to the straggly furze triumphantly. Kilgore could see nothing and said so. Skanderbeg tolerantly pointed out two crushed twigs and a bit of disturbed earth. A falling butterfly could not have left less of a clue. Then he observed how the dragon head on Skanderbeg's staff glowed a pale red whenever it passed wizard signs. So that was how the old fox did his sleuthing.

The trail led them further into the mountains, over trackless barren stretches where only trolls knew the way. Unerringly, Skanderbeg led the way, always tapping ahead with his staff. They camped in places they would have quickly passed before. Spirits sagged until everyone was grumbling and cross. Even Skanderbeg complained. "I don't know why we even go on," he said. "We'll be out of food in a matter of days. It will take at least a week to get to Gardar at

118

the rate we're going, even if there wasn't one troll in the Gap. But if we have to chase Warth all over the Trident to get the sword and then come back and expect to find a way down to the road, we'll be troll bait. And finding a way down those sheer walls is no easy matter, unless you're a troll or a bat."

"There's a way without coming back," Asny said slowly, frowning as she remembered. "It's terribly dangerous, though. It would take us right through the hunting grounds of the vargulfs. Now that they have stalked us once they won't give up, no matter which side of the Gap we are on, so the less time we spend, the better off we'll be."

"My dear uncrowned queen, what are you trying to suggest?" Skanderbeg demanded. "I feel my blood turning cold. You aren't possibly suggesting that we go over the top of the Trident, are you?"

"Yes, I am," Asny said, folding her arms and scowling. "Fortune may not wait for us to come back to here. And it has been done by one party, since the Second War, though two men froze, one was lost over a precipice, one was eaten by something, and one died of wounds from a troll arrow. But it may have been mere bad luck, you know. A man must die when his time comes, and Fortune is not always kind."

"If all that happens to us," Kilgore said, "there'll be no one to carry the sword to slay Surt."

"Well, that's true," Asny agreed. "We don't know if it will, though. Skanderbeg, what do you think? Is the risk worth it?"

Skanderbeg had been pondering in silence. After a moment, he stood up to his full height and began striding back and forth, scowling. Then he stopped and declared, "We shall do it nevertheless. There are many advantages, one being that nobody will expect us to attempt it. Also, it will save backtracking. And time. We must ride the winds of luck, and if they carry us to the Trident, then we shall let them carry us over the top. It shall be done."

With no further discussion, he and Asny plotted the course from their knowledge of the land, while

Kilgore watched with growing excitement. "Here lies the old kingdom of Wickness," and "This place used to be dreaded for its white wolves," and "No mortal ever set foot through this country, so this is the way we shall go," were only some of the clues he got about the Trident side of the Gap. It sounded frightening, and very heroic to his ears. That night he could scarcely sleep for the visions of ancient lands and strange creatures.

In high spirits, they set forth the next morning. They were not surprised or disappointed to see the trail bend directly to the east, toward the Gap and the Trident.

As they drew nearer the Gardar Gap, they could hear the far-off bellow of the wind from Gardar as it thundered through the Gap to the coastlands. It shrieked among the crags or muttered deep in the rocky throat of the Gap. The land approaching it was wind-hewn, and heaps of stone and earth were shaped through the ages until they resembled weird temples and altars. The travelers spoke little as they hurried through, ever scanning the terrain warily, and stopping seldom except in carefully chosen campsites.

The red sun was glowering in a muffler of black clouds when they arrived at the rim of the Gap. Here they were baffled. Warth's trail went right over the edge—his troll ancestry let him climb down the perpendicular wall as easily as a spider. An easier crossing place would have to be discovered before they could descend. And then they would have to find the trail again.

While Skanderbeg and Asny fumed and plotted another course, Kilgore stared in awe at the Gap. It was a huge and ragged gorge so deep he could not see the Old Road below through the gloom. To him the Gap looked like a monstrous black crack in the mountains with vertical sides. He shuddered, partly because of the icy draft blowing up from the Gap, and partly because of the sudden dread in his heart. If the sword had gone down that black gorge, he feared it would never again see the light of day. There, just below, he knew the legions of trolls were crouching and waiting for travelers, eager for destruction and death. He backed away from the gaping, evil maw before him, imagining the gray figures flitting to and fro and perhaps watching him even now, waiting for the opportunity—he shook his head angrily and tried to think of Wulther and Valsidda to bolster his courage. But the fear he felt settled in a determined knot in his throat and he spoke little.

"What's the matter?" Asny asked. "You're not afraid of a few trolls, are you?"

Kilgore shrugged in a noncommittal way, then he exclaimed, "Why, of course I am, and if you have any sense at all you ought to be scared too. Talking of heroes is very well, but that's all it is, just talk. Those are real trolls down there."

Asny gulped. "You're right. I'm scared too, and now that I've said so, I think I feel better."

Kilgore nodded. Skanderbeg silently pointed to the west and they followed him without arguing. By the time they found the downward path, snow was coming down in earnest, hiding most of the Gap's gloomy gorge in a billowing curtain of white. Goats would have had a difficult time navigating the path; it was steep and dangerous enough without the added slipperiness of the snow. All they heard was hissing snow. As they descended, the two rims of the Gap seemed to draw together overhead and it became gloomier and quieter and more frightening.

By the time they reached the bottom they were in deep gray twilight. The winds howled and moaned faraway down the Gap, answered by a moaning bellow from above, and the snow curtain gusted furiously. They floundered through brush and rocks until they reached the road. Its expanse was smooth and white until they reached the far side. Myriads of troll tracks crisscrossed the snow like giant bird prints around a mess of broken boxes and barrels and packs. A cart lay overturned and the tracks of the horses

121

disappeared in the troll prints. No trace remained of the human occupants of the cart.

Hurriedly, they put the ominous scene behind them. They found the trail going up the other side and scrambled up the cliff in what must have been record time. Kilgore was haunted by the scene of the tragedy below, and he imagined the hot breath of pursuing trolls behind him.

Skanderbeg immediately began searching for traces of Warth. But no traces were to be found, not even on the opposite side from the place he had gone down into the Gap.

After about an hour of futile searching, Skanderbeg sat down on a rock. "It's plain what has happened," he said with a sigh.

"Warth didn't come up this side," Asny replied. "He went either up or down the road, knowing we wouldn't dare follow."

"And we don't," Kilgore said. A dull ache settled in the middle of his back, and his feet were wet. "We'd better find a safe place to camp tonight. Up here there probably aren't any fewer trolls than below."

Silently they slogged through the snow. Kilgore concentrated on Skanderbeg's footprints to forget how utterly miserable he felt. He was jarred out of his stupor by colliding with Skanderbeg's shoulder blades. When he looked up to complain, he saw the dark mouth of a cave against the blue hillside. In an instant he knew what it was.

"A troll hole!" he whispered piercingly. "Let's get out of here!"

Skanderbeg didn't move. "No trolls are inside. The door is standing wide open. I wouldn't be at all surprised to find a lot of food and firewood down there."

"I would, for nothing could persuade me to investigate," Kilgore said.

CHAPTER 9

"So you want to wait out here in the cold and storm and trolls while Asny and I warm ourselves by a crackling hot fire and stuff ourselves with the troll's provisions? And it is getting dark too."

"I never said that. If you are so sure there's food and no trolls in that cave, I suppose all I can do is go along."

"Almost certainly there's food. Trolls always have quantities of it. They steal it from travelers and eat the travelers and so have no use for the food. I've never yet known a troll who did anything inconvenient like cooking soups and bread and gravy. They'd much rather stick to simple meals and never mind the delicacies. However, they just can't resist stealing everything they can get their paws on, even if they never use it. That's what I call unthrifty theft." All the while Skanderbeg was marching resolutely up to the troll hole.

It was a dreary place sunk into a hillside. An arched door with rusty iron bands and no handle stood halfway open, and the hinges screeched crazily.

Skanderbeg thrust his head inside and shouted, "Hullo the troll hole! Anybody home?" Nobody was, so in they trooped.

A bed of coals was banked on the hearth and a great black kettle hung there burbling sullenly. With a quick sniff, Skanderbeg banished it and found another pot. It wanted scouring. Stuff had been burnt and baked into it for years. The whole cave, in fact, smelled like the kitchen of a very bad cook. Suspicious rotting smells hovered around the carelessly piled provisions, and some rats had a large shaggy nest in the beams overhead. The beams themselves were covered with soot which sifted down finely into everything. Broken crockery was shoved into a corner but not with a broom; there wasn't one and hadn't been for some time. Smashed chairs, parts of which were half-charred in the fireplace, animal pelts and horns tacked on the walls or thrown into a corner, rags and clothing, blackened bones—all these were the furnishings of the troll hole. And the smell alone was enough to make Kilgore wonder if he shouldn't have waited outside.

Skanderbeg built up the fire and clambered about in the pots and kettles, preparing a great feast. Meanwhile, Kilgore and Asny stuffed quantities of supplies into their packs. Kilgore often glanced anxiously toward the door, expecting to see an angry horde of trolls glaring at him in outrage.

"Skanderbeg, are you ready to go?" he asked after filling his pack almost to bursting.

"Go? Certainly not. We'll stay until we're warm and dry and we've had supper." He did not even remove his head from the kettle he was stirring.

"But the trolls! They'll be coming any time now!"

"Not if the door's locked, they won't."

Kilgore was speechless. He stalked about the cave distractedly, his horror increasing every moment. This time tomorrow, he told himself, their own bones would be charring in the fireplace. He knew it was useless to try to budge Skanderbeg once the wizard's mind was made up. However—it would be nice to warm up and dry out and have a decent meal for a change. Finding the last whole chair, he drew it up to the fireplace. Skanderbeg promptly sat on it with a cheerful "Thank you!"

"The pleasure is mine," Kilgore grunted, sitting on a stone.

"I think this troll hole has been abandoned," Asny said, stretching out on the hide of some unfortunate creature beside the fire.

"Troll holes always look abandoned," Skanderbeg replied, "whether two or twenty live in it."

"I hope there aren't twenty trolls living in this one," Asny said. "I suspect they'll be coming in soon, and the fewer there are, the better fighting chances we have."

"Of course, we'll be on our way before they do, won't we, Skanderbeg' Kilgore asked pointedly.

The wizard was sound asleep in his chair, clutching the ladle in one hand.

"Skanderbeg!" Kilgore said indignantly.

"I heard every word you said and I quite agree with everything. Now let's eat. I hope no one's too upset about eating stolen troll provisions. Smells wonderful anyway." He handed round the bowls of stew.

Everyone was beginning to eat with gusto when suddenly there was a commotion at the door. Somebody was pounding and kicking at it. A hoarse voice called out, "Who's that in my troll hole? Open up at once, I say. Whatcha got the door locked for? Is that you, Skulfing?"

"Are you alone?" asked Skanderbeg gruffly.

"Certainly! There's no one to be trusted! You ought to know that!"

Skanderbeg quickly shot back the bolts, reached out, and snatched the fellow inside. It was a troll all right, and his fright at seeing his uninvited guests was almost equal to theirs at seeing him. He gave a little screech and turned quite pale under the black hairs on his face. His small features convulsed with fear or hatred, and he was noticeably trembling in his outsized greatcoat that trailed down to his heels.

"What's this?" he cried in such a hoarse voice it was difficult to understand him. "You'd murder a poor old troll besides invade his own home and eat up all his food? In all my life I've never heard of such inhospitality, ingratitude, churlishness, and spitefulness!"

"Trollishness you mean!" Skanderbeg said. "Any troll would do the same, wouldn't he?"

The troll blinked rapidly with passion. "And you never were even invited!" he said.

"We couldn't wait for an invitation," Skanderbeg said. "It was a frightful imposition."

Kilgore felt like laughing. The troll didn't seem

125

quite so fierce now. In fact, he looked more like an apprehensive little old beggar in a stolen greatcoat.

The creature blustered, "Well, what do you want with me? Can't you set a fellow down?"

"Not until you tell us where Warth the wizard is hiding," Skanderbeg said.

"There are no wizards in these mountains," the troll snapped. "No decent troll would be seen with one for all the gold in Gardar if there were any wizards here. We have no use for their mumblings and herbs and spells and charms." And he looked hard at Skanderbeg as he said so.

Kilgore almost laughed. "Then you haven't seen a miserable little old rogue who walks with a limp carrying a huge sword as long as himself?" he asked. "And a dirty red cloak and hood and big boots with curling toes?"

"With a blue muffler and ragged gloves?"

"Yes!"

"And an evil rolling eye?"

"That's him!"

"And a knotty old staff?"

"To be sure, that's the fellow!"

"Then I haven't seen him," the troll said shortly and folded his arms.

"Tell me, friend Asny," Skanderbeg said, poking at the troll critically. "Do they still eat trolls in Gardar?"

Asny replied, "More than ever." She drew out a knife and began to whet it. "A great favorite, roast troll."

The little troll's swarthy complexion slowly blanched as he looked at his captors. He gibbered nervously in troll, then said, "Beastly uncivilized louts. How could you think to eat another intelligent being?"

"We wouldn't dream of it," said Kilgore. "Trolls are a different matter, though."

"Eat me, then. See if I care. But you're doing yourselves a monstrous disservice."

"Nonsense. Troll is very agreeable provender," Asny said. "Find a large kettle. And some garlic. I don't suppose, old man, you'd have a few potatoes and fragrant herbs?" she asked the troll.

"It's very stupid of you to put into your gullets that which would better enrich your brains," blustered the troll, blinking in alarm.

"That sounds like a riddle," Skanderbeg said, skaking the frightened creature reprimandingly. "No more riddles. At least, not before supper."

The troll began to tremble harder than ever as he watched the preparations. "Now see here!" he exclaimed.

"There's plenty of fodder more tender than an aged troll. You're welcome to it all—more than welcome, in fact—in exchange for my worthless little self." He blinked his green eyes apologetically.

"Indeed! What a strange offer," Skanderbeg said. "What has that got to do with dashing out brains—wasn't that what you spoke of?"

"No, no, no! Not at all! I meant that I could tell you something that perhaps you want to know, if I weren't eaten, that is." He lowered his dry voice almost to a whisper.

"What did you say? You almost sound like you're conniving against someone!" Skanderbeg roared.

"Shh, shh! There may be ears listening!" the troll squeaked in terror.

"Well, why not? That's what they're made for," Skanderbeg grumbled.

"But these ears are no friends to either of us, really," the troll went on. "If you'll put me down, sir, I'll tell you whatever you want to know."

"Fair enough." Skanderbeg lowered the creature to the floor and the troll scuttled away from the light, grumbling, and found a dark corner. He sat hissing and muttering with his head withdrawn into his coat.

"Well?" Skanderbeg said impatiently.

"What do you want to know?" the troll asked sullenly, not quite so frightened now.

"Where is Warth?" Skanderbeg demanded sternly.

"What difficult questions!" the troll murmured with a yawn. He had yellow teeth that looked long and sharp to Kilgore.

127

"Kilgore!" Skanderbeg bellowed. "Get the kettle ready!"

"But not that difficult!" the troll added hastily. "I need time to think, you know. It's hard to remember what these wizards do with themselves, especially when one is so distraught."

"Just go right ahead and think all you want," Skanderbeg said soothingly. "Meanwhile, we'll get the kettle ready."

"Quite unnecessary! I just remembered," the troll exclaimed.

"Excellent. Now where is he?"

"Why—er, I forgot again."

"Kilgore!"

"But memory, a fragile thing, is quick to mend," the troll babbled knotting its clawlike hands together anxiously and darting furtive glances at Kilgore. "Warth the wizard—um, let's see. Warth the magician —no, ah—Warth the sorcerer—"

"Wrong, wrong, wrong!" Skanderbeg declared. "I wouldn't demean any of those titles by applying it to him."

"Oh? I wager he can out-wizard any wizard you know," the troll smirked.

For an answer, Skanderbeg nodded at the fire, which instantly roared like a furnace and made the room hot and bright as noonday. It was so brilliant that the rats in the rafters scuttled away squeaking to find the darkness.

"So! A fire wizard!" the troll growled. "And what might the likes of you be wanting with the likes of Warth?"

"Much wickedness," Skanderbeg snapped.

"Good enough business, I suppose," the troll said. "I knew there was something disagreeable about the lot of you wizards."

"Reserve your character judgments, troll. I suspect there are a good deal more disagreeable things in this room than wizards," said Skanderbeg. "And answer my question or I'll have you boiled up at once."

128

"Humph. Empty threats," the troll muttered under his breath.

"You may not think so very long if you don't tell us where Warth is," Skanderbeg replied, and he drew a sharp little sword from his waist and looked lovingly at its blade.

"It'll be the death of me if I do," the troll said. "And the death of me if I don't." Skanderbeg had taken up a pair of menacing tongs. "Looks like I'm a dead troll either way. Yes, I have seen Warth dragging away a great sword, not three days ago. I'm sure he's headed for the old capital of Reekness, Trondheim."

"Trondheim," Skanderbeg said. "It's been a long time since I've been there."

"You'll get there quite quickly if you go by way of Blight Peak, and I doubt you'll reach it alive." The little creature grimaced, or smiled, very cheerfully.

"What is Warth doing at old Trondheim?" Asny asked sternly.

"Warth is the new emperor of the trolls, he says," the troll replied. "With King Trond still in prison, Warth seized command—it wasn't hard, since nobody has worried about such truck as kings and kingdoms since we decided that government was illegal. It's rather upsetting to many of us—rebels, we're called—because Warth broke our most cherished law; and besides that, he's only half troll, and worse-tempered than any meek and mild troll born. Mortal blood, no doubt, makes him that way."

"Hold your tongue, troll," Asny warned.

"Certainly. But first I must warn you. Beware of three travelers. It is said that they seek to destroy the great lord of darkness himself, Surt. Personally, I'd say they haven't got a bat's chance—"

"Bah on your warnings," Skanderbeg said. "Now peace!"

"Of course. You needn't worry about those three. Every troll, ogre, giant, and other citizens of the nether worlds is sworn to rip, rend, or otherwise destroy them. Warth's orders."

Skanderbeg roared, "Where's that kettle?" and rose

129

to his feet purposefully. The troll gibbered in fright and scuttled to another corner and eyed his captors sulkily. He whispered smugly, "And it is a very valuable sword, and, strange. Elvish, so they . . . say." The little creature closed his eyes. In two breaths he was asleep and snoring like a whistling teakettle.

"He knows us," said Kilgore in a low voice.

Skanderbeg nodded soberly as he polished off his plate of stew. "The bread is very stale," he said.

The troll snored on while supper was finished. Outside, it was completely dark. Still Skanderbeg showed no signs of leaving. To Kilgore, there were more pleasant places to spend the night than in a troll hole, with the troll still in it.

"Skanderbeg!" He poked the wizard to waken him. "We can't stay here tonight. This is a horrid, filthy hole, and I will not trust your friend not to stick a knife between my ribs."

"But it's warm here, at least."

"I'd rather sleep in a tent than in the same room as a troll. What if he's hungry?"

"There's stew, you know. And it's all his supplies."

"There's also us. Let's get out of here. Now!"

"Oh, plagues and poxes! All right, if it'll make you feel better—"

Something went *crash!* and they felt a gust of cold air.

"The troll!" Asny shouted, awake in a flash.

The troll was gone. They plunged to the door and dashed into the night. Not a sign of the creature anywhere, but that was to be expected, since trolls were very adept at blending into the shadows and skulking along so quietly on their crow feet that an unwary traveler had no idea they were there until too late.

"Well! Now we shall absolutely have to leave," Kilgore said. "He knows who we are. Warth must have warned the trolls not to let us pass. Now he's off to tell Warth, or tell his friends. Either way, we're in trouble if we stay."

"At least we know where to find Warth. Reekness," Asny said. "I can just remember the troll civil wars

130

when I was a child. I don't think it's far from here. We can be there tomorrow—if the trolls don't smell us out tonight."

"I can prevent that," Skanderbeg said. "One pinch of white powder—"

"Let's get going," Kilgore urged, more nervous than ever. He could imagine legions of trolls advancing on their hiding place and whisking them off to some damp old dungeon in Trondheim.

After they got the packs stuffed, they set out at a rapid pace. The snow had let up somewhat; it now sifted down in little hard crystals. Skanderbeg led the way with his dragon's head glowing to show the path, and with his compass in one hand. Several times it warned them not a moment too soon and they flattened themselves among the rocks while a brigade of trolls galloped by.

"This will never do," Skanderbeg said. "It's much too dangerous. If nothing else, they'll trample on us before morning."

"The whole mountainside is alive with trolls!" Asny reported. "Too many to fight and have a chance to survive. And you wouldn't even get to have a decent funeral, since these fellows would eat you without a moment's hesitation. How ignoble!" She balanced the hammer in her hand and looked about cautiously.

"There's only one safe place to go," Skanderbeg said. "Back to the troll hole."

"You've lost your mind!" Kilgore exclaimed.

"Nonsense! That's the first place they looked and we weren't there. And we haven't a chance on these slopes tonight, with every troll from here to Haelfsknoll looking for us. Come along. One ignominious death is as good as another, you heroes." Turning a deaf ear to further protest, he hastened back to the troll hole. The place was a worse mess than before. It looked as if an army had trampled through it, smashing all in its path. But Skanderbeg threw more chair legs on the fire and spread out his blankets and fleeces. In another moment he was asleep and snoring as if the Trident Mountains had never seen a troll.

131

CHAPTER 10

"Well, there it is," said Skanderbeg, about midday. They stopped on the crest of a ridge and looked down into a deep rocky valley. On the other side of a small frozen fjord was Trondheim, or rather the remains of it. Once there had been dozens of troll holes in the steep fellside, but now most had fallen in or were clogged with rubbish. Bones and antlers and hides were scattered around three main caves with rough wooden doors. Muddy paths angled all over the hillside, converging at last at the central cave where there was the most mud and the most trash. A heap of broken barrels and boxes had been tossed out and allowed to roll a short distance down the slope.

"No mistaking troll holes these days," Asny said. "They used to be a bit more discreet. At least there's no mistaking Trondheim for some other place."

"What do we do?" Kilgore asked. "Go knock politely on their door and ask if Warth is there?"

"Is there a better idea?" Skanderbeg snapped, studying the area with a small spyglass. Snow had settled in the creases of his cloak and was collecting in his beard. "Well, well! What on earth can this mean?" he suddenly exclaimed, swinging his glass to the left toward the fjord. He pointed to a long dark line that eddied and scurried among the rocks, around the end of the ice, up the fell, and into the main troll hole. It consisted of about a hundred trolls hurrying along in single file with a purposefulness seldom seen in trolls.

"Gray trolls," Skanderbeg murmured. "All sizes. It's been a long time since I've seen trolls like that and I don't like it. Unless I knew better, I would say old

132

Trond the troll king was back, in which case I wonder what became of Warth and my satchel and Kildurin." He briskly put away his spyglass and took a firm grip on his staff and started marching straight for the main troll hole of Reekness. Kilgore and Asny walked cautiously behind him, waiting for the inevitable fight to begin when they were spotted by the trolls. Kilgore kept his hand on Warth's sword, although it wasn't at all as reassuring to touch. If it had been Kildurin, he was sure it would have been howling as they approached the trolls' door. The place was filthy and smelly with old black bones, skulls, rotting potatoes, and hides with the hair shedding.

With no hesitation, Skanderbeg thundered on the door with the head of his staff. The sound echoed as if a vast cavern lay on the other side. With a scuttling sound, something wheezed, "Who goes there?"

"Trunt, trunt, and the trolls of the fell!" Skanderbeg said in a deep voice. The bolts began sliding and chains rattled on the other side of the door. Whispering, the wizard said, "Stay close to me and keep your mouths shut."

A small troll peered out at them fearlessly, although he was hardly as high as Kilgore's waist. "Who are you, and how do you know the secret passwords to Trondheim?" the troll asked.

"I am an old acquaintance of Trond," Skanderbeg said. "I heard that he had escaped from dwarf prison, so I came to pay my respects. Send him the name Skanderbeg and he will know who I am."

The small troll scratched his ear with his foot. "This is a bit irregular, you know, allowing you creatures into Trondheim, but since you know the passwords—" The big door grated further open and the troll waved them inside.

Kilgore almost fell twice on the wet, slimy stairs. Crude steps led them down and around and further down to a huge room lit by two bonfires. Hundreds of trolls scuttled in all directions, carrying a variety of brooms, mops, pails, rags, carpets, furniture, plus any movables they could get their paws on. In a moment,

Kilgore realized they were cleaning house. Part of the process seemed to be chasing out the former occupants of Trondheim. Kicking and shrieking, the less favored trolls were forcibly evicted, which action consisted of tossing them bodily out the front door in a hail of other refuse.

Kilgore immediately lost track of their guide. There were dozens of small, wizened trolls dashing in and out of about twenty holes that led to the great chamber. Skanderbeg seemed to know exactly where he was going, striding among the trolls without so much as a by-your-leave. The trolls glanced curiously at the three strangers. The younger ones stopped their work to stare, until a sharp nip on the ear restored their sense of duty.

A largish troll blocked their entrance to a side tunnel, demanding, "What's this intrusion? Are these prisoners? You can't take men into Trondheim! King Trond is too busy right now to disturb. He'll have our heads if you bother him."

"It's none of your business," their guide said, kicking the other troll aside and ushering the travelers into another large chamber. A great number of trolls were huddled in the center of the room before a big chair where sat the largest troll Kilgore had seen yet. Two fires burned on either side of the chair for illumination and Kilgore looked at King Trond in awe. His head was large and furrowed between the ears, one of which had a chewed appearance, and the fur around his small facial features was slightly silvered. He sat with one leg crossed over the other, flexing his scaly gray feet with long talons on each toe. With a wave of one paw, he banished the trolls huddling at his feet and gave a contemptuous yawn as they were hauled away by the gray trolls with a chorus of hysterical screeches.

"What's next, Blygli?" King Trond asked of a small troll sitting on the head of a barrel. "Not more of these vandals, I hope. Have you ever seen such degenerates in all you life?"

"No, never," Blygli said. "It's one thing to be a

134

troll, but quite another to be an anarchist besides. The way these fools have been running the Gap is a disgrace, a distinct disgrace. Now what we have next is the case of that hopeless wretch you've locked away in the dungeon. I'll send Blofi to drag him up here, if he's still alive. I tell you, we had to trounce on that one. He's quite insane. I'm not at all sure he's a troll born, as he claims. There's something very odd about him. I recommend we use him if we can. But if we can't, he will be a dangerous enemy—not like these idiots we've kicked out. A little persecution will work wonders for them, but this one is too dull for sophisticated teaching."

"Well, the least we can do is listen to his case." Trond sighed, admiring his claws. "We're only just, you know."

Blygli scurried past Skanderbeg and Kilgore and Asny, turning his head to stare as he ran. Their guide pounced on him and bit him by way of greeting, saying, "What's the odds of getting an audience with the king? These creatures knocked on the door and I didn't send them away because they knew the passwords. Can Trond spare a moment?"

"Certainly," Blygli said, blinking at the strangers. "Mercy, I haven't seen a man in a thousand years. Is it true the outlaws have been eating men for food lately?"

"Aye, it is true, just like uncivilized savages."

"Well! Speaking of savages, I must go fetch one upstairs for his hearing. You ought to come watch. He's the madman, you remember."

"No! I wouldn't miss that for the underside of the moon." He gave Skanderbeg a shove toward Trond and began shouting, "Skanderbeg to see King Trond! Important acquaintance of the king, he says."

Trond sat up, his fur bristling slightly. "Well, it *is* Skanderbeg," he declared, his nose twitching. "My favorite old enemy. Curse your bones, Skanderbeg, how have you been these past thousand years? I thought of you often in dwarf prison."

Skanderbeg advanced and solemnly bowed over the

extended claw of King Trond. "I was entombed myself by one of Surt's wizards for two hundred years," he said. "And you should have thought of me, since I helped put you in dwarf prison. But now you've escaped and soon Trondheim will be bigger and better than before, I suppose."

"Ah, yes," Trond sighed pleasurably. "It's lovely to be back, in spite of this frightful mess. How could you let such a thing happen, Skanderbeg? I'll be busy until the Fimbul Winter trying to get all this trash cleaned out."

"What do you hear about the Fimbul Winter lately?" inquired Skanderbeg casually, leaning on his staff.

Trond eyed him craftily. "Not a great deal, except that soon I can expect to quit worrying about overexposure to the sun and our former ranges on the surface will be restored to us, instead of these filthy holes in the ground. A very important person informed me of all this with his very own words when I was freed from my cell. And what do you hear of the Fimbul Winter lately, Skanderbeg?"

"Nothing at all, since it isn't going to come off," Skanderbeg said. "The sword has turned up again, you've probably heard."

Trond's grin widened. "Yes indeed, I'd heard, but it shall never again see the light of day. I have it right here in Trondheim, and it will never leave. Now then, enough of this gabble. I can see you're positively starving, as usual. You and your friends are invited to a troll feast. Blygli! You old rat, where are you? We're having a feast for our guests. Bring out the tables and benches, the best drink and the best food. No honor is great enough for my old enemy and these two potential enemies. You know, I hate the friends around me, but there's nothing I cherish like an enemy."

"What about this baggage?" Blygli poked and pummeled a bundle into the throne room, leaping back to keep from being bitten. "You better interview him now, because I won't mess with him again. He bites!"

"Skanderbeg, you must pardon me a moment,"

Trond said. "I'll handle this business as quickly as I can."

"Skanderbeg? Skanderbeg?" a familiar voice shrieked. The prisoner hurled himself at Skanderbeg's boots and refused to be dislodged. "Friend wizard! Fellow magician! You've got to rescue me from these inhuman trolls! You can't imagine how glad I am to see you!"

"Nor you I, Warth," Skanderbeg said. "Particularly in such circumstances. It gives me great delight, when I recall how you left us defenseless against the var-gulfs, which you no doubt summoned. And that nykur hoax was as bad as any, when you stole my satchel."

"I rescued it only to return to you," Warth said righteously, drawing himself up with pride in spite of his ragged appearance. "In spite of our differences, you know that we are working toward a common goal against a common enemy."

"Well! A day or so ago you were a troll," said Trond. "Now you're a wizard. What an adaptable fellow. Maybe you would make a better king than I would."

The darkness beyond the firelight tittered, where a multitude of trolls squatted to watch. A few small ones capered about in trollish glee, throwing themselves in-to the air and jumping nimbly on the backs of the big trolls. All sorts of misbehavior and rudeness seemed to be the privilege of the little trolls.

Warth gathered his shreds around him. "I was do-ing my best. It was I who prepared the trolls to ac-cept a king again, and didn't I gladly relinquish my throne to the rightful king? Once the lawful king re-turned, I had no intention of resisting his divine right to rule."

"If that's true, then I wonder how come you at-tacked my gray trolls with tooth and nail and threat-ened them with sorcery of all sorts? We had to throw you in a dungeon to protect ourselves," Trond de-clared, lazily crossing his legs the other way and spreading his toes. "Once we got that little black

137

satchel away he was quite helpless, Skanderbeg. I wonder if that's the way one disarms all wizards?"

Skanderbeg sat down in a large chair and began puffing clouds of smoke. "I won't answer that," he said. "As you see I have no such satchel and if you once suspected I was powerless I'd be troll bait in an instant, which you well know already."

"How well we know each other!" Trond curled his toes and chuckled. "I can see you're bluffing, old man, but I can't tell which way."

"It's his satchel you took from me," Warth blustered. "He's completely helpless. And those two fellows with him are plain ordinary mortals. The scroungy one is supposed to be the only one who can use that Alfar sword you took away. There now, I think I've told enough to save my life, and I hope you'll have the sense to realize I'm telling the truth."

Trond blinked his eyes and yawned again. "Dear me. This is something to think about, but not before dinner. Blygli, put this troll wizard in the corner where I won't forget about him and let's organize some contests. Skanderbeg, you're acquainted with my contests, of course. Explain to your friends what my stakes always are."

Skanderbeg looked at Asny and Kilgore. "I'm sure my friends know that their lives depend upon the outcome of the contests. Bring on your games and we shall see who will have the upper hand in Trondheim."

"Aye. But one penalty if you lose will be that the sword bearer, if indeed this mortal is he, must translate the runes on the sword of Andurich. If he cannot, then I shall persuade this trickster to try it. A troll wizard might be useful after all. The Alfar and the wizards have their magic, but we trolls seem to be a dull lot when it comes to the craft. I have studied it and you'll no doubt see an improvement, Skanderbeg, when you see the riddles I have for you."

"Then let's see them," Skanderbeg said. "I can't wait to give my opinion. Your riddles and contests are always very interesting."

"But first," Kilgore spoke up, ignoring Skanderbeg's warning, "I want to see the sword and the satchel to be sure they are the ones we've lost and intend to regain."

"A shrewd request!" Trond said, sitting up to stare at Kilgore. "You shall see you sword at once. Blygli! The Alfar sword!"

"And the satchel," Skanderbeg added. "Ha, what's this? The feast or the first contest?" He eyed the tables being set up under his nose and loaded with delicacies the travelers hadn't seen since Shieldbroad. Pickled whale, sheep's heads and feet, cheeses of every description, fish of all types from fresh water and salt, breads, skyr and berries, and so much more it was boggling to the hungry travelers.

"I see you are starving," said Trond. "But I will wager that the three of you are not able to outeat my smallest gray troll Hrim."

Hrim was so shriveled and small that he was scarcely larger than a beer jug. He climbed onto the table by the corner of the cloth and sat down facing the travelers on an overturned cup.

"Well, I should think we can manage to eat more than an overgrown rat of a troll," Skanderbeg said. "To make it more fair, only two of us will challenge the little fellow."

Trond grinned and shook his head. "It is, of course, enchanted food. You are wise to leave one of your party to free you from the spell, if that is the way the curse is working. Which of you will not eat or drink anything in Trondheim?"

Kilgore looked at the pickled whale meat and sheep's heads. They certainly looked like any other examples he'd seen, and svid was his particular weakness. He whispered to Skanderbeg. "What will happen if we are enchanted by eating it?"

"Nothing pleasant. Whoever doesn't eat will have to draw blood for us if it is enchanted. But it might not be. Perhaps it will work the other way round, and whoever doesn't eat it falls under the spell."

"I'll be the one," Asny said determinedly. "I don't

relish the idea of eating stuff that may be something else. Besides, I don't think I'd be much good in the contest, and Kilgore is a natural."

"We're ready to begin," Skanderbeg said.

"And here are your possessions," Trond said, as Blygli and two trolls staggered in carrying the sword among them. They placed it on a dais nearby, along with the satchel. "Of course I shall return them to you if you win even one of my contests. You may begin now."

This was Kilgore's kind of contest exactly. He devoured the food without looking up and had made a sizeable dent in about four days' of supplies, but Skanderbeg was eating at twice the rate. When he was beginning to feel slightly stuffed, Kilgore looked down at the troll's end of the table with a pitying eye and was transfixed. The little troll was eating a roast pig bones and all, including the wooden platter it sat upon, and there was a large portion of the table chewed out and swallowed. The pig vanished in moments and the troll fastened his sharp little teeth in a horn cup and ate that too. Then he sampled the table cloth and took several more bites out of the table.

"I can see we're beaten," Skanderbeg said, and the tables were removed, with Hrim still gnawing on one of them.

"Well, you weren't as hungry as you thought," Trond said. "But I know how Skanderbeg can drink. Bring my great cup out here, Blygli. Skanderbeg, if you can drain this cup in two breaths I shall say you've won both contests."

"To make it more fair, I'll drain it in one," Skanderbeg said as Blygli handed him a huge gold cup filled to the brim. The wizard began swallowing the mead and did not stop until his face was purple, but the cup still looked brim full.

"A pity," Trond said. "But perhaps your sword bearer is a wrestler. Young fellow, if you can throw your opponent, I'll say that you've won all three contests. Is that fair enough?"

"Fair enough," Kilgore said eagerly, glad for the opportunity to get his hands on a troll.

"Your opponent will be old Nagli," Trond said, and a frail old troll hobbled into the firelight to shake hands with Kilgore. The poor creature was so skinny his arms were like strings hanging from his thin shoulders. Kilgore was appalled; he was certain if he grabbed the old troll it would fall apart in his hands like an old dead leaf.

There was no time to protest. Blygli gave a sharp whistle and the wrestling match began. Before Kilgore could even twitch a muscle, Nagli seized him by the belt and tossed him into the air like a bundle of hay; he landed with a terrific thump. For a moment he didn't know what had happened, but gradually the world stopped spinning and he sat up, greatly embarrassed. Trond was shaking his head and Skanderbeg looked worried.

"Another defeat," Trond sighed.

"Not quite," Skanderbeg said. "I don't think your champion has clearly defeated Kilgore."

Trond sat up and stared at old Nagli, who was bent almost in half, his face pinched up like an old walnut. "My back," he croaked. "I've thrown it out. That young sprat's too much for me."

"You'll see" Asny said triumphantly. "That old bag of bones couldn't beat Kilgore in a rematch now, could he?"

Nagli waved a paw and began hobbling away. "No, no, not now. Maybe in about seventy years I'll get him, but for now I'll have to cede the contest."

"Then Kilgore wins," Asny said, folding her arms.

Trond rubbed his ear, looking a little sour. "We'll be magnanimous and call it a draw."

"A draw! By my grandmother's old socks, Kilgore ought to be the winner. Nagli is in far worse shape," Asny muttered to Skanderbeg, who was trying to shush her. Instead, she stepped forward and demanded, "Let me have a try at one of your contests, in case your enchanted feast has done some harm to my friends."

"Then you shall try your luck," Trond said. "Come forward, my dear, and we'll see what you can do. Unless I'm mistaken, you have the look of a great and noble family of Gardar that I used to know rather well because of their warfare on my people. You are a Wolfganger, are you not?"

"I am," said Asny. "My mother was the last queen and I shall be the next. I am called Asny."

"I am honored indeed," said Trond, rising to make a low bow and grin with his pointed teeth. "The Wolfgangers are almost as dear foes to me as old Skanderbeg here. Particularly if you are to be the the next queen of Gardar, should you happen to succeed at my next riddle. What you must do is simple. You see my lazy old cat sleeping there by the fire, don't you? He's not a large or vicious cat, but he is exceptionally heavy. If you can lift him, my dear young queen of Gardar, you have my word that you and your friends shall depart in peace."

Asny immediately seized the cat and began pulling. It seemed that the beast was fastened to the floor with spikes, or else that she was trying to move a mountain. She couldn't even manage to pry one paw from the floor, although he did lift the tip of his tail a very little bit.

"I can't do it," she finally panted, very red and furious. "You're tricking us. All these things are enchanted so we can't expect to win."

"That is right, of course," Trond said. "Did you expect it to be any other way when you came down into Trondheim? I am your enemy, and if you come to challenge your enemy you must be prepared."

"I am prepared," Asny said, grasping her hammer and holding it aloft. "Unless you restore our property to us at once I shall use this to end your existence."

"Tush! No need to threaten," Trond said. "I see that is an Alfar weapon. Would you like one more contest to end this little dispute? I shall give you my great cup and you see if you can smash it with that Alfar hammer. And then I shall give you the sword and the satchel back and you may resume your mission of destruction. I know I may lose my chance to destroy Surt's worst threat, but there is nothing I love like a contest of wits and strength. Here, my dear, take this cup and break it into bits." He smiled tolerantly and extended the cup to Asny.

She examined it cautiously to see what magic had made it. Runes dyed with blood were carven into it to protect Trond from poison. She could not read the runes nor decipher its maker's mark on the bottom. Placing the cup on the floor she dealt it a smashing blow, using all her strength and all the strength of the magic hammer. The cup rang a clear note and bounced away unharmed, not even dented or scratched. Asny did not strike at it again. Instead she picked it up and looked at it with a thoughtful expression.

"Another contest," Skanderbeg said. "And this will be the last one. If we lose we shall forfeit all."

Trond shook his head. "You have already lost and all is forfeit. You shall now translate the runes on the Alfar sword."

Over in his corner Warth gave a loud chuckle and cut a caper that certainly looked trollish in origin. "Skanderbeg, I've longed to see you get your comeuppance ever since the first light. Not so smart now, are you? Where's all your magic now? Well, I'll tell you, it's in that black satchel and with the stuff inside that bag I shall become a better wizard than you ever thought of becoming, and King Trond and I shall rule all the underworld as well as the surface, when we have used the sword to kill Surt. Then it shall all be ours!"

"A noteworthy idea, wizard," said Trond. "If you can become half the wizard Skanderbeg is, it shall be enough. Blygli, bring our friend and ally Warth a seat of honor."

Warth sprang from his corner and executed a triumphant jig. "I am your servant, most excellent prince of trolls. Command me and I shall do it. Nothing is beyond me with Skanderbeg's satchel. Did I not fool the old fox himself and steal the Alfar sword right out from under his nose? What is your first request? Shall

143

I dispose of these boorish invaders for you? It is a task I yearn to perform!" He made faces at Skanderbeg and plumped himself in his seat of honor with a delighted sigh. "At last—recognition for my great abilities. Power, you know, was always my weakness."

Kilgore glanced uneasily at Skanderbeg, who smoked his pipe, unperturbed by the sinister turn the situation was taking. As for Asny, she was gazing at the cup with a faraway look on her face and paying no attention.

Trond rubbed his hands together, looking mighty pleased. "The best thing to do would be to hold a contest of magical skills," he said. "On one side, Warth and the satchel, with Skanderbeg alone on the other. It will be a monumental spectacle, will it not?" The trolls watching from the shadows chuckled and gibbered and the small trolls' transports of unholy joy were frenzied.

Warth took a dramatic pose with Skanderbeg's book of spells in one hand, raising his black old staff in the other. When the room was perfectly silent he began uttering strange words in a deep voice and making peculiar gestures. Skanderbeg sat up to watch with interest but made no move to weave a counter spell, other than crossing one dusty boot over his knee and puffing steadily on his pipe. Suddenly the air was full of bats and blue smoke, which dissipated harmlessly as snowflakes.

"That was a spell I concocted myself," said Skanderbeg. "Of course you can't make it work against me. And I suppose I had better warn you that at least half of the spells in that bag are booby-trapped so they work backwards. I always knew some inferior magician was liable to steal my satchel and try to use my magic, so I made spells that look particularly inviting, but if you try to invoke them the magic will work on you instead. Which is the case of that transformation spell you are looking at now, Warth."

Warth hastily slapped the book shut, glancing anxiously at King Trond. "I'm sure Your Grace has no desire to see me change myself by accident into a gollup or a blue gosset," he said with an endearing leer.

"Quite the contrary," said Trond. "It would be most entertaining. Do get on with the contest. I haven't had such rich entertainment since I was freed from prison. Skanderbeg, what can you do? A little wizard fire? How about making it rain boiling water again?"

Skanderbeg arose and folded his arms. "This is one you might not have seen before." Tapping his staff gently on the floor with a word or two, the wizard managed to change Blygli into a merman. For a moment the little troll sat unaware of his transformation, then he happened to notice that his lower half had become like a seal. After the initial surprise wore off, Blygli looked pleased and said, "Ask me some boons, friends, now that I'm a merman and bound to give them to you."

Warth glared glumly and spoke up in a sour tone, "Give me some new boots and a set of fine clothes that will never wear out in a lifetime, Merman."

"Why, that's easy enough," Blygli said, immediately pulling off Warth's own worn-out boots and handing them to him. "Since I doubt if you'll live longer than three days in Trondheim, these will last you all your life." He simpered at Trond and gave a booming laugh. "All mermen are supposed to laugh because men are so stupid. Anyone can see that Skanderbeg is the chiefest wizard with or without his book of spells, and Warth here is trying to weasel himself into Trondheim."

"I'm still not convinced," Trond said. "After all, Skanderbeg could solve none of my simple contests or riddles. Warth is of no consequence in the battle against Surt, but Skanderbeg and these mortals may be terribly important. How about it, Skanderbeg? What do you think of my little magic tricks which I have learned?"

Skanderbeg waved absently and Blygli's legs were restored, which he used to leap repeatedly into the air and turn in somersaults. The wizard strolled partway across the room, scowling in thought. "There is something vaguely familiar about it," he said consideringly. "The feast, the drink, the wrestling contest, the cup, the cat—"

"He doesn't know," Warth said. "He's stalling for time."

"Do you admit it, Skanderbeg? You can't decipher the magic? That could be a grave experience, you know." Trond chuckled as he clicked his black claws on the arm of his chair.

Skanderbeg shook his head in perplexity. "If I had my references in my satchel—"

"Ah! Then it is true! The satchel is Skanderbeg's power!" Trond gave a gleeful bellow and stood up to his full height. "He can only do harmless tricks without it and there's nothing he can do to harm us now!"

"Didn't I tell you so?" Warth demanded in the general uproar. "I told you so first, if you'll remember. That should be worth something."

"Indeed it is," Trond said. "You shall be my second advisor after Blygli and your title will be Chief Troll Wizard of Trondheim. Your first duty will be to dispose of our enemies here in any way you see fit. Make sure these mortals shall never live to escape and a spell must be woven that will bind Skanderbeg until the Fimbul Winter is absolute. Then let him try his fire arts in a world with no sun or cursed light to turn good trolls to stone." The trolls all roared and jigged up and down and stood on their heads. Warth hugged himself and swelled up with importance.

Kilgore stayed close beside Skanderbeg. Now he whispered, "What are we going to do? Will the wizard fire keep them away long enough to escape? If I could get my hands on the sword—"

"I have one more trick to try on him," Skanderbeg said quietly. "If that doesn't work, we'll try some desperation tactics, for we are in a truly desperate situation." Then the wizard cleared his throat and began in a loud voice, "Are you sure you aren't being a bit hasty, Trond? I seem to recall how you were captured last time. I am famous for my bluffing, as you well know."

146

"Indeed, no one but a fool or a wizard would come into Trondheim with no protection," Trond said. "This time I am sure you are bluffing. Warth stole your satchel and you came to find him because you are virtually powerless without it. This time I have you, Skanderbeg, and I shall make sure this time you won't ever trouble me again."

"Stop," Asny said in a quiet voice, still holding Trond's cup. "Give us the sword and the satchel. We are leaving Trondheim. If you refuse I shall break this cup and with it you will lose what pitiful magic you possess. I know these riddles now."

Trond looked at her closely and shook his head. "You had your chance and you failed to break the cup with your Alfar hammer, so the contest was forfeit. But I can't resist this sort of thing. Are you trying to fool me or not? Go ahead and see if you can break the cup. I lose nothing if you fail; if you succeed it is Surt's problem."

Asny stood holding the cup in both hands. Then she walked to the foot of Trond's throne, almost within touching distance of his huge savage talons. In one smooth motion she drew back her arm and threw the cup with all her might straight at Trond's head. It struck the center of his forehead and shattered into fragments. Trond rubbed his head ruefully. "And what about the other riddles?"

"The small troll was a spell. Really he was fire, which eats everything. The drink in the cup was actually the sea and of course Skanderbeg could not swallow the sea. Old Nagli was no wrestler at all until you consider that he is old age, which eventually wins the battle every time. Your cat is really the Midgard snake, which is so large it encircles all the earth, so of course I could not lift it. These tricks once fooled Odin and Thor and we sing about them in our most ancient songs. That is also where I learned about breaking the cup on your forehead. So now we see that your magic was really nothing at all, Trond, and we have beaten you. We will leave now and take our

147

possessions with us." Asny stared at the huge troll fearlessly, although he was twice the size she was.

Trond appeared to deliberate, a deep scowl wrinkling the fur on his skull. "I see that I've been beaten by a Wolfganger again! As long as the vicious breed survives, gray trolls will never be safe."

"Whatever are you thinking of?" Warth shrieked, standing on his chair. "Don't let them get that sword or that satchel or we're all doomed. Since when is a troll's word good for anything? It's your right to lie and cheat. You don't need to let them go merely because you said you would. What are words? Mere air! All trolls lie their heads off. They'd lie to their own grandmothers. You've taken leave of your senses if you think you have to keep your word."

Trond blinked and stared at Warth with a suddenly hostile expression. "What is this creature doing out of his cell? Blygli! Guard! Take him off. What an insulting blot upon Trondheim. Skanderbeg, it has been a marvelous round in our game and you have won again, but it was a very near thing. If you hadn't brought this young Gardar along I would have had you in an instant. She is worthy of a kingdom." With great dignity Trond bowed to Asny, who was looking very pale. To Kilgore he extended one claw for a handshake and said, "May we never meet on the battlefield with the sword of Andurich in your hand. I have only fear and sympathy for Surt at your hands."

Kilgore at last touched the smooth metal of Kildurin and slipped the sword into its sheath. The trolls murmured and cowered back from its glow. With great satisfaction Skanderbeg tucked his satchel under one arm and saluted to Trond. Blygli himself ushered them up the steps to the door. Kilgore could hardly wait to get through it to the safe sane world outside, but Skanderbeg hesitated.

"I have a last gift for King Trond," the wizard said solemnly, withdrawing Warth's imitation Kildurin from his cloak. "Send this to Trond with our deepest gratitude and wishes for a long and prosperous life. Tell him this sword is a very good one manufactured

148

by a great and noble wizard. May it serve him well."

Blygli looked at the sword in amazement and stole a glance at Kilgore's sword. "I shall take it to him at once." Bearing his prize away in both arms, he vanished into the darkness of the tunnel of Trondheim, pausing only to slam shut the door and bolt it.

"Now we need to flee at top speed," Skanderbeg said. "Up this valley we'll find the way to the fells of Beortstad. When Trond deciphers Warth's runes, he'll be in a mood fit for murder."

"What did those runes say? I thought they were fakes," Kilgore said, stepping in Skanderbeg's long strides.

"They said, 'Whoso uses this dies by this. Warth's sword.' I thought it would make a very touching gift to Trond."

"After he violated every principle of troll nature by letting us go? You gave him a sword that will kill him?" Kilgore demanded.

"Yes, indeed, and we don't know yet what nasty surprise he had in store for us by letting us go, either," Skanderbeg retorted. "We'll not rest until we're out of his immediate territory. Asny! You'll have to keep up better than that or we'll leave you for the trolls."

Asny made no reply and stumbled along a little faster. A driving snow made the stones slick underfoot as they followed the rocky path of a glacier. The snow also buried or blew away their footprints and hid their scent from sniffing troll noses that were bound to follow. By dark, a good many fells were between the travelers and Trondheim, and the huge icy bulk of the Trident hung over them like a wall. The terrain was bristly with basalt crags once poured out of volcanoes, where a few demented trees scrabbled for existence in a sea of rock. Clear little rivulets clattered everywhere in the lava, coating the rocks with a clear and fatal glaze of ice. They climbed over one large glacier that steamed and burbled deep within, where a hot spring or geyser was hidden. Crevasses that seemed bottomless looked back with quiet water like mirrors.

They stopped to rest on a rocky outcropping that overlooked a small cold lake. Skanderbeg rearranged the contents of his satchel, throwing some things out with great disdain. "A packrat has more sophistication than this," he grumbled, hurling a dead lizard away.

"Do you know where we are, Skanderbeg?" Kilgore looked up at the imposing Trident. Hundreds of hills lay between them and it and there were any number of ways that all led up.

"Beortstad, of course," Skanderbeg said. "Home of the vargulfs of Grimshalg. If we were only vargulfs we'd be inside Grimshalg by tomorrow dawn."

Kilgore looked around with an uneasy chill. "And we're going to stop here tonight? How do you expect us to fight off legions of vargulfs and possibly Trond's trolls besides?"

"I don't. With any luck they won't even get a smell of us. I happen to know where there's an old Alfar fortress not a half hour's walk from here. There may still be some Alfar at this outpost, or if it's deserted we can still get in, since I was given the key to it a good many years ago." Skanderbeg shook his satchel and smelled it with a satisfied manner and took up his staff. "Well, come along and we'll have a delightful supper tonight, now that we have the satchel."

Kilgore followed thoughtfully. He had reached the bottom of the hill before he stopped and looked around. "Where's Asny?" he asked in alarm. "She's gone, Skanderbeg."

They hurried back up the hill. She was asleep among the rocks as comfortably as if they were feather cushions. Skanderbeg shook her gently, and then not so gently. "Blast!" he exclaimed. "I was wondering when this would happen, and which of us it would happen to. It seems that Asny was the unlucky one. The spell was on the ones who refused to eat troll food. Well, there's nothing we can do but carry her to the Beortstad outpost. I hope we make it by vargulf time."

"I've never seen anyone under a spell before," Kilgore mused. "How do you wake her from it? You said something about drawing blood."

"Aye, I did." Skanderbeg was searching through his satchel. At last he found a long slender knife in a jeweled sheath. Taking one of Asny's fingers, he pricked it with the knife so a dark red bead of blood welled up in the little wound. "That's how it is done. Or you can punch a fellow in the nose and make it bleed. In a bit she will wake up, but there isn't time to wait." Sighing and groaning, he hoisted the sleeping girl to his shoulders like a sack of grain and started plodding resolutely through the rubble of glaciers and lava flows.

The wind stiffened and the sky began to lower. With awesome rapidity, the massive Trident disappeared in a thick cloying cloud. The snow smote down with fury, until Kilgore could see only a few paces ahead when he looked up from the convenient windbreak of Skanderbeg's cloak. The black rocks became white like the sky, and he was reminded of the dismal landscape of his dream the night the sword had been stolen. He touched it to be sure it was still there. Ominously, it was humming slightly.

Skanderbeg stopped a moment to consult a small device and to shift his limp burden. Then he grumbled. "We've got to hurry faster, Kilgore. Dusk will be early tonight."

As if in answer to his words, a long howl came from the Gap behind them, muffled in the snow.

CHAPTER 11

The gloom purpled around them and the snow was as deep as their ankles. Puffing and slithering, they halted again on a hilltop to listen to the querulous howls around them. The vargulfs seemed confused by the snow. Then a wild howl sounded close behind them, triumphantly ringing out the discovery of the scent.

"It sounds as if they're converging on us," Kilgore said. The humming of the sword had intensified to an urgent note of warning.

Skanderbeg shifted Asny's limp form and hurried away at a faster pace. "Hurry, Kilgore. They can smell a magic spell as if it were a pickled herring. Beortstad isn't far now."

"It's not entirely dark yet, but the vargulfs came straight after us. They knew we were here, didn't they?"

"Most likely. Trond sent a courier for them before we left, or my name isn't Skanderbeg."

"Now they've found our scent, how can we hope to outrun them?" called Kilgore, running alongside Skanderbeg.

"Don't waste your breath," Skanderbeg replied. "Just hurry!"

They ran, slipping and stumbling, and twice Kilgore stepped into an icy streamlet, numbing both feet. Just as he was about to ask how much farther, he saw a faint glowing light ahead at the foot of a huge black crag.

"Beortstad!" Skanderbeg panted, putting on a burst of speed. The ground underfoot was still slick, but it wasn't as treacherous with rocks and holes. Dimly, Kilgore could see great black dumps of rock piled on both sides of the cliff. It was almost completely dark.

Kilgore saw the streaking black shadow first and yelled a warning to Skanderbeg. The wizard went down soundlessly as the vargulf leaped with snapping fangs and a chilling snarl. Then without pausing, the beast lunged at Kilgore, who had the sword in hand, willing to fight. As he raised it to protect himself, the vargulf leaped at his arm instead. Searing needles sank into his forearm. Icy breath frosted his face and the vargulf's terrible human eyes glared only inches away. The sword fell from his numb hand with a clatter. The vargulf released its hold and bowled him over, trying to seize his throat. Kilgore wrestled it away with desperate strength, grappling for a stranglehold on a whirling, snapping, snarling nightmare. Suddenly the vargulf was knocked aside like a doll, half smothering him in its fur.

"Kilgore!" Asny called in a panicky voice. "Skanderbeg, help! He's been bitten!"

Kilgore shoved aside the vargulf and sat up. "It's not so bad. How did you get released? You were out cold for at least an hour."

"You're talking nonsense," she snapped. "I've been right here every moment. But wait, this isn't the hill I remember. What's that light, Skanderbeg? And I see a lot of men coming."

The wailing notes of many horns pierced the snowy atmosphere. Kilgore saw two long files of men marching slowly among the stone hills in a serpentine manner. He also heard the thrum and whisper of arrows being launched, along with the dying cries of the vargulfs. The howling took on a note of bafflement. In the dying light Kilgore could see the vargulfs retreating in long black lines that skimmed over the snowy earth. He sheathed the sword with his left hand, since his right was still without sensation. Skanderbeg quickly wrapped a bandage on his arm and bound it very tightly with hands that seemed to be shaking.

"Are you hurt, Skanderbeg?" Kilgore asked.

153

"Not in the least. Now then, to Beortstad. Asny, watch for any vargulfs that might break through again. We must hurry." There was a strained, urgent tone in his voice.

"What happens to people who are bitten by vargulfs?" Kilgore asked. "Will I die or become a vargulf?"

Reluctantly Skanderbeg answered, "Well, not much research has been done on the subject. Don't trouble yourself about it; leave it all to me, since I was the one who led us into Beortstad." He took a firm grip on Kilgore's good arm, as if it were his staff, and led him along with great energy.

"It's the Alfar," Asny said over her shoulder, delighted.

"Who is that there?" a voice called. "Is someone injured?"

"Aye!" Skanderbeg called back strongly. "It is Skanderbeg the wizard and two friends. We were traveling to Beortstad outpost to ask for shelter for the night. We are on an urgent mission for Elbegast and I have the passwords for Beortstad."

The files had stopped marching, but the playing continued, which seemed to distress the ears of the vargulfs. Only a few faraway howls mourned with the echoes of the Gap. Then a small body of Alfar advanced to meet Skanderbeg. Nothing could be seen of them in the swirling dark, except whipping cloaks drawn up to their eyes and snow-clotted hoods drawn down low. The leader motioned to his men, and they turned about and began piping their way back to the entrance of Beortstad.

"I am Eldjarn, the captain of this outpost," the leader said. "I shall take you to Beortstad for the night. If your friend is badly bitten, we will have to hurry to save him. We've been watching for you on both sides of the Gap, knowing that Elbegast had placed the sword in mortal hands. You are lucky to have come this far."

By this time Kilgore was feeling very much like putting his cold feet up to a brisk fire and getting on the outside of a generous feast. In his head were visions of the Brandstok hall on a winter night, warm with merriment, good food, and companionship. He could almost see his father sitting in his carven chair, as was his habit, but what Kilgore was seeing was keener than a memory. Valsidur was holding the old bent sword which Kilgore had played with, and his face was sad and old. Kilgore was sure he could feel the warmth of the Brandstok hall as surely as he could feel the sadness of his father. He longed to say something to cheer the poor fellow, knowing that his absence was the cause of his father's grief. Then he saw Valsidur rise impatiently from his seat and cry out, "I know that my son is in terrible peril on this night! Curse that elven sword! I wish I had never seen it."

"Don't worry, I'm all right," Kilgore murmured. "We're going to the elven outpost at Beortstad."

Valsidur seemed to freeze, listening. Kilgore could feel the familiar warmth of the Brandstok hall settling around him. He could almost imagine himself sitting in his favorite place by the fire with the nine old retainers arguing at his back.

"Did you hear? Did you hear anything at all?" demanded Valsidur. "I thought I heard Kilgore talking to me. Kilgore, where are you?"

His voice changed to Skanderbeg's. "Kilgore! Kilgore, can you hear me? Are you still alive, lad?"

Kilgore opened his eyes to darkness and snow blowing in his face. He was being carried along at a rapid clip on some sort of litter. Never had he been so cold in all his life. A bone-gripping chill seemed to well from his right arm and he could make no answer except to blink. He could see Skanderbeg and Asny in a peculiar light of some sort and an archway passed overhead and then they were inside Beortstad. From a strange distance he saw the golden-bearded Alfar with their colorful cloaks and gold ornaments; then the colors melted and ran, and he fell into a deep cold sleep.

The Alfar physician was sent for the moment Eldjarn set foot in Beortstad. By the time the procession had wound its way down the tunnels to the halls below, Bergljot was waiting with her satchel. She and Skanderbeg exchanged a formal, professional nod at the door of a small but elaborately furnished chamber as Kilgore's litter was carried inside. The Bergljot declared, "I must have absolute silence in order to work against the vargulf spell. Send for two swordsmen to be on hand at the door in case my medicine has not worked by dawn. I need a hot fire at once and someone has to go out and find me some fjallagros."

"Fjallagros? At this season?" murmured the Alfar, clustering around the physician's door. "And with all the vargulfs on the prowl?"

"It shall be done," Skanderbeg said, striding into the room and instantly striking a scorching blaze in the hearth, which sent the Alfar back a pace or two. For a moment he laid a palm on Kilgore's pale brow and looked at Bergljot in dismay. "Ice cold," he murmured. "Is there any hope at all?"

"Very little, and none without the fjallagros," answered Bergljot calmly, inspecting the toothmarks in Kilgore's stiffening forearm.

"Then we shall find the fjallagros," said Asny, hovering at the shoulder of Skanderbeg. She was familiar with the little brown or gray moss plant, although it wasn't common or easy to find. Its healing power was legendary.

"You shall stay here," said Skanderbeg, delving in his satchel and pulling out a peculiar fur cloak. "It's a night for beasts, not men. If I happen not to return, you at least will be able to continue into Gardar with the sword; and perhaps the means will be opened up to you, if you are required to use it. Don't try to detain me; every moment is precious." Swinging the cloak over his shoulder, he strode away toward the tunnel to the outside. Just as he rounded the last corner, Asny saw a puff of smoke and briefly glimpsed a large white wolf racing away at a gallop.

Suddenly she felt very tired and lonely. She looked at the door of Bergljot's chamber, from which she had been shut out, and around her at the unfamiliar grandeur of Beortstad. The floors of the halls were padded with rushes and carpets, and sconces twinkled like jewels every pace or two so the darkness was utterly banished. Alfar clad like kings hurried about, carrying trays or brooms and other menial implements. A delicate Alfar maiden dressed in silk the color of apricots politely curtsied and said, "If you please, I'll show you to your room where you can rest and refresh yourself."

"I can't leave this spot until dawn," Asny said, sitting down in a comfortable little alcove. "You can bring me a drink of something hot and I shall take my boots off, but that is quite enough comfort for me until I know whether the sword bearer will live."

The maid curtsied and disappeared in a silken swirl. Asny sighed unhappily, wishing she had insisted that Skanderbeg take her along with him. Waiting idly was worse than any kind of desperate combat. From somewhere in the Alfar halls she heard music lilting sweetly from stringed instruments. After listening a moment, she felt her nerves relax and her thoughts became more peaceful. The chair she sat in was soft and she was already half asleep. The sconce in the alcove had gone out, making a pleasantly shadowy corner for her to curl up in and sleep for awhile.

She awakened quickly at the sound of quiet footsteps coming down the hall. It was Eldjarn himself, in a silver and blue cloak. He tapped lightly at Bergljot's door and it was opened a crack.

"Is it the fjallagros?" inquired Bergljot sharply.

"No, it is Eldjarn. I came to ask about the young mortal's condition," replied Eldjarn with dignity.

Bergljot sighed impatiently. "I'll send word if there's anything you should know. And you must do something about all these people who keep coming and breathing in the keyhole, trying to see something or hear what is happening. Tell everyone he is sleeping and nothing else. If I catch anybody prowling around here, I'll have their ears." With a slight bang she closed the door in his face.

Eldjarn nodded to the door and stood thoughtfully

staring at it, twisting a gold chain between his fingers. He paced up and down a time or two, then he discerned Asny sitting in the shadows watching him.

"You're here?" he asked in disbelief. "I sent my daughter to show you to the best rooms in Beortstad, but she must have forgotten. I apologize for this neglect; you must be exhausted."

"No, I'm waiting," Asny said. "I have no use for comfort when my friend's life is in peril. I'm very comfortable where I am, sir, thank you most kindly. As a soldier I am accustomed to fatigue and discipline."

"Soldier?" Eldjarn's smooth features puckered in confusion.

"I am Asny Wolfganger, queen of Gardar. You are familiar with the fighting women of Gardar, I presume?"

"Indeed, I had the highest respect for them, but they are all gone now, along with everything else in Gardar. How is it that you have survived, when your existence is a threat to Surt?" He frowned and his voice was low.

Asny glanced around for possible eavesdroppers. "I was freed from a wizard spell by Kilgore with the sword. I had been suspended in that spell for sixty-five years and now I am freed in time to assume the crown of my country when Surt is killed. I cannot help believe it was planned by a greater fate than my own."

"Indeed! Indeed!" Eldjarn agreed, rubbing his chin. "I wish you success in your venture. But your life is in terrible danger. Surt is the most powerful wizard we have ever seen. At least he is too strong for the Alfar to contain any longer, and I doubt if there is any way you can deal with him yourself. We extend to you our asylum here until you decide to go back to your own kind somewhere to the south. I understand there are many pleasant lands governed by men beyond these mountains."

Asny looked at him in amazement. "But Surt wants them, too. He's conjured a cloud over Heroness and Whaleness and other northerly lands and it's moving southward every day. Surely you are aware of this, and how Surt's wizards are making life miserable for many of the people. How could I abandon my homeland? Have you not heard about the Fimbul Winter, which Surt is bringing down on Skarpsey?"

"We have heard such talk," Eldjarn said cautiously, "but we receive very little information from Elbegast himself. Perhaps I had better explain. I am Eldjarn, Prime Minister in exile, formerly Prime Minister to Elbegast, King of the Alfar. We have suffered a division of the Alfar over the issue of Andurich's sword being placed in mortal hands. I relinquished my position, my home, my future, and a good many friends rather than share the responsibility for what may happen. That sword will be the cause of the banishment of all Alfar from Skarpsey, once it is unearthed and given to men. On the other hand, if left to himself in Gardar, Surt may content himself with what he has and leave the rest of Skarpsey to be shared among men and Alfar."

"But we see now that Surt is not content with Gardar. He wants to bring down the Fimbul Winter and he must be stopped, forever," Asny said. "We are sorry to be a trouble to you, knowing how you believe. As soon as Kilgore is out of danger, we shall be on our way. We are terribly grateful to you for rescuing us from the vargulfs, when no doubt you would rather they tore us to pieces. I understand that your physician is only doing her duty to her profession by saving Kilgore."

"I believe her loyalties lie more closely with yours," Eldjarn said with a slight bow. "She will save the sword king if he is to be saved at all. I hope I have not seemed inhospitable. Beortstad is your home as long as you choose to stay, and I wish you would stay here forever, rather than enrage Surt to further bloodshed. What I really mean to say is, we will do what we can for you as individuals, but we cannot help you in your cause beyond providing you supplies and equipment, as we have no wish to send you

159

to your deaths. I will spare you no men and I will not let you use our tunnels to Gardar."

"Thank you," said Asny with regal formality, although her eyes were flashing. "I believe you will regret your estrangement from our cause when I am back on my throne. You are not quite an enemy, but you are not a friend either. When Skanderbeg returns I shall inform him of your position."

Eldjarn made a stiff bow, his gold ornaments clattering softly, and took his leave from her. Leaping up the minute he was gone, Asny strode fiercely up and down the hall, clenching her fists and her teeth.

"Coward!" she muttered. "I thought he wore too much gold to be a warrior. Deserters! Every one of them!"

Bergljot's door opened an inch as Asny stalked by again. A low voice urged, "Come inside. I wish to speak to you." Bergljot opened the door wide and closed it immediately after Asny. "I was listening. It's a characteristic of Alfar to eavesdrop."

Asny was looking at Kilgore, not listening. He was almost blue, although the room was as hot as an oven. Bergljot kept him wrapped in fire-warmed blankets and a small elf child was in charge of hot stones for his feet.

"He looks frozen," Asny said with a dead feeling in her chest.

Bergljot only looked at her with level, violet eyes. She was not as fair as most Alfar and almost as tall as Asny. "The wizard isn't back yet," she said. "The time is almost gone. What will you do?"

Asny moved impatiently. "I won't stay here with these traitors. If you're sympathetic to Elbegast, why don't you leave here?"

Bergljot never removed her calm eyes from Asny. "Because I am a mortal, not an Alfar. I have no Tarnkappe to travel with in the unseen realm. Many years ago I came here as a midwife. I decided to stay. I don't regret it a moment, but you should know that if you stay you will never leave. If the wizard doesn't return, you will be faced with that decision."

"A life of ease would drive me mad," Asny said. "I will take the sword and go as far as I can."

"Eldjarn would never let you take it. He will destroy it so Surt won't get it to use against us," Bergljot said.

"Then we had better do all we can to make sure Kilgore lives," Asny said grimly. "It will be the death of all of us and all of Skarpsey and all the world if he perishes."

Bergljot nodded. She took up a long black cloak and hood and fastened them on. "I shall leave you here for a short while. Since so much is at stake, I am going to risk the wrath of Eldjarn and send for Hrafngrimr. I'll answer your questions later, when I get back."

Asny sat down and waited. A large hourglass was slowly pouring out the grains of the night and there were not many left. For a long time Asny watched Kilgore. His breathing was almost imperceptible and barely warm. In another few hours it would be either stopped or it would become the icy breath of the vargulf. She shuddered and turned away with unsoldierly tears in her eyes. Absently she patted the head of the wide-eyed elf child. Her eye lit upon Kildurin, placed on a high cabinet in its sheath. Slowly she crossed the room and put her hands upon it. Nothing happened, so she pulled the sword from the sheath. Its light was dim with sporadic flashes that traveled from one end of the blade to the other. The magic runes were black, indecipherable marks etched from the hilt to the very point. Resting the heavy sword on the cabinet, she put one finger to the point cautiously and felt the acute sharpness that was impossible to obtain on a sword of drosser materials. She was sure the sword was sharp enough for the purpose she had in mind, but the outcome was questionable. Skanderbeg ought to be here, she thought, if he were still alive. Looking at the almost empty hour glass she knew she could not wait for his advice.

161

The dawn was raw and windy. As the last of the vargulfs melted into the gloom of the Gap, Skanderbeg made his escape from the crevice where the vargulfs had cornered him. He had not found any fjallagros. Like a swift silent streak, the white wolf raced toward Beortstad. He threw off the fur cloak at the doorstep and strode down the halls to the chamber of the physician. Quite a crowd of Alfar had gathered, their silken clothing rustling and smelling of warm fires and wine. Eldjarn and his ministers had just left Bergljot's room and the Alfar people began to babble and buzz with questions. Some were obviously angry. Everyone was talking about someone named Hrafngrimr. When they saw Skanderbeg they fell away to make a path for him to the door. No one spoke until he had closed the door behind them and then the angry rustling began again. He scarcely heard. Asny was sitting beside Kilgore's cot, and Bergljot and a dark-clad stranger were talking apart in low tones. But what arrested his attention was Kilgore. He was no longer icy and pale; his face had faint color now and he was sleeping heavily.

"What happened?" Skanderbeg demanded. "Did someone bring the fjallagros?"

"No," said Bergljot, her face puzzled. "I went out for half an hour to summon Hrafngrimr from Murad, knowing he was all we had left to try. When I came back, the young man was warm, the spell was gone, and even the tooth marks were partially gone. As you see now, there is not a trace of a wound on his arm. I have never seen anything like it, nor has Hrafngrimr, who is one of the last Alfar sorcerers. The only people in the room were Bersi the Alfar child and your companion Asny. Neither are capable of such magic."

"Do you have any theories, sir?" asked Skanderbeg sternly of the Alfar sorcerer.

Hrafngrimr was a lean, brown fellow with dark narrow features and long tapering hands. In his eye there was a watchful, brooding look as he said, "I have traveled several hundred miles tonight after receiving Bergljot's message, taking less than an

162

hour to get here. With all modesty I can say I am the best Alfar sorcerer in existence today and I have studied other forms of magic, including the kind used by Surt. But I know of nothing that could dispel the bite of the vargulf so thoroughly. Nothing, that is, known previously by wizards and sorcerers. This is something new, or most likely something very old brought again to light. What I would suggest is talking to the girl and the child who were in the room at the time."

Before Asny could open her mouth to deny any knowledge of magic, Eldjarn put his head in. "We wish to speak to Hrafngrimr the outlaw," he said. "If he has finished his business, that is."

"He has," Bergljot said. "But either come in or go outside. I have no wish to leave that door open longer than a moment."

Eldjarn and three others came inside wearing solemn expressions. "Since this was an emergency we are willing to excuse you for returning to Beortstad," Eldjarn said to Hrafngrimr. "But you must leave at once, never to be seen here again, as the conditions stated. No one is glad to see you here. I shall give you one hour to be as far from Beortstad as you can get."

"In that amount of time," Hrafngrimr said, "I could go there and back. You needn't worry, I have no desire to remain. Your climate is getting far too cold for my taste."

Eldjarn turned sharply and departed with his ministers. Hrafngrimr began gathering his satchel and staff and fastening his cloak on with a large gold clasp.

"Before I go," he said, "I have one question, though I make it a habit never to ask questions. May I see the sword of Andurich? You do have it, don't you?"

"We do," Asny said, standing up protectively beside the cabinet where Kildurin lay. "But why should you have such an interest in it? We have discovered that the Alfar are not all friendly to our cause. How do your sympathies lie in the business of Surt and the sword?"

"As you see, I am an outlaw in Beortstad," Hrafngrimr said. "I have committed no crime except that of voicing my opinions. At one time I was the chief advisor to Eldjarn, after following him into exile. We once shared the same views of the dangers of the sword and believed that Surt would limit himself in his excesses. But as any rational being can see, Surt will not be stopped. I used my position of eminence to try to convince the Alfar of Beortstad to rejoin Elbegast. Needless to say, my warnings were not acceptable to Eldjarn, so I was outlawed, little to my sorrow. My magical experiments were also cause for alarm among these comfort-loving people. Under certain disguises I would go to the halls of the Dark Alfar to learn their crafts. One should take any possible opportunity to learn more about one's enemies. It was completely misunderstood by Eldjarn, of course, and I was labeled as a turncoat. I have now withdrawn myself completely from the dispute and spend my time conducting experiments in my castle in Murad. I wish to see this instrument, partly because it destroyed me and partly because I have a purely scientific curiosity about the magic that formed it."

Skanderbeg wrinkled his forehead dubiously. "You can't so much as lay a finger on it if I do show it to you. If you have as much power as I suspect, you could damage it purposely for the benefit of Surt. I see that great changes have come over the Alfar, with splinter groups off splinter groups, until everyone is disorganized and useless. We can trust no one, although my sympathies are with you as another member of my profession. I am sorry, but I don't trust you, old man. Perhaps you had better leave for Murad."

"Perhaps I had," said Hrafngrimr with a quick bow.

"No," said Bergljot, turning her back to the fire and folding her arms into her sleeves. "Let's not be hasty. We've all had a dreadful night, but it looks as if the crisis is past. The question now is the success of the sword king. Skanderbeg, you are of a cautious nature, but I urge you to think again. The mention of

Dark Alfar has made you suspicious of Hrafngrimr. This much I can tell you, however: he is an honest Alfar and he knows a great deal about the Dark Alfar. Without his knowledge you will get no further than Wolfinden in Gardar. Although I am only a mortal, I know almost as much as Eldjarn himself about the situation at the other end of the tunnels. There are wounded people from the sentry positions and it seems that they must tell someone of the horrors they have witnessed and I listen. I urge you to make use of Hrafngrimr for the sake of this mission."

Hrafngrimr shrugged in the dying light of the fire. "Whatever is mine to give I will share if it will help," he said in a low tone. "But we are not safe talking here now. I must let Eldjarn's timid people see me leaving so they can return to their harps and wine and peace of mind. We shall talk more later. Expect me back in the evening." In a swirl of cloak and gleaming leather boots he opened the door to meet the disapproving Alfar faces on the other side. In a moment he was gone, walking quickly away without a backward glance.

"So," Skanderbeg said, sinking into a chair and pulling off his boots with the aid of little Bersi, who ran and brought him a warm drink. "I had not expected this in Beortstad. Alfar against Alfar. This was the way Dark Alfar came into existence long ago. What will come of it? Nothing but ill, I fear. Oh, my back feels as if it will break. I had to hide in a crack all night while a hundred vargulfs tried to get at me. It's a very bad business, being a wizard. Bergljot, how much help can we count on from the Alfar?"

"Just enough to get you out of Beortstad," the physician answered. She glanced at Asny who was still sitting beside Kilgore.

Asny looked up with an inspired expression. "Bergljot, if you want to leave Beortstad, why don't you come with us? I can tell you have the heart and mind of a warrior. I have no doubt that you could make it."

Bergljot smiled. "I shall be fine right here until it is

165

all over. When the roads are safe to travel again, perhaps I will return to my family. But I don't wish to talk of myself. What I want to hear is how you cured the sword king of his fatal wound."

Asny looked warily around the room. "I didn't want Eldjarn to know Kilgore had recovered. I believe he thinks Hrafngrimr did it. What I want to do now is let Eldjarn go on thinking Kilgore is in a very perilous state. I shall let him think Skanderbeg and I will continue alone and that he has a chance to wrest the sword from us. He will be eager to see us gone and we will be able to talk him out of the equipment and supplies we will need to climb the Trident. At all costs, we will keep Eldjarn thinking he is winning the contest."

"That will be easy to arrange," Bergljot said. "I shall order this hall quarantined."

"Now tell us how you did it," Skanderbeg said.

"I was afraid there was not time left to cure him by any other means," Asny said, rising and crossing to the cabinet that held the sword. "Drawing blood is an old-fashioned way of thwarting a spell, as you did to free me from Trond's little spell. I wondered if the same procedure would work for Kilgore, but I knew this spell was more intricate and dangerous than anything Trond can ever aspire to. I know I have a tendency to oversimplify the situation, but I had to try it. I took Kildurin to Kilgore's cot and I pierced his finger on the point. The blood ran out on the blade and I felt a tremendously powerful magic loosed in the room that clashed with the ice magic. In a moment it was over. The sword stopped flashing and settled down to a steady glow, as you see when I pull it out a bit. I think of sunlight when I see it shining like this and I believe it means that Kilgore is recovering. I hope I did the right thing. I was afraid he might die for certain, since a wound from that sword is always fatal. but since it is his own magic sword, I thought there was a chance that it might work."

Skanderbeg was nodding his head. "I should have thought of it myself, but I have a tendency to over-

complicate things. Never let it be said that I gave anyone a compliment but, Asny, you are worthy indeed
to be Gardar's queen when we have freed it. Now why
don't we send Bersi to fetch us something to eat? At
least we are relatively safe here for a little while." He
yawned and rubbed his eyes wearily, settling himself
in his chair as if he intended to stay there awhile.
Hardly had his eyes closed when someone tapped
briskly on the door. Bergljot opened it to a messenger
clad in scarlet and purple, ornamented with feathers
and tassels. With a flourishing bow the fellow reported, "His Honor the Prime Minister in Exile
wishes to confer with the honorable Skanderbeg at
the earliest possible convenience. In private chambers."

Dismissing the gaudy parrot, Skanderbeg growl-
ingly pulled on his boots. Taking up his staff, he strode
away at the heels of his guide, treading upon them
occasionally, and the black scowl on his face sent
curious onlookers scuttling out of his way.

CHAPTER 12

Eldjarn's rooms were warmed by a crackling coal fire fragranced with boughs of evergreen. Part of the walls were the natural stone, polished to rich gleaming black, and part were covered with wood and draperies. The furniture was sumptuous and dozens of examples of Alfar goldsmithing gleamed softly in the shadows or brazenly glittered in the light of the fire. Eldjarn himself was displaying the Alfar crafts in the gold chains, rings, and amulets he wore. In the old days, or in Elbegast's halls, such devices would be magical, but Skanderbeg sensed that Eldjarn's baubles were powerless pretenses. He had felt little magic in Beortstad, except for that of Hrafngrimr, which was a far more potent variety than usual for an Alfar sorcerer.

After the customary overpolite greetings were exchanged, Eldjarn beckoned Skanderbeg into the best chair in the room, drew up a footstool so the wizard could warm his feet in sheep fleece slippers, and invited him to light his pipe and smoke it, which Skanderbeg did, puffing up an inscrutable smoke screen. When the cloud was sufficiently thick, the wizard cleared his throat. "I've had a terribly hard journey, and what I want more than talking and flattery is a good long sleep. What is it you wished to say, Eldjarn? You don't invite all your guests to your own chambers. Are there any ears listening here?"

Eldjarn looked shocked and put down his gold cup. "You are an honored guest, Skanderbeg, in spite of our differences of opinion. Nothing less than the best treatment will do for you and your friends. Which reminds me, how is the sword king doing now? We were all relieved when the spell was lifted, even if it meant suffering the presence of that infidel Hrafngrimr. I meant to warn you about him, but since I have a peculiar premonition that he will be back, I shall tell you all I know about him, and I speak from experience, you know. Hrafngrimr was a very dear friend at one time, as staunch a supporter as I ever wished when we made the break with Elbegast, but soon after we moved into this old outpost and refurbished it, we discovered that some of our tunnels provided easy access to regions near the tunnels of the Dark Alfar on the other side of the Trident. Hrafngrimr began taking an unhealthy interest in them almost at once. He began practicing the old Alfar magic with some ice magic thrown in. Some of his experiments were so terrifying and dangerous that we were forced to outlaw magic and any sorcerers already among us. Hrafngrimr refused to abandon his evil practices so we outlawed him, which I truly hated to do. Later we heard the news that he had joined the ranks of Gorm, king of the Dark Alfar. I don't know what possessed Bergljot to send a message for him to come back here, but it was a good thing that she did. Or so I hope, unless Hrafngrimr was able to put some sort of spell on her for evil purposes of his own. He is very skilled in the arts of healing magic, I must admit, but you will watch the young man very closely in case the wounds should reappear. It would be well if you never saw Hrafngrimr again, and since I have this premonition that he will return tonight, I've done everything I can to make sure he doesn't get into Beortstad."

"Well, bless you for your efforts," Skanderbeg said dryly. "If I have any premonitions myself I shall certainly relay them to you to act upon. How many premonitions do you have listening in Bergljot's room to everything we have said?"

Eldjarn attempted to smile. "These are dangerous times, my friend. I would not have you deceived by Hrafngrimr for the world. If you so wish, we'll capture him when he appears tonight and this time we shall make sure he and his pestilential sorcery are imprisoned forever."

Skanderbeg's pipe bowl glowed red a moment. "Whatever you do suits me," he said. "Your selfless concern for our safety is touching indeed. I had thought you would do your best to thwart our mission. Eldjarn, I do apologize for such an unworthy thought. You've been a gentleman from first to last, in spite of your premonitions. Asny and I were terribly discouraged at the thought of leaving Kilgore behind to recover, but with such generosity and nobility of soul as yours we shall succeed in carrying the sword ourselves somehow."

"Ah but is that a good idea?" asked Eldjarn. "Only the sword king can use it, you know. It will only be a hindrance to you. I am sure you could not translate those runes, even with all your skill in magic. I shall keep it for you, if need be, in the safest vaults in Beortstad, some of which I alone know the locations of." His mellow voice dropped to a conspiratorial whisper. The polished table he leaned upon reflected his image in the wavering grain of the wood.

"I shall think about that," Skanderbeg replied, nodding his head. "When there are no premonitions listening I shall give you our answer."

"That is a wise decision," Eldjarn said. "You know as well as I that nothing shall ever break into these halls—as if the sword could be found again once I have hidden it. You are most sensible, Skanderbeg. The bite of a vargulf is not a matter to take lightly. I would say that the sword king ought to remain here until spring before you dare remove him. There is no safer place for him than here, where nothing can get in or out to harm him." Eldjarn lovingly touched a bow and quiver hanging on a convenient hook. "And now I know you are anxious to begin planning the next part of your journey. Be assured that all the resources of Beortstad are at your disposal—excepting of course the neccessary impedimentia of war, such as troops, horses, and weapons."

"The two of us will not need much," Skanderbeg

said, rising from his seat. "I expect to be leaving at dawn tomorrow. You must show me what stores I have to choose from and I would like to see a sample of your secret vaults before I go."

"It shall be done," Eldjarn declared. "We'll heap up your supplies on our way to the vaults. I had hoped we would have time for at least one grand feast and merrymaking before you depart. Tonight, perhaps, a very small celebration to send you off."

"How very appropriate," Skanderbeg murmured with a bow.

In a short while, Skanderbeg returned to Bergljot's chamber. He put his satchel on the table and at once wove a spell around the room that could not be heard through.

"That takes care of the premonitions," the wizard said, opening his satchel and hauling out the contents. Ropes, parcels of grain and flour, extra clothing, boxes, bags, and bundles were all piled untidily in the middle of the floor. Asny examined everything gleefully and helped Skanderbeg divide it all into three piles.

"We shall be ready to go at the first opportunity," Skanderbeg said. "There will be a small celebration tonight which will easily last all night and render most of Beortstad insensible by dawn. And now how do we warn Hrafngrimr that Eldjarn knows he's coming here tonight?"

Bergljot did not appear concerned. "He knows already. I expect he knew at the same instant you did. There is a small glass sphere in the chambers of Eldjarn—but doubtless you know all about such things. He placed it there himself long ago when he first came to suspect he was going to become an outlaw."

"Do you think Kilgore will awaken in time?" Asny asked, already trying on her pack and striding up and down in a pair of new boots.

Skanderbeg pulled tight the strings on a parcel and they tied themselves obligingly in a firm knot. "He

171

hasn't any choice," he said in a preoccupied manner. "We aren't leaving him here."

Kilgore still slept as the day waned toward dusk. As the vargulfs swarmed howling from the Gap, the Alfar minstrels tuned their instruments and the cooks strained their every nerve and sinew to create the most splendid concoctions ever for the evening celebration. More torches and sconces were lit in the halls and fineries and plumeries sprouted by the scores.

A mountainous heap of silks and scarlets was delivered to Asny and Skanderbeg by Eldjarn's own Chief of the Wardrobe, a feathery personage who floated along in a cloud of purple. Asny disdainfully examined the apparel and rejected it. "I won't go if I have to look like this," she declared. "What's wrong with my own clothes? Much more durable and suitable to warfare. Now if they had a set of armor my size that I could borrow, I just might be vain enough to wear it. I would gladly stay and watch Kilgore, though. These state affairs are always poisonously dull. But since I am the future queen, I don't suppose it would do for me to absent myself. You can wear all this gauzy flummery, Skanderbeg. It would suit you exactly."

"Not I. You are the queen. I'm only a wizard. I'm lucky to be able to go at all with all you notable personages. Now what do you suppose that is?" He listened intently to several sets of feet tramping in step right up to the door. He stooped to peer through the keyhole.

Bergljot snatched the door open in his face to confront six Alfar carrying bows and swords. They too were dressed for the festive occasion and they bowed politely before assuming a protective stance on both sides of the door.

"Fools," Bergljot said, closing the door. "They think they are going to stop Hrafngrimr from coming here tonight." She shook her head as if she had not encountered such stupidity in a long time.

"They have lost touch with magic entirely," Skanderbeg said, rubbing his ear; at once a slick blue

172

snake slipped away under the door and caused a terrific outburst among the soldiers.

While they were still chattering about it, someone else knocked, a small, stout fellow soberly clad in gray. In a gruffish voice he introduced himself. "Bjolfr, the Captain of the Guard, sent by Eldjarn to fetch the sword of Andurich. He wants to put it into safekeeping now before the celebration."

"Do come in, good fellow," Skanderbeg said. "We'll do all we can for you. How would you like to be a raven for just a moment while we collect our parcels and leave? There now, don't complain, have a bit of bread and behave yourself."

Where one moment had stood a sober old fellow with an incredulous expression, there was now a large raven with his beak open. Cackling, the bird hopped onto the table and flew to the back of a chair with a bread crust.

"Bravo," said a familiar voice as Hrafngrimr slowly materialized on the hearthstone. "That's the best I've ever seen old Bjolfr looking in many a year. What do you intend to do now? Eldjarn is waiting with great impatience for Bjolfr to deliver the sword."

"If he believes I am that stupid, he deserves the disappointment," Skanderbeg retorted. "Really, I am insulted. Even Trond would have more subtlety." The raven cackled appreciatively. "I asked you to come back to tell me what you know of the Dark Alfar, but it seems there will be too little time. What we do must be decided upon quickly. Asny, you shall speak your opinion too, of course. What I propose is that we take Hrafngrimr along with us, if he cares to go on a little expedition at least as far as Wolfinden. The pay will not be extraordinary, but the company is excellent. From talking to Eldjarn, I am convinced that you are honest and also deeply committed to the same cause as we are. Won't you consider sharing our perils and possible death with us?"

Hrafngrimr inclined his head. "I came here with the specific purpose of attaching myself somehow to the sword mission. All of my life I have waited for

173

the prophecies to come true so that I would have a chance to be a part of the restoration of Gardar and the downfall of Surt. But certainly the young queen had better voice her opinion first, and the lad too if he awakens soon."

"Well, it all sounds very good," Asny said, "but can you fight if we are attacked? I see you don't carry a weapon and that is reason for doubt in my mind."

"I fight with sorcery," Hrafngrimr said. "In my youth I was proficient with a sword and axe and bow, and I doubt if my hands have forgotten how to use them."

"Then I suppose you'll do," Asny said. "Skanderbeg, when shall we depart? I'm heartily sick of this place."

"With the vargulfs on the prowl, we will remain in Beortstad and go to Eldjarn's celebration. Hrafngrimr and Bjolfr and Bergljot can keep an eye on Kilgore and the sword. I expect Eldjarn is wondering what became of Bjolfr and perhaps he will pay you a visit, being the conscientious fellow that he is. We'd best make the situation look as normal as possible. Bjolfr has never showed his nose around here as far as we know. Too much wine under his belt perhaps. Asny and I will do our best to keep him beside us every moment." Skanderbeg took up his staff with a sigh. "If it comes to a fight over possession of the sword, use your powers, Hrafngrimr. I have the uneasy feeling this celebration tonight is an unpleasant trick intended to thwart our mission."

"Then let's not go," said Asny. "It won't matter a whit to us." She watched Hrafngrimr closely to see if he would betray any emotion, but his face remained as bland as ever. More than once, the thought had occurred to her that perhaps Hrafngrimr and Bergljot should not be trusted either. Looking at the half-drawn sword, she saw it glowing gently, with none of the lightning flickers she had observed before in times of peril when evil-intentioned creatures had been close by.

Skanderbeg opened the door with one grand swoop,

174

declaring, "Come along, fair queen of Gardar. I'm sure there are those who are anxious to see you. Ha, what's this? Eldjarn has come to check on his premonitions. Strangely silent, I believe."

Eldjarn was indeed standing outside the door, splendidly dressed in his ceremonial Prime Minister's garb, minus the silvery Tarnkappe. He bowed a trifle to Skanderbeg and Asny and glanced within the room, now empty of Hrafngrimr, as if that one had vanished like smoke. The raven uttered a deep chuckle and resumed dipping his beak in a wine cup.

"There has been a suspicious occurrence," Eldjarn said in a low voice. "Has not Bjolfr come to collect the sword?" He looked at their blank expressions a moment, then shrugged elegantly. "It is nothing but a problem of internal discipline. I beg you not to be concerned. Shall we ascend to the main hall? We shall use my private entrance to avoid the crowds." He led them up a cleverly hidden spiral stair which issued them like magic into the main hall, which was brilliant with lights and glittering decorations and the costumes of the Alfar. The music and the eating and drinking never stopped a moment, except for a speech by a dignitary or official which no one listened to anyway. From their places of honor on the dais, Skanderbeg and Asny could see the whole display of the exiled Alfar wealth and luxury. Men and women alike wore jewels that would ransom a king, glittering and throwing light on the walls until the room seemed to be filled with flying sparks. Even Skanderbeg was silent with awe. Asny had seen many a state assembly, but never anything so grand and mysterious. Her eyes began to be dazzled and her senses dulled as the evening wore on with greater and greater grandeur, more music, and more food and drink. It seemed that hours passed on feet of lead, and still there was no end to the costumes and merrymaking. Her head became so heavy that she had to lean on Skanderbeg; her eyes would not stay open and she fell instantly into a deep and comfortable sleep.

In only a moment, it seemed, she was awakened

175

by Skanderbeg, but the hall was almost dark and two drunken musicians were struggling to stay awake to play their instruments. Most of the candles had burned down to nothing and the tables were covered with the rubble of the feasting. Everywhere the exhausted Alfar were sleeping, careless of their finery and jewels now.

"It's time to go," Skanderbeg said. "I should have warned you about the wine. Terrible stuff for mortals or Alfar."

"Where's Eldjarn?" Her throat felt raspy and her head ached.

"Sleeping under the table. I confess I slipped a bit of powder into his glass once to encourage it, but I don't believe he needed it. By the time he wakes up and remembers us, we'll be halfway up the Trident." Skanderbeg lit his staff and searched among the draperies for the spiral stair. Asny looked around thoughtfully at the opulence of the exiled Alfar, thinking of the hardship and frugality of the war camps she had seen. Shaking her head, she followed Skanderbeg in silence.

Bergljot, Hrafngrimr, and Kilgore were exactly as they had left them. Hrafngrimr sat reading with his satchel at his feet and Bergljot was spinning wool. The sword glowed brightly, its light trembling when Skanderbeg brushed by it. In a loud, cheerful tone he commanded, "Wake up, Kilgore! It's morning and time we were on our way."

Kilgore sat up immediately. "Why didn't someone wake me before?" he grumbled. "Look how light it is. Trond will have a score of trolls hunting for us by now. Where are my boots?" His voice trailed away as he looked around at the four stone walls, the hearth, the stout wooden door, and the shelves and cases and cabinets of Bergljot's supplies. "What happened to the vargulfs?" he finally demanded. "How did I get here? This must be Beortstad, but I don't remember a thing about last night. Where are all the Alfar?"

"You shall hear all about it later," Skanderbeg said. "But right now we must get ready to leave. Our hosts are in no condition to see us off, but they will understand, I hope."

"I'd hoped for one grand breakfast," Kilgore hinted. "It seems terribly rude to throw ourselves on their doormat with a thousand vargulfs one night and depart without thanks early the next morning."

"It would if that's what we'd done," Skanderbeg replied testily. "Yesterday you snored your head off while we worried around trying to keep the sword from being taken by Eldjarn and you from being kept here indefinitely, and now you worry about breakfast. On with your boots and I'll tell you all about it as we walk."

"But—" Kilgore was looking at Bergljot and Hrafngrimr.

"Hrafngrimr is an outlaw Alfar sorcerer and he is coming along so you can pester him to death with your questions; and Bergljot is the mortal physician of the Alfar who attempted to save your life," the wizard snapped. "You nearly died of a vargulf bite, if you will recall."

"I recall nothing of the sort," Kilgore said indignantly, stamping into a fine pair of boots and fastening the clasp of a new cloak before pausing to admire his outfit. "Is it a Tarnkappe?" he asked, drawing the cloak around him.

"Nonsense!" Skanderbeg said. "No one in Beortstad has a Tarnkappe. Are we ready? The vargulfs are all in the Gap by now and there's a low warm cloud cover with a hint of snow. It looks like an excellent day for walking. Bergljot, we bid you farewell and thank you many times over. When the roads are safe again we hope to see you back among your people. Give Eldjarn my regrets for leaving so abruptly, and thank him warmly for being such a help with the provisions."

Bergljot nodded her head gracefully. "Remember, it was not I who saved the life of the sword king, so you needn't be that grateful. I shall see you again when Gardar is restored and Surt slain. May the gods protect you." Then she gave gold rings to Asny and

Skanderbeg and Hrafngrimr and a gold-embossed sword belt to Kilgore, with the words, "These are gifts from the Alfar. Not these Alfar you have seen, but from the southern tunnels and forges where golden things are given power of their own to help their masters. These rings will give you strength and this sword belt will add power to the swordsman. Such a sword was meant to be carried on a belt like this. It was the very last made by an old smith called Alfarekkar. He would be pleased to know it had fallen into the hands of a warrior at last."

Kilgore could only hold it and stare. Gold and gems twinkled in intricate designs and he could feel power tingling in his fingertips.

"Thank you," he murmured. "Thank you! It's a noble gift."

Before he could thank her enough, Skanderbeg was whisking everyone out the door into the hall. Then Hrafngrimr led them at a brisk pace to a small dirty tunnel with slippery steps and a cold draft. They saw no one and did not pass one elaborate chamber or brightly lit hall. Beortstad was lifeless and silent, nothing like the enchanted place it had been the night before.

The tunnel ended at a wooden door which Hrafngrimr pushed open cautiously. After glancing all around, he motioned the others to follow. A cloud of snowflakes blew in their faces.

"Will you look at this," the Alfar said. "No sentry on duty. This whole place is wide open to attack. If only Trond knew this." His voice was grim as he shook his head silently.

For a moment, the party stood looking at the snow drifting down in curtains, almost obscuring the blue hulking shadow of the Trident. All the rocks and defiles were white hummocks and deceptive shadows softly muffled in layers of white. Skanderbeg was looking at his map for a moment; then he pointed. "That is the way. Past that highest foothill on the north. I hear there are trees and meadows on the other side and not quite as many vargulfs." Sticking his staff into the snow with each step, he led the way, leaving a curious trail to follow. The blowing snow began filling their footsteps as fast as they made them, and they traveled rapidly in the half-gloom of the snow storm. Spirits were high as Asny tried to tell Kilgore about the splendor of Beortstad and the exotic costumes of the Alfar at the celebration, but he was not inclined to believe any of it, having seen nothing but the cold desolation of Beortstad on the morning after. Then Skanderbeg described the narrow escape from the vargulf death and how Asny had saved him.

"That's twice now that she has pulled our bacon out of the fire," Kilgore said. "Getting lost in the Slough was one of the better things I've done on this trip. My deepest thanks, Asny."

"Tush, I daresay it won't be the last time either," Asny said with her usual lack of tact, but she looked very pleased.

At noonday the weather took a bitter turn. As they rounded the foothills, they came into the icy teeth of the Trident wind. The terrain was forbidding, with mazes of scrub trees that defied penetration. A foreboding, watched feeling soon stifled all idle chatter.

The rest of that day and half the next was spent in silent, grueling travel. They stopped only to unthaw their hands and feet and warm a little tea. Then it was more hiking again. The wooded hills and vales gradually gave way to upthrusting crags and sliding sheets of scree. The silence was broken only by their puffing breath and the clatter of dislodged rocks rolling and bouncing down. The sound seemed to echo from the black muffler of cloud just above them. Nothing grew on the slopes of the Trident, not even lichen or thorns. It was bare and gray, and the longer Kilgore climbed the more uneasy he felt. They were totally exposed here to any attack Surt might choose.

The last stages of their ascent were the worst. By the time they reached the black cloud, they were climbing with ropes and spikes. They hesitated a long time just under the cloud while the two wizards wove spells to protect them when they were in it; then

179

slowly they ascended into the cloud. It was thicker than any fog in Shieldbroad, and smelled as if fifty ancient mouldy cellars had been thrown open. It was damp, and caused the rocks to be coated with a cunning film of ice that made the going even slower and more treacherous. In addition to that, the cloud seemed to contain a nasty snarling wind within it that threatened to pick them off the Trident's icy face and hurl them to the rocks below.

When the weak daylight was finally swallowed by darkness, the party found themselves on a rocky shelf, exhausted. Snow began whirling madly in the strange musty air currents. Kilgore finally broke the despondent silence.

"I suppose we could camp here somehow. It looks as if we'll have to."

"The four of us might well be frozen stiff by morning," Asny said. "But at least I am not spoiled by a life of ease, such as Eldjarn's Alfar. How are you managing, Hrafngrimr? You can magic yourself to a warmer place at any time you wish, since you are a wizard."

"I am well enough, thank you. This reminds me of crossing the Hrimfast Mountains with Wulther, only that was farther north. We didn't have quite such nice clothing or food, I believe." Hrafngrimr made a small fire of dry brush that grew in the fissures of the mountain face. From his satchel he took a package of dried cod and put it into a pot.

"I'll shut my mouth if you were with Wulther," Asny said contritely. "That was easily the worst of it. But if Wulther and Valsidda had not become separated at Gunnarsmound, the war would have gone very differently and Gardar would not be what it is today."

"And I would have never joined with a fellow like Eldjarn," Hrafngrimr said. "I was disillusioned with war and he promised a life of peace and harmony and great beauty. I must say that it prompted me toward my natural inclination, sorcery, because I soon became bored with the safe life. Boredom and curiosity

180

sent me to the halls of Gorm and I learned a great deal more besides magic. From him I discovered the plot about the Fimbul Winter." He sighed deeply. "The rest you know."

Kilgore nodded. Asny had told him about Hrafngrimr, out of the Alfar's hearing, and added her suspicions to the telling. He had not liked the part about his interest in Kildurin. The sword registered no disapproval, but perhaps a clever sorcerer could fool it.

"What do you know about the sword?" he asked rather abruptly. "I would like to hear the Alfar side of the story."

Hrafngrimr added a few more sticks to the cooking fire and everyone huddled around it on the narrow ledge. Hrafngrimr began, "This sword was forged about a thousand years ago by Andurich, who was really a black dwarf and not an Alfar. He was captured and forced to make it rather against his will by the Alfar king, but he was paid for it handsomely and assigned an apprentice, a young and promising lad named Hrafngrimr. So I was there with Andurich when the sword was forged down in the depths of Muspell, which is the only place that is hot enough to melt the substance it is made from. We mined it ourselves in a shaft that is now filled with terrible spells so another such sword can never be made. I was there when old Andurich hammered out the metal and beat it to impossible fineness, weaving magic into it all the while with words I never understood. It took him three years of steady work to perfect it, when the king had ordered it in less than a year. It was the time of Surt's third attempt to bring down the Fimbul Winter. Since then he has made two more major attempts, as you doubtless know, and is gaining in power each time he is defeated. At the time he was hardly offensive enough to be taken seriously—just another mad wizard who had spent too much time with the trolls. King Ellidagrimr, however, was known to be a seer. With the aid of his wizards, he had discerned that such a sword could not be made at any other time by any other hand, and they also knew that Surt would

181

turn into the greedy monster he is now. In spite of terrific opposition from the Alfar, he ordered the sword made and hid it away quietly where it was soon forgotten. Old Andurich went up into his mound soon after, and I was sent out to be a goldsmith and the time passed peaceably enough in spite of repeated uprisings from Surt. Few Alfar noticed he was getting more difficult to handle each time. Then the men in ships came and immediately settled in the land you call Gardar, which was the stronghold of Surt's armies when he was in power and his hideaway when he was not. They trampled among the mounds and planted fields and built houses, which Surt cannot tolerate. Since men have come, he has doubled his power. He intends to have all of Skarpsey, which was a thing some Alfar could not understand. When Elbegast came to the throne during the last war, he had few who shared his conviction that the sword should be unearthed and put to use against Surt. Some believed it would not work well enough to deal him the double death, some were afraid it would fall into the wrong hands, and some like Eldjarn thought there was no need. Elbegast ignored them all and followed the advice of his father Ellidagrimr. He delivered the sword himself to the hall of the Brandstok and thrust it into the tree, where the only hand that could pull it out was the hand that could slay Surt. The fact that the sword had fallen into mortal hands was enough to divide the Alfar forever. I found myself outcast from both groups, although I now have pledged my aid to the sword king. The sword has great personal attraction and I am interested in studying its magic because I was present when it was forged. You might say that I am also an apprentice to the sword itself. I have always felt there was a bond forged between us, although I am not the chosen bearer. Once I asked Andurich about the sword king, hoping that it might be me, but the old dwarf only promised me that I would someday be the right hand of the sword king if I lived long enough. I am not certain even he could visualize who would possess the

182

sword. Now I am glad I was not the chosen one. It is much easier to be the follower than the leader."

For a moment the fire crackled cheerily in the silence. Skanderbeg cleared his throat. "After the sword was placed in the tree, Elbegast stopped by the Wizards' Guild, where I happened to be staying, and asked if I wouldn't undertake a small errand for him to Gardar to escort the sword. I really supposed it was less of a participating role—a mere representative accompanying a large body of horse and foot soldiers; but I saw at once that Elbegast had understated my significance considerably. Which is fortunate; otherwise I'd never have consented to such a journey. Well, perhaps I would have."

"I wouldn't have missed it for the world," Asny said cheerfully. "This has been a real lark so far. And to think that tomorrow we will be in Gardar. I can hardly believe it."

"And then we'll have to start calling you 'Your Highness' and 'Your Majesty'," Kilgore said gloomily.

"Oh, nonsense. I'm not crowned yet. You can't be a queen without subjects. I only hope there are more than trolls and wizards left. In a few hours we shall see Gardar for the first time I have seen it in sixty-five years. Just in time for the harvest and the pig-killing and the beer-brewing. But I suppose there will be none of that." Asny sighed and helped herself to more boiled cod.

"No indeed," said Hrafngrimr. "I have seen it. Everything will have to be rebuilt."

Skanderbeg yawned tremendously and began shaking out his sleeping blanket as a hint for everyone else to do likewise. Kilgore situated himself as far from the edge of the gulf as possible and still felt as if he were going to roll over it any second. He grumbled, "I feel like a bat hanging on this cliff. I don't think I can sleep like this." His answer was a throaty snore from Skanderbeg.

True to his expectations, he was entertained all

183

night by dreams of someone stealing out of the shadows and rolling him over the edge like a hogshead of ale. He awakened several times, always relieved to find it was only a dream. Each time he heard Skanderbeg snoring nearby in the damp darkness and he was aware of Hrafngrimr crouching over the tiny fire with the wind whipping at his beard. Once he thought he heard a wizardly chant raised, but it might have been a combination of the wind and his imagination. It could have been the wind that dislodged the pebbles that pattered down the face of the cliff above from time to time, and once he thought it sounded like boots scraping on stone. But of course it was only the wind. Skanderbeg was sleeping soundly, or at least it sounded like him, which was not quite as reassuring. The wind whispered and moaned around their camp with sounds barely concealed under its voice.

Hrafngrimr's staff poked him awake. It was still dark, but he supposed dawn was somewhere imminent. He greeted the Alfar. "Did you sleep well last night?"

"Sleep is a mortal's luxury, and curse also. No, I watched the cliffs and saw wondrous things."

"We're being followed!" Kilgore said, touching the sword to see if an enemy was at hand. It was silent. "What did you see."

"A strange little chap. Looked rather like a troll, minus the claws. I suspect he was a wizard of the baser sort. He came crawling up in our very tracks. Ragged like a beggar he was, with a villainous eye and a greasy yellow beard. When I asked him politely what he wanted, he quavered fiercely, 'Vengeance for the betrayal of Trondheim!' and waved a horrible little sword. 'What rot,' I said. 'The trolls wouldn't take you if they were paid.' Then he declared that you had deserted him to a terrible fate at the hands of King Trond and turned all the trolls against him. I could make nothing of it, and he became quite ugly, so I was forced to change him into a hare. It will take him awhile to get out of that one. He prowled around here

184

all last night, dreadfully noisy for one hare. Do you suppose you know him?"

Kilgore smothered a grin. "Aye. It's old Warth."

Skanderbeg appeared above and called down, "Warth, did you say? I thought we'd seen the last of him. He's worse than a burr in your beard."

"Not much he can do to stop us now," Asny said, uncoiling a rope and tossing it up to Skanderbeg. "Today we'll be in Gardar."

"There's still plenty of time before we get to Surt," Skanderbeg said. "And I've got uneasy feelings about this musty fog. It can't mean anything good in this territory." So saying, he hauled out his book of magic. "Let's see. Flies, focal distance, fogs, foot baths, fox—fogs. 1149–1150." Pages rustled. "Aha. Green fogs. Swamp and Marsh fogs. Manufacturing fogs. White fogs. Ah, here. Cold magic black fogs. 'Caused by distillations of the—' Oh bother. 'Cold fogs, black, encountered in territory known to be infested with any type of giant.' Yes, that's it. 'It is best to evacuate yourself at once. There is little known fire magic effective against giants, particularly of the mountain variety, due to a peculiarity of their physical composition, which is impervious to all manner of mortal shafts or bolts, and wizard power when employing some mortal means of destruction; however most giants are susceptible to stone implements applied directly to their most vulnerable parts, whatever they might be, if one is reckless enough to attempt it.' What rot! No help at all." And he stuffed the book back into his satchel.

With that warning, the travelers inched away up the mountain. At midday they stopped on another ledge to rest and brew tea; at least, they estimated it was midday, for the fog still hid the sun. Thankfully they threw down their packs and collapsed on the rocky shelf. Asny set off to explore the extent of the shelf and was lost from sight at twenty paces.

Suddenly the mountain quivered under their feet, and a few rocks came bouncing down.

"Asny! What are you doing?" Skanderbeg demanded.

"Don't be alarmed," Hrafngrimr said. "It must mean old Bulthor is stretching his legs."

"Who?" asked Asny, who came hurrying back when the shaking began.

"Bulthor. He's the mountain giant of the Trident. Very old, hasn't moved for centuries. I suppose Surt has roused him so he can prevent us from reaching Gardar," was the reply of Hrafngrimr.

"What do mountain giants do?" Kilgore asked.

"Oh, they stalk around until someone notices them, and then they disguise themselves as a mountain. Bulthor remains mostly mountain now, except for a part of him far within that no one sees."

"Does every mountain have a giant inside it?" Kilgore asked.

"You never know," Hrafngrimr answered.

Another tremor shook the ground. The shaking and quivering continued until the party was packed again and moving on. As they climbed, the mountain trembled several times, and once they heard a snarling rumble far within as if something were stretching. Then unexpectedly, the mountain's steep face leveled to a gentler incline, and they were walking on level ground. They stopped to coil the ropes before advancing slowly, looking around on all sides. In the fog, they could discern little, but directly ahead they dimly saw two black mountain shoulders rising and disappearing above into the cloud. Cautiously, they approached. Quite abruptly, the fog fell behind them. They stopped to stare upward at the two soaring peaks. To the west was the third, equally mighty and malignant. Ice sheathed peaks as far up as Kilgore could see, and their heads were hidden sullenly in dirty tatters of cloud.

"We must hurry," Hrafngrimr was urging. "This is not the place to—"

"Hulloa!" boomed a voice like a thunderclap. "Who goes there? Who's that sneaking among my spires?"

186

CHAPTER 13

The voice vibrated all around them, but the author of those stentorian tones did not emerge from the cloud to challenge them. Kilgore put his hand on the sword and found it quivering and humming.

"Greetings, Bulthor," called Hrafngrimr. "Is that you in the ice caves? You sound as hale and hearty as you did nine centuries ago. Did you have a pleasant rest?"

"Yes, indeed. Slept over seven hundred years, but some mischief has disturbed me. As you see, I'm not in a very good humor. Somebody has put out one of my eyes and it's been eons since I ate anything. What are those creatures with you, Alfar?"

"Two children of Ask and Embla and a most dangerous and despicable fire wizard. I'm afraid he'd melt you down to the last rock and block of ice you have, if you don't humor him."

"Well! Pleased to make your acquaintance!" the mountain giant said less volubly.

Skanderbeg bowed curtly, doing his best to look dangerous and despicable. "Skanderbeg's the name. Most honored."

"Won't you all come nearer so I can see you? I've only one eye and it's very weak when it comes to viewing small objects. So these are mortals, eh? Look like a runty species of giant, shrunken almost to nothing, or a hairless troll. Speak, mortals. I presume you have names."

Kilgore moved a step closer to the glittering ice cave. Some sort of life seemed to flicker in the black ice. "I'm called Kilgore of Shieldbroad," he said.

"I see. I've never seen a Kilgore before. Let alone a

187

mortal. Have those old, gloomy prophecies truly come to pass, and the lands become infested with barbarians?"

"We call them mortals now," Hrafngrimr said. "They've advanced a bit since they arrived seven centuries ago."

"Might have possibilities," the giant said.

Suddenly a crack split the earth at their very feet. The travelers sprang back, astonished. It closed slowly with a grating noise.

"Dear me, I'm sorry for yawning right in your faces," Bulthor said contritely. "I've had such a long sleep. I'd be a-sleeping yet if it weren't for all this hullabaloo about Surt and that silly sword Andurich was making. Do come closer; I can't see a thing. Drat that—er, Skyr, Scour—I forgot his name."

"Surt," Kilgore said.

"Ha! Then you know him!" The earth quivered alarmingly.

"Only by his name," Kilgore said hastily. "No more than I know Andurich except by his name."

A crack snapped open behind the travelers and swallowed up the coiled heap of climbing ropes.

"Andurich!" The giant uttered a muted roar. "Nine centuries ago I swore on Surt's imprisoned bones I'd swallow Andurich and that sword of his if ever they passed this way. Why don't you come closer? I get tired of shouting. But stay! You can tell me about Andurich. Surely he and his friends are dead by now? Surt certainly hasn't let them live on, has he?"

"No, they are both safely dead," Hrafngrimr answered. "And you remember Elbegast's promise about the sword. It probably lies buried yet."

"The only thing that lies is you, elf. Surt himself told me that the sword has been taken from its hiding place and given to the barbarians. And it is now in the hands of a large and eminent king from the south, who is on his way to Grimshalg to slay Surt and all the Twelve. Why did you try to fool me, elf? Don't you know that I am the heart of the Trident, the highest of the high? No one can fool Bulthor!" With a throaty rumble, an immense crack opened almost beneath their feet and would have swallowed them up, had they not scurried to safety.

"Peace! Let us pass!" Hrafngrimr cried.

"Nay, not by the roots of all the mountains!" Bulthor thundered. "It's you that Surt wants. It's you who dare to presume to halt the return of the Fimbul Winter, you who weren't even there. Well, let me tell you, neither you nor that great sword that Kilgore carries shall ever pass these three peaks. I know you, you earth-spoilers. Show me the sword, for I know you have it." The ground heaved, and another crack sent them sprawling.

Skanderbeg picked himself up, a fiery light in his eye. "See here, you pile of gravel and stone, let us pass or it'll go the worse for you. Andurich's sword is far more powerful than one tottery old mountain giant with scarcely one eye. Aside, villain, or we shall use it on you."

"Ha! Then the truth is out! Which of you is the large king? Him I shall swallow first!" Rocks and ice came thundering down from the triple peaks, which seemed to sway with Bulthor's fury.

"Try a little wizard fire first!" Skanderbeg bellowed. Raising his staff, he sent fire up the eastern peak above the ice cave in somersault disks and half-moons.

"Wizards and demons!" roared the mountain giant, and the earth rippled with cracks that opened and shut in the wink of an eye.

"Wizards and Alfar, if you please!" Hrafngrimr replied. Calling to the others, he raced for the pass, directly under what would have been Bulthor's nose. At this, Bulthor gave a great bellow that must have been heard in Shieldbroad as his quarry escaped. More fire and sparks raced up to the sky and ignited the hovering mist. The cloud burned with a brilliant blue glare, lighting up the mountain top as brightly as noonday.

"I see you now!" the giant thundered. "Death to the sword king!" A rock the size of two draft horses galloped down the center peak toward the fleeing travelers.

Seeing it, Kilgore stopped at once. The others put on a burst of speed, and the rock smashed down behind them like a plug between the two peaks.

The mountain giant roared in triumph. The Trident shook to its very roots. For an instant Kilgore was blinded and choked by flying dust and ice particles. A terrific cold breath suddenly gusted from the ice caves. Kilgore shrank behind a stone, instantly numbed by the giant's deadly breath. At his side, the sword howled for battle, audible even over the crash and thunder of Bulthor's rage and the hurricane of icy wind. Kilgore drew it stiffly, wondering what damage he could do to an enemy of stone and ice. He ventured a glance around his rock and saw the ice caves not a bowshot away. One cave glittered with ages of dark ice—the eye of Bulthor. From the other cave, his blinded eye, roared the awful breath of the giant and all the noise and chunks of ice and rock.

Kilgore tried to argue himself out of the only plan he could think of. It was a desperate plan, and risky, but he was freezing. He had to act. Taking up a rock, he hurled it away from him down the slope. At once a crevice snapped open in that area, followed by others.

"Har! So I've got you now!" the giant roared. An avalanche of ice and snow crashed toward the place.

Kilgore sprang from his hiding place, sword in hand. He had covered half the distance before Bulthor's attention was drawn to him. Then the giant roared, enraged at the sight of the gleaming sword. "By Surt's body, you're doomed! Andurich, Elbegast, die!"

"For the children of Ask and Embla! Die!" Kilgore shouted, swinging the sword against flying rocks shooting from the blind eye. He bounded up the cliff face in an instant. The sword plunged into the green-black ice up to the hilt. With a shattering crash, the ice fell into the black void behind it. The wind nearly

190

took Kilgore off his feet and added impetus to his flight as he raced toward the pass.

Bulthor bellowed, "You've put out my other eye! Treachery! Villains! Kill!" The earth shook and heaved with billows of rage. Cracks split open a dozen at a time, and the icy breath of the giant raged from their gaping jaws. Bulthor raged, Bulthor bellowed. Rocks the size of cottages lumbered down, jolted from their frozen moorings high in the triple peaks.

On the Gardar side, it was no safer. Boulders came rolling down with retinues of sliding snow, and chunks of ice fell from perilous heights to explode into a million stinging needles.

Manfully, Asny swung the hammer at the crashing boulders. At the same time, Hrafngrimr threw spells over his shoulder as he ran. Another furious outburst nearly shook the fleeing runners off their feet, and Skanderbeg called down a dazzling bolt of pure fire to dance upon the spires of the Trident. Then the ice water came down with a vengeance and they fled before the dirty cascades of water and rubble.

When the dust and dirty snow cleared, they had outrun the fury of Bulthor. Skanderbeg and Hrafngrimr crouched under a ledge far down the slope, overlooking the land of Gardar. In the sudden silence, they studied the desolate landscape. A half-day's descent would place them among the shoulders of black stone and clumps of dark scrub forest. Mist hung in tatters on the broken spines of barren ridges and clung to the tops of the once-magnificent forests, now dead and replaced with scrub. Nothing stirred below the lead-gray ceiling of cloud. All living creatures, if there were any, seemed to be watchfully waiting.

"Can you see the way?" Skanderbeg whispered.

"The fog obscures most of it, but Wolfinden lies to the north. It commands the only pass to the high plain within." Hrafngrimr pointed to the dim black line that barred their way. "Once we pass through the Dark Alfar realm, we are clear all the way to

191

Grimshalg. All there will be is barrows from ages of wars. Perhaps a few native Gardars. I understand some of them have escaped Surt's control and become quite savage. And there will be the vargulfs' runs every morning and night, but for the most part they will be further south of us, nearer the Gap. By far the worst of it will be Wolfinden, if the weather is dark. Hope for a relatively bright day, Skanderbeg."

"What I hope for right now is a quick descent into some better cover," Skanderbeg growled, peering anxiously up the mountain slope. "I see Asny coming down but Kilgore is nowhere in sight. You don't suppose he got stranded on the other side, do you?"

"If he did, Bulthor has got him by now."

Asny almost stepped on Skanderbeg before she saw him. She could hardly remove her eyes from the land below. "It looks pretty bleak," she said briskly. "All the trees have died, but another twenty years will see them return. The Wolfindensgade is gone, grown under with scrub, but I expect it can be cleared again. Have you seen any signs of houses or homesteads? I haven't seen one yet."

"Have you seen Kilgore?" Skanderbeg asked.

Asny looked around in surprise. "He's not here? I thought he was ahead of me, since I stopped to look at my domain for a moment. I'll go back and find him."

"No, we'll wait and let Bulthor cool down a bit," Hrafngrimr said. "We have no way of knowing what attention we've attracted already."

They sat down in the lee of the ledge to wait. A few flakes of snow blew purposelessly at intervals and the gloom became grayer. To pass the time, Skanderbeg brewed tea and handed around some dry biscuits. Still there was no sign of Kilgore and the night was drawing down.

When Bulthor ceased his wrathful convulsions, Kilgore was bounding downhill on the Gardar side. The others were not in sight, as he had expected after scrambling over the stone blocking the pass. He kept pausing to look back. It was a spectacular sight, really, with bursts of ice crystals and flickering wizard fire sudden and brilliant. A last sudden heave set the mountain trembling. Kilgore lost his footing and skidded on his elbows and knees into a bed of sliding shale. By the time he got to his feet again, the shale was on the move. It slithered down the steepest parts of the mountain, pouring rapidly in and out between crags and dead trees. He could see its silvery back far, far below, cascading like a waterfall down the mountain. To his alarm, the shale jerked and rushed in a most uncharacteristic manner. He tried to scramble toward the edge unsuccessfully; the slide moved too fast and erratically. Strangely, there seemed to be no rock rolling down on top of him from above, and all the pieces were the same size and color and reminded him more of scales than shale. He looked down to the jagged valley floor again, then back the way the shale poured down. No end was in sight either way. Uneasily he redoubled his efforts to get away from the sliding creature. What if it were the great Midgard serpent about which superstitious old Grandam had always told him? He'd supposed it was merely a myth that a monstrous snake encircled the earth, always in pursuit of its own tail. If the story was true, however, he could easily be carried around the entire known earth and through the east and west seas. Determinedly, he scrabbled his way to the side of the monster by means of handholds among the huge scales. Exercising great caution not to fall clumsily between the grinding sides of the serpent and the rough rocks, he flung himself clear. He rolled head over heels several times and came to rest against the mossy knees of a tree.

When he had recovered his breath and a few scattered possessions, he took a last incredulous look at the shining back of the Midgard snake and turned to examine the forest he'd been thrown into. The serpent had carried him nearly to the bottom of the mountain. These same trees had looked like short dark furze from the summit. Now he could see they were tremendous and ancient. Their mossy branches were

193

interwoven like gnarled old fingers. Centuries of storms had twisted and blasted and killed, and still the ancients clung tenaciously to their rocky soil.

"How pleasant to stroll along a shady path for a change!" Kilgore said to himself, stepping within the wood. At once he noticed the hiss and thresh of the branches overhead. The trees seemed to bend toward the earth smotheringly. "Maybe not just yet," he added hastily, and thought of the others. He must find them as they came down. It was unfortunate the others hadn't managed to fall onto the snake's back. But all he had to do was wait. To entertain himself, he sauntered along the edge of the wood, just under the eaves of its black and gray roof. Although it was late fall, the limbs still had leaves of greenish black that looked like old leather left out in the sun. It was dark and odorous under the trees. Small rustlings caught his attention. He looked sharply into the mossy gloom, but saw nothing. Something or someone was in there watching, he thought with a chilly sensation. He wished Skanderbeg were along to laugh scoffingly at him and perhaps send a fire bolt into the rustling duskiness.

His nervous wanderings brought him to what had been a road into the Trident mountain, or into the gloomy forest. Grass had grown up in it and rocks had pushed through the once-packed surface under the insistent auspices of the weather. As was the custom, a stone had been erected there to guide the traveler. Kilgore approached the stone curiously. The chiseled letters were nearly gone. In the dim light he managed to read *Wolfindensgade* and *Tridentsgade* and what he thought must be *Grim*— something. Possibly Grimshalg, he thought with excitement. He looked in the direction the stone indicated. A grassy, grown-over flatness that may have once been a path rambled off into the wood, choked with young beech and sumac and thorn tangles. No one had been along that path—if it were a path—for many years.

As Kilgore stood gazing into the deepening gloom of the forest and smelling the rotting odor of old wood, a sudden loud crashing to his right startled him. Whirling, he saw squat shapes blundering through the underbrush. He half drew the sword. One never knew the form his enemy might take. The creatures carelessly crackled the branches, making peculiar grunting noises. Then in a group they trotted out of the wood toward him, heads low and uttering the same grunts.

Kilgore laughed aloud with relief. They were nothing but a herd of swine. Nonetheless, he moved closer to the stone tower, which he might climb if they proved ill-tempered. He supposed they were the wild descendants of the swine herds of the Gardars. When the people had been driven out or killed, he remembered Skanderbeg saying, the livestock roamed the woods and meadows unattended. It was possible these beasts were quite wild and vicious, if they had never learned to fear men.

Morosely the swine began tearing at the ground with their tusks. A few eyed him suspiciously. He dared not make a move to run away. Being pursued by a herd of wild pigs across the slopes of the Trident would set him far off the course of Skanderbeg, Asny, and Hrafngrimr. Then it occurred to him all in a flash how delicious one of the swine would taste roasted over coals. Drawing a short sword from his pack, carried just for such purposes, he edged toward the closest porker. Disdainfully it stared at him, squint-eyed, as if it knew exactly all his intentions and cared not a whit. With a grunt it shuffled off. Kilgore made a flying dive after it and caught it by one leg. Such a squealing and kicking and thrashing! Battered but not discouraged, Kilgore was about to put an end to the pig when a voice cried, "Ho there, you waylaying robber! Would you brutally slay a poor man's only livelihood and send him starving into the woods?"

Still holding the squealing swine, Kilgore looked around in amazement. His eye lit on the speaker and his fears were quickly dispelled. For an instant he had envisioned a large and angry herder twirling a hand-axe and advancing upon him. Instead, a spritely little old fellow sat comfortably on a tree root not fifteen paces off. He was clad in a single garment made from

195

the hide of some unidentifiable and long-dead animal. It covered him from neck to knees and was cinched around the middle with a wide belt with a brass buckle. From it hung several pouches, a double-edged knife, an old silver horn, and a crude but serviceable battle-axe, well-rusted and probably taken from a barrow. Laced gaiters protected his legs from the thorns he encountered herding the swine. A shapeless hat with an owl's feather hung over one eye, and he peered out from under it with an amused expression as he smoothed his pale yellow beard.

Kilgore answered the fellow's challenge. "Certainly I would allow no man to starve. I'll gladly give you half of your pig, and you may share my fire while I eat my half. And wait for my friends," he added, "who are coming presently."

"Ah! That is nobly generous," the little fellow said, nodding. "I shall build the fire at once. It's not every day I'm given half a hog."

"Who are you, and what do you do in this desolation?" Kilgore asked.

"I am Schimmelpfinning, and I herd swine," the fellow replied, scooping together a heap of twigs. He turned with a jerk to snatch up larger branches. Kilgore saw a tiny flame already devouring the twigs and wondered if the swineherd had sulfur matches like Skanderbeg's, so quickly was his fire started.

Shrugging, he dispatched the pig. In almost no time, he was roasting a piece of pork on the end of a stick, facing Schimmelpfinning over the fire. The fellow talked on and on about his swine, the woods, and the giants, and never seemed to run out of words. And questions. He wanted to know everything about Kilgore, who was hard pressed to avoid lying outright and to avoid telling all.

"Are you a wizard by nature?" asked Schimmelpfinning, very friendly. "I've seen nothing but the magical folk in this wood, all on business with Surt, I wot. At least if they're heading north, they are. I can tell you're a wizard by your stern countenance. Great matters are weighing you down."

196

"Appearances are always deceiving, Schimmelpfinning," Kilgore said, making his countenance very stern. "Now look at yourself, for instance. To look at you, anyone would think you are nothing but a humble churl who wanders around all day with his swine. That is almost too obvious, so I would suspect that in truth you were really something else, say one of Surt's ice wizards; and the moment I turn my back perhaps you'll blast me with one of your dreadful spells. What do you have to say about that?"

"Only that you'd be a fool to turn your back on me, if that were the case," Schimmelpfinning said with twinkling eyes. "Not to mention being rude. But now as I look at you, I see an average young mortal, rather ragged around the edges, as if you'd walked quite a distance through some rough country, but otherwise common enough. Almost too common in this place at this time. Nobody in Gardar looks just ordinary, unless he is up to something. You need to look suspicious if you want to conceal yourself from the watchful eyes that are under every stone."

"But what can be more suspicious?" Kilgore inquired. "It's not at all like men to leave a comfortable fire and snug shelter to brave the trolls and giants and vargulfs of Gardar, not to mention ice wizards. Is it not madness to come to battle an enemy such as Surt?"

"Battle Surt? Battle Surt? Is that what you've come to do?" gasped the old swineherd.

"Yes, and you may tell him so if you see him," Kilgore said, shutting his mouth firmly.

"Well, so I shall. But tell me now, since you are a traveler and have seen a great deal, what do you know of Shieldbroad? Horrid, all bog, fens, trolls by the caveful, and hostile natives—"

"What!" Kilgore exclaimed. "It's a lovely land. You've never seen better hay fields and clearer firths and such hospitable people. Forests and harbors and fire-halls and not a troll any nearer than Haelfsknoll or Heroness—" Suddenly he was nearly overcome with homesickness, just talking about Shieldbroad. He heaved a sigh and sat morosely watching the fat sizzling on his pork.

Schimmelpfinning chuckled. "Aye, you're right. Who's ring-lord there these days? Wulther? Valsidda?"

"Valsidur," Kilgore said, his thoughts far away within the ancient and polished walls of the Brandstok hall.

"It seems to me," the swine herd mused, examining his meat, "that I heard a strange tale about Valsidursknoll and the Brandstok."

"Oh?" Kilgore murmured. "Well, this far away, one never knows what is fact and what is rumor." Rapidly he added, "You must never believe rumors about far-away places. Nor even nearby places. No, it is best not to pay any attention to rumors."

"My goodness, I haven't even told you about it yet," Schimmelpfinning said. "That is very peculiar. If you are a wizard, you must have known the thoughts in my head before I could speak them."

"No, I didn't. I mean, I couldn't if I wanted to, since I'm no wizard. You see, I've heard that exact same story before about Valsidur's son and that sword."

"I never mentioned anything of the sort!' the swineherd said truimphantly. "I wasn't even thinking about that boy and the sword. Why are you so anxious not to talk about it? You looked positively frightened when I mentioned it. And speaking of swords, that's a beauty you've got there, although you keep it muffled so cleverly in your cloak. I'd say it looked Alfar if ever I saw an Alfar sword." He winked conspiratorially.

"And I doubt if you have, being only a swineherd. See here. Schim—Schmelling—whatever your name is—" He swallowed his exasperation. "—I think your meat is burning."

"Eh! So it is. I hadn't noticed," Schimmelpfinning said cheerfully. "But that's no matter. And back to our original topic, I'd say that's just the type of sword a fellow needs in these parts, if he runs into old Surt and his wizards. Most of the peaceable inhabitants lock themselves in their houses and don't put their noses out, but if a body should go looking for Surt to challenge him, all he'd have to do is follow the old Wolfinden road, where it's possible he might find some aid. I would stay out of the woods and those low gray hills, if I were you, because you never know when one of those hills might be a sleeping giant. The frost giants love to hunt the forests for small game, as we do for rabbits, only they hunt men and not rabbits. Don't be afraid to pass Svartheim, which is the Dark Alfar name for Wolfinden. There shall be reinforcements standing by in case you need them. You may think the reinforcements are worse than the Dark Alfar, but don't be deceived. You will be taken to the barrow plain and from there it is an easy walk to Grimshalg. Getting inside will present no difficulties and you will find a friend there even among your enemies. Challenge Surt one blow for one and he will accept. Like all wicked creatures, he has a tremendous sense of justice and will not attempt to cheat. Strike the first blow, need I add, or you are surely doomed."

Before Kilgore could do anything but gape in amazement, Schimmelpfinning wiped his fingers on his hem and proceeded to carve off a hind leg of the pig, saying, "And now I've got matters of importance to attend to. Sorry to rush away." He stuffed the joint into a pouch. "Good luck, Kilgore Valsidursson, we'll meet again."

"What?" Kilgore stammered. "How do you know—"

"Now I hear your friends coming, so I needn't worry about you any longer. You've chosen some admirable companions." His eyes twinkled as he settled his feathered cap on his head. "Do be cautious of the people you meet in Gardar. Most of them are not at all what they seem. You must guard yourself against hasty condemnations of character. Farewell."

He shook hands with Kilgore, who could say nothing but, "Wait a moment, Schmilling, Schmelp—"

"Be of good cheer!" called the swineherd from the edge of the trees. But he was back before Kilgore could stop stammering.

"I forgot one thing." He presented his old silver horn and hung it around Kilgore's neck. "That is a gift to you from me. I got it one day in the barrow mounds and I promised its owner I would place it in the proper hands someday. Farewell again, Kilgore."

"Farewell!" Kilgore sat down, shaking his head. But Schimmelpfinning was back again.

"If you ever need help desperately, sound this horn and I shall be at your side with sword and buckler at the third mot. Don't forget."

Looking at the old horn in confusion, Kilgore said, "Goodbye!" There had to be another explanation. He stood for a moment waiting for the fellow to reappear; finally he sat down to eat his meat and wonderingly examine the old horn. There were runes on it—what didn't have runes? he thought—which Skanderbeg would have to translate. It was also clogged with dirt. That supported Kilgore's notion that Schimmelpfinning had robbed the barrow mounds of the old warriors for most of his appointments. With a shudder, Kilgore tossed the horn into the trees. He wanted nothing to do with any dead barrow wraith's horn. The fellow might come stealing foglike after him to get it. Besides, who was he to deprive a stout warrior of his horn, which he would need in the hall of dead heroes?

He heard the horn thump against a trunk in the blackness of the wood. It rolled and bounced against other roots and rocks and things and suddenly came rolling out again, tumbling into the clearing, and lay shining in the glow of his fire. If he threw it back, he feared the same thing would happen again. Very reluctantly, he went and picked it up. Its hard-packed dirt sifted out as he did so, and he shook it to remove the last clots of earth. Sighing, he hung it round his neck. Obviously it wasn't going to let him get rid of it. Therefore, it must be rightfully his.

As he finished the piece of meat he had been eating, he heard Skanderbeg's voice grumbling from afar and the tramp of boots.

"Blasts and fogs!" the wizard was saying. "Can't

200

find the dratted signpost, lost that nuisance Kilgore, and now benighted. What next!"

"Halloo!" Kilgore called, taking up a brand and hurrying to show them where he was.

"Ha!" Skanderbeg exclaimed. "We're being attacked by flaming salamanders! I knew for fair something worse had to happen."

"Skanderbeg!" Kilgore called.

"What's that? Identify yourself or you'll be a crumpet in about an instant!"

"It's Kilgore, and you are Skanderbeg, Hrafngrimr, and Asny. Hurry up, I've just killed a swine for our supper."

They emerged from the rocks and brush of the slope somewhat suspiciously. Seeing it was indeed Kilgore, they advanced confidently to the fire and fell upon the pork with delight.

"How did you manage this, Kilgore?" Hrafngrimr asked when he had finished a crisp morsel of meat.

"And where did that old silver horn come from?" Asny asked.

"How did you manage to arrive at the bottom so speedily?" Skanderbeg asked. "It took us the better part of the afternoon. Looking for you, of course—"

"You'd never believe it," Kilgore said with a laugh. "I rode down on the Midgard serpent. It looked like sliding shale, but it wasn't."

"Serpent? Absurd!" Skanderbeg snorted in wonder.

"But it was," Kilgore insisted, and he went on to tell about the swine and the funny little old swineherd —strange, but he had forgotten the name already— and the horn and how it had come bouncing back to him, and that in case of great danger he was supposed to use it to summon help from the swineherd. The others laughed at his recount. Then he told them of the directions and warnings the swineherd had given them, and showed Skanderbeg and Hrafngrimr the runes. They examined the horn closely and were silent as they listened.

"Well," Hrafngrimr said uneasily, "the horn he could have dug up from the barrows. Keep it, because

201

these are elven runes. And about the rest, I'd guess that he received word from someone about us. Eldjarn, maybe. But at any rate, it never hurts to be cautious. We shall follow the Wolfindensgade more warily now, according to our first plans."

"But I don't like having our route known," Asny said. "And also we don't know the changes that have taken place. I suggest we plot another course across country, following the general direction of the old road."

"Good idea," Hrafngrimr said, spreading his map on his knee to study the faint lines. "There's a lot of woods and rivers and hills between us and Wolfinden. We'll need to cover it quickly, in order to finish our business in Gardar before the winter storms come. Kilgore, you don't suppose that swineherd will return, do you? He could escort us to Wolfinden safely, I imagine, knowing the wood as well as he must."

"Not unless we run into him and his swine by chance," Kilgore said. "He was a very busy type, if you know what I mean. Seemed rather pressed for time."

"Perhaps," Asny said, half to herself as she gazed into the woods, "he is calling together the other peasants for some kind of resistance. Maybe we shall have the help we need after all."

"Let us hope that he is on our side," Skanderbeg replied darkly.

"Certainly the peasants would be against Surt," Asny said. "If they were themselves, I mean. But if that swineherd survived the devastation, surely there are others, and Surt couldn't control them all."

"Devastation?" Kilgore said. "It looks pretty fierce and bushy to me. Not at all devastated."

Asny shook her head. "You should have known Gardar before. It used to rival the coastland for granges and fields and meadows. Now you see that Surt's wizards have made it wild and ugly with these perverted trees and thorns and poison plants. The air is even hostile. Nothing but wickedness can grow where Surt has smitten the earth. A thousand plagues

202

upon him! Of all his crimes, the death of a beautiful and pure land is by far the worst." She fell into a gloom that lasted the rest of the evening, which helped their surroundings to inflict the others with the same melancholia. After more course plotting and map comparing and wizard book consultations, the guardian rings were drawn and they all tried to sleep. A pair of owls kept the night lively with their dolorous hooting, and every time Kilgore awakened he was sure to hear suspicious sounds in the wood. He dreaded the thoughts of plunging into that unfriendly gloom on the morrow.

He still had the same feeling about the forest the next morning when they struck camp. In no time he was scratched and itchy from brushing against whitish, sticky plants of some vile sort. Their progress was painfully slow. Everyone's patience was exhausted by noon. They had covered scarcely a league in half a day.

"This will get us to Wolfinden by approximately another fortnight," announced Skanderbeg, pulling tenacious little burrs from his cloak, beard and satchel.

Hrafngrimr sighed. Asny suggested using their swords to chop a way through the brush. Kilgore glared at an inflamed scratch across his arm and declared, "I vote for the road. We can go four times as fast. This way, we're muddling along like snails and giving the whole forest ample warning we're coming and fine proof we've passed. So what if there's frost giants? Now that we know about them, we can watch for them. I don't know what the difference is between being frozen by winter snows or frozen by a frost giant."

In dispirited silence the others considered his retort. Then Hrafngrimr nodded. "I too vote for the road."

"It's just as well," Skanderbeg agreed. "At least we'll know we're going in the right direction. Let's only hope that swineherd is what he seemed and not what he might be."

"I think he is a friend," Asny said. "I'm sure he

had a purpose for sending us down the Wolfinden road."

To everyone's satisfaction and relief, the road was discovered without trouble. Travel was significantly faster. The poisonous plants and thorns, however, grew in riotous profusion, as if planted there for the very purpose of discouraging travel. But no one complained. The joy of walking on an actual road made by men—if overgrown and gullied—more than compensated for the discomforts of the undergrowth.

They moved quickly for the rest of the day, and the musty gloom of the forest closed around them. The gray and black branches formed a net overhead almost continuously. In spaces where the trees cleared, it was almost pleasurable to see the leaden sky brooding above them instead of the scraggly, grasping limbs.

That night they were forced to camp among the trees. Both wizards wove spells all around their camp. Nevertheless, it was an uneasy night. Two of the wizards' alarms went off when something tried to get through. The trees kept up a running conversation all night, although there was no wind, and the owls were merciless. Small screeches and crackling brush all around added to the general uneasiness of the travelers. Sap oozed out of the branches and dripped on them. They were sticky for two days after. To add to their woes, in the morning it was raining lightly.

"Is there no end to this loathly forest?" grumbled Hrafngrimr, who scarcely ever complained. "I swear the ground under these trees is harder, the wood slower to burn, and even our food seems more miserable."

"I agree," Kilgore grunted. His back felt as if he had been pummeled all night long.

They got off to a late start and grumbled until noon. The rain didn't worsen enough to call a halt, and didn't let up. In self-pitying silence they ate a sparse lunch, while hoarse bird voices croaked in the trees overhead.

"I always loved to be in the forest when it rained,"

Kilgore said, looking around at the wet leaves and mossy trunks. The others glared at him until he hastily added, "In Shieldbroad, anyway."

The rain continued. With the perversity of nature and men's creations, it seemed to form the deepest puddles on the old road. The travelers marched along grimly, scarcely noticing when the road began to rise.

They noticed, however, the increasing elevation when they found themselves on the crest of a hill. Before them wound the road through glades and dells and among scattered clumps of trees. It seemed almost pleasant, except for the squat, ugly hills dumped here and there.

Hrafngrimr didn't share everyone else's relief. He scowled and muttered, "Giant country, if ever I've seen it."

With their weapons ready under their hands, they started into the open lands. All the rest of the afternoon they were watchful. Then it came time for supper and camp and Kilgore began saying, "What's wrong with this place?"

Hrafngrimr and Skanderbeg refused to listen. The sky darkened as they hurried along.

"It's going to be a dark night for wandering among the woods," Kilgore warned. "We'd better stop."

"In giant territory?" Skanderbeg demanded. "Not unless you want to become the main attraction at some giant's supper."

"Are we going to walk all night?" Kilgore asked. "More giants are out at night than day. Why don't we—" He paused, listening. Faintly he heard muffled crashes and he was almost certain a roar or two. "Why don't we hurry?" he demanded. "We can go much faster."

They left the exposed surface of the road to dash from clump to clump of trees. The earth trembled underfoot with great blows. Suddenly there was a terrific crunch and ripping sound just behind them. Kilgore looked back to the stand of trees they'd just deserted. There, waist deep in the foliage, were two frost giants. He could tell at once by their flowing

205

white hair and beards, which were frozen with icicles and frost by their breath. They carried stone weapons and wore rough leather garments and barbarous helmets of a lost age of warriors. One giant was standing with his arms akimbo while the other smashed a swath through the trees. Their small heads were inclined; they were carefully searching the ground. They cast about like hunters after the hare, poking with their clubs and walking softly. Then they shouldered their cudgels and passed swiftly, uprooting a few trees for practice. Their glancing eyes filled the air with snow and their breath was like the coldest night in deepest winter.

When the ground stopped trembling underfoot, the companions began breathing again. Kilgore murmured, "Those were larger frost giants than the one old Mord created. Do you suppose these were made by Surt himself?"

"By Surt and Surt alone," Hrafngrimr said. "Such creatures have not been seen on the surface of the earth since the end of the first Fimbul Winter, when there were vast numbers of them."

Kilgore watched the giants making their leisurely way across the landscape until they had crossed several low ranges of mountains and disappeared into a storm cloud. "Say, look at that!" he exclaimed, seeing something else now that the land had darkened. "I see a light!"

"A light? In this land? Impossible!" Skanderbeg said. "Hardly anyone can have a fire or it draws evil beasts. Where is it?"

"There in that thick patch of woods ahead."

"I knew there had to be people left!" Asny said, crunching Kilgore in a breathless hug. "All my people are waiting for us to lead them to the final battle with Surt."

"It may be only a woodcutter," Hrafngrimr suggested cautiously. "Or an air vent for the Dark Alfar. We better be careful."

"I'm certain it's a good sign," Asny said, striking off into the darkening woods toward the light.

CHAPTER 14

By the time they reached the light, they were swallowed up in the thick of the Gardar night. No stars or moon cast the least particle of light, and distantly they heard the howling of vargulfs and crashing which may have been frost giants. They blundered right into the dooryard of a rude little hut with firelight pouring from its open door.

"Hello! Anybody home?" Skanderbeg called.

At once about twenty dogs rushed out of the hut and from under it, baying at the tops of heir lungs. A head with a long waggling beard peered warily from the doorway. It bellowed, "Down, you curs! Quiet there, you mongrels! Peace!" When the clamor continued, the fellow sprang out and began vigorously laying about on all sides with his staff. Chastened, the dogs crawled back to their places, still growling and whining.

"Now who's out there that causes such a din?" demanded the man, twirling his staff very capably.

"Just a few homeless wanderers in need of refuge," Skanderbeg said.

"Ha! More than likely you're wizards, come to pound out my brains, burn my hut, and seize my meager property. In days like these, a wise man trusts no one." He planted himself in the doorway of his miserable hut and looked ready to defend it to the finish.

"We're just as unfortunate as you, friend," Skanderbeg began.

"All the more reason to distrust you!" was the sharp reply. "Begone, or I'll call the dogs."

The dogs whined and yelped and crept out of their hiding places with bushy tails awag.

"My good man," Hrafngrimr said, "we are not the least bit interested in your hut and food. We have lost the road following your light. Set us right and we shall be gone."

"Get off my property. I shall tell you nothing. Your days are numbered, you brigands, you wizards. A king is on his way here to return the Wolfgangers to the throne of Gardar, and there's nothing you can do to stop him. The Alfar have returned, just as they promised they would to our grandsires. Faugh on you, wizards!" Boldly he twirled his staff over his head and took a step forward.

"Wait, Njal!" cried a voice in the hut behind him. "Remember what the swineherd said. He said the new queen of Gardar would be barked at by dogs, and driven out as a beggar and a thief before she assumes the crown. Mark me, Njal, the dogs never created such a howl over the other bandits, and they're whining still. And the swineherd is not often wrong."

The woodsman hesitated. "Come into the light," he commanded.

The travelers stepped forward, and the dogs came whimpering out from under the hut and crouched fawningly at their feet, bushy tails beating the ground humbly.

"Schimmel—Schmeil—anyway, the swineherd said the dogs would know the queen," the voice in the hut said, and they saw that it was a woman. She stepped forward. "Everybody knows that the evil folk can't fool hounds," she said.

"But still it may be some kind of trick," Njal. mused. "Show me some sign that you are the travelers the swineherd told us about."

"Aye, tell us the name of the swineherd," added the woman.

Kilgore felt the others looking at him. That name! He touched the old silver horn, and the name returned to him in a flash. "Schimmelpfinning!" he almost shouted. "And I have his silver horn, which he gave me with the promise of aid should we need it. Now let us pass, kind guardians."

"Nay, not by the beard of Elbegast," the woodsman said. "You shall stay the night here. That is, if you don't find my hut and provender too humble, since I suspect the young woman is the Wolfganger princess."

"Humble!" Asny said. "Any house of my countrymen is noble in my eyes. Since I left my mother at Grimshalg during the Wars, I have not slept in a bed except of stones and worries, fearing that there were no true Gardars left to defend the country when I returned."

"Ah! Then you were the princess that Surt held hostage, the beast."

"Best not speak of it, Njal," his wife warned. "It brings 'em every time, like ugly moths to a light."

"Brings who?" Kilgore asked. "We've a weapon that can conquer any creature that comes to harm you."

"Surt's twelve," Njal said grimly. "They know the swineherd's prophecy too. Do come inside, noble guests. Hildegunn makes a fine stew."

"Who is this swineherd?" Asny asked.

"Don't know. He's been here as long as we have, and probably longer. Everyone around knows of him." Njal frowned thoughtfully. "And it may sound odd, but I don't think he has aged a whit since I was a boy. He tells us much of the young queen elect who rode away and never returned, who is the hope and promise of Gardar."

"Aye," his wife said. "Now come inside so we can hide the fire. If they knew we had it, we'd lose half of all we own." She led them inside the hut, where it was warm and orderly. Also it was small, and the four travelers seemed to fill it from ceiling to floor.

Njal and Hildegunn knelt at once and kissed Asny's hands. She told them to rise, adding. "I haven't been crowned yet, my friends. Until then we are all soldiers together and Kilgore is the key figure. It is he who carries the Alfar death to Surt."

"Well then," Hildegunn said, busying herself at the

fireplace. Large steaming bowls of deliciously fragrant stew appeared on the table. "We're safe enough here, for the time being. Njal, close that door and put out some of the fire. It's served its purpose. Let us eat."

"Not I," Njal said, struggling into a huge hide cloak. "I'm off to alert the rest of the Regulars. Now that the wolf has returned to the lair, the foxes are soon to be homeless." Quietly he slipped out into the dark.

"Then there are others," Asny said with a glowing face.

"Oh yes, there are many," Hildegunn said. "From our fathers and grandfathers we inherited the legends, the hopes, and the hatred. Wait until the wolf returns to the lair, they told us, and for all these years we have waited. Few of the ones who truly remember are left. Most are dead, captured in the vargulf spell, or held captive in any of a dozen hateful enchantments. There are some hiding in the hills where Surt and his minions hunt them like animals, but they are a law unto themselves. If you could only know how we hoped and waited and fought off the despair that kills a man's spirit! I can't yet quite believe the queen is here."

Skanderbeg nodded and puffed his pipe. "The wait has been long. You have suffered the most, but there are others in this land who will rejoice when Surt is dead. You are true Gardars and your long vigil and sufferings shall be more than rewarded. I promise."

Hildegunn's eyes filled with tears and she smiled. "Ah, if only you could do one thing for Njal and me. We raised six sons for the return of the Wolfgangers, and every one was taken by Surt from the craddle and enslaved. They now run and howl with the Grimshalg vargulfs. And not only just Njal and me. All the families around have lost their hope, their sons."

Skanderbeg patted her hand and said gruffly, with a terrible frown, "When Surt is slain, all his foul spells will melt like smoke and all will be as it was. And we have come to hasten his death."

"But he can't die," Hildegunn said. "He is not mortal."

"And neither is the death we carry for him," Kilgore said, laying his hand on the golden hilt of the sword.

"Then the old prophecies of the swineherd and others are all true," Hildegunn said, shaking her head. "I scarcely believed it before tonight. I thought the Regulars just a way to stay alive inside. For the first time, I feel as if I shall see freedom. Freedom! To keep what is my own, to have no fear, to know that tomorrow I shall be alive, and no giant or wizard is going to murder me for no reason. Schimmel—the swineherd tells us that Surt has been warned of an Alfar death. Is this sword—?" She didn't finish, but the others all nodded in reply to her question. "Then this is cause for celebration," she said, and produced a stone flagon from a secret hiding place in the rush matting on the floor and handed it around. "To the Alfar death!" she declared.

The rest of the evening was spent in amiable chatter, over a golden round of bread Hildegunn took from the ashes. The travelers learned much of the changes wrought in Gardar since the wizards' rule began. Giants were sent out to stalk the land and seize any night-faring peasant, for, as Surt decreed, anybody out at night was conspiring against the crown. Hildegunn went on to tell them that half of everything they produced on their homesteads and granges was paid to Grimshalg as tax. If anyone were remiss in his taxes, his land was appropriated; then, if he were still remiss the next season—which was inevitable without any land—he was done away with, and that was the last of him. The herd of petty magicians that surrounded Surt preyed upon the poor peasants and abused them worse than the mightier wizards. They thought nothing of taking whatever they wanted, no matter how it affected anybody. Surt and his twelve people seldom saw, except in fast-riding processions to or from some mission of destruction. Hildegunn spoke of them with fear and loathing.

They knew something was up, she said, and gave her and Njal little peace. When they decided they had excuse enough, Hildegunn and Njal would disappear too. And already the wizards were suspicious. The least harm the wizards would do was curse their farmlands so that not a blade of grass would show itself. By riding across their fields once, such a crop of thorns as had never been seen would spring up, if they took the notion. The sight of the twelve scarlet-cloaked riders flying across the trackless bogs and fens without leaving a hoofprint or broken stem of grass sent any wise-headed farmer into hiding until they had passed. One nod or evil word and a field would wither.

The tales of dread could have continued far into the night, but Hildegunn shook her head and said. "It's bad luck. It draws 'em. We had neighbors who were too free with what they said. Now there's naught behind but burned wood and thorns and nettles—all plagues on Surt!"

Clean mats and straw were provided for bedding, and the low fire was allowed to burn lower. Hildegunn knew how to make the coals burn all night to warm the house. Smoke, she said, attracted unfavorable attention. In fact, until that evening they never had had a fire blaze enough to show at the door. But the swineherd had directed them to do so and told them once again his prophecy about the dogs and the queen.

After Hildegunn buried the coals in peat, the inside of the poor hut glowed ruddily with a warmth the travelers hadn't enjoyed for days. Before long, Skanderberg's appreciative snores began. All slept soundly on their straw mats until the dead hours just before dawn. Suddenly the dogs began howling dismally, and distantly, like a rattle of thunder, they heard the approach of horses' hooves.

"The wizards!" Hildegunn cried in alarm, running to the door at the sound of a knock. She threw back the bar, and Njal flung himself inside breathlessly, livid with excitement.

"Hide them, quickly!" he ordered, snatching his

longbow and stringing it. "To the cellar! The wizards followed me! This may be the end of it for us, but the plan is working now. Tell them about the tunnel."

Hildegunn pushed aside the rude table and removed a strip of turf, earth side up, which cleverly concealed a narrow wooden door. The tramp of hooves and clatter of harness surrounded the hut outside. A voice shouted, "Halloo, Njal! Open up the door!"

Hildegunn bundled the four travelers into the cellar, together with their mats and possessions and a few things the wizards should not find. The door was closed quickly, the turf replaced, and the table restored to its position. They found themselves in a small underground room. Longbows were standing against the walls and, from the barrows, no doubt, a heap of rusty axes, swords, helmets, spears, and some armor. All glowed briefly in the light of the dragon-staff. Then they waited in darkness.

The horses' hooves were silent. In a moment they heard a powerful thundering knock on Njal's crude door. "Open up, peasant, or we'll blast your filthy hut into splinters," a hoarse voice said above.

"The door is not locked," the calm voice of Njal said.

"Where is the mortal with the sword?" the hoarse voice asked, with no emotion. "He travels with two wizards and a girl and his tracks lead to your door. If you are hiding Surt's enemies, the penalty will be death. Stand aside while we search."

"As you can see at one glance, there is no one in our house but us two," Njal said. "The trail you followed was probably mine. I just returned from some business not a moment ago."

"That is death," the wizards muttered with a sound like dead reeds rustling together. "Conspiring against the crown. Death to him."

"I was doing nothing of the sort. Were I not loyal to Surt and my homeland, I wouldn't remain here so peacefully," Njal said.

"You needn't lie, Njal," Hildegunn spoke up. "We

213

hate Surt and the only reason we survive is because of our hope that someday we'll have our homeland back again. A pox on all wizards! I wish the Alfar death were here in my house and I would summon the sword king to slay the lot of you. When the enchanted Wolfganger queen returns, all of you will be slain and your heads put on the battlements of Grimshalg!"

There was a tight silence above. Then more boots began tramping into the hut, and loud angry voices were raised. With splintering crashes, thumps, and the smashing sounds of crockery, something dreadful happened. Kilgore wanted to snatch the trembling sword from its sheath and spring to the aid of Njal and Hildegunn, but wordlessly Hrafngrimr gripped his arm. The sounds ceased, and the boots trooped outside. Faintly they heard the clatter of armor and harness, then the thunder of hooves, followed by perfect silence.

In silence the company stood motionlessly. Kilgore tugged at Skanderbeg's sleeve and received a sharp nudge in answer. The lighted dragon's head pointed out the narrow earthy tunnel leading from the chamber. Kilgore held back, looking up at the trap door. Asny stood beside him.

"Come on," Skanderbeg whispered.

"Not until we see if they are all right," Asny said firmly.

"As you wish," Hrafngrimr replied, after a pause. "They are your countrymen, after all. And they were helpful."

Suddenly the door overhead was snatched open and everyone started.

Njal's welcome voice cried out, "Well, the rogues are gone. Drat them for the wicked demons they are. I'm sorry this happened. But it's common enough these days. Nobody, nothing is safe. We've learned to hide what we want. And of course we have to conceal the weapons." He held out a hand to help them out of the cellar.

"Very good planning, Njal," Hrafngrimr said, looking back into the dark hole below. "They didn't even suspect you had such a place."

"You certainly saved our lives," Kilgore said, "and the entire plan to save Gardar and the Quarters. Those wizards would have—" He didn't know what they would have done, but he shuddered to imagine the possibilities.

"Yes, they would have, indeed," Hildegunn said. "Curse their cruel hearts! What a menace they've been since they heard you were coming. I almost wish they would get to Grimshalg and begin their dreadful business. My fiery tongue will be the death of us someday."

"What have you heard about their business?" Skanderbeg asked.

"Not much, but what we have is from good sources. Surt is preparing a great spell in Grimshalg. We don't know what it could be, but I'm sure it will far surpass any of the sorrow he's inflicted upon us so far."

"A shrewd guess," Skanderbeg grunted. "We know his spell—from the best sources that are."

"The Alfar?" Njal asked quietly, and Skanderbeg nodded. Hildegunn almost burst into tears of joy.

"It's been so long since we've had any news from the Alfar!" she said. "We feared they'd left us. Now tell us what they said."

"It's worse than anything you would suppose," Hrafngrimr said, speaking for the Alfar. "Surt is casting an enchantment to return the Fimbul Winter."

"I've heard of it," Njal said levelly. "That means the death of the sun, and every decent living creature on the earth. How could he be so vile?" He sighed tiredly and sat down on the one unsmashed chair in the wreckage of his house. "What shall we do? We have an army all ready and waiting, but you can't fight darkness and cold with spears and swords. We were foolish to think that our weapons could drive Surt away, I guess."

"Now don't get discouraged, or we're beaten before we've tried," Asny said, righting the table. "How many fighters can we count on?"

215

"Twenty longbows, thirty spears and lances, eighteen broadswords and axes, fifty with slings and stones, and perhaps a hundred with clubs, knives, flails, hooks —whatever they can lay their hands on."

"No horsemen?" Asny asked.

"Horses are rare nowadays. All instruments of war were confiscated, and that included horses," Njal said. "We thought we could do as well or better without them. Our warriors are trained to walk through the woods without a rustle or snapped twig. They can hide like the wild beasts themselves in places where there is no cover. You could walk through fifty of them and not realize it until the single fatal arrow is flown." Njal spoke proudly of his men, and his courage returned.

"A map, if you please, of Grimshalg and the barrow plain surrounding it," Asny said to the wizards.

Skanderbeg unrolled his map with a flourish, and Asny took charge of the planning. "You must send out the call at once, Njal, to advance to Grimshalg. On this side of the Grimstrom we shall meet and scatter in a chain around the fortress so not one wizard shall escape after Kilgore kills Surt. On this side is a secret tunnel entrance which we'll have to watch carefully, so we shall place your stealthiest spies there. And on this side—" In no time the map was covered with chips and pebbles and moved from place to place until Grimshalg had fallen a dozen times.

"Fall indeed," Skanderbeg said, his eyes great pits of shadow. "I've translated the runes on the old silver horn, and it is indeed Wulther's horn. I remember an old riddle about an Alfar horn: 'What sounds thrice, what sounds elven, what sounds the end of the rule of ice?' The answer of course was Wulther's horn, but he was killed, unfortunately, and buried before we could devise an experiment. But a direct descendant of his such as Kilgore might be capable of the same effect."

"It's an old riddle," Hrafngrimr said. "Something to do with old spring rituals. Odd you should remember it. What do the runes say?"

" 'Thrice the silver throat shall sound to bring the

Alfar hosts around,' " Skanderbeg read. "There's another line, but it's too dim to read. I tell you, this has to be Wulther's horn. Your old swineherd said three mots would bring help, and Alfar horns have supernatural carrying abilities. Blow this three times, and perhaps we'll be summoning Elbegast from his hiding place to battle for us when we need him the most."

Kilgore took the battered old horn and held it in his hands. "I'd like to believe it, but it would be difficult to count on a miraculous reappearance of the Alfar when we haven't seen hide nor hair of one since we left Shieldbroad. Except Hrafngrimr, of course, and I don't count Eldjarn and his crew. We could have used a lot of help, many times. Where is Elbegast, and why hasn't he helped us?" He looked straight at Hrafngrimr.

The only answer was silence and a shrug. "It does no good to speculate," Hrafngrimr said. "Elbegast will appear when the time is right."

The plotting ended at midnight and the travelers slept until dawn. Hildegunn prepared an ample breakfast and filled their packs with almost all her meager stores, sending them on their way cheerfully, insisting that she would be repaid when Grimshalg fell.

"Bless you," Asny called from the edge of the clearing. "You shall be repaid a thousand times when I am crowned queen."

The new day was more somber than the one before. Quickly they lost themselves among the trees, traveling with light steps until they found the road again. Asny strode along with her own thoughts for company and Kilgore felt a widening gulf between her and her companions. Once Surt was slain, she would become a queen and Kilgore would go back to Shieldbroad and obscurity. For the first time Kilgore realized the journey was almost over. Then there would be nothing to hold their group together any longer and they would all part forever. All he would have left were a lot of stories to tell and his walking muscles.

He glanced around appreciatively to remember the

moment, and instantly noticed the great white shapes towering above the treetops over them.

"Skanderbeg! Frost giants!" he whispered sharply.

"Great Hod," the wizard breathed, stopping in his tracks. "We almost walked right into them. Everyone hold still and don't make a sound. I think they'll pass if we don't show ourselves. Giants are lazy louts when it comes to pursuing unseen quarry. But if one spots you, it's all over, particularly if he had a sweet tooth."

"You mean they just eat people?" Kilgore whispered.

"Yes, and in an instant," Skanderbeg said.

"With great relish," Hrafngrimr added. "Although two fire wizards would give them a whopping case of indigestion."

They hid themselves in a tangled deadfall and waited. The ground thumped and trees gave way with groaning, rending sounds. Suddenly a monstrous pair of legs and feet came crashing through the wood. A voice that dwarfed the thunder bellowed, "They're in here! I can smell them and hear them rustling like mice. Get on the other side of the thicket and walk toward me. We'll flush them out, by gore!"

The trees seemed to be flattened by a tremendous icy wind as the frost giants smashed their way into the wood. The sounds came from all sides at once.

"Run!" Skanderbeg was preparing to utter a spell. "I'll divert their attention. Go on, I'll catch up."

"We'll stay or fly together!" Kilgore said.

"Better one of us than all of us be eaten," Skanderbeg replied. "Now get you gone before I turn you into something! Scat!"

Kilgore sprang to his feet as the mighty feet shuffled closer. He drew the sword and gave a shout. "Kildurin! Giants ho!" He dashed at the huge gaitered leg that stood before him like a tree trunk. The sword sang gleefully as he swung on the leg, hewing at it fiercely. The giant howled suddenly and the leg was snatched away in two monstrous hands. Kilgore thrust at the other leg, and barely avoided being crushed as the first came stamping down.

218

"Help, help! Arr!" the giant bawled with a terrific smashing of trees. "They bite or sting with swords like fire! I'm wounded, fatally burned with Alfar magic!" The giant thrashed away, clearing a swath through the forest like a tornado, leaving pools of black ice water behind.

Kilgore stood gasping, both at the sensation he had caused and because he was nearly frozen. Nobody had told him a giant's veins contained nothing but ice, and his blows had melted the giant's icy blood. Freezing water and black slush had almost drowned him. Before he could get his breath back, Hrafngrimr snatched him away, and they all ran as hard as they could until the giant-racket was left behind.

"Wasn't that astounding!" was all Kilgore could say when they stopped. "Ice! And water! Imagine that."

"Well, that interesting discovery could have been the death of us," Skanderbeg snapped, puffing and wheezing and glaring. "Next time let me handle it with simple sorcery!"

"And leave you behind?" Kilgore asked.

Skanderbeg snorted and squeezed the water from his beard. "I am an old wizard and accustomed to taking care of myself. But at any rate, there's one less frost giant in Gardar and one more dump of stone. I only hope we shall be able to find the road again after that disturbance."

Kilgore shivered in his wet clothes but he felt good, particularly when Asny grinned at him and declared, "I thought it was downright bold of you, Kilgore. I longed to do the same thing myself."

"There's the road," the quiet voice of Hrafngrimr said before they had searched very long.

"You seem to know this country rather well," Asny said to him. "I noticed you never were really lost after the giants chased us. I suppose you've traveled through here more than once to visit your friends in Svartheim."

"No, not my friends," Hrafngrimr said. "I don't spy upon my friends. I have been here many times, it is true, in preparation for the day I would lead the sword king through Wolfinden pass to Grimshalg."

"Then lead on," Skanderbeg said. "It looks like a poor day to tread upon Dark Alfar territory, but it can't be helped when there are frost giants hunting for you."

Hrafngrimr took the lead, forsaking the road almost immediately for a small, well-beaten track that wound through the darkest parts of the woods and around the gloomy feet of outcroppings. He paused to listen several times and consult one of his instruments before hurrying onward. Once he led them quickly off the side into the underbrush where they hid while a long file of many pattering feet went by on the path. Not a word was spoken after they came out of hiding. Everyone knew that the Dark Alfar had passed by within touching distance.

At midday they stopped to rest on the windy crest of a rocky ridge. All around them rose eddies of mist. Blue and smokey hills rose from the dark growth of trees like islands in a gray and black sea. On one rough hill, a tower rose from a jumble of black stone, aloof on its high perch above the brume below.

The travelers stared at it silently. The hills it protected rose like battlements as far as they could see. Dimly the road faltered toward Wolfinden, offering scant cover. Anyone traveling that way would be in view for hours from Wolfinden.

"We'll camp as soon as we find a place," Hrafngrimr said. "The day is getting too dark to get any nearer Svartheim. These hills we are in will be quite safe, if we don't light any fires."

It was a silent and uneasy camp. Asny was acting peculiar, as if she didn't trust Hrafngrimr. She kept her hammer in her hand and watched him with the indifferent alertness of a cat watching a bird. When Skanderbeg made the guardian rings around their camp and rolled himself in his blanket to snore, she only wrapped her cloak around her shoulders and didn't move from the spot she had warmed as she sat.

Kilgore noticed and felt uneasy. If Hrafngrimr noticed, he wasn't going to comment on it. He sat on the other side of the camp facing her and smoking his pipe in the clammy darkness. Kilgore watched them until he couldn't stay awake any longer and fell into a restless doze filled with unpleasant dreams.

In the morning he was awakened by a great debate between Skanderbeg and Hrafngrimr. They were stooping over something on the ground and consulting a variety of devices while Asny circled the camp warily with the hammer in her hand.

"What is it?" he asked her without much interest. For an answer she pointed to the damp earth, beckoning him to see for himself.

What he saw was footprints, large bare footprints that came from several pairs of feet that had prowled all around their camp in the shelter of boulders and clumps of brush.

"There were about ten more hiding behind that outcropping," Asny said, nodding toward a hump of rock not a good bowshot away. "And they had weapons. I found this snagged in a bush." She held up a broken piece of feather that had been trimmed for fletching an arrow.

Kilgore went to peer over Skanderbeg's shoulder as the wizard was passing a small glowing disk back and forth over a footprint.

"Not an hour old," grunted the wizard. "Or at least that's what I thought until Kilgore came and breathed all over my device so it won't react properly. Probably some of those wild Gardars Njal and Hildegunn mentioned. Whoever they are, I don't intend to run into them. Let's strike camp and hie ourselves to Wolfinden with all haste."

Hrafngrimr agreed and began packing up. Asny, however, stood studying the Wolfinden road as it wound across the bald flatlands.

"I don't like this Dark Alfar trail we're on," she said. "The swineherd said to follow the Wolfinden road and that we would have no trouble passing through the ruins. If that is so, why are we muddling around so far from the road where hundreds of Dark Alfar go trooping by all night long?"

"My thoughts exactly," Skanderbeg said worriedly. "But I vote to trust Hrafngrimr. I've never been to Wolfinden since it became a ruin hundreds of years ago, before men landed. Hrafngrimr, say something to alleviate our worries."

Hrafngrimr only shrugged. "There is nothing to be said, except that we are in dreadfully perilous country for those who do not know the ways of the Dark Alfar. You must trust me and believe that I am leading you along the best way possible if we are to pass Wolfinden safely."

"I still don't like it," Asny said, turning away with a scowl. "We shall follow you, but I for one will have my weapon in my hand every instant and I advise everyone else to do the same."

The day was gloomy, with squalls of rain or snow and sailing banks of mist that swallowed up the trail; the Wolfinden rampart, trees, everything was lost in the dripping, clammy cloud. Twice in the middle of a fog interval they had to dive into the scanty cover of rocks and brush while the Dark Alfar clattered by. Kilgore ventured a small peek at them and saw nothing but a long file of small, dark-clad men trotting away into the mist, intent on some business of their own. At his elbow Skanderbeg wore an expression of worried resignation.

Kilgore thought they were traveling with agonizing slowness until suddenly a huge blackness loomed out of the mist not fifty paces away and Hrafngrimr whipered, "There's the path the Dark Alfar use to climb up the rampart. We shall have to hurry, since there's nothing to hide us once we start to ascend."

The path bent sharply around shoulders of stone and squeezed up narrow chutes. In places it was only a series of steps chiseled into the black lava. They crept around noses of rock with unpleasant abysses below and sometimes the track was little more than a scratch on a sheer wall falling away to the plain with not so much as a handhold to break the fall. The mist blew away while they were toiling up the path, revealing a clear view of Gardar that was so depressing and

222

grim that Kilgore was chilled to the heart. Murky forests squatted like black fungus on the hills of gray stone. Rocky ridges like fishbones had been bared on the mountain back by years of wind and storm. Frozen rivers like iron bands bound the land in gloomy silence. The back side of the Trident was veiled in a shroud of murk that was slowly spreading northward.

They gained the summit by midday, which was darker than it had been at dawn. The ruins lay before them, hardly more than grassy heaps where the stone had been grown over and a few crumbling walls with vacant windows. One black tower still stood, and the great arched gateway into the courtyard led them to a field of cobbles with tuffets of dry grass among the stones. They felt no inclination to loiter. Before them lay the vast empty expanse of the barrow plains, once green but now gray and misty. The ship rings of the dead lay in large ovals in a random pattern among the barrows. Kilgore stared in fascination, remembering that these graves had been here at the time of the first landing of men on Skarpsey.

As they silently picked their way among the ruins of great halls with lofty choirs, Kilgore sensed the awesome size of the place when it had still been in use. It looked like a hall of the giants compared to the cozy turf and timber houses built by the coast settlers. He had always supposed in his pride that the Brandstok hall was the grandest and most noble dwelling on Skarpsey, but in comparison it seemed like a tiny place.

"What a doleful spot," Kilgore observed, clutching his cloak as the wind snatched at it wildly.

"And the sooner we're out of here, the better it is," Asny said.

In the lee of a grass-topped wall, Hrafngrimr halted the party and began shuffling maps with Skanderbeg to decide the best approach to the barrow plain and Grimshalg beyond it, while Kilgore and Asny stood guard. To amuse himself, Kilgore looked around the old wall for evidence of the dwellers of such a noble edifice, but found little that wasn't related to small animals and birds. Without losing sight of Skanderbeg and Hrafngrimr, he crossed to another weedy wall and for a moment stepped into its lee to get out of the tiresome wind. Another wall had collapsed in a great slab, slanting at an obliging angle, so he could walk on it to its edge and look over. A smooth look to the earth suggested a path. Perhaps some animal had its den under the slab. He jumped down to peer under it cautiously; as his eyes became accustomed to the dark he saw that the earth had indeed been hollowed out under the slab and there was even a neat wall of stone and mortar. In amazement, he stared at it, wondering if his eyes were tricking him. Next he discerned a low door with a large brass handle and three short steps leading down to it. He hesitated, wondering if such a small and humble abode could be part of Svartheim, which seemed very unlikely. It could be the home of more survivors like Njal, or most likely it was only an abandoned cellar. Abandoned places always fascinated Kilgore, so in a moment he was down the steps and pulling the brass handle.

To his surprise, the door fell inward instead of outward and he felt hands grasp his wrists and yank him inside before he could open his mouth to shout a warning. The door slammed shut with a crash. Kilgore leaped to his feet, drawing the humming sword. It flashed in the half-darkness, showing him a rude little room of beaten earth not quite as nice as the troll hole. He also saw five crouching figures lined up against the door staring at him in disbelief, their eyes flinty with hatred. Then, with a chilling yell and a clashing of swords, all five attacked. With one stroke Kilgore shattered two swords, and the next silenced forever one fellow with an axe. The remaining four backed away for a whispered consultation. At that moment a distant clamor came from the direction of the back of the room and Kilgore realized there was a tunnel behind him. Whirling around, he saw a glow bobbing toward him and heard the racket of many feet approaching. Dark Alfar. He knew it now. Drawing the sword, he waited.

CHAPTER 15

The bearer of a torch flung himself into the room, leaping back with great agility when he saw Kilgore and the sword. "It's one of the barbarians!" he called back to the main body.

"Barbarian yourself," Kilgore challenged. "Stand aside or I'll carve right through you and your door, and woe to the one who tries to stop me." He flashed the sword and advanced upon the party guarding the door. They cowered but did not retreat.

"It's a wizard," one said.

"No, not a wizard, a mortal," Kilgore said. "But this sword has powers. It is singing for the blood of Dark Alfar and all other wicked creatures who follow Surt."

"Peace, peace!" a placating voice cried. "We mean no harm to you. My name is Gorm and you have my word we bear you personally no grudges. Will you please sheath that dreadful weapon so we can converse like intelligent beings?"

"We have nothing to converse about," Kilgore said. "I'm leaving, if I have to slay the lot of you. If you want to live, you may get out of my path." He menaced the group at the door again.

"Oh, surely there's no need for this unpleasantness," Gorm said anxiously, coming into the light to wring his hands and wrinkle up his large bald forehead. He was a very ugly little brute, with liver-colored spots on his face and hands, large teeth, and small sly eyes. He grimaced at Kilgore and said, "Can't you just accompany me peacefully to my conference room and we shall discuss this misunderstanding?"

"I have no intention of doing such a thing," Kilgore

declared. "I know who you are. Dark Alfar, who are my enemies and Elbegast's."

Gorm sighed and rubbed his hands together nervously. "It grieves me to hear you speak of enemies, but it is to be expected. I fear you may need some persuading before you'll do what you know you ought to. I beg of you to put away that terrible instrument and come along quietly. I assure you that we wish you no evil."

Kilgore shook his head. "I can walk away from here any time I choose. There is no way you can stop me. Do you think I'm a fool?"

The Dark Alfar smiled ruefully and sighed. "Yes, I'm afraid I do." He removed a small wand of wood from his sleeve and held it aloft. "Do you know what this is?"

Instantly the sword's light was snuffed out and it became leaden in Kilgore's hands. Kilgore stared at it in horror. "What have you done?"

Gorm patted the wand in his palm. "Mistletoe. It's the bane of Alfar things. As you know, Baldur, the god of light and beauty, was killed by his blind brother Hod with an arrow of mistletoe. You are properly amazed; this is the greatest secret Elbegast had, until we discovered it through the services of a talented spy. You know him, I believe. It was Hrafngrimr, who led you here with so much care. Eldjarn tried to warn you, bless him for an honest soul, but you and your friends insisted upon trusting him. Hrafngrimr became a Dark Alfar with us many years ago. He has attained a very high rank already. Why, it is rumored that Surt is considering him as an alternate to his Twelve. Had you asked anyone this side of the Trident you would have learned the fame of Hrafngrimr as an ice wizard."

Kilgore was almost reeling with the shock. With trembling hands, he put the sword into its sheath. He might have used it as an ordinary sword, but it was tremendously heavy now, and in any case he was no match for about twenty practiced Dark Alfar. Taking a deep breath, he looked squarely at Gorm and said, "All right, now what do you want? Don't try to deceive me with a lot of talk about meaning no harm.

226

I know your intentions are evil, or you wouldn't be a Dark Alfar."

Gorm shrugged and held out his hands suppliantly. "Please give us a chance, young fellow. We only do what we must do with our lives, you know. Once you learn this fact, everything is much easier. Now please follow me. I believe you'll find Svartheim quite interesting."

Numbly Kilgore followed, stooping slightly in the low tunnel. It soon led into a vast underground amphitheater hollowed out by the Dark Alfar. A balcony of stone ran all around the edge; when Kilgore looked over it his breath was taken away. A bottomless semi-dark pit bored straight down into the earth, with a spiral roadway following it down. Torches spaced at intervals lit the road with a smokey red light, and thousands of Alfar were toiling upward with huge baskets of ore on their backs or hurrying briskly downward with empty baskets. Kilgore could not see as far as the bottom.

"We have always been miners," Gorm said pleasantly. "From the very beginning we have had a great love for treasure. This is not a very good mine you see here. We've gotten little out of it for all our trouble. If Surt's plan works this time, he has promised us unlimited privileges for mining on the surface. It gets dreadfully hot down at the botttom. In one spot we have actually tapped the fire in Muspell's kettle. A few specialized Alfar have adapted to the terrible heat, but the rest of us can't exist beyond the two-hundred-and-sixtieth spiral. Of course no one can get very near the molten rock itself, which is at the bottom of a long shaft on the two-hundred-and-sixtieth spiral. I shall show it to you tomorrow."

"Halloo, Gorm! More barbarians and wizards!" a messenger shouted trotting importantly toward them with a torch. "And Hrafngrimr has returned to Svartheim with them. He asks to see you immediately."

"Send him here at once," Gorm said with a wide grin. "He will want to bid his friends farewell, and they no doubt will be glad to see him for the last time."

Kilgore was unable to speak. Asny and Skanderbeg were led into the mine amphitheater by a crowd of

Dark Alfar. Skanderbeg was bound with thin cords and Asny was without her hammer. Hrafngrimr followed at a distance, half-concealed in the shadows.

"So this is where friendship gets us," Skanderbeg said angrily. "Bound with mistletoe in the hands of Dark Alfar. Eldjarn didn't have his head on backwards after all. Kilgore, this is all my doing. If I had been the least bit cautious, I could have foreseen everything, but I was deceived by a great deceiver."

Gorm smiled almost sympathetically. "You needn't blame yourself, Skanderbeg. Hrafngrimr is a master of lies and deception. He could deceive even me, I fear. But it was a wonder that he could fool you, Skanderbeg. I've admired you ever since you came into your own as a fire wizard."

"I imagine!" Skanderbeg snorted.

"But it's true," Gorm insisted. "All the Dark Alfar remember how you diverted the River Rang so it would flood our fire holes, and it was you, of course, who devastated our stronghold in the Ragnhold, and a thousand other exploits that proved most costly in lives and gold. Were it not for you, our realm would be much more powerful and widespread than it is. That is the reason we are so utterly pleased to entertain you and your guests in Svartheim. Who would ever have dreamed that we would have such an honor in this humble fortress?"

"Who indeed?" Skanderbeg snapped. "I would have come sooner, but you never sent me an invitation. Before I leave, I hope to see you roasting on skewers over the fires of Muspell."

"I'll remember your words," Gorm said, bowing low and smiling. "If I am not mistaken, we shall see much of the fires you just mentioned. I hope you are not too distressed by the heat here. By tomorrow you should be more accustomed to it. The sword of Elbegast should be glad to return to a place so like its birthplace."

"Then you're going to melt it in the fires of Muspell?" Kilgore demanded, grasping the dead hilt.

Gorm rubbed his hands together apologetically. "Is

228

there any other fire hot enough to destroy it? Now we have discussed unpleasant things enough. Come, you can refresh yourselves before the feasting begins. For tonight, you are honored guests in Svartheim. It's not every day we are favored by the presence of the most famous of the fire wizards and the sword king of Elbegast and the nobility of Gardar." He made a bow to each one as he spoke.

"Not yet nobility," Asny said haughtily. "I shall be the next queen as soon as I am crowned. By then you shall be food for the ravens."

"Who knows? Perhaps I shall," Gorm said cheerfully, leading the way with a brisk pattering of feet. "No one knows what Fate shall deal him next. It is an intriguing topic for discussion. We'll have to discuss it tonight over dinner."

The rooms they were taken to were the private chambers of Gorm himself. Two guards took the sword from Kilgore and staggered with its cold weight to a table where it was placed with Asny's hammer and Skanderbeg's battered satchel. Kilgore watched narrowly, wondering if he should attempt to rush the table and seize the sword, and whether or not it was still impotent from the effects of the mistletoe. More of the hateful stuff was placed near the weapons when Skanderbeg's bonds were removed.

Kilgore was only half aware of the darkly sumptuous furnishings of the room. Gorm and Skanderbeg sat down beside a small fire, chatting companionably like old friends. As for following or participating in the conversation, Kilgore was too upset to be coherent. He could dwell upon nothing but the treachery of Hrafngrimr.

"How could he do such a thing?" he muttered to Asny, smoldering beside him.

"I had my suspicions," Asny said, "and I didn't act upon them. It was more my fault than anyone's. I just had a feeling he wasn't to be trusted when he seemed to know Wolfinden so well. Now we know why."

"If I hadn't found that tunnel entrance and gone blundering into it, we wouldn't be here," Kilgore said in misery. "We would have gone right into the barrow plains as we should have. I suppose after they captured me, they rushed right out and grabbed everyone else."

"Aye. Only they hailed Hrafngrimr as a comrade instead of tying him up with mistletoe." Asny sighed and clenched her hands. "If ever I get the opportunity, you can be sure there will be one less traitor in Svartheim when I get through."

Overhearing, Gorm turned and said, "Traitor, you say? Isn't that rather a harsh word for one who is only doing his duty, as he sees it? Hrafngrimr is a rare and valuable pawn in this great battle. One doesn't find a truly dedicated turncoat often these days, for a decent price. But for this secret, it was worth twice what I had to pay him." He held up the wand of mistletoe. "The only mistletoe in Skarpsey, and I possess it. I hope it shall become much more abundant—one arrow for every Light Alfar heart."

Skanderbeg puffed his pipe, eying the smoke rings he blew from time to time. "I suppose there's a catch somewhere, Gorm. How do you know the mistletoe isn't the bane of the Svartalfar also? After all, Light and Dark Alfar have the same origins, much as you hate admitting it. Don't you rather suspect it would be a good idea to drop that stuff into the fiery pit before it damages Svartheim?"

Gorm turned away to hide a quick scowl. He studied the slender wand of wood. "I shall take precautions. You needn't suppose I haven't thought of all this already."

"No, indeed. I'm sure you already realize you don't want it spread throughout Svartheim, or your willing workers might decide to act for themselves and take a larger share of the loot they dig for—and perhaps dispose of any petty despots in their way."

Gorm seemed to swell with indignation. "They won't get it, not so much as a single leaf. Only Elbegast, Hrafngrimr, and I know about the powers of mistletoe, and I have plans for Elbegast and Hrafngrimr, you can be sure of that." He was so angry he knocked a cup to the floor with a loud, unnerving clatter.

"Magical powers slipping already, eh?" Skanderbeg appraised him critically. "It's the mistletoe, isn't it? Getting to you so soon, and nobody knows if its reversible. Pretty soon you may be absolutely powerless. Rather a high price to pay for your part in bringing down the Fimbul Winter. Surt won't have much use for powerless drones."

Gorm tried to smile through the ugly, angry flush that dyed his blotchy skin. "Then I shall dispose of the stuff. Just as soon as I've destroyed the three of you and that hateful sword."

Kilgore bestirred himself from his gloom. "I wonder whose side Hrafngrimr is really on. Seems as if he's plotting against both Elbegast and Gorm."

Gorm leaped to his feet and stalked to the door. "You must excuse me. There's something I must see to." He shut the door and summoned another guard for the outside.

"He looked upset about something," Skanderbeg said. "I wonder if he's going to an assignation or an assassination?"

They said no more until the festival of the Dark Alfar had begun. In a great, gloomy, natural cavern in the earth they convened, with tables for the feasting and platforms for the honored guests and musicians. Torches glowed eerily through the stone formations with strange phosphorescence. The prisoners were seated in heavy, carved chairs on the dais of honor, and Gorm sat between Skanderbeg and Kilgore, glorying in the adulation. For the occasion, he had lent his prisoners splendid black cloaks of the finest stuff, trimmed in the Dark Alfar tradition with red and gold. They made a wonderful spectacle for the scores of Dark Alfar that presented themselves under the direction of their captains, making low obeisances and staring respectfully at the Alfar weapons displayed for public view.

After hours of feasting, which Kilgore and Asny took no part, the speeches began, with much enthusiastic applause and cheering, but Kilgore was unable to listen. Yearningly, he looked at his sword. He jumped

231

when Gorm whispered in his ear, "A great pity, is it not? To be forged with so much trouble and never used. If only we could be sensible about the whole matter."

Kilgore drew away with a shudder. "You needn't even think about getting me to give you the runic key. I simply won't, so don't waste your breath."

Gorm puckered up his head in sorrow. "Such a great waste, though. Since you are doomed, would it not be a good idea to leave the sword to the rest of the world, just to keep things interesting? Perhaps Surt needs to know that somewhere there is a weapon to control him if he oversteps himself after the Fimbul Winter. Perhaps there is someone who doesn't believe Surt will be a good ruler after he takes control, although he is the only one who can bring down the Fimbul Winter. When his purpose is fulfilled, perhaps it would be well if we got rid of him again."

"That will be your problem," Kilgore said.

Gorm said no more to Kilgore. He sat with his chin on his fist in deep thought until it was his turn to speak. He gave a long-drawn-out oration that aroused little enthusiasm from the audience, who were mostly asleep by this time. Kilgore had never seen such a frightful collection of misshapen heads, blackened faces, burned faces, colorless faces, and hideous blotches. Their appearance was nothing like the refined Alfar of Eldjarn; they were more like trolls from their greedy moiling for gold.

Kilgore cast his eyes upward to avoid the awful spectacle. The murky torches sputtering among the rock formations threw little light, but that probably seemed like blinding brilliance to the Dark Alfar's unaccustomed eyes. As he gazed upward at the unseen dome of the cavern, he thought he saw a movement near one of the torches. Searching for it again, he saw something else he hadn't noticed before. Against the blackness of the cave he saw a streak of gray light from the outside; there was an opening up there somewhere that might be reached by climbing; also, dawn was not far off and the march to the bottom of the pit was all too near. He managed to nudge Asny and convey his knowledge to her. Her eyes widened and grew dark with thought; but with thousands of Dark Alfar surrounding them, there seemed no opportunity for escape.

Suddenly he noticed that the chamber was beginning to empty. From the sounds, Kilgore realized the Alfar were trooping down into the spiral pit to witness the burnings.

"And now it is time," Gorm said, rising from his chair. "Follow me, comrades. Under different circumstances we might have been friends."

"Never," Asny said.

"Our friends and the enemies of Dark Alfar are often hard to distinguish," Skanderbeg said. "But all I ask is that my staff be in my hand when I am cast over the edge. I couldn't bear to see it destroyed first."

Solemnly, the procession wound downward, with some Alfar carrying torches so the lights swirled down like pearls diminishing in the blackness. The air became difficult to breath and increasingly sulfurous. Thousands of Dark Alfar were crowding each level as Gorm and the prisoners descended, rustling like dead leaves as they craned to see the victims. The farther they descended, the more blotched and blackened the faces that watched.

When the air was acrid and searing to the lungs, they reached the bottom at last—the two-hundred-and-sixtieth spiral. The heat was almost insufferable. Everything glowed red as if molten, bathed in the fiery light that glared from the bottom of a large vertical shaft.

Kilgore kept one hand in front of his face to shield his eyes from the glare, but his skin still felt dry and seared. Touching a silver button on the Alfar cloak Gorm had given him, he jerked his hand away and put a blistered finger in his mouth. Beside him, Asny had her eyes closed, her face very red in the fiery glow. Skanderbeg's hair stood out in a halo around his head as he watched the sword and hammer and his staff and satchel being brought down the ramp to the final level.

Gorm was rubbing his hands together and grinning, not noticing the terrible heat. "At last we're ready," he said in a dry voice, and the great pit became hushed except for the muted hissing and burbling of the fire. Gorm held aloft the wand of mistletoe with a beautiful smile on his face. "This is the most glorious hour for Svartheim," he said in ringing tones, that somehow sounded flat in the intense atmosphere. "The world will not forget this day, when Elbegast was confounded by the revelation of his long-kept secret, which now reposes with me and which I shall make known to every Dark Alfar for his own benefit in the war against the Light Alfar. The secret lies in this wand of wood—"

"Your honor, I wish to speak to you immediately!" came an imperative voice from one of the side tunnels. A dark figure hurried forward.

"Later, Hrafngrimr! Begone, deceiver, and don't trouble me again," Gorm snapped. "You've been paid for your services, a little too well if you ask me."

Hrafngrimr replied bitterly, "Is that the way it works? You take all the glory and I am forgotten? Was it not I who brought you Elbegast's secret, which you never would have discovered yourself?"

"Take yourself away, traitor, or I shall have my guard remove you with force," Gorm said. "And don't let your face be seen again in Svartheim. I still cannot trust a traitor and a spy, even one of my own."

"Is that the way it stands? Then you shall die with that precious secret of Elbegast!" Hrafngrimr leaped forward, his sword flashing in his hand. After a brief scuffle, Gorm uttered a shrill shriek, staggering and collapsing to his knees at the edge of the pit. His hands scrabbled desperately, shoving Kildurin toward the fire. Everyone who was near enough to see what was happening was too paralyzed with shock to move, except Kilgore. He flung himself forward and seized the sword in both hands before it could fall.

Then Gorm's guards and retainers rushed forward with a furious roar, axes upraised. Hrafngrimr grappled with Gorm, who was feebly croaking the word "Mistletoe," but no one could hear above the sudden pandemonium. He struggled with something in one of his pockets as Hrafngrimr bore him steadily nearer the edge of the abyss. Suddenly the wand of mistletoe popped from his pocket and fell to the earth, eluding a dozen hands that pounced after it, and tumbled over the edge into the fire. Gorm shrieked, diving into another pocket and pulling out a bundle of rope made of mistletoe, but this time Hrafngrimr gave a tremendous shove, and Gorm toppled over the edge of the pit.

Hrafngrimr whirled around to face the howling mob descending upon him, brandishing his short sword like a cornered rat snapping its teeth. Suddenly Kildurin burst into life as the tide of Dark Alfar almost engulfed Kilgore and Hrafngrimr. Asny dived for her hammer and sent it flying among the attackers, gleefully beating swathes in their ranks. A tremendous yellow flash, followed by a thunderous explosion, sent the rest scurrying from Skanderbeg's wrath and from a hail of swords and spiked maces. In the brilliance Kilgore saw the Dark Alfar fleeing up the ramps, completely routed. He also saw half a dozen tall, bearded mortals swinging swords against the hardy few who stayed to fight. A strong hand caught his arm and a voice shouted in his ear, "Follow us if you want to escape alive! They'll turn in a moment!" and he was forcibly towed toward a side tunnel. Several small horn lamps bobbed ahead of him and his rescuer, and he was satisfied when he recognized Skanderbeg's white beard and Asny's hammer flashing as she struck a Dark Alfar out of the way.

They raced in silence up the winding tunnel until their lungs were bursting, stopped several times to fight where other tunnels intersected, and at last they stumbled into the silent coolness of the huge natural amphitheater where the celebration had been held. Pausing only to count themselves, they began climbing up the flowstone and wedging their way up fissures. The small horn lamps lit the way dimly, but Kilgore was not aware where he placed his hands and feet; he climbed in silent desperation after the others. Far below, he heard the sounds of pursuit, resounding from

235

all sides of the cave until he was sure there were Dark Alfar above and below and beside him. From somewhere ahead there came a flash of purple light and something zipped past Kilgore to explode below with a splendid, fiery report. The fire did not go out, but grew instead into a huge, serpentine lingorm with orange scales and an eye that darted fire. Immediately it fell upon the swarming Dark Alfar, greedily collecting every bit of gold it could see, and finally slithered off down a tunnel in quest of more.

The next thing Kilgore knew, he was stumbling along a low passage, bumping his head at every step and tripping over rocks in the blinding light that poured in from the sky. Someone caught him and half dragged him over the rocks until suddenly they were running down a prickly slope in the murky, red glow of a Gardar dawn. Six tall, bearded men loped along with them, bearing swords and bows pilfered from Svartheim. Skanderbeg slowed to watch behind them as the great serpent set up housekeeping in Svartheim. Dark Alfar stumbled out of a dozen entrances, some perishing instantly in the red glow of the sun, others finding their way into the shelter of a rock or fallen wall. For a moment Kilgore had a glimpse of glowing orange scales as the lingorm slithered out of the cave they had just left, but a word from Skanderbeg sent it back.

"I raised that one from just a little fellow about a foot long," Skanderbeg said proudly. "He's just a puppy yet, but well trained."

"A real lingorm!" Kilgore puffed. "Do they really get bigger with every bit of gold they have, or is that an old wives' tale?"

"Old wives aren't so misinformed," the wizard retorted.

The leader of their strange escort called back urgently, "This way and be quick!" Everyone altered his course suddenly to dive into the shelter of a rocky hill. A few arrows clattered on the stones or arched overhead harmlessly, and the men bent their bows to send back a similar reply. Kilgore felt a thrill of alarm as he studied them for the first time. They were all larger than most Shieldbroad men and clad in crude hauberks of animal hides. Their feet were bare and as tough as hooves as they ran lightly over the rock and prickly clumps of brush. Their weapons were ancient iron dug from barrows, and some were chipped from stone.

"Skanderbeg, are these the wild men?" Kilgore panted as they ran over yet another hilltop.

One of the fellows heard and laughed. "Yes, we're the wild men of Gardar," he said. "Only a bit better than the Dark Alfar!"

Before Kilgore could reply, they were trotting downhill into a large camp. Cooking fires pencilled smoke lightly into the sky and a score of small children snatched up miniature bows and raced silently at the heels of their elders, staring at the newcomers curiously.

One side of the camp was under a natural overhang, where the important men of the tribe waited.

"Well done, Injyald," said the one in the center with silver in his beard. "You have the three important ones. What of the Alfar one?"

Injyald shrugged and Skanderbeg stepped forward. "Hrafngrimr is a traitor. He betrayed us into the hands of his old friend Gorm, whom he also betrayed. Let his name not be mentioned in my hearing, because just the thought of him makes me lose my temper. If I am not mistaken, we owe to you a great debt of gratitude for sending your men to rescue us. To you and to all of them, we extend our most humble thanks and beg that we may serve you in any way." Skanderbeg made a very low bow.

"My name is Skuld," the leader said with a welcoming grin. "Let's not talk of gratitude. We are only too glad to be of service to you for bringing our queen back to us." He knelt and kissed Asny's hand. "We are completely at your bidding, Exalted Lady."

Asny placed her hands on his shoulders. "You, Skuld, shall be my chieftain of the armies. From your years of hardship, wandering through this blighted land, you are as canny as the foxes. I believe you

237

have the look of the Wolfgangers. Was not your grandfather named Hoskuld?"

"Aye, he was. He perished in the Wars when we were driven from our homes. My father Hrosthjof took his family into the mountains along with others who also fled for their lives when the great light of the Wolfgangers was extinguished. I was born in the wilderness. There is not one of us here who was not. Life has been cruel, Exalted Lady. Where once there were thousands of free Gardars, there are now mounds or scattered bones. We wild ones grow fewer every year as the winters and the vargulfs take the weak old ones and the very young. My father told me that the returning queen would be blood kin of mine, which same blood I will gladly shed to see a Wolfganger queen again rule our land." There were tears in his eyes when he finished speaking and the rest of the wild people had gathered round to listen to their leader. Respectfully they bowed and knelt on the ground.

"This winter you will all have houses," Asny said, "and there will not be one vargulf left. We are going to march to Grimshalg and with the sword of Elbegast end the death reign of Surt." Her face shone as she mingled with her people, shaking their hands and learning their names.

Finally the leaders took refuge in the cave and began plotting Skuld's part in the overthrow. Skanderbeg and Kilgore sat down in an honored spot on the ground where the nasty, whipping wind did not reach. It ruffled the shaggy pelts of the wild men as they squatted in rows to listen to the council of war. Wrapped snugly in Gorm's black cloak, Kilgore felt deliciously warm; in half a second, he was asleep against Skanderbeg's shoulder in a pose that looked as if he were deep in profound thought.

When he awakened, the council was over. Guiltily, he wished he had stayed awake for it and taken part, perhaps; but after all, what did he know about warfare? And the sleep had done him good.

"We'll meet again in victory," Asny said, clasping

the huge hand of Skuld, and the rest of the Gardars echoed her words.

Silently, Skuld crushed Kilgore's hand in his own. "We will be at your back all the way to Grimshalg. Our Exalted Lady has told me of your limitless courage in carrying this sword, and I am humbled to meet such a warrior as you. Never as long as I have a tongue to speak and breath for words will I let your fame be forgotten. May the war god go with you, Kilgore of the Brandstok."

Skuld did not waste time trying to persuade them to stay with him, even for the rest of the day. "Enough time and lives have been wasted," he said, adding a few pitiful supplies to their packs. Then he and most of the wild people accompanied the travelers to the next hilltop to see them away. Looking back, Kilgore could see only a rough rocky mountain, but he knew Skuld's people were there, blending perfectly with the rocks and scanty vegetation; and they were watching with hope in their hearts.

As Kilgore turned for one last look, a bush stirred in the wind and seemed to come tumbling down the hillside. It was Injyald, racing after them with the speed and agility of a hare.

"My father Skuld sent me after you to guide you safely to the land of the barrow hills," he said, falling into step with Skanderbeg easily. "It will save you a good deal of time, since we know the land from years of living with it. We've only a few miles to go together."

The arrangement was highly agreeable, and they traveled hard until the sun vanished behind the grim ranks of the mountains. Injyald was enthralled by the everyday magic Skanderbeg used in making guardian rings and cooking fires, so the wizard could not resist a few small tricks like exhaling pink smoke and conjuring huge crackling sparks in his hair and beard.

"I only wish you could conjure this dried meat into the real thing," Asny said with a sigh. "I remember the cattle and the swine and the grain that used to grow in my land. Perhaps in this very spot there was

239

once a field of golden wheat." She rose to stalk about in a fever of impatience.

In the afternoon of the next day, they arrived at the foot of the first barrow mound. Looking back, the hills of Svartheim were misted with rain and distance. Ahead, the white scar of an old road wound among the gray mounds and disappeared in the low-hanging mist.

"That's the road to Grimshalg," Asny said, letting the wind whip her cloak. "It hasn't changed much since I saw it last. Now we are on the old dragon's doorstep. Injyald, I thank you for showing us the way through the hills. You can return our thanks to Skuld."

"Can't I go with you?" Injyald asked wistfully. "You are our queen and I want to fight by your side and die defending you. My father will understand if I don't return."

"No, you must return to Skuld as we agreed," Asny said, unaffected by the admiration in Injyald's eyes. "You are needed far more with him than with us. Your chances of dying in my service are far too great if you go with us, and I would rather be served by a living Injyald than flattered by his memory. Go back, my friend, and we'll meet later. You shall be on my right hand when Grimshalg is ours."

Injyald's disappointed face brightened. Taking Asny's proffered hand, he kissed it, declaring, "We'll meet again in victory!" With his bow over his shoulder, he loped away toward Skuld and vanished into the mist.

"It's an awesome feeling to have an army at your back," Kilgore said as they started on the last miles that would take them to Grimshalg.

"Especially considering," Asny added thoughtfully, "that we only began with a green boy and one burnt-out old wizard and one nuisance of a girl. Probably the improbability of it is what enabled us to get so far into Surt's heartland."

Skanderbeg only snorted indignantly. "I have never at any time considered myself burnt-out."

"I would consider myself frozen, perhaps," Kilgore said through chattering teeth. "This rain is like ice water. Are we going to stand here talking until we're

240

frozen to death or are we going to travel while the light is good on this excellent road?"

The rain did not let up for the rest of the day. They made their camp in it on the leeward side of a large barrow with a flat top like an anvil. Asny said that it was a king's barrow and she could remember attending her mother's coronation ceremonies on its top when she was very young. The wind whistled over it now with a vengeance and slipped around the sides cunningly so the travelers could not make themselves comfortable. Huddling grimly in their cloaks, they resigned themselves to a sleepless night.

"I wish Skanderbeg could conjure us a cozy little house," Asny said, her teeth rattling uncontrollably.

"I'd conjure us a castle in a moment and three goose down feather beds and twenty fires and a dozen roast pigs, but every troll and Dark Alfar this side of the Trident would know about it if we so much as sit on a rock too long and get it warm," Skanderbeg grunted.

"At least Skuld's people are still in the protection of the hills," Asny mused, her thoughts suddenly miles away from her discomfort. "He ought to be at this very spot in six hours, and at the edge of the Grimstrom river by tomorrow—"

Skanderbeg sat up attentively and looked at Kilgore. "Did you hear something? I thought I heard a halloo."

"It's just a barrow ghost," Kilgore said, discovering some warmth in his sodden cloak and burrowing into it. "I didn't hear a thing."

"Nor I," Asny said, "but I wasn't really listening."

"Imagined it, I guess." Skanderbeg unwrapped his head to the teeth of the wind and listened.

"Halloo!"

It came from the top of the barrow mound, too clearly to question. Looking up, they saw a black figure against the bloody sky; or at least it was a cloak flapping in the wind and carrying a staff.

"A shepherd?" Kilgore suggested, stirring himself reluctantly.

"Here?" Skanderbeg snorted. Rising, he took his staff and waited for the strange figure to descend.

241

CHAPTER 16

The stranger advanced slowly, leaning on his staff. He carried no light and they could see nothing of his face. Stopping at a cautious distance, he peered through the gloom at them.

"I'm not hospitable by nature," he called, "but I can't have you freezing on my very steps. My house is small, but I have a fire and it is just over the barrow from here. Come along, it's seldom enough I'm disturbed by travelers." He started stumping back to the top of the barrow as if he didn't really care if they followed or not. At the top he paused a moment until they caught up.

"My name is Vatnarr," he said, his face lurid in the dying light. "I made my house to be near the barrow of the king I am named for."

"Vatnarrsmound. I remember now," Asny murmured, taking a closer look at Vatnarr.

"I ask no questions and I want none asked of me," Vatnarr continued, turning toward the house below. Kilgore could now see that he was rather a short individual, but powerfully built—so powerfully that he had an almost brooding, forbidding appearance. The hand that gripped his staff was easily twice as big as Kilgore's. Kilgore began to feel the stirrings of awe within him.

The house and several barns and small buildings were built into the side of the barrow with turf piled on the roofs. The main house was small, with two rooms downstairs and a sleeping loft above, with a kitchen annex down the passageway. When they entered, Kilgore nearly fell over backward with shock when a female troll scuttled away from her weaving, knocking over her stool with a crash at the sight of the guests. Kilgore touched the sword and found it quivering more violently than he had ever experienced before. Curiously he looked at the small green-eyed creature as she peered at him from the kitchen passage.

"Gillitrut, bring my guests something to eat," Vatnarr commanded. "You may put your cloaks before the fire to dry while we eat." Then they sat down at the table and the troll brought out curd and cream and a thick soup with some sort of meat in it.

"Sit down to your weaving and don't disturb us."

As if there were a conversation to disturb. The meal was eaten in total silence and Vatnarr did not look at his guests. Kilgore stole nervous glances at the curious sight of a troll weaving; he was bursting with questions but he restrained himself. The looks of Vatnarr in full light was enough to quell any man's curiosity. He had a smooth, sharp face like polished stone, with two vertical lines etched permanently in his wide brow. Reddish brown hair and beard framed his piercing eyes of the same peculiar color. When he breathed, his nostrils flared as if he were inwardly suppressing great aversion or anger.

After the meal was finished and the bowls and cups cleared away, there was a long silence. Finally Skanderbeg spoke and Vatnarr did not lift his eyes from his two clenched fists. "We're grateful for your hospitality on a night like this. We've come exceedingly far and we're weary."

"Then you may take your slumber at once. However, I have only one bed, which you shall draw lots for. I myself choose to sleep in the barn."

Skanderbeg bowed gravely. "Thank you for your hospitality. It is a generous host who will give up his own bed to his guest."

"I insist," Vatnarr said shortly. "I never sleep there myself. Whoever draws the short straw shall sleep in the bed." He held up three straws in one massive hand.

Asny drew the short straw. She shrugged and said, "Where I rest my back makes no difference to me, but it has been a long time indeed since I slept in a real bed."

"Then I shall leave you," Vatnarr said. "I must caution you not to open this door before sunrise, no matter who you think may be knocking. This ground is of course haunted by many ghosts. You may think you hear horsemen in the yard, but there will be nothing; if you should hear something, don't show a light or as much as the ends of your noses. If you do, I shall not be responsible for what may happen to you."

"Thank you. We shall not be any trouble," Skanderbeg said.

"Then I bid you goodnight. Gillitrut, attend to the fire and see that it doesn't go out tonight." With a final lowering glare, Vatnarr closed the door and paused to listen while Kilgore slid the bar in place. Then his footsteps went away in the direction of the stable.

Kilgore sighted with relief and exchanged a glance with Skanderbeg. "Not a very genial host, is he?" Kilgore remarked as they stretched their weary bones out to soak up the warmth of a real fire. The troll anxiously poked at the fire, although it was already banked and stoked to perfection.

"You needn't worry," Skanderbeg said to her. "It won't go out. If it does, I'll mend it myself."

Gillitrut clasped her paws and squeezed shut her eyes in a shudder. "I daren't leave it for a moment," she declared, trembling to the tips of her large ears, which were shaped like a cat's. "If it goes out, I'll be in the soup tomorrow, and that's not an exaggeration. The soup tonight was my cousin Bligr, and last week it was a wild troll he trapped on the barrow plain, so please don't suppose he wouldn't really do it."

"Troll soup?" Kilgore said in an odd voice.

"Well, there's nothing to be done about it now," Asny said in a practical manner. "It wasn't bad, you know."

"One has to eat something out here," Skanderbeg said, "and trolls are certainly plentiful enough." With that he rolled himself up in his cloak and sighed blissfully, as if the hearth stone were a feather bed. Gillitrut pointed out the bedroom to Asny, where quite an ordinary-looking bed stood against one wall. The troll then lay down on the mat beside the door.

"What do you think of our host" Kilgore whispered, nudging Skanderbeg.

"A very impervious sort." Skanderbeg yawned. "Go to sleep and forget him. Anybody who eats trolls is bound to get peculiar." The last word became a snore almost before it was spoken.

"Skanderbeg." Kilgore had to poke him sharply.

"What is it?" the wizard growled.

"The sword. It's been having a fit since we arrived here. Do you think it's Gillitrut?"

Skanderbeg was silent a moment. "Could be. Also could be the ghosts Vatnarr mentioned. Be on your guard, Kilgore, and protect us."

Kilgore sighed restlessly. The sword's unease kept him awake; it was quivering and humming insistently as he tried to sleep. Finally he managed to doze off, but a shout from Asny awakened him instantly. Seizing the sword, he thrust open the door, letting the firelight into the room. Asny was trying to light the lamp.

"What's wrong?" he asked.

"There was a cat walking around in the rafters," she said, holding up the lamp to illuminate the ceiling. "Did you see it run out when you opened the door?"

"Cat? No, and there's no cat in here. What harm could a cat do?" Kilgore was on the point of laughing until he saw Asny's face. She was pale with fright and her eyes were wide. "What kind of cat was it? Are you sure you didn't dream it?"

"I heard it rustling around up there, then it jumped down on the bed and sat on my chest," she said in a low voice. "It got heavier and heavier, until it seemed as heavy as a horse. I could scarcely draw a breath to yell. If I hadn't, it would have suffocated me."

Kilgore and Asny looked at Skanderbeg in silence. He glanced quickly around the room. "A sending," he said. "Someone wishes you harm. Was there anything in your hand when you awakened?"

"A piece of straw. Is that what it changed to when Kilgore opened the door?"

"Probably," Skanderbeg said. "You take my place by the fire. I'll lie down in the bed and we'll see if it dares to return." His staff's head glowed a sinister red. "There's something still about."

Asny curled up by the fire, wide awake, staring at the bedroom door. "If that beast comes back, I'll dash him to pieces with the hammer. I'll be listening. If Skanderbeg misses a snore, I'll break that door in. I wish we hadn't come to this place. I'd rather be freezing on the moor than fighting for my life with ghosts and sendings."

Gillitrut stirred on her mat by the door. "Everyone who sleeps in that bed dies by morning," she said apologetically. "It's been so since I came here. If you want to live, you must wear a sheep's rib next to your skin."

"I'd rather have a sword," Kilgore said grimly. "So that's how it is. A sending's bed. How many guests has he offered it to?"

"Many," Gillitrut said with a yawn. "I lost count long ago."

"We'll see how the sending likes dealing with a wizard," Asny said.

The fire died low and Kilgore began to nod and dream. He dreamed he heard horses milling around in the yard outside. One neighed shrilly, which jarred him awake. It was no dream; there were horses and voices in front of the house.

Rising quietly, he stepped over Gillitrut and peered out the crack between the shutters. Three horsemen were riding up the side of the barrow toward a flickering blue light at the top. Kilgore strained his eye against the crack to see better, his heart suddenly thudding. From the ancient folklore of his people, he knew a blue light in a barrow mound meant there was treasure inside. He fumbled for the latch on the shutters to open the window.

"No, don't!" Gillitrut whispered in terror. "He'll boil us all, if he suspects you were looking out tonight of all nights."

"There's treasure up there," Kilgore said. "Who are those men? Treasure seekers?"

She shook her head. "They aren't men. They're wizards, and that is positively all I dare tell you. What are you doing? You're not going to open the door, are you? He'll strangle me for the kettle for sure if he finds out."

Kilgore paused with his hand on the door latch. "Why don't you run away then? There's nothing to stop you."

"And leave this place for a filthy troll hole? I'd rather be stuffed and roasted," Gillitrut said scornfully.

"Then if you are, it is your own choice," Kilgore replied, opening the door. "Asny," he whispered, and she made a noise of assent. "I'm going up there. Let me in again when I knock four times."

"Treasure or no treasure," Asny muttered, "those wizards are three of Surt's and you know it. I wish we had never stopped at this place. I'd get more sleep on the moor in a thunder storm."

Kilgore slipped outside, flattening himself in the shadow of the house. The sword hummed and quivered intensely, with an angry buzzing like disturbed bees and unlike the warning throb caused by Gillitrut. He followed the way the wizards had gone, ducking from shadow to shadow. The wind on the mound whipped at him and stung him with a few pellets of ice as he crouched, listening behind a boulder. Hearing the snort of a horse, he was able to discern the outlines of three horses tied in the shelter of a thicket. He was not far from the top, but the blue light had vanished. Cautiously he crept toward the end of the barrow where he thought the opening should be, shielding his face from the teeth of the wind. It occurred to him that anyone upwind from him might not be able to hear any noise he made as he approached, but it was possible that he would be warned well in advance if anyone was coming.

The wind suddenly carried a voice to him as if it were a disembodied spirit speaking. The words were either garbled by distance and wind or else spoken in a foreign language. Kilgore circled uphill to get the advantage if he had to fight and crouched behind a rock to wait.

Talking with their heads bent low, the three wizards hurried by without glancing right or left, plainly expecting no interference. They seemed to be carrying nothing but the usual staffs and satchels and weapons. Obviously not treasure seekers. They had come here for some peculiar meeting of their own, perhaps with the ghosts of the barrow. Uneasily, Kilgore wondered if he ought to go back. He wanted no dealings in the affairs of the dead.

While he hesitated, the blue light flickered like a bit of flame in a dark recess under a great flat stone. Clutching the sword, which was trembling furiously under his hand, he crept toward the hole and ventured to peek inside. It was, of course, pitch black, and he could see nothing, but he could smell musty air and ancient rotting things. With the sword in one hand partially lighting the way, he slithered inside the small opening without too much difficulty. In the flickering of the sword he saw a small dirty hole, littered with scraps of rotting cloth and wood and what may have been bones. It looked harmless enough, so he boldly crawled all the way inside. In disappointment, he looked around at the muddy walls and stones. There was no treasure here. Skanderbeg would scoff and make testy remarks about wandering around old barrows alone at night in a hostile land. The thought of it suddenly chilled Kilgore to the marrow of his bones. Hurriedly, he groped for the small hole to the outside; but just as he was putting his head through, he heard a sound behind him. Immediately he whirled around, seeing nothing but shadows dancing in the light of the sword, which now set up a fearful warning racket. Something hissed and scratched against stone. Holding up the sword, he could see something move. Two orbs of light gleamed redly from a ledge where crouched a hissing, bristling cat. When he spoke to it and advanced his hand, it gave a wild shriek and leaped over his head like a thing demented. It raced around the room twice and vanished behind a stone. Kilgore investigated with care, not wanting to get bitten; to his surprise he found, not a cornered cat, but a tunnel leading further into the mound. The room he was in was only an antechamber to the real barrow. Rolling aside a few stones, he made the tunnel large enough for him to crawl through and was rewarded with a blast of stale barrow breath in his face. He had been told many times that often men dropped dead the instant they broke open an old barrow from the effects of deadly vapors within. Cautiously he looked through the opening.

The light of the sword flashed into the room beyond with twice the usual brilliance. It commanded him to enter, but he hesitated, staring in awe at the treasure that filled the room beyond. The floor was covered with a jumble of golden things of all sizes: cups, urns, vessels large and small, plain and ornate; helmets and shields, armor, jewelry, and a vast lot more, all tangled together in a glittering carpet of wealth. Kilgore's heart almost stopped beating at the sight of so much gold and silver and jewels. Plunder from all the castles and wealthy houses in Gardar, and probably most of it was the Wolfganger treasury. Never before had Kilgore beheld such a sight. He was about to climb through the hole he had made, when his eye lit upon a stone bier in the center of the room. The corpse of a king lay there, resplendent yet in a scarlet-embroidered gown. The shriveled hands clutched a long bright sword, and all around were the usual elaborately carven wooden carts that once had contained offerings, before the rot had almost consumed them. For a moment, Kilgore had the prickly sensation that the dead king was watching him from the corner of one sunken eye, as if he had little intention of relinquishing his treasure. Quietly, Kilgore withdrew into the antechamber. Hearing a sound in the treasure vault, he looked back and saw the cat sitting fearlessly on the chest of the dead king and eying him with malevolent distaste.

Quickly, Kilgore replaced the stones and crept out the hole back into the wind. He was not entirely sure what it was that he had discovered. Gladly, he let the wind blow the barrow dust off him as he hurried back to the house. He found the door shattered off its hinges.

When Asny answered his knock, he found the house full of sulfurous smoke and Gillitrut was gibbering and moaning from the loft above the room in trollish hysterics.

"You've taken long enough," said Asny in a strained voice. "We've had a rather bad experience. We wished you and the sword were here."

"Pooh, it was nothing so serious," Skanderbeg said, wrapped in a cloak beside the roaring fire and visibly shivering.

Kilgore looked in amazement at the bedroom. All the walls were thoroughly charred and the bed was a pile of smouldering straw.

"The sending descended on Skanderbeg and he blasted it with fire and burned the whole room in the process, but it escaped unharmed," said Asny. "I tried to kill it as it rushed through, but the hammer annoyed it about as much as a gnat would have done. The beast is indestructible."

"Was it the cat again?" asked Kilgore, looking at the door.

Skanderbeg shook his head, looking gray and old. In a low whisper he replied, "It was the flayed bull again, Kilgore. All that saved us was the fact that it seemed to be looking for you. I saw it seeping through the keyhole like a fog and I blasted it with every ounce of magic I knew, but it wasn't even touched. Asny smashed the door, and it charged out at her and went through the outside door and up the side of the barrow. I don't know what changed its mind. You didn't see it as you returned?"

Kilgore shook his head. "I did see the cat, though. It was with me in the mound and that is where I left it. I suppose the cat and the bull are both the same sending. The bull must have visited you while I was climbing the barrow and followed me inside as the cat."

"He did nothing to you?" asked Asny.

"No, just stared and growled, but I thought nothing of it," Kilgore said. "But it must have something to do with the dead king I found inside the mound. I saw the cat sitting on the corpse."

"Vatnarr," Asny murmured, frowning. "There's something familiar about the name. I learned all the kings of Gardar once and there were a hundred Vatnarrs, but one stuck in my mind. A prophecy, a curse—"

"Well, it's not important now," Skanderbeg said anxiously. "What else did you see in that mound?"

"The dead king was holding a sword that wasn't a bit rusty, the way you'd expect, and it had a black hilt. I had the feeling the king wasn't exactly—well, I had the feeling he was watching me. Then the cat sat on his chest and looked at me with real hate, so I left. But the treasure was stupendous. It must have been all the gold of the Gardar kings."

"No doubt it is," Asny said. "And that sword sounds like the one called Tyrfing. It was supposed to have magical qualities and it belonged to the Tyrfingrs, who ruled Gardar before the Wolfgangers. It belonged in my mother's treasury, not in a barrow with a Vatnarr. The Vatnarrs ruled Gardar almost six hundred years ago. There is no way that sword could have been buried with a Vatnarr."

"Then how did it get there, if it is the same sword?" Kilgore asked. "Someone might have placed it there as an homage, perhaps."

"I know Tyrfing was in our treasury," Asny said.

"But knowing who stole our treasury, I can't imagine them putting a sword in the hands of an old corpse. I wish I could remember what I heard about the Vatnarrs."

"It's of little consequence," Skanderbeg said. "What worries me is explaining this mess to the flesh-and-blood Vatnarr when he returns in the morning. We can't say we left a candle burning."

"We'll explain nothing to Vatnarr," Kilgore said. "We're going to leave at once. We may be cold, but we won't be on haunted soil. The sunrise is not far off."

"That's incomparably rude, you know," Skanderbeg said.

"He's not a polite host either," Kilgore said. "He knows that was a sending's bed. If he's just an old eccentric, he'll be glad to see us gone without having to feed us again. I'm not sure my stomach is up to troll stew again anyway." He spoke lightly and began gathering up his tattered pack, aware that he was making an unreasonable request that he had no desire to explain.

"Then let's not waste any time," Skanderbeg said. "Anything is better than a sending's bed and troll soup."

They left Vatnarrsmound with many backward glances, but no one came to pursue them. Not so much as a dog barked. When they had put several hours of fast walking between them and the place, they slowed to an easier pace. The dawn was not far off, what dawn there would be through the clouds and mizzling rain. Wandering among the barrows of the dead on such a gray, miserable day filled Kilgore with gloomy thoughts and forebodings. Often he touched the sword, wondering what the outcome would be when he confronted Surt. Here he was, a presumptuous mortal, daring to challenge the most powerful of all ice wizards—one powerful enough to kill the very sun. Looking at the pallid glow in the east, he thought it might not be much of a battle.

Undaunted by the rain and gloom, Asny led the

252

way with swinging strides, impatiently scanning their course from every rise. With more confidence, she led them from the road up a long, low ridge. When they reached its crest, they saw the land fall steeply away to a low, gray plain, corrugated by black lava flows. A river had carved a deep grave for itself, cutting into the heart of Skarpsey and leaving fantastic shapes in its wake. In the center of the plain stood a large island of black stone, rising from the river like a huge pedestal for the fortress that was built upon it. Banners of mist clung to the spires and pinnacles. It was Grimshalg.

CHAPTER 17

Kilgore lay flat in the dead grass, peering between two crusty bolders. For at least an hour, he had studied Grimshalg as the sky became light. At his elbow, Asny poured out all she knew about the fortress. She was saying, "The island is all made of the black stone that comes from the volcanoes. It is thought that Grimshalg itself is the core of an old volcano that the river discovered and was unable to wash away, so it went all around it. Inside, the whole island is like a honeycomb, with tunnels everywhere and steps made in the stone by all the kings who have lived there. There are many secret entrances and one very large main one that is hidden in the rock. It leads to a tunnel under the river, which is never flooded, even in spring when the ice melts up in the mountains. And the other entrances—but there's no sense wasting time talking about it. You'll see it for yourself when we get inside. Skanderbeg, is it time yet?" she inquired for the fourth time.

Skanderbeg was earnestly consulting some devices. "Well, according to these sensitive and delicate instruments"—he paused to rap one smartly against a rock—"almost any time now they'll come."

"I could have figured that out for myself without any magical instruments," Asny said. "What good is a wizard if common sense—"

"There they are," Kilgore said suddenly, pointing across the plain. A long, ragged, black line was loping toward Grimshalg. As they watched, more shapes appeared from other sides, all bent on the same destination.

"By the great wizard's gizzards," Skanderbeg said. "So this is the migration of the vargulfs. Blow me to Padbury if I've ever seen such a thing in all my days. Why, there must be thousands of them."

"We'd better be on our guard in case—" Kilgore began. Stones clattered on the slopes behind them, and Kilgore whirled to face the attack. His right arm throbbed, remembering savage teeth crushing flesh and bone together. The sword hummed in his hand eagerly.

The vargulfs burst upon them, about ten in number, and leaped aside startled; but to Kilgore's amazement, they only glanced worriedly at the companions and made a detour around them. Six more followed, scarcely glancing at the intruders, and raced toward Grimshalg with irresistible determination. More passed on either side, hardly pausing to sniff and bristle their black fur. A few growled and whined over their shoulders, but nothing could stop their flight toward the entrance, which was at the base of a large, black abutment of stone. Just as the last pack of vargulfs vanished, the red rim of the sun crept wearily out of the clouds where it had been smothered for many hours. Its light was watery and faint, not even enough to cast a shadow.

"The poor beasts," Asny said quietly. "But at least it's a comfort to know there are so many of my countrymen left alive, if we could only break the vargulf spell. How about it, Skanderbeg? Would you dare try?"

"Not for all the fire wizards' pensions in the Wizards' Guild," Skanderbeg said gloomily. "You'll have to get it from Surt himself." He collected his staff and satchel and straightened his clothing, like a wet, miserable but still proud beggar. "Lead us to one of the side entrances, Asny. Now that the vargulfs are safely inside where we want to be also, we'll crawl right in with them and cozy right up to old Surt and all those wizards and trolls. I suppose by now he senses that he'll be having company for dinner tonight."

"Right," Asny said, eager to get started. "To the

north there's an old portal very few know about. It will serve us fine."

"No," Kilgore said, sitting down on a mossy rock. "I've been thinking this over. We are not going inside Grimshalg."

"But of course we are!" Asy exclaimed. "You've lost your nerve?"

"No," Kilgore said. "I am the only one going inside. You will both wait here where you won't be in my way. And that is my last word." Asny started to protest, but he went on, "I am the one Elbegast chose to battle Surt, although I certainly wouldn't be here without both of you. I know this is the way it must be. One or three against Surt makes little difference if this sword isn't able to do the job. If I'm not back by dawn tomorrow, you'll know I've failed. If I can, I'll use the swineherd's old horn and signal you and Skuld and Njal to start the battle without me. Three mots and you'll know something calamitous has happened—if I have time. Perhaps old Schmelling—whatever, will come to my aid," he added lightly, but no one smiled.

"But it's my country," Asny burst out in disappointment. "Why can't I go along to help?"

"It's my battle to get your country back from Surt," Kilgore said.

Skanderbeg sat down and began warming his hands over the glowing head of his staff. "We shall be here at dawn tomorrow waiting for you, if you don't come back sooner. I knew from the start you'd have to face Surt alone, like a man. Good luck, and may the thunder god favor you." He shook hands solemnly with Kilgore. "I hope you don't feel deserted, but the battle is now in your hands, Kilgore."

Asny turned away stiffly and mumbled, "Goodbye, Kilgore. Good luck." When she turned around again he was gone. She peered over the edge of the ridge to catch a glimpse of him but all she saw was the lifeless expanse of cold lava tumbled about like giants' play. Of course he would be invisible, after so many

256

weeks of experience at hiding. Dismally, she sat down beside Skanderbeg. "What now, wizard?"

"We wait. How about some very weak tea and soggy stale toast?"

The gloomy day deepened into gloomier rain mingled with snow. Watching for Kilgore was impossible. Even Grimshalg was completely invisible in the murk. Skanderbeg bestirred himself to locate an old barrow that had been broken into long ago by robbers and investigated it suspiciously to see if somebody or something was already in possession.

"It's almost sundown," he said to Asny, who had steadfastly refused to give up her watching position all day. She was now sodden to the skin and still stubborn. "It will be time for the vargulfs to start hunting. If they don't remember us and come back for a look at us, I'm your grandfather's old nanny goat. We'd better fortify our barrow against them. At least we'll be out of this confounded weather."

"I suppose," Asny said, glad for an excuse to move. All she had done all day was strain her eyes into the joyless weather and exclaim unexpectedly, "I wonder what Kilgore's doing now?"

Competently she scanned the bit of terrain she could see and circled the barrow before stepping aside. Nothing in it except dust and bones and a few rotten artifacts. At least it was dry. Skanderbeg had lit a small fire and was wringing the water out of his beard. When he finished, he helped her block up part of the opening. Wrapping her wet cloak around her, she sat in the doorway waiting for the vargulfs to appear at sunset. Behind her, Skanderbeg callously fell asleep, nodding over the small bed of glowing coals.

At first it was only a peculiar feeling. Gradually she became certain there were people on the hill above her doorway and on the brow of the ridge on both sides. Listening, she could hear nothing but the throaty roaring of the rocky Grimstrom as it poured through its torturous channels. As she listened, she heard the first distant howling of the vargulfs at the gates of Grimshalg. Gripping the hammer, she rose

257

to look outside as the vargulfs streaked across the plain, howling with blood lust. As Skanderbeg suspected, they all raced straight for the ridge where they had encountered the travelers. Positioning herself for battle, she experienced a curious reluctance and her hands were slick with sweat as unwelcome thoughts came crowding into her mind. Long ago she once had seven younger brothers. Were they now running with the vargulfs, held these three score and five years in thrall to Surt? Had they possibly been slain at her own hand in defense of Kilgore that night at Beortstad? Or had they died when Surt seized power in Gardar?

The howling of the vargulfs came up the slope. The first black shapes raced toward her, heads low. Snapping white, vicious fangs, the leader reached the cave in two leaps. In the dismal light of the dying sun, Asny could see his eyes, pale and sad in the furry, black face. They were human eyes, and Asny stood frozen with her hammer upraised, unable to strike the beast. He gathered himself for another leap, snarling.

In mid-leap, the monster whirled aside with a yelp. A flaming torch blazed up suddenly from the other side of the ridge and descended upon the vargulfs. Asny could scarcely discern her rescuer's rough, hairy garb as he waved the torch at the startled vargulfs and planted himself before the cave. Other torches leaped up over the ridge one by one until they formed a barrier all along the ridge, extending down the slope and across the plain and river and encircling Grimshalg like a finely etched line of gold on black.

Behind her Skanderbeg said, "Right on time. I knew we could count on Skuld. And there's Njal's fires on the far side."

Asny sighed with relief and fastened her hammer at her belt. "Now all we need to do is wait for Kilgore to appear at dawn. The vargulfs are contained and Surt is baffled, for one night at least. And may it be his last night in Grimshalg, or even this side of the grave. Look at the vargulfs, Skanderbeg. They're standing like timid sheep. Are they so utterly terrified of light and fire?"

"So it seems," Skanderbeg said, staring into the darkness that was gathering around them with a flavor of snow to it. "Halloo! Is that Skuld the wild man up there on the ridge?"

"It is," came the reply, and Skuld himself came striding down with a torch in each hand. "It was a stroke of choice luck that we happened to come to this place to start, and that you were here too. Take this torch, Exalted Lady, and enlarge your fire for more torches. As long as we have fire and light, they won't attack. In all my chieftaincy, we haven't been forced to kill any of our brothers—even temporarily. Poor brutes, you shall be freed by dawn or, by the gods, I'll be one with you." He strode forward to thrust his torch at a bold vargulf.

"I hope not," Skanderbeg said, breathing fragrant clouds of smoke from his pipe. "I expect you'd make a particularly objectionable vargulf. Besides, we shall not fail."

"But I expected Kilgore would be back by now," Asny said with no attempt to hide her unease.

"Perhaps he can't get out if the vargulfs are in," Skuld suggested. "Or possibly he's hiding somewhere this instant, waiting for the vargulfs to return to their dungeons at dawn so he can cross the plain."

"Dungeons?" asked Asny.

"Yes. As you know, these creatures become themselves in the hours of daylight, so Surt must keep them imprisoned while his spell is not in effect. We know this from a hapless few who have escaped." Skuld's face looked grim in the flickering light of his torch. "We could not keep them with us, of course, because of the curse, and they were terrified to be caught in the daylight and wondering what terrible fate was going to befall them. We never saw it, we never knew, but I suspect Grimshalg is the best place for them until the curse is lifted. The curse wears thin at times, on a full moon night or just before dawn when Grimshalg is about to call them home. They are at their worst just after sunset, and I expect we shall have a battle on our hands tonight, if the torches don't hold them at bay."

"But if we don't hold them, our plan will fail," Asny said. "How can we keep Grimshalg surrounded until the hour of reckoning? We must slay the wizards of Surt and whatever else comes out to fight for him, or there is no sense to getting rid of Surt. Skuld, the torches must hold them at bay. There can be no other way."

Skuld clasped her hands reassuringly. "Exalted Lady, have no fear. I have every confidence that the line will hold them. It is our destiny to restore Gardar to the Wolfgangers." Then he strode away grimly to supervise the replenishing of the torches.

The vargulfs milled around and squabbled restlessly. Fierce attacks on weak places in the line grew more frequent as the sky blackened to midnight, but no blood was shed on either side. Bonfires burned at regular intervals in the line, where torches were rekindled. Skuld raced from fire to fire, making sure the supply of torches was not running low. The wild men had manufactured and stockpiled bundles of torches made of hard, slow-burning wood, hundreds of them, for defense against the vargulfs. It was a secret that had been handed down; it was the only known defense against the vargulf attacks that had plagued Gardar since the Wars.

Asny fanned a torch into flame by swinging it around her head, and stood gazing vainly toward Grimshalg. All there was to be seen of it was one significant light on the rocky top. Skuld appeared in the ring of firelight to report. He looked tired and grim. "We can't hold our lines much longer than tomorrow dawn," he said. "Kilgore must return by dawn, or we'll have to take up defensive positions—a definite disadvantage for us, if we have to fight Surt ourselves."

Asny said nothing, turning away sharply. Everyone seemed so sure that Kilgore had failed, yet dawn was hours away. She noticed some of the vargulfs lying down sleepily, and the savage howling had diminished to an occasional mournful cry. In the east the sky was deep blue, hinting of the dawn soon to come, but Asny tried to ignore it. She saw that the torches were being put out to save them, leaving only the signal fires. The vargulfs were not interested. They all seemed to be waiting for the signal from Grimshalg.

By the time the sky was gray with light, Asny and Skanderbeg and Skuld were standing silently together, watching the vargulfs streaming homeward like homing bats in flight.

"Now," Asny said, "Kilgore will come."

They watched until the last vargulf was gone and the sun had risen, shining briefly as in the old days; then a solid cloud of gray swallowed it up like a sullen bruise around the eye of doom. As the sun was blotted out, the wind sharpened, nipping into the old barrow where Asny and Skanderbeg sat. Watching the snow beginning to sift around the black rocks of the Grimstrom, Skanderbeg shook his head and said, "I can't imagine Kilgore failing utterly. You mustn't fret yourself, Asny, I know he's coming out of there triumphant. The Wizards' Guild wouldn't back a loser. You mustn't get upset now. Remember these things take time. It's very important not to rush something like this, and Kilgore always was the deliberate type. Confound it, where is that boy? He ought to know better than to worry me this way." Anxiously Skanderbeg bit on the nose of his dragon staff until it spat sparks.

Asny busied herself making a tempting pot of tea and some ash cakes from the meal Skuld had given them. The day seemed endless, but at last the snow clouds darkened into early gloom of evening. Before long the vargulfs would be out, and the return to activity was a welcome relief. Almost cheerful, she declared to Skanderbeg, "He'll make it tonight, wizard. He's only a bit late, one day. He was waiting for the darkness."

"And the vargulfs?" grunted Skanderbeg gloomily.

"At least he hasn't blown the horn." Asny thrust a

torch into his hands and nearly set his beard ablaze. "To the battlements, troops, and prepare to hail the returning hero."

No hero appeared. The vargulfs broke through Njal's line in two places and harried the Regulars with frequent lightning attacks from the rear. Their success made them bold, and even the torches began to lose some of their menace. The vargulfs swirled and snarled, singeing their whiskers in the flames. In desperation, Skanderbeg wove a mighty incantation that drove the vargulfs back in a towering wall of purple and orange flame, but only temporarily. After recovering from their initial terror and confusion, the vargulfs came pouring back with renewed fury.

The moon did not show itself that night and the dense snow clouds hung to the earth, obscuring moon and stars, making it a prime vargulf night. Skuld rushed from fire to fire trying to make too few torches do the work of twice as many.

"It's no use," he finally said on his last report to Asny. His face was blackened and desperate. "They've broken through and carried off two of my men and the torches are burned down to nothing. Njal is worse off then we are. We'll have to hide and defend ourselves as best we can until dawn. Then we'll have to draw up some new plans, in safer country."

"And give up Kilgore for dead?" Asny said. "You may do as you see fit for the protection of your people, but Skanderbeg and I will not leave this place until we know what has happened to Kilgore, or until he comes back. I shall still remember you well and reward you when I am queen, Skuld." She spoke with dignity, in spite of the charcoal blackening her face.

"We aren't deserting you," Skuld said. "I mean to withdraw and get more torches, or take up weapons against the vargulfs. We'll stay here and battle barehanded; never let it be said that Skuld the Wild Man deserted his queen. But desperate measures must be taken now if any of us are to survive to see the dawn, Exalted Lady. We must withdraw from our positions."

Midnight was a dismal hour, filled with blizzarding snow and the savage, exulting cries of the vargulfs. Njal and Skuld withdrew their men so cunningly the vargulfs did not realize what had happened until the men were all huddled in compact rings around large fires with torches facing outward. Howling with frustration, the vargulfs swarmed around them, searching for an opening and lunging boldly into the very face of the flaming torches.

In a brief respite in the battle, Asny relit the stub of her torch and whispered nervously to Skuld, "If they attack us in a mass we are finished. I'm glad dawn is not far off. I feel a great worry for Kilgore. He ought to have been back by now."

Skuld glanced around to make sure no one else could overhear. "I don't believe he's coming back, Exalted Lady. The odds were too great. Surt is too clever to allow that sword anywhere near him. I fear the young sword king has been killed. When dawn comes, we had better begin to consider dispersing and going back into hiding."

Asny turned away to stalk along the ridge of the hill, staring into the gloom. "Shall we retreat, Skuld? Or shall we attack Grimshalg and hurl ourselves to certain doom, rather than live as outlaws and slaves?" Bitterly, she turned to look over the dark plain at the ring of fires surrounding Grimshalg. "Every man of Gardar is here, but will it be a wasted effort? By dawn they could all be scattered like so many dry leaves in an autumn wind, never to be gathered again. If we stay, our doom will almost certainly be sealed. The wizards will ferret us out and destroy us. But at least we will not die in the awful lightless cold of the Fimbul Winter."

Skuld nodded his head. "What you say is true, Exalted Lady. Never let it be said that Skuld got out while the getting was good. We shall stay with you, whatever your decision."

"Bless you, Skuld. We'll wait a little longer, just until dawn. There is nothing to be lost now."

CHAPTER 18

Kilgore had less trouble gaining access to Grimshalg than he had expected. Huddling the hood of Gorm's black cloak over his face, he scurried from rock to rock until he was within a bowshot of the main entrance, where a gang of trolls stood guard. When he stepped boldly from behind his rock they stared at him, bristling with suspicion until he extended his hand in a quick gesture which he had observed the Dark Alfar use as a greeting in Svartheim.

"Dark Alfar!" squeaked one of the small trolls, springing back in alarm, and the others abandoned their guard posts to race ahead of him down the long black tunnel. It was wide enough for four horsemen abreast and high enough that even a tall man on horseback needn't fear for his skull. Smoking torches were thrust into the crevices in the stone to light the way, so he had no lasting fears of getting lost. Besides, as he progressed, the tunnel became more crowded with others hurrying along in the same direction, glancing at him as mistrustfully as he at them.

A beady-eyed old wizard with a wooden foot fell into step with him, whispering and chuckling to himself. When the tunnel gave way to a winding stairway, the old wizard darted ahead to club a half dozen trolls out of the way for no apparent reason, other than for pure enjoyment of their shrieks and shouts. With a wink, he snatched Kilgore's arm and whispered, "So it's you, is it? I thought I recognized the cloak of Svartheim. Welcome to the ranks. A pity about old Haukr, but one does not rebel against Surt and expect to boast about it. Well, we mustn't be late, eh?" With

264

that, the old barrow robber bounded up the thousand or so stone steps to the top without pausing once for a breath, towing Kilgore after him. If anyone or anything got in his way, he simply trod upon them or shoved them down the steps behind him.

The steps gave way to ramps, and the ramps to natural tunnels, gleaming black tubes lit by scutcheons and whale oil lamps. A thousand more steps, and suddenly Kilgore almost fell flat on the level surface. He was at the top of Grimshalg.

"Over here," the old wizard commanded, pointing to an open door across the gloomy court. "Hurry, we can't be late. I wouldn't miss this for all the blood in Gardar."

"Neither would I," Kilgore said, his lungs burning like fire as he let the wizard shove him into the main hall, already jammed with the motley cloaks of ice wizards and the hairy backs of trolls. Mercifully, in the confusion of fighting his way through the crowd, the wizard lost track of Kilgore, who darted into the protection of a large stone column to watch. A spacious place was cleared before the hearth and thirteen massive chairs were set up in a semi-circle. Most of the chairs were filled, except the central one. Kilgore recognized the old wizard in dirty white with the wooden foot; he was arguing violently with the wizards seated on either side of him, one magnificently clad in purple and the other a ragged beggarly sort in orange. With a mild shock, Kilgore also recognized his five acquaintances from the Sloughs of Heroness, occupying prominent positions in the front row of spectators. After a moment of tense wariness, he decided no one was going to recognize him. The hall had a festival atmosphere, and from time to time a troll capered across the front, making grimaces. A table was arranged there with some oddly shaped objects on it, shrouded in a black cloth, which seemed to be the focus for much whispering and speculation.

A few more important wizards took their seats as members of Surt's twelve. All were now present except Surt and the thirteenth wizard who would occupy the last chair. Finally the fellow appeared, slipping quietly through the crowd and sitting down before anyone was really aware of him. Kilgore stared, scarcely breathing, realizing the old wizard with the wooden foot had confused him with this fellow, because they both wore the black cloaks of Svartheim. It could be no one else. When the wizard threw back his hood, Kilgore was certain. It was Hrafngrimr.

The room chilled unexpectedly with an icy gust. At once the wizard in purple arose and commanded: "Silence! Our master Surt is coming. Any of you caught misbehaving will be tossed off the battlements."

Kilgore gripped the sword; Kildurin was trembling with tremendous force. He shrank further into the shadow and waited for his first glimpse of the being that was Surt. The crowd had parted with alacrity but Kilgore still could not see his adversary. He took a step closer, and accidentally trod on someone's foot. The owner whirled around with a startled snarl. With yet another horrible shock of recognition, Kilgore found himself staring into the yellowish eyes of Warth the wizard.

Warth gasped with fear—then a cunning light spread across his face. "Oho! Oho!" he cried with a gleeful grin, clapping both hands over his mouth as if he could scarcely restrain himself.

"Silence, or I'll—" Kilgore's hand moved toward the sword. Warth scuttled away with a frightened giggle. "Hold your tongue, Warth, or I'll make you a gift of your head," Kilgore snapped in a fierce whisper.

Warth made a face and disappeared into the crowd. Kilgore changed hiding places immediately, but he was haunted by a nasty feeling that something was going to go hideously wrong.

A cold wind gusted through the hall, making his neck hair bristle with a barrow-mound sensation. The wind ran around the hall, over the heads of the crowd and Kilgore felt its clamminess touch him, linger to brush his face and hair. Drawing back with a shudder, he touched the sword and pulled about an inch of it from its sheath. Immediately the cold sensation passed. Then everyone in the hall uttered a roar of respectful greeting as Surt appeared in the doorway. Without glancing right or left, he glided toward his chair and sat down. He was a stout, powerfully built individual, draped from the shoulders with a magnificent, scarlet-embroidered cloak. In his hands he carried a staff with a gold knob and he wore a magician's headdress of animal pelts. Kilgore could only stare disbelievingly. It was Vatnarr of Vatnarrsmound, dressed in the scarlet cloak of the dead king in the mound.

Vatnarr seemed to stare directly at him through the stone pillar. With a slight nod in Kilgore's direction he began to speak in a deep, mesmerizing tone. "We are assembled here to try our powers against the pernicious powers of Elbegast and his forces. The time is right for the return of the Fimbul Winter, if only we can prove our powers superior and muster our strength together for this worthy purpose. Now I demand silence in the hall. Whatever powers those here have to offer must be contributed to the communal effort."

There was a scuffling somewhere in the rear, near the doors. A reedy voice called out, "Wait a moment, most noble of masters. I happen to know there is a traitor in our midst and, as a loyal servant of yours, I'd be happy to point him out for only a small reward, you can be sure."

The motley assemblage shrank away from the speaker, revealing Warth crouching and fawning with one hand on the door handle for a quick escape. Voices rose in a sinister chorus and a few wicked-looking knives were drawn.

"Let no one leave this hall," Surt spoke to one of his lieutenants. "And seize that stunted wizard who dares to make himself so bold."

With a muffled shriek, Warth was collared and brought before Surt.

"Now point out this traitor and be quick about it, while your throat is yet unsliced."

Warth began to babble and point, and finally manage to sputter, "That's him there, in the black cloak of Svartheim."

Surt stared at Kilgore. "Clear out this rabble instantly. Leave only that fellow in the black cloak."

The hall was cleared in a trice, with no demurrers or backward lookers. Warth seized the opportunity, lunging for the door and not caring whom or what he clawed and shoved in his progress.

A couple of trolls slunk under Surt's chair and glowered sullenly at Kilgore as he stepped closer. The twelve wizards began to scowl and mutter when he flung back his cloak to get it out of the way of the sword.

Vatnarr-Surt looked at him with no expression on his impervious face. "So you didn't care for my hospitality at Vatnarrsmound. And now you have come to inspect the lodgings at my castle. I knew from the moment you appeared at Vatnarrsmound that you fancied yourselves a group of heroes come to kill me. In fact, I knew your purpose at Haelfsknoll. You have come far through many perils for this day, and I too have prepared myself for centuries to meet this sword of Andurich. It has been severely tested, but I am still not convinced that it is more powerful than I. Yet it may be a useful tool for my purposes."

"Even an Alfar sword is no use to a dead corpse," Kilgore said with a peculiar calm feeling. He unsheathed the brilliant sword and stepped closer. "I have come to challenge you and you will accept my terms, if you have any of the courage of the Scipling's form which you inhabit. I challenge you one blow for one until one of us is dead. As the challenger, I request the first stroke."

Surt sat a moment frowning at him and Kilgore felt cold, evil currents flowing over him like a river of blackness. The twelve wizards murmured among themselves, looking bored and impatient with the interruption of their business. One malevolent fellow with only one eye rose and demanded, "Let's get on with the business at hand. This is only a mortal with no power. We can kill him like a fly any time we care to. Most noble Surt, allow one of us to remove this annoyance. Then we shall continue with the glorious project of bringing down the Fimbul Winter."

"I forbid it," Kilgore said in a carrying tone. "The Fimbul Winter will never rule as long as I am here to prevent it. I shall slay you all if you attempt to stop me."

"Well! If you are as immovable as Surt, then we shall have a fine battle," the wizard in purple said, sitting down with his arms folded.

"A battle it shall be," Surt said, "for I accept the terms of the challenger."

The wizards looked balefully at Kilgore, and the old one in white said, "It makes little difference if the stranger does manage to kill the body of Surt. We know there is nothing that can destroy the living essence of Surt, and he will return stronger the next time in the space of a few short seasons. The only pity is the delay involved."

"There shall be no delay, you fools," Surt said in a thunderous voice, grasping the arms of his chair until the wood protested. "You are ignorant idiots if you know nothing of the sword this stranger carries. I have seen from the past three efforts we have made to call down the Fimbul Winter that there is not enough power in the lot of you to blow out a small candle. Either you are all paltry tricksters or some of you are treacherously working against me, which would be a tremendous lot of magic indeed, if someone is deceiving me, the master sorcerer of all. But with this sword of Andurich, I shall have enough power alone to call down the Fimbul Winter, or to destroy entirely the earth we walk upon. I do not need the services of cowards. Whoever desires may leave."

Not a muscle stirred. They knew the fate of deserters or rebels. One would not reach the door alive or have time to utter the second word of an incantation before Vatnarr-Surt struck.

"Then let us hear no more whining about death and delays," Surt continued, his eyes smoldering. "All that stands between us and the Fimbul Winter is one helpless mortal. There is nothing he can do to stop us."

"Then let us begin the battle and we shall see," Kilgore said, with the sword humming powerfully in his hand.

"In good time," Surt said, rising and removing the black cloth from the objects before him on a low table. He spread his hands out, and Kilgore again felt the evil tide rippling all around him. Surt raised a dismal chant, echoed by the twelve wizards. Kilgore watched suspiciously as the objects on the table began to move. There was a green disk representing the earth. Around it were moving two chariots drawn by horses, one gold and the smaller one silver. He recognized Hrimfaxi, the horse of the night with frost dripping from his mane, and Skinfaxi, the bright horse of the sun. As the wizards' chant grew more intense, Kilgore saw not only the metal representations of horses and chariots, he saw real horses striding across a field of blue or black with tremendous strides, accompanied by the clatter of harness and the thunder of wheels and the loud cracking of a whip. He saw the fiery flashing of Skinfaxi's eyes and heard the whistle of wind through his mane. Then the great horse seemed to pass by. Kilgore even thought he could smell sweating horseflesh, and the last thing he heard was a horse's disdainful snort.

Or perhaps it was Vatnarr-Surt. In disgust he exclaimed, "Enough! It is worse than before, now that this stranger is here. He has some power after all." He threw off his hat of animal pelts and glared at Kilgore with hatred, sending again the currents of evil at him.

Kilgore mentally recited the sword runes: "No night can overtake the sons of Ask and Embla."

Surt rose to his feet and paced impatiently up and down the line of wizards, then whirled to face Kilgore. "I am ready for the battle," he said. "You have friends in this hall, but I am more powerful. I have met nineteen others like you with swords or maces or axes; once I was assassinated in a most cowardly way with an arrow in the back, and twenty times I permitted myself to be slain so I could return more powerful than when I died. In all those cases, I turned the celebrations into funeral feasts. If your Wolfganger princess were here, she would remember the legend of the first Vatnarr who said he would not die until he ruled as the last king, deathless and absolute. It was I who uttered those words as I died in battle, and I shall live to see those words become truth." He unsheathed his sword Tyrfing and held it aloft.

Kilgore thought of the dried husk in Vatnarrsmound with a cold chill of dread between his shoulders. Vatnarr-Surt was a barrow ghost, capable of inhabiting mortal bodies as long as they served his purpose, then taking refuge in the corpse of Vatnarr in the mound until he could contrive to become mortal again. He had already done so twenty times; each time it was thought that the world was rid of Surt, but in a short while he would be back again, stronger than ever and more versed in evil.

"You shall not live to see the dawn," Kilgore said coldly. "Come forward and receive the death stroke."

"Remember me at your celebration feast," Vatnarr-Surt said. "I shall announce myself with a single knock at the door, as all barrow spirits do. I hope you have your grave mold prepared when I arrive." Vatnarr-Surt bared his teeth in a grimace and planted his feet firmly, his eyes burning with a savage, fearless fire.

Kilgore took a breath and whispered the sword runes, then swung Kildurin aloft with both hands, whirling the blade in a brilliant circle to bring it down upon the skull of Surt. At the precise instant the blow connected, a searing needle of agony shot up his right arm where the vargulf had bitten him, and the arm seemed to rebel with a power of its own to deflect the edge of the blade.

With a triumphant shout Vatnarr parried with his

own sword, twisting Kildurin out of Kilgore's left hand and sending it spinning across the floor in a shower of sparks.

"That hand will always be the vargulf's hand," Surt said with a mirthless laugh. "So of course it will not rise against its master. Oblad, Berserker, he is yours to do with as you wish. Destroy him!" He strode away to retrieve Kildurin.

The wizards rose up in fury. Kilgore ducked as a blood-encrusted axe went end-over-end above his head. A wizard in purple surged forward with a sword driving inexorably toward him. In that split instant, he knew he was dead, and then darkness slammed down on his senses. A shout lingered in his ears briefly, then it was all nothingness.

CHAPTER 19

When he became aware again, he still thought he was dead. The place he found himself in was cold and damp and absolutely lightless, as if it had never seen the face of the sun. Indeed, it probably had not, if he were truly in the realm of the goddess Hel and the dead. Cautiously he felt around, finding cold, sweaty rock. It felt bubbly and pitted, like the lava tunnels of Grimshalg. When he stood up, his head touched the roof of the tunnel before he could straighten fully. Carefully, he felt the air in front and in back and found open tunnel. Wondering which way to go, and since it made no difference, he turned the opposite way from his original position and began slithering along the wall. Almost at once, he stumbled into another tunnel. After exploring it on hands and knees for a short distance, he came to the edge of a pit. A pebble or two rattled down its sides and, after a long time, he heard a faraway splash. Shivering, he backed away carefully and found yet another tunnel. This one was large enough to stand up in. The ground inclined downward and he stopped, not wanting to go any deeper, if he were ever to find his way to the surface again. Pausing a moment to analyze that thought, he decided that he didn't really believe he was dead. He was probably alive and lost in the maze of tunnels under Grimshalg.

How he came to be there was a stupefying puzzle. Thoughtfully, he rubbed a throbbing knot on his head after ramming it against an unsuspected outcropping of rocks. It seemed only moments ago that a sword was about to make a lasting part in his hair, but instead, at the last instant, some sort of powerful magic had transported him here. For what dismal purpose he couldn't imagine, except as a tasty tidbit for the first vargulf to come strolling by, unless Surt kept worthings in his cellar for the entertainment of his captives. But certainly that would be an ungratifying execution for an important enemy, from the wizards' viewpoint.

Kilgore sighed in the darkness, thinking of Hrafngrimr for no particular reason. It was an uneasy thought. Maybe Hrafngrimr had sent him here for some private confrontation of his own—to extract the runic key to Kildurin so he could use it himself. Kilgore's spirit hardened against such a possibility. Hrafngrimr would be sadly disappointed.

Perhaps Skanderbeg had somehow intervened and preserved him from instant death by incanting him into the tunnels. But that was a slender possibility. Kilgore decided, with a mental shrug, that the only thing to do was to make the best of a queer quirk of fate.

Turning around carefully from the deep well, he felt his way back. Or at least he supposed he hadn't mixed up his directions too badly, until he found himself in a crooked tunnel that suddenly dumped him over the edge of the much-to-be-dreaded pit. Scrabbling frantically, he made a despairing attempt to save himself, but the sides of the pit were too smooth. He dropped possibly ten feet and landed in soft sand. Feeling it thoughtfully between his fingers, he knew there had to be an outlet to the outside somewhere, since sand was usually carried by water. Eagerly, he sloshed along in the sand, feeling it growing wetter and wetter until he was feeling his way through knee-deep water, and the ceiling was about waist high and getting lower. He turned around slowly and, when the sand became dry enough, he sat down, wondering how he could ever expect to see the topside again. Bitterly, he blamed himself for losing the sword to Surt. Of all the fiends who had tried to steal it, Surt was the most disastrous, and Surt had succeeded. Skanderbeg would choke if he knew. Kilgore rested his head on his forearms, not

274

caring at the moment if his bones rotted away to dust under Grimshalg. He had failed, and he had a great series of failures leading up to this ultimate disaster, all brought on because of his foolish impulsive actions. The worst impulse had been ever consenting in the beginning to going with Skanderbeg on this hateful trip. He thought of Shieldbroad basking in the sun like a jewel and the comfortable old Brandstok hall which he would never see again. It made him angry to think how he had been cheated.

"By all the gods!" he exclaimed, standing up and bumping his head unnoticed, "I'll get out of here somehow and strangle that wizard Surt with my bare hands, if it's the last thing I do!"

Time was meaningless to him, blundering around underground as blind as a mole. All he could use as an estimate was the knowledge that he had been searching long enough to get himself almost exhausted. He leaned his forehead against the rock at the end of a long tunnel which had dead-ended without so much as a by-your-leave. Above was a long vertical shaft with a strong down-draft, so he knew he was getting closer. As soon as he had rested and rubbed the bruises on his head, he would attempt to climb up. Looking up, he of course saw nothing; he could only judge by the feel of the place what it looked like. For an instant, he thought he heard something above, and then he saw a glow of light on the rock about thirty feet up. He almost opened his mouth to shout, but wisely did not, knowing there was a greater chance it would be an enemy, not someone who would help him. In a moment the light was gone.

By bracing his back and feet against the walls, he was able to chimney up the shaft to the tunnel above. The breeze was stronger now, and he followed it with exhilaration, bumping into winding walls and occasionally stumbling into dead-air side tunnels. At last he saw the light at the end, a faraway speck that became larger as he stumbled toward it.

When he reached the opening, he was still almost blinded by the light, although it was the pale dimness of the Gardar dawn. Some instinct made him hesitate before venturing a look outside. He heard a thumping of feet and suddenly he was face to face with a big, black vargulf, galloping at top speed. The beast did not have time to slow down before bowling Kilgore over in a tangle of arms and legs. After the impact, they wrestled violently a moment before the vargulf disentangled himself and fled. Then the rest of the pack galloped over Kilgore with their huge feet, stumbling in their haste and sprawling under the noses of other vargulfs. Kilgore got up when he could and ran back into the tunnel to save himself, meaning to dive into a side tunnel; but he could not seem to find one. Vargulfs passed him on both sides and the tunnel filled up with them, until Kilgore was trapped in the press of hairy bodies. The vargulfs carried him along like a piece of bark in a river. Sometimes he lost his footing and rolled across their backs. All he could think was that he would never find the tunnel to the outside again, even if he wasn't devoured by the vargulfs.

Abruptly the migration halted. Kilgore had the feeling he was in a high, vaulted chamber. Where its walls were he could not guess. The vargulfs brushed against him on all sides, and he sensed there were no more coming in. He could hear the padding of hundreds of paws going by in the tunnel outside, all without a growl or a howl. Around him they seemed to be bedding down in the sand with weary sighs. There was some kind of stirring among them, and he wondered uneasily if they had just remembered him. Not moving, he crouched in the sand in readiness. A nose count began, each vargulf grunting his number. Curious murmurs arose around him and he was bumped several times. Suddenly he was siezed and thrown roughly to the sand. Before the fangs closed on his throat, he yelled defiantly, "Death to Surt! Long live the last Wolfganger Queen Asny! Confusion to the vargulfs and the wizards!"

His attackers did not move, but an excited rumble filled the chamber. Hands felt his face. A human voice declared, "This isn't one of us, and he's not one of them either. He's gotten in from the outside!"

Voices babbled in excitement. Kilgore sat up and exclaimed, "I thought you were vargulfs. What happened to them? Not a moment ago there were hundreds of them—"

In the sudden silence, a voice said grimly, "Yes, you're right, there were hundreds of vargulfs, and they still remain. We are the vargulfs, by night anyway. By day we are men of Gardar. Who are you and how did you get into Grimshalg?"

They clustered around him while he told his story. When he finished, they were all silent. The one who was the leader said, "We have heard the legends of the sword king and the return of the last queen. But to kill Surt? Do you have any idea how powerful he is? You are just a lad, are you not"

"Not at all," Kilgore said quietly. "I have met with Surt twice and twice I have met with his sending, forms, the flayed bull and the cat. Because of his curse that runs in my sword arm from the bite of a vargulf on Beortstad, I could not use the sword properly against him. But if I get it again, I know how I can destroy him forever. I don't know why I was sent here, instead of being killed instantly. As long as I am alive Surt knows he is in deadly peril, since I am the destined one who will kill him, body and ghost."

"But if you are here when the planets reach the morning positions, you'll be killed by the vargulfs," another voice said flatly. "Although we are now men like you, in a few hours we shall become beasts. If you do not escape immediately, then neither you nor anyone else ever again will see the face of the sun."

"Then we shall have to help him escape," the leader said.

This led to a mixture of protests and eager agreement. Someone finally said, "Rolfr, I think the time has come to light the last candle. I believe we shall have no need of it presently."

Sparks were struck; in a moment the candle flared, a tiny stub of wax. Kilgore sat in the middle of a ring of bearded men sparsely clad in rags and pelts. They were even more wretched than Skuld's wild men. Their eyes were hollow and haunted with the misery of their curse. One of the men was wiping tears from his eyes and murmuring, "Never again did I expect to see a man decently clad in respectable clothes among us. But your garb is unfamiliar, friend. Tell us what land you hail from."

"Shieldbroad, on the western coast, south of Heroness. You know the Brandstok hall, which is the hall of my fathers. In three score and five years since the fall of Gardar, everything has changed."

"That long?" Everyone murmured and marveled.

"The candle is wasting," Rolfr said. "Who is going with me to lead Kilgore of Shieldbroad back to the upper levels? I want at least four others to be eyes before and behind. Glam. Helgi. Raud-skeggi. And Wittorf. Good."

"And your other two brothers Avangr and Skarp," another voice said. "We intend to do all we can to see the queen returned to her throne."

"Then you shall come along," Rolfr said. "The rest of you know what to do if we don't return. You will know nothing of our disappearance."

"And if we are caught," one of Rolfr's brothers said "The world will be rid of seven vargulfs and one mortal."

The seven vargulf men led Kilgore at a trot through the passages as easily as if they could see every side tunnel and pitfall. Rolfr explained that there was nothing else to do during the long summer days, when there was hardly any night, so they explored the tunnels of Grimshalg until almost every step of every tunnel was well known, even in absolute darkness. But even so, it was senseless to attempt to escape, although they knew of a dozen unguarded exits. As Rolfr put it, one does not run away from a curse.

"And shall you never grow old and die?" Kilgore asked.

"Yes, we are aging," one of the brothers said. "When we were captured, we were all scarcely more than children. Rolfr was fourteen, and I was a child of six, being the youngest of the seven brothers. And now you see that we are grown men. I suppose we age normally as long as we are in the human phase, so we are half as aged as we ought to be."

Kilgore was about to ask another question when Glam whispered sharply, "Look there. A light. Coming from below where we just were."

"Today of all days they have decided to count the prisoners," Rolfr said. "Don't make a sound. We shall have to kill him swiftly if he's a wizard."

"He's coming up," Avangr warned. "Let me deal with him."

Boots scraped against stone, inching upward; then they stopped. A voice spoke distinctly. "Kilgore, tell your friends to let me come up. I must speak to you. You do know who I am, don't you?"

"Indeed I do," Kilgore said levelly, in spite of the surge of anger rising within him. "It is Hrafngrimr the traitor, who is now one of the twelve wizards of Surt. You are, I recollect, the thirteenth wizard."

"One of Surt's wizards!" Rolfr breathed. "We are done."

"No, let me speak," Hrafngrimr said. "Kilgore, I know you believe I betrayed you to Gorm, but things are not always as they seem."

"Svartheim was certainly very real," Kilgore said. "Gorm was not feigning his friendship or the money that must have exchanged hands. And how can you possibly explain how you do not really occupy the thirteenth seat in the hall of Surt, when I saw you there myself?"

Hrafngrimr sighed and lit the head of his staff so he could see. "There is hardly time for explanations, but I will tell you that it was I who slew Gorm and it was not for jealous reasons; it was for the glory of Elbegast. During the celebration, I was tracking down Skuld and persuading him to send rescuers to you, and it was difficult to convince him that it wasn't a senseless risk of his men's lives. If not for Asny, he could not have been moved. Do you begin to see, Kilgore?"

"No. All I can see is you in the thirteenth chair. Whose idea was it to send me here to be torn to pieces by the vargulfs? Yours?"

Hrafngrimr answered quietly, "It was in fact I who sent you here. It was preferable to allowing you to be destroyed instantly on the end of a wizard's sword, which was inevitable, as I am sure you were aware. It was the work of an instant and none of the others know where you are, save Surt, possibly, if he is interested. Now that he has Kildurin, there is not much to concern him, except waiting for the proper position of the sun and moon for their destruction. Unless he is stopped tonight, he will bring down the Fimbul Winter with Elbegast's sword. There's not much time, as short as the days are now. In just a few hours, Surt will reconvene the wizards, and you had better be there to stop him, since nobody else can. How are you going to manage it? The vargulfs will be no use to you when you reach the door at the end of that tunnel. You will never get beyond it, let alone into Surt's hall with the twelve wizards."

Kilgore looked away into the impenetrable darkness around him. "I shall have to think about it, but I'm sure there is a way without trusting one of Surt's henchmen. Why did you come here, anyway? Is it some wizardish game?"

Hrafngrimr made an impatient sound. "There's no time for this nonsense, Kilgore. I know you have a right to be angry after what seemed to happen at Svartheim, but you can't risk everything because you're still sulking. I've told you as much as I can. now are you going to allow me to come up and take you out of here to face Surt, or are you going to lose everything because you can't make up your mind? Either you know I'm honest or you know I'm lying. What shall it be, Kilgore?"

Kilgore hesitated a moment, knowing it was true. He remembered the nights on the Trident and the trek along the Dark Alfar trail to Svartheim. Skanderbeg had trusted Hrafngrimr and so had he. "All right," he said with a sigh. "Come up. I'll try to forget what happened at Svartheim. I promise that my friends won't harm you."

"It's a terrible risk," Rolfr said dubiously. "But it would be odd if one of Surt's wizards was indeed playing such strange tricks. For all our sakes, I hope he is to be trusted. He seems to have a record of past treachery. But it is true, we could not get you out of the tunnel. We wish you good luck, Kilgore. We'll go back now to the others. Maybe we'll meet again when the vargulf curse is lifted." They all vanished in the blackness, leaving Kilgore and Hrafngrimr.

. . Hrafngrimr climbed out of the shaft, his staff glowing brightly. "You've done the right thing, Kilgore. Your instincts are good. Now follow me closely. I won't be able to keep this light for long without making Surt suspicious. We ought to be out of here at dusk. This time, when you get your hands on the sword, don't touch it with your right hand when you strike Surt or he will escape again."

"But how am I to get near enough to touch it?" Kilgore said. "I don't have even an ordinary sword to challenge him with."

"Don't worry. I shall get you inside the hall, and you'll see your opportunity. I have a short sword you can borrow, but it takes more wits and muscle to use it than magic."

They emerged from the tunnels on an obscure part of the battlements just at sundown, in time to see the vargulfs streaming away toward the chain of torches encircling Grimshalg. Uneasily, Kilgore thought of his promise that he would return at dawn, which was long past and another dawn not far away. The sight of the torches was encouraging. Surely they had not given up on him yet.

Hrafngrimr told him to pull his hood over his face and stay close. When they reached the entrance to the hall, they stopped in an alcove of stone.

"You and I are about the same size," he said. "Keep your cloak close and hide my sword under it.

When it comes time to use it, remember that Surt cannot be dealt the lasting death by any sword other than Kildurin."

Kilgore looked at the other wizards filing into the hall in somber silence. "Where shall you be?" he asked. "I might need your help. You'll be there, won't you?"

"I'll be at your side every moment, but you'll do everything yourself. Remember to make the first move before the presence of Surt weakens your courage. Good luck."

Kilgore glided in quietly with the last of the wizards. No one looked twice at him as he took the thirteenth seat and kept his hood pulled low. The wizard with the wooden foot leaned over to cackle in his ear, "It was a pleasant diversion last night, was it not? But it was a pity the wretched little beast escaped from us at the last instant. It was a wizard spell that did it, and I smelled fire in the hall as surely as I live to make old bones. Perhaps it is one of us that is the traitor. I'd relish dealing with another traitor, wouldn't you?" He nudged Kilgore slyly and tried to peer nearsightedly under his hood.

On the other side of the old wizard, someone growled, "I see that rat-tongued Warth is back. Itching for one of our chairs, he is, with all this talk of traitors in Svartheim's cloak." He looked hard at Kilgore, his eyes challenging.

Kilgore did not answer. His eyes were riveted on the door and his hand rested on the sword hilt. Warth was strutting and boasting around the rear of the hall, but Kilmore paid him scarcely any attention. The door opened, sending everyone scuttling aside into their places, and the icy wind filtered slowly through the room, stirring hangings and waving strands of the wizards' beards. Kilgore was braced when it finally came to him. It halted suddenly, as if smelling him. Kilgore again felt the evil presence of Surt, and this time he had no protction but Bergljot's belt and an ordinary sword.

Suddenly, with a cracking sound like lightning,

the ominous mass of cold was rebuffed. The wizards looked around in astonishment, sniffing the sulfurous smell of the incantation and grasping their staffs in readiness.

"Fire magic in Surt's hall," one of the twelve wizards declared in the sudden silence. The trolls snarled and rolled their eyes warily.

"Fire magic, bah!" the others snapped, but they all glared around the hall, sifting the rabble for possible fire wizards.

Kilgore did not dare twitch a muscle. His eyes found Warth, who was sidling back and forth in great excitement and watching him with bright, knowing eyes.

In a shrill voice, Warth cried out, "I said the traitor was in the cloak of Svartheim, but now you see there's one more black cloak among us. Unveil him and you'll see it's the sword king, back again to slay Surt!"

"Sword king! Nonsense, he's dead," someone said. "Or is he?"

Kilgore sat still, with an icy trickle of sweat between his shoulders. His stillness seemed to quell the suspicious rumblings around him. No one offered to approach him and tear off his hood, no doubt out of respect for Hrafngrimr and his abilities.

"Cowards," the voice of Surt said. He stalked into the hall, bearing Kildurin in his right hand. A heavy metal glove protected his hand but, even so, the glove smoked sullenly with a noxious smell. "What do we care for a sword king without his sword? There might be a thousand fire wizards in here and they would be powerless to stop me from bringing about my purpose." He raised the sword aloft and everyone cringed. He sat down and continued, "With this sword I am the most powerful being ever to descend from the darkness. In spite of your weakness and lack of faith in me, I shall spare your worthless lives to serve me as lord of the Fimbul Winter."

A bright globe of greenish fire appeared over his head and burst in a hail of brilliant sparks. Surt lifted one hand and the sparks were instantly extinguished. The wizards leaped to their feet, muttering curses and peering balefully at the cowering spectators.

"Sit down, you fools. There is no reason to concern yourselves." Surt arose and approached the shrouded table. The glove on his hand was smoking more than before, black and acrid. "We shall get on with out purpose, unless there is anyone who dares confront me in defiance. Who dares to challenge me in this hall, when all the earth trembles at the mention of my name?"

In an awful silence, a mouse ran across Kilgore's foot. It winked its bright eye knowingly and twitched its silky whiskers, and Kilgore felt reassured. Without knowing quite how he did it, he found himself standing and walking slowly toward Vatnarr-Surt. In a strong clear voice, he heard himself say, "I dare challenge Vatnarr-Surt and I do not tremble."

Surt sat grasping the arms of his chair in speechless fury. The other wizards clamored among themselves and one exclaimed, "Hrafngrimr, don't be a fool! You're throwing your life and your magic away."

"I'm not Hrafngrimr," Kilgore said, throwing aside the cloak to get it out of his way. "Although Hrafngrimr is standing by with his fire magic to thwart anything any of you might attempt until I am finished with the business I have come to do, which is the slaying of this impostor from a barrow mound, Vatnarr-Surt. Do you accept my challenge again? Or shall you be called a coward?"

Vatnarr-Surt clutched the sword and rose to his feet, filling the hall with his power. "I shall answer your challenge again," he said in a thunderous tone, "and you can strike the first blow, being the weaker fighter; then I shall use the sword of Andurich to send you to oblivion. As you know, there is no chance that you can kill me, now that I have your sword. I have a particular fate in mind for you as a warning to other would-be heroes. Your head shall join my collection of enemies' heads, who are enchanted so that they are still possessed with speech. But yours will be the most prized, since I have learned to despise you with every fiber of my being. Are you ready to make your attempt? I see you have only a toy for a weapon. How could you be such a fool as to think of facing the immortal Surt with such a farce for a weapon?"

"I do not really need so much as it." Kilgore unsheathed it. "The hour of your destruction is appointed, Surt, and I am the appointed destroyer. A man hates that which he fears, as you hate and fear me, knowing that I shall succeed."

Vatnarr-Surt took a step closer, swinging the sword so it burned into his hand with a hot blue flame. "I could make you as powerful as I am," he said, his eyes probing into Kilgore's with a cold light.

Kilgore raised his short sword involuntarily against the wave of power that crashed over him. A bright crackle of flame exploded between them and vanished. "I have come for my sword," he said. "Fight for it if you will, but the end will be the same."

"Then strike your blow, and I shall strike mine," Surt said, baring his head of the black helmet he wore. "But perhaps you will find that your sword has found a new master and it will no longer work for you."

"That can never happen." Mentally Kilgore recited the runes, concentrating upon Kildurin as it burned with the unnatural blue light. Instantly it flashed gold and the runes blazed a moment before subsiding into a sullen glow.

Surt did not flinch, although his hand was burning. "Strike your blow. Or are you wondering where Hrafngrimr is when you need him? Has he led you into your doom and abandoned you?"

"Here, but not seen," Kilgore retorted, despite a rising wave of uncertainty.

Surt's reply was a derisive snort. "Then make your peace with whatever gods you mortals worship. Your doom is in my hand." With massive dignity he lowered himself to one knee to receive the blow from Kilgore's sword.

Kilgore drew a deep breath and took a double-handed grip. Then a voice seemed to murmur right in his ear—the voice of Hrafngrimr. "The horn. Remember the riddle and the prophecy."

Kilgore hesitated, wondering if the message was only a trick employed by Surt. He touched the old silver horn at his side, still slung on its rotten leather strap which had once hung over the shoulder of his ancestor Wulther. He saw no sign that Hrafngrimr was anywhere near.

"The horn!" the voice insisted.

"The horn," Kilgore echoed aloud.

"What? His first blow shall be a note on an old horn?" The wizards were amazed and delighted.

Surt's face darkened, then paled as he stared at the horn. "I know that horn. It was Wulther's, who was destroyed by my hand and left to be picked by ravens and kites. You also shall find a nameless grave on the moors if you believe that prophecy about Wulther's horn."

"What prophecy?" demanded one of the wizards warily. "We want nothing to do with any prophecy!"

" 'Thrice the Alfar throat shall sound to bring the Alfar hosts around; River-island of Grim's name then shall fall in smoke and flame,'" the wizard in purple quoted.

"A foolish myth invented by ignorant Sciplings," Surt growled. "Who gave you that horn? It must have been Elbegast himself."

"No, only an old swineherd."

"Swineherd!" The wizards were silenced a moment, then began whispering among themselves.

Surt uttered an exclamation of rage, which was cut short by Kilgore's long quivering note that echoed throughout the hall and drifted out to the battlements and pinnacles. After Kilgore lowered the horn, they could hear the note echoing across the barrow hills. The wizards looked at one another in suspense, some replying with snorts and some clutching their staffs in genuine alarm.

Vatnarr-Surt chuckled and swung the sword experimentally, which caused it to burn more hotly into the metal glove. The hall was filled with the smell of scorched flesh. Kilgore felt the hairs of his neck prickle and he knew that Surt was weaving a spell to accompany the stroke of the sword. Silently, he recited the runes over and over, and the sword responded with a tormented wail, alternately gleaming gold for its true master and blue for Surt.

There was no warning when Surt struck. The sword was suddenly in the air and fanning Kilgore's face with a hot breath as it whistled past his head and bit into the stone pillar with a resounding clang and a shower of pebbles and ice. Kilgore gasped at the speed of it, marveling that he was still alive.

"Kildurin refuses to kill its master," he said. "You will end by destroying yourself."

Surt rested the point of the sword on the floor and bored his eyes into Kilgore with consuming hatred. He did not seem to pay the least heed to the smoking glove or the hand inside it.

Kilgore blew the second note on Wulther's horn and Surt attacked before he could lower the horn from his lips. Again the sword narrowly missed him, despite Vatnarr's powerful two-handed grip. The wizards raised a clamor of fury and advanced with a battery of spells, but Surt waved them back contemptuously. His face and arms glistened with the power of his concentration. "Blow your third note but remember—I shall have the last stroke."

"And it too will miss," Kilgore snapped, raising the horn and drawing his breath to sound it. Before he could do so, Surt uttered a sudden furious roar and drove the sword at him. It veered at the last instant and gouged a shattering slash in the stone floor. With another enraged bellow, Surt hewed repeatedly at Kilgore, so there was no chance to blow the third note. Kilgore retreated, his protests unheard in the din of exploding stone and howling sword. He ducked behind pillars, which Surt smashed into fragments with one blow. A shower of rocks from above sent the wizards scuttling for a safer observation point. The crowd of wizards and trolls scrambled frantically away from the battle.

Surt grasped the sword with both hands, oblivious to the terrible burning, and swung with all his might. The blade screamed past Kilgore's ear, so near he felt its breath. It was a battle of wills between Surt and sword, and Surt had nearly won that time. Kilgore leaped out of his way repeatedly with strength and agility—not entirely his own—which was an even match for Surt's ice spells. All the while, he noted that Surt was expertly maneuvering him into a corner where the wizard could easily finish him off. Kilgore looked around for Hrafngrimr and saw no indication that the Alfar was in the hall. Desperately, he tried to escape, but Surt blocked the way each time. With a triumphant roar, Surt lunged forward murderously as Kilgore felt the clammy stone wall against his back. The sword struck the wall as he ducked, dusting him with rocks and mortar. A handful of gravel sent his feet skidding, causing him to dive straight at Vatnarr-Surt, who fell back to raise the sword over his head as Kilgore tangled around his boots. The sword flashed as it descended. Kilgore squirmed out of the way and rolled clear of Surt's feet as the sword struck, scratching one arm slightly. Surt gave a terrible bellow of fury and frustration, and Kilgore saw that he had cut off half of his own left foot with Kildurin.

In the sudden shocked silence, Surt dropped the smoking sword with a loud clangor. Slowly he turned to face Kilgore with a fearful grimace of hatred. Harshly he said, "So you have won. This time I have beaten myself and this carcass of the Vatnarr dies. But the real Surt will live on, stalking you for vengeance. I leave you now to wonder in what form I shall next appear, renewed and stronger than before."

He sank to the floor in the widening pool of his own blood. The eleven wizards gradually separated themselves from the shadows and gathered around, ignoring Kilgore.

"Shall we save you from bleeding to death, great Surt?" asked the old one in white, kneeling beside the still body of Vatnarr. There was no answer. The wizard stood up and said to the others, "I do not suppose he would want to live in a maimed body when he can so easily take another stronger one. The Vatnarr was a good servant."

"But that is the last of them," the stump-footed one said. "And this time Surt is weakened. It will take him a long time to recover, in a special place. I know where, but I'm not saying its name."

"Then you'd prefer to let the name die with you?" The form of Hrafngrimr materialized at the edge of the shadows, staff in hand.

The wizards drew back, making signs to ward off evil. The stump-footed wizard growled, "Vatnarrsmound then, and the trolls take you. I still doubt you'll kill him."

"Kilgore, fetch the sword," Hrafngrimr said. "We'll get him while his power is at ebb."

Kilgore retrieved the sword, putting it into its sheath and keeping his hand upon the cool metal of its hilt. "There's something I want to finish," he said, starting to lift the horn to his lips again.

"No!" Hrafngrimr gripped his arm and pointed to the body of Vatnarr. The wizards began muttering and backing away, shielding their faces with their arms. A fierce coldness gathered over Vatnarr, growing more intense by the moment. Kilgore backed away without taking his eyes off the swirling icy motes that clustered and began to take form. Hrafngrimr yanked at him, urging him to hurry. Trolls and wizards were clawing desperately to crowd out the door.

"It's the bull," Kilgore whispered, his hackles rising in revulsion. He raised the sword before him like a shield as the hideous creature took on an almost-solid form, tossing its huge head and rumbling deep in its chest with menace. It was immense and bloody, its hide flayed away in strips along its ribs and back.

Black maddened eyes glared at Kilgore. The wizards, transfixed for a moment, suddenly bolted for the door, and the bull lunged after them with terrifying speed, hooking his horns left and right. Kilgore started to lower the sword, and the creature jammed to a skidding, whirling halt, abruptly switching his hatred back to his original enemy. For a long moment he stood glowering, head down, slowly raking one hoof on the floor.

Kilgore and Hrafngrimr stood motionless. Batting drops of sweat from his eyes, Kilgore whispered, "What is this cursed thing? Is it real or is it a ghost? Can I kill it?"

"Easy now," murmured Hrafngrimr. "One never knows what a ghost will do. I think he's trying to frighten you into doing something foolish so he can escape. You'd better let him go before you make a real mistake—"

Kilgore seized Wulther's horn, knowing it would banish Surt's frightful apparition, and sent the final note braying into the corridors of Grimshalg and over the battlements to the plain below.

The flayed bull threw its head aloft and vanished with a ghostly bellow that echoed mockingly through the halls of Grimshalg.

"Now you've done it!" Hrafngrimr cried. "We'll have to run for our lives!"

A deep ominous rumble sounded from far below in the bowels of Grimshalg. In the courtyard outside, trolls were fleeing in silent, single-minded desperation. A cracking report shook the fortress under their feet. The whole fortress began to sway. From far below, they heard the rumbling clatter as the tunnels collapsed, forever closing all the portals of Grimshalg.

Asny and Skanderbeg kept their vigil alone through the long night. They did not speak or move until the dawn was approaching and the vargulfs would soon be thronging back to Grimshalg. Then Asny rose and called for Njal and Skuld. "It's time to

290

give the order to disperse," she said. "For three days Gardar was alive again."

Skanderbeg roused himself from his black reverie. "It was my fault. Why didn't I insist on going? I was afraid, that's why. Just an old coward."

"Tush, wizard," Asny began. "Hark, what was that? Did you hear it."

"Aye," Skanderbeg said after a moment as the last echoes of a horn faded away among the barrow mounds. Another note rang quiveringly, like a dirge. After a long silence, the third and final note followed, carrying on the crisp cold air until it too diminished into mocking echoes.

Skanderbeg leaped up on the highest point of the barrow, staring toward Grimshalg with no regard for the wind or the vargulfs. He shook one fist at the fortress and uttered a wild wizard's curse that chilled Asny's blood, and there were tears in his beard.

The men of Skuld murmured, "What is it? Whose horn is that?"

"Wulther's horn," an old man said wonderingly. "Elbegast made a prophecy about that horn. Listen to me, I'm not daft—" But no one listened in the sudden flurry of anxiety.

"It's Kilgore." Asny spoke woodenly. "We've failed, old man. Come down from there before a vargulf carries you off."

"Let him," Skanderbeg said, suddenly dispirited. His shoulders sagged and he let his staff fall to the earth. "Kilgore must be dead, or very nearly so. So bright and promising, and now I've led him to his destruction. This is the last mission for Skanderbeg the wizard. I'll break this staff, renounce magic, and never forget the sorrow of this day."

"Skanderbeg—" Asny could scarcely speak, but a shout from many throats stopped her. They both whirled to look toward Grimshalg, expecting to see Surt and his wizards roiling out on clouds of fury and destruction.

Instead, they saw a brilliant yellow coil of smoking yellow lava pouring from a crack near the base of the fortress mountain. Scalding geysers hissed like fountains as their subterranean hiding places were disturbed. The earth groaned and trembled. A sharp cracking sound, echoed by staccato reports, filled the air with noise and dust. Another fissure in the riverbed opened, turning the water instantly to steam and spattering the walls of the fortress with gobs of spurting orange. A mighty molten wave welled up and poured down the river channel as another fissure burst open. By the weird and brilliant light, the besiegers could see the inhabitants of Grimshalg scuttling away in terror from their doomed fortress, straight toward the waiting ranks of Gardars.

The men of Gardar seized their weapons with shouts of fierce jubilation. They surged toward Asny, surrounding the barrow mound where she stood.

"Give us the order and we'll attack!" Skuld came leaping up the hill in great excitement. "They're trapped between Grimshalg and our lines. It's our opportunity to rid Skarpsey of a good many wizards and trolls. What is your wish, Exalted Lady?"

Asny wavered only a moment. Raising her hammer in a flashing arc, she cried, "Attack! Death to the imposters! Vengeance for Kilgore!"

The challenge was echoed by the men of Skuld and Njal, and the fighting began as the first groups of the enemy came rushing unsuspecting right into their lines. By the lurid half-light beneath clouds of smoke and dust, the minions of Surt perished in great confusion.

Then the earth shook for the last time with a final violent convulsion. The mountain that was Grimshalg revealed that it was nothing more than a plug in the vast firepot of Muspell. The pressure became too great and the plug suddenly exploded with a thunderous report. Grimshalg vanished and the pieces plummeted down into the glacier fields and lonely mountains miles away. Clouds of belching dust and ash filled the pale sky with a new species of night and the rain fell like heavy black tears.

CHAPTER 20

As Kilgore and Hrafngrimr picked their way along the battlements, trolls dashed in all directions like demented things, paying no heed to them. From their high vantage point, they could see a brilliant orange fissure near the main entrance, pouring out a coil of molten lava. With groans and tremors, the whole fortress seemed to be rending asunder with the force of great unknown pressures. Often they stumbled as they made their way up the high pinnacle on the north. By the light of Hrafngrimr's staff, they located the pile of ropes and spikes cached there by Hrafngrimr long before discovering Kilgore in the vargulf tunnels. As they descended the smooth black face of the cliff, Hrafngrimr removed the spikes and ropes to prevent a stream of trolls from following them down. Several times they were shaken loose from their precarious handholds by massive tremors, like flies being twitched off the withers of a horse. Fortunately their ropes saved them, while a few well-placed spells protected them from the rocks that bounced down from above, ranging from pebble size to huge crashing monsters that shook the mountain. The sounds of shrieking, sizzling magma mingled with the hiss of geysers and the scream of cold water meeting molten rock. The faraway savage din of the battle filled every momentary silence.

By the time they reached the foot of Grimshalg, the sky was beginning to show light. The heaving of the mountain was slackening, as if gathering strength for a final convulsion which could come at any instant. Kilgore looked in dismay at the smoking piles of new stone and hoped there was a way among them to the river. The earth seared their feet as they hurried gingerly over it. When they finally threaded a treacherous path to the river, they found it steaming like a cauldron. Geysers spouted from its bed, hiding the far side in clouds of steam.

"We'll be boiled alive if we try to swim that," Kilgore said, staring vainly toward the far side. He could see unidentified forms flitting among the steaming rocks. Out on the plain he heard the vargulfs moaning and wailing in confusion, as dawn neared with no dark haven to flee to.

Hrafngrimr beckoned him to the lee of a large rock beside the river, where a small boat had been miraculously spared from the conflagration that had consumed every burnable thing. Without a word, they pushed away from the bank and the boiling current snatched the boat like a leaf. At once the pitch caulking softened and the boat began to fill with scalding water. Paddling desperately, they brought the boat aground on the other side before it sank and left it behind without a second glance.

"The fighting must be going well," Hrafngrimr observed as they passed a heap of dead trolls and wizards. "Skanderbeg and Asny must believe you are dead to risk an attack with you still inside."

"It couldn't be helped," Kilgore said, striding ahead resolutely. "The destruction of Grimshalg has put Surt and his followers to flight. Njal and Skuld shall take care of the followers, and Surt will be finished at Vatnarrsmound." He spoke without slowing his pace, recognizing the row of old cairns along the road to Vatnarrsmound, marking the graves of executed criminals and standing in the gloomy half-light like black prison towers.

"You were there once," Hrafngrimr said. "Tell me what we are likely to find when we get there. He must have a body of some sort to finish his battle with you."

"There's an old king's barrow, and the old king is scarcely more than rags and dust and bones, but I suspect Surt once inhabited that Vatnarr also—perhaps the one who claimed he would someday rule absolute over Skarpsey. It feels like a place of powerful magic. The treasure hoard is there, and Surt held audiences with his wizards." Briefly he told Hrafngrimr about the sending appearing in the form of the flayed bull and the cat who had sat upon the dry husk of the Vatnarr in the barrow.

Hrafngrimr walked along in silence, nodding from time to time as Kilgore talked. Suddenly he stretched out his hand to point. "Look there, in the soft ground. Tracks of the bull." Great cloven prints led straight toward Vatnarrsmound. They were edged with frost, which was beginning to melt. "Evidently his wound isn't slowing him down much. We haven't much chance of overtaking him before he reaches the safety and further power of his mound. He is, of course, far too clever to get himself trapped outside his barrow when the sun comes up." Grimly he nodded toward the southeast, where the sun was making a faint showing behind the clouds.

Kilgore also glanced toward the pale sun, and his eye caught a movement in the bleak dark landscape. "Horsemen!" he cried, pointing.

"And they've seen us." Hrafngrimr drew his sword. The riders came racing along the top of a barrow mound where the light could barely reach them. They appeared to be riding in the air over the shadowy earth. Kilgore wished he could see them better. The sword gave no warning as they plunged downhill into the shadow. Their cloaks billowed in indiscernible colors and they carried lances in their stirrups. There were six riders, closely followed by two riderless horses. One of the riders sounded a mellow blast on a horn, which was answered by others from various points around Grimshalg, some near and some far. At a slight distance, they slowed and approached at a peaceable walk. The leader lifted a hand in salute.

"Halloo, young Kilgore! My advice has brought you a long way from the foot of the Trident."

"Schimmelpfinning! Where's your herd of pigs?" Kilgore stepped forward gladly to grasp his outstretched hand. "When I find out who you really are some day, I'll thank you properly for all the help you've been. Grimshalg is burning, and Surt is dispossessed of a body until he gets to Vatnarrsmound." Kilgore glanced at the two riderless horses and opened his mouth to ask for them just as Schimmelpfinning called them forward by their names.

"That's excellent news, lad, and here's the means you need to get you to Vatnarrsmound before Surt changes hiding places. Ride like the wind, and we'll talk later."

Kilgore found himself tossed into the saddle and the reins were thrust into his hands. At once, the horse leaped away at a full gallop with Hrafngrimr flying along behind. Schimmelpfinning and his companions watched a moment from the top of a barrow, then vanished in the direction of Grimshalg. The gray air bit through Kilgore's worn-out clothing, and the white horse snorted clouds of steam as he ran surefootedly up the frosty sides of barrow hills to plunge down the other side. Kilgore warmed his hands on the horse's neck until the buildings of Vatnarrsmound appeared out of the mists that hung sullenly among the mounds.

They surged into the muddy courtyard. The door of the house stood open and the inside was pillaged and smashed. A last troll skittered out with a sack over its shoulder and dashed wild-eyed toward the barrows.

Kilgore satisfied himself that no one was left inside and turned toward the treasure mound. Forcing himself to move deliberately, he rode slowly up the steep slope to the barrow opening. He dismounted, his hand on the sword, and knelt to peer inside. It all looked perfectly commonplace, except for the massive hoof prints that vanished at the entrance. Hrafngrimr knelt beside him. "I'll go in with you. He may try magic."

"I'll go in alone. I prefer to face him by myself, in spite of his magic. If Kildurin can't protect me, then even your power isn't enough."

Kilgore poked the sword in ahead of him and crept

inside. The antechamber was thick with darkness. He had a feeling he had cut a tunnel into the very heart of the night. It oppressed him on all sides until he found it hard to breathe. Smiling grimly, he said aloud to the darkness, "So you're home already, Surt. It's a pity I didn't deal with you the first time I was here."

"A pity indeed, mortal," came the answer from beyond the wall. "You would be dead now if you had tried."

"You knew who I was, so why didn't you destroy me then?" he asked.

"Every great ruler eventually makes a fatal mistake. That was mine. I did not think you could ever get inside Grimshalg so easily. And without the treachery of the Alfar sorcerer, you might not have managed it a second time. And now what are you waiting for? You have come a long way to die with me in this mound."

Kilgore removed the stones and stepped through onto a carpet of gold. The sword lit up the chamber like a torch, striking fire off a thousand golden points. A whisper of movement alerted him in time to raise Kildurin against the spell that was hurled at him. A long spear of black ice shattered and dissolved into particles and fell musically among the gold artifacts underfoot.

The corpse of the dead king was rising stiffly from its bier, clutching Tyrfing in its skeletal claws. With astounding agility, the ghost attacked, swirling and dodging with the clashing of the swords. Tyrfing burned bright blue, throwing orange sparks when it met Kildurin's force, but it did not break as an ordinary sword would have done. Kilgore muttered the runes continuously, aware that the sword's magic was being tested to its limit. A dozen times he swept the limbs off the ghost, but each time they clattered swiftly back into place and the ghost was more furious and desperate. Without pause, they battled until Tyrfing was chipped in four places and its sharp point broken off. Although Kildurin was unscarred, Kilgore was nearly exhausted. He felt little pain from the several superficial wounds he had received, but the fury of the fighting was telling on him. The ghost capered around as spryly as ever, having no mortal body to tire and suffer from pain.

In a final desperate attack, the ghost launched itself straight at Kilgore and wrestled him down with incredible strength. Kilgore let the sword drop to match his might against the ghost, whose bony fingers were trying to get at his throat to strangle him. The nearness of the dreadful apparition and the feel of those blackened fingers almost overpowered Kilgore with revulsion. With a yell, he tore away the fingers and buffeted the dusty body away from him. For all its supernatural strength, it was disgustingly light. He pounced on it, pinning it under him. It scrabbled desperately with beetle-brittle arms and legs. Kilgore seized the sword and severed the moldering head from its shoulders. Then he clapped the skull alongside his thigh in the prescribed formula for destroying evil ghosts, and the wretched carcass of the long-dead King Vatnarr stirred no longer.

Looking at the corpse, he saw only a heap of rags and bones lying on the mass of gold and silver, like a bundle of trash. He tried to call out to Hrafngrimr, but all he could muster was a feeble croak.

The voice of Hrafngrimr had been calling for some time. "Kilgore! Kilgore! Answer if you're still alive. Drat it, I'm going inside."

Hrafngrimr appeared in the opening and stared at the scene before him, heaps of silver and gold, and Kilgore leaning on the sword and staring at the old king's corpse.

"Surt is dead," said Kilgore, sheathing the sword.

"Good heavens, you're wounded!"

"Not seriously."

They looked at the small pile of rags and bones that had been the old king. Quietly, Hrafngrimr clapped his shoulder and said, "We had better burn the rest of him to ashes to be safe. Then let's go find Asny and Skanderbeg."

In a short while, a black cloud of smoke was rising from Vatnarrsmound, and there was hardly anyone to

298

notice. Kilgore and Hrafngrimr left the fire to burn itself out and started back toward Grimshalg. The day
was dawning black and dreary, particularly toward
the south where roiling clouds of dust and smoke ascended into the sky.

On the crest of a barrow, they stopped to watch as
the black cloud gathered itself together like a thunder-
storm. The earth trembled and a geyser of dust and
smoke burst into the air, high over Grimshalg, loaded
with gigantic pieces of stone. With a mighty cracking
sound that shook the earth, Grimshalg vanished utterly, leaving nothing but a roaring abyss that heaved
out orange tongues of magma. The Grimstrom met
with the molten stone and was vanquished in clouds of
vapor. When the dust had settled a bit, there was
nothing left of the fortress but a sea of boiling, steaming water and hot new lava flows, smoking in the pale
gray light of dawn.

Kilgore sent his horse racing toward the hilltop
where he had left Asny and Skanderbeg. A group of
Skuld's men were gathered there talking, so he dismounted and walked somewhat blindly toward them,
as if he were apart and watching himself from a
distance. Skuld's men at first took him for another of
themselves, tattered and war-weary, but suddenly
they recognized him. With a bellow of greeting and
glee, they rushed forward and carried him bodily to
the cave where their leaders had convened. Asny
rushed out, her eyes suspiciously red for a warrior,
and exclaimed, "We thought you were dead! We were
going to build a lovely memorial on the top of the hill
for you and now you've spoiled all our plans. Where
have you been and what have you been doing? Surt's
minions are dead or scattered and full of the fear we
put into them, and Grimshalg is burned. It was a pity
you weren't here to see the return of Elbegast and the
Alfar after you blew your horn, and—oh, you're
bloody, Kilgore! Whom have you been fighting? Surely
not—you did fight him, and you did win? Surt is
dead!" Her words raised a storm of excited voices as
the news spread outward from the cave.

Kilgore nodded and sat down on a stone. "Vatnarr-Surt is dead, by his own hand and mine. And with the aid of Elbegast and the Alfar and old Schimmelpfinning and the men of Njal and Skuld." He paused suddenly and began looking around at the gathering circle of well-wishers. "But there is one other who was at my side every minute in the wizard's hall and behind me at Vatnarrsmound. He has gone through more than all of us and he is by far the bravest man I have ever seen. And now he's gone and I never spoke a word of thanks to him."

Skanderbeg came shoving through the crowd importantly. "Never mind any others. You look as if you've been through ninety years of captivity with the legions of Hel. Now you can just relax and let Asny take over the worrying, since this is her country now."

"So it is. The fighting is all over," Kilgore murmured, looking down at the misty plain below. It looked no different for its redemption; it was still in his mind the dismal running ground for the vargulfs.

"Vargulfs!" He leaped up and looked around for a sign of them. "What happened when the sun touched them?"

He dreaded the answer, but Asny only beckoned. "Rolfr, Glam, Wittorf, Helgi, Raud-Skeggi, Skarp, Avangr! Come here and meet the sword king."

Rolfr and his brothers were there, freed of their curse, and wreathed in smiles. "We met already in the tunnels of Grimshalg. The stroke that ended Surt freed us from the spell. We turned our hands to fight wizards and trolls—whole men again, not half beast."

"Welcome back," Kilgore said with heartfelt relief.

Happy reunions were taking place on all sides among the former vargulfs and the men of Skuld and Njal. Kilgore and Skanderbeg were the only ones there without family members to find, so they retreated to the cave, where Skanderbeg dressed Kilgore's wounds. Kilgore felt a little dejected in the midst of all the happiness. His family was hundreds of miles away in Shieldbroad and he would not be home until at least spring.

"I wish I could start home tomorrow, Skanderbeg," he said as he sipped a cup of hot tea. "I don't mean to sound sentimental or anything like that, but I rather imagine old Valsidur has missed me somewhat. Asny doesn't really need us now that Gardar has been won back from Surt."

"Aye, we could leave tomorrow." Skanderbeg placed a cobweb on the last wound and bandaged it. "Neither of us care for crowds and all that heroic mush. I imagine every person in Gardar will idolize us both with songs and scalds and all that sort of thing. Wulther and Valsidda were dead, at least, before they became heroes. I don't know how we'll stand it. We don't really want to stay and see Asny crowned queen either, after so many years of being without a queen in Gardar, and after all we've been through with her. No, and I don't suppose you'll feel a bit sad about saying goodbye to these struggling people who hold you so dear in their hearts."

"You're right. We'll stay." Kilgore stretched out on the ground wearily. "I need to catch up on my sleep anyway. Tomorrow I want to hear about the way the battle went here, but for now—" He yawned, suddenly aware that he had not really slept for four nights. The ground under him was lumpy and damp, but he did not even feel it.

When he awoke again, it was mid-morning. Stiffly he sat up and looked around for a cloak. Although the sun streaming in was bright and cheerful, the air was freezing. In the night it had snowed, covering the ground with a layer of fluff that was now sparkling like fields and hills of diamonds. It squeaked underfoot with a cheery sound and made the dismal landscape look clean and less harsh. Overhead, the sky was a rich blue, a great source of amazement and rejoicing for the Gardars. They had taken shelter in caves and open barrows for the night, and now everyone was involved with preparations for a grand celebration.

Limping gingerly, Kilgore climbed to the windy crest of the ridge and found Skanderbeg directing the construction of a huge bonfire for the burning of the

301

heroes who had fallen in the battle. Already the smoke ascended in a glorious thick column straight toward Valhalla.

Spying Kilgore, Skanderbeg left his business to point out the hill they had selected at one time for Kilgore's memorial. "It would have been breathtaking, and we intended to begin on it as soon as we'd had breakfast, but you showed up too soon. Speaking of breakfast—"

"Yes, I was wondering how so many people are going to be fed," Kilgore said with a frown. "Being free is well enough, but starvation is a dreadful possibility, this far into winter. What has been done for the general welfare of these people?"

"Many are returning to their old homes with their families, along the foot of the mountains where we found Njal and the Regulars. Skuld has organized hunting parties, and houses are being built for the homeless. For the time being, Asny will rule from Vatnarrsmound. In the spring, a new Grimshalg will be built for her. But there's a problem you'll be interested in," Skanderbeg said, suddenly reminded of something. "I'd almost forgotten. We have some prisoners for you to dispose of. We didn't take many. I was forced to deal rather harshly with Surt's wizards, for the most part. Exile, imprisonment, spontaneous combustion, changing of forms, and so forth accounted for nearly all of them."

Skanderbeg showed him to a cave in a hillside where two of Skuld's men guarded the opening. Looking inside, Kilgore saw three wizards looking much the worse for wear. He barely recognized Mord and the old wizard with the wooden foot and one of the splendid fellows in purple, now as sad and bedraggled as a half-plucked rooster. They looked at him dejectedly and said nothing.

"But here is the prize, Kilgore," Skanderbeg said, reaching into a dark corner and dragging out a small squeaking object.

"Oh, spare me, kind sirs! Don't kill me, I never meant any harm at all with my clumsy tricks. I never

302

intended to help Surt or Trond or anyone evil. Please spare me and my poor worthless skin." The fellow prostrated himself at their feet in abject humility.

Kilgore prodded him with his toe. "Get to your feet, you miserable excuse of a wizard. From the very beginning in Shieldbroad, you've threatened this entire enterprise. You nasty little brute, your big mouth very nearly put an end to me in Grimshalg. You remember that, don't you?"

Warth sniveled, blinked, and trembled. One of his long, hairy ears looked as if it had been bitten nearly off and his cloak was nothing but holes held together by threads. "Oh, but that was entirely against my better wishes. Let me explain; those wizards are so coercive. I never once intended—"

"I think it's time we put a plug in that mouth," Skanderbeg said with menacing relish, "and I have something very pleasant in mind for you, Warth. I've burnt all these fellows' magical apparatus, if you could call it that in Warth's case. I've seen cannibals with more sophistication."

Warth began to wail and grovel, rolling his eyes cunningly at Kilgore and looking as miserable as he could. "I beg your kindness, dear masters, most desperately. I promise I'll never misbehave again."

"Kindness only encourages such scum as you," Kilgore said. "Your tricks are absolutely unforgiveable, Warth."

Warth shriveled visibly and clasped his hands. "I had already decided to reform and spend the rest of my days doing good deeds. I thought noble souls such as yourselves were always merciful, generous, kind, and—"

"Enough!" Skanderbeg roared, his eyes red with rage. He seized Warth by the scruff of his neck and dropped him with a thump beside the other wizards.

"Now for the final settlement." Skanderbeg held aloft his staff. "I banish you forever from the island of Skarpsey. Never let so much as one of your whiskers be seen here again, or I shall blast you with everlasting fire. I order you to surrender yourselves to the Fire Wizards' Guild for their judgment for this profanation of magical powers which you call ice wizardry. The forms I now confer upon you will endure until the Guild members free you. Farewell! Enjoy your journey!"

Incanting some foreign words, he passed his staff over the four wizards, and instantly everyone was swallowed in a choking orange cloud of smoke. When it cleared, nothing of the wizards remained except four hairy lumps that revealed themselves to be the most despicable and disagreeable of rats. Three scuttled away with enraged squeals, but the fourth sat up in rage and gnashed its teeth and squalled balefully until Kilgore put it to flight with a rock.

"Warth will always have the last word if it kills him," he growled.

As they returned to the hilltop, horns sounded to the south across the river. Everyone stopped to watch as a long column of horsemen cantered through the river and across the plain toward the mound where the funeral fire burned.

"It's Elbegast and his Alfar come back," Skanderbeg said. "Look at them, Kilgore. Few men have ever seen such a sight, and after this day possibly no man will ever see the Alfar again."

Kilgore was unable to speak. He gripped the hilt of the sword, fighting down a lump in his throat, partly caused by the impressive appearance of the Alfar, and mostly because he knew there was no need for such a sword as Kildurin anymore; Elbegast must have come to take it back to the Alfar halls where it had been forged.

By the time the Alfar horses had climbed the hill and the Alfar dismounted, Asny was standing beside Kilgore. Elbegast himself, resplendent in gold helmet and silvery Tarnkappe, strode forward to greet them. Grasping Kilgore's hand, he exclaimed, "So you followed the advice of the old swineherd and blew Wulther's horn! Bless you, how you've changed since we first met. There's an eagle's look in your eye now and, if I'm not mistaken, you're the very image of your ancestor Wulther. He was a fine friend to me, laddie, and he'd be proud of you today, as I am."

Kilgore could only grin until his face felt as if it would crack. "Schimmelpfinning," he said. "I tried to throw the horn back into the woods, but it was you who threw it back. And now—" He stopped suddenly, clapping his hand to his side in dismay. "It's gone!"

"The horn? Aye, lost again," Elbegast said, with the sun glinting in his wiry gold beard. "It's gone and melted with Grimshalg, as I intended it should be. Now that its call has gathered the Alfar and caused the destruction of Grimshalg, there is no further need for it. Lad, you just can't know how long the Alfar have waited to hear Wulther's horn calling them to the last battle with Surt, blown by a true descendant of that great man. He'd be wonderfully pleased to see this day. Now tell us all about your travels and your fight with Surt. Gather around, Alfar and Gardars, and we shall hear the whole story from the mouth of the hero himself so we can teach it to our children and grandchildren."

Kilgore took a seat on a stone where they could all see. The Alfar sat in a cluster to one side and the Gardars crowded all around the hill from the top to the bottom. Asny sat near his feet with her seven brothers. Compared to the beautiful capes of the Alfar, everyone's clothing was mere tattered rags, fluttering in the slight breeze.

Kilgor spoke in a clear, carrying voice, beginning at the very beginning in Shieldbroad. He told of his astonishment when he was the one who removed the sword from the tree. Again he traversed the Sloughs of Heroness and discovered Asny imprisoned in Surt's spell and freed her with the aid of the sword. The Gardars smiled and looked proudly at their young queen when he described the way she saved them at Trondheim, and many laughed aloud at the misadventures with Warth and the nykurs. But many of the freed vargulfs shed tears of remorse because they had been there that night at Beortstad when Kilgore had nearly joined the vargulfs. Elbegast and the Alfar exchanged thoughtful, sardonic glances as he described the grandeur of Eldjarn's fortress where no troublesome outside business was permitted.

With no betraying enotion he reported the defection of Hrafngrimr at Svartheim. He told them of the night at Vatnarrsmound, about the flayed bull and the cat. He described his entrance to Grimshalg and the loss of the sword to Vatnarr-Surt. He did not mention the name of Hrafngrimr until he had finished the final battle with Surt in the treasure mound.

By this time everyone was eagerly awaiting the name of this new hero. Kilgore continued, "I don't know where he is now, but he is surely a greater hero than I am. From the beginning he had to take the difficult road of appearing to be something else, even to the extent of deceiving his close friends. I do not doubt that he was absolutely loyal from the very beginning, but we judged him too hastily and even deserted him. Without him, we would have failed and I, at least, would certainly be dead at the hands of Surt's wizards. I wish he were here to see our victory and to receive our deepest apologies for ever doubting him. I can't find the right words to praise him enough, so I'll tell you his name and let it be remembered with mine—Hrafngrimr, the Alfar wizard." A murmur went through the crowd and suddenly Kilgore jumped up and exclaimed. "Hrafngrimr! You are here!"

The people let forth a roar of acclaim as Hrafngrimr quietly stood up in the back ranks of the Alfar. Elbegast beckoned to him and he came forward through a sea of faces bright with admiration and gratitude. Many hands touched his cloak reverently and the boast would live for generations: "My great-great-great-great-grandfather touched the cloak of one of Skarpsey's greatest heroes!"

Skanderbeg rose and clasped his hand wordlessly.

Asny said, "I take back every suspicious thought or word I ever had about you. Please forgive me for ever doubting you."

"Forgive me for being forced to deceive you,"

Hrafngrimr said with a hearty handshake for each of them.

Elbegast took the speaker's position on the stone, standing on top of it with one hand resting upon Hrafngrimr and one upon Kilgore. When everyone was silent, he spoke. "My friends, Gardars, and Alfar, few of us appreciate the difficulties our comrade Hrafngrimr has endured. Not only has he successfully completed one of the most important missions Skarpsey has ever seen, he has spent almost his entire life preparing the groundwork for it. It took years to win the confidence of our enemies to the extent that he deceived even Surt, the greatest of deceivers. Through his skill and intelligence, we ferreted out the halls of the Dark Alfar and learned their secrets and eventually led them to their doom. Svartheim is no more, thanks to Hrafngrimr and Skanderbeg together, who destroyed their king and drove them from their tunnels. Only his years of careful preparation saved the sword mission, but at the cost of seeming to betray his friends. This was perhaps the greatest agony of all, knowing that they would have to travel through a dark and dangerous land without his help, and wondering whether they would ever trust him again so the sword mission would succeed. All this great weight fell upon him alone and at every moment this brave Alfar was in peril of his life lest his disguise be discovered by the hideous creatures he was forced to associate with. However, he was undismayed by his own importance. To the very last stroke of the sword of Andurich, he was at the side of the sword king to do his bidding and lend his arts when they were needed. And now to the point of what I am saying. For outstanding bravery and noble conduct in the halls of the enemy, for unswerving loyalty to the sword king and the Wolfganger queen of Gardar, even in the face of the wizard Surt in the barrow of the dead king, and for surpassing all limits of the science and art of sorcery, I, Elbegast, King of the Light Alfar, do bestow upon you the highest honor of all Alfarim—the Tarnkappe."

He held up a cloak that seemed spun of moonlight and rainbows. It shimmered and tossed in the breeze as if it were of no substance. The sun caught it eagerly as if it were part of the same fiber, and all the mortals present were awed by the rare sight, knowing they were seeing what no men had ever been privileged to see, and would never see again.

Hrafngrimr knelt while Elbegast fastened the gold clasps, then he straightened and with a brisk salute took his place among the ranks of the select Alfar who had earned the Tarnkappe.

"And now, dear friends, before I go," Elbegast said, turning to Kilgore and Asny and Skanderbeg, "I wish to leave you with something to remember the Alfar."

From his pocket, he took a gold ring for Asny and placed it upon her finger, where it fitted comfortably as if it had been made for her. "This ring, beautiful queen, is a ring of truth. With it you will always be able to discern true from false, a friend from a foe. If you attempt to be dishonest in your dealings as queen, it will cut your finger to remind you to be honest. I hope you shall never be parted from it."

"I won't," Asny said in awe. "It shall never leave my hand."

"And for you, Skanderbeg—I wish there were more wizards like you—I extend to you an invitation to become my right-hand sorcerer, and advise me with all the concerns of the Alfar realm, with the assistance of your good magic."

Skanderbeg looked startled, then intensely grave. "I thank you, but I cannot accept. The truth of the matter is, I must return a wandering son to a gruff old man in Shieldbroad whose heart is grieving. After that, I plan to remain to meddle in the affairs of these wretched mortals and help them unsnarl the mess they've gotten themselves into. I desire no reward for doing my duty as I see fit—except perhaps your promise that there will be a scruffy swineherd prowling about in case something like Surt ever arises again."

Elbegast bowed to the wizard. "We'll never be far away, Skanderbeg."

Then he turned to Kilgore, who was still struggling with a choking lump in his throat. "And now, Kilgore. What shall I give you to remember me by?"

"Nothing. I shall carry this day forever in my head. I need nothing to remind me. And now since the journey is over and the fight fought, I return your sword to you and thank you for the honor of being its bearer. Kildurin has served me well. May it find an honorable resting place in your hall." He could scarcely speak the last words. He held out the sword, gleaming in the sunlight like a ribbon of the sun itself, inscribed with the magic gold runes that he knew by heart. For the last time, he read them: "No night can overtake the sons of Ask and Embla."

Elbegast took it and turned it over lovingly in his hands. "These runes have become a prophecy fulfilled. From the first parents of the race of mankind and far into the misty future, these runes will always ring true. This sword was fashioned hundreds of years before you were born and for your hand alone it was made. Take it and keep it safe in the heart of your old Brandstok tree to remind you of Surt and the Alfar, and perhaps an old swineherd who wanders in these green hills of Gardar. There is nothing I can give you that would not seem a tawdry bauble after all you have endured. But as an affectionate memento I would like to leave you my stallion Cloud-stepper as a means to carry you swiftly home to Shieldbroad. You know him well, he is the one that carried you to the barrow mound of Surt. May he carry you back to your friends here just as swiftly. Goodbye, laddie. I'll visit you in the future to see if my predictions come true of a united Gardar and Shieldbroad. Farewell, dear friends."

Amid many blessings and farewells, the Alfar mounted their white horses and rode across the plain and the river and into the mist on the far side and did not reappear. Kilgore stared after them a long time, holding Kildurin as if it would melt away like

309

a dream object. He realized what a cold and vast kingdom Gardar was, and the numbers of difficulties surrounding its rebuilding. It was a far cry from the cozy comforts of Shieldbroad, which he had missed so much and boasted of so often, but he knew with a sudden fierce yearning that this wild land had claimed his heart. He had to stay.

He turned to Asny.

She looked away quickly and busied herself with intently stabbing a tuffet of moss with her knife. "So I guess you'll be leaving us soon, too. Well, I wish you a happy journey. I hope you'll come back for a visit sometime?"

Kilgore shook his head. "No. I'm not leaving. I can't explain it, but I like this awful place and I know I have to stay."

Asny cut a caper of high glee. "Let's go tell Skanderbeg you've decided to save him a trip back through the Trident."

They found Skanderbeg vigorously ransacking his scanty possessions in preparation for the journey back to Shieldbroad, six days from now.

"Skanderbeg, I've decided not to go back," announced Kilgore.

Skanderbeg sat down and cocked his head to one side. "Oh really? I suppose you've forgotten about Valsidur? He's an old man and you're his only son, Kilgore. In spite of his meanness, he won't live forever. You need to make your peace with him. Then you can come back. I expect the old roarer will be rather proud of you now. Stay with him a year or so, and I'll come for you myself. It'll be just like old times."

"But a year or so is such a long time," protested Kilgore. "Everything will be changed by then. What if something happens to one of us?"

"Not afraid of a few trolls between here and there, are you?" Skanderbeg demanded.

"Of course not, but—"

"He's afraid he's going to miss out on all the fun," Asny said. "Hunting out the last of the trolls and wizards and fighting the frost giants, and such things. Kilgore, I promise we'll save you your share, and more. It's going to take all our lifetimes before Gardar is as safe and peaceful as Shieldbroad."

"Longer, I hope," Kilgore muttered, but he was beginning to feel a little better. "I suppose I had better go—for now. But you can bet I'll be back here the spring after next. I promise."

"And I shall hold you to that promise," said Asny, and they solemnly shook hands.

Six days passed impossibly fast and found the three friends standing again on the same hill. "I only hope a year and a half passes just as fast," Kilgore said around a lump in his throat, gruffly shaking hands with Asny.

"You mortals," Skanderbeg snorted, shaking out his cloak and giving his satchel a hearty pummeling to shape it up. "A year is nothing, a mere blink of an eye, and you carry on like it's forever. It's scarcely even worth a goodbye." He bounded astride his horse, an Alfar steed like Cloud-stepper, who was pawing the earth impatiently.

"Scarcely worth it at all," agreed Asny, not fooled by Skanderbeg's growling. "But I'll say it anyway. Goodbye, and have a safe journey!" Then, in a low voice, she added, "And, Kilgore—come back to me."

Kilgore swung aboard Cloud-stepper and the two horses leaped forward as if it were a race, striking sparks from their hooves on the stony but free earth of Gardar.

ABOUT THE AUTHOR

Elizabeth Boyer began planning her writing career during junior high school in her rural Idaho hometown. She read almost anything the Bookmobile brought, and learned a great love for Nature and wilderness. Science fiction in large quantities led her to Tolkien's writings, after which she developed a great curiosity about Scandinavian folklore. Ms. Boyer is Scandinavian by descent and hopes to visit the homeland of her ancestors. She has a B.A. from Brigham Young University, at Provo, Utah, in English literature.

She now lives in the Rocky Mountain wilderness at Scofield State Park in central Utah. She and her ranger husband Allan write and photograph outdoor recreation articles. They met on a desert survival trip in the canyons of southern Utah. They share their home with two daughters, a Siamese cat, and a pet skunk named Chanel. Ms. Boyer enjoys backpacking, cross-country skiing, painting, and reading.

Dear Reader,

Your opinions are very important to us so please take a few moments to tell us your thoughts. It will help us give you more enjoyable DEL REY Books in the future.

1. Where did you obtain this book?   5

Bookstore ☐1	Department Store ☐4	Airport ☐7
Supermarket ☐2	Drug Store ☐5	From A Friend ☐8
Variety/Discount Store ☐3	Newsstand ☐6	Other_____

(Write In)

2. On an overall basis, how would you rate this book?   6

Excellent ☐1   Very Good ☐2   Good ☐3   Fair ☐4   Poor ☐5

3. What is the main reason that you purchased this book?   7

Author ☐1   It Was Recommended To Me ☐3
Like The Cover ☐2   Other_____
(Write In)

4. In the same subject category as this book, who are your *two* favorite authors?

_____   8
                            9
_____   10
                            11

5. Which of the following categories of paperback books have you purchased in the past 3 months?

Adventure/ Suspense ☐12-1	Biography ☐4	Horror/ Terror ☐8	Science Fiction ☐x
Bestselling Fiction ☐2	Classics ☐5	Mystery ☐9	Self-Help ☐y
Bestselling Non-Fiction ☐3	Fantasy ☐6	Romance ☐0	War ☐13-
	Historical Romance ☐7		Westerns ☐2

6. What magazines do you subscribe to, or read regularly, that is, 3 out of every 4 issues?

_____   14
                            15
_____   16
                            17

7. Are you: Male ☐1   Female ☐2   18

8. Please indicate your age group.   19

Under 18 ☐1   25-34 ☐3   50 or older ☐5
18-24 ☐2   35-49 ☐4

9. What is the highest level of education that you have completed?   20

Post Graduate Degree ☐1   College Graduate ☐3   Some High
Some Post Graduate   1-3 Years College ☐4   School
Schooling   ☐2   High School   or Less ☐6
    Graduate ☐5

(Optional)

If you would like to learn about future publications and participate in future surveys, please fill in your name and address.

NAME_____

ADDRESS_____

CITY_____ STATE_____ ZIP_____   21

Please mail to: Ballantine Books
DEL REY Research, Dept.
516 Fifth Avenue — Suite 606
New York, N.Y. 10036

F-13